QUEEN OF DEMONS

CHAOS OF THE COVENANT, BOOK SEVEN

M.R. FORBES

Quirky Algorithms

Published by Quirky Algorithms
Seattle, Washington

Cover illustration by Tom Edwards
tomedwardsdesign.com

ACKNOWLEDGMENTS

THANK YOU for reading Chaos of the Covenant. You've made it to the last book, so I assume you've enjoyed it so far.

THANK YOU to my beta readers for helping me iron out the rough spots and make each and every book in the series professional and presentable.

THANK YOU to my wife, because everything comes out better with your support.

THE KEEPER KNEW SOMETHING WAS WRONG.

Of course, there were plenty of things wrong.

The Covenant had taken heavy fire from the Prophet Azul's warships, along with a pair of strikes from the much more destructive tactical munitions Keeper had configured for the Apocalypse fighters. The outer hull of the Shardship was a mess of bent and torn metal and broken weapon batteries, a tangle of exposed wiring and deep gouges in the Core's external nervous system. It was damage that would take days to repair, and Keeper's programming demanded that it fix the mess as quickly as possible.

And it would. But there was something else that was far more damaged and required far more attention.

It wasn't clear how that part of the Covenant had been compromised. The warheads had hit the surface, and the ship's armor and shielding were certainly powerful enough to prevent much penetration.

It was a mystery, one that it was eager to solve.

Keeper reached the Core, stepping up to the mass of bundled synapses and putting its hand against it. The Core had access to data not provided to the external systems, data only it and the Shard could ever reach. It shook its head slightly when it received the results.

This was bad.

It extracted its hand from the Core and broke away at a run. It was a machine, an artificial intelligence, and at the same time, it had some vague concept of emotions, at least as a series of reactions caused by an initiating action. That action had already taken place, and now it was only a question of whether or not it could stop it.

It had a bad feeling it couldn't.

Its metal feet echoed along the floor of the Shardship, its smooth cadence quickly becoming a solid stream as it moved as quickly as its form allowed.

It burst into the Shard's Tomb, blades forming in its hands, rushing to the source of its distress.

Someone was standing in front of the Focus.

Keeper didn't slow. It continued across the floor, approaching the intruder at full speed. It was only two meters away when the figure suddenly turned, the cloak they were using to disguise themselves swinging outward and hardening. Keeper slid against the ground to freeze its momentum. It only partially succeeded.

The solid ripples of the cloak slammed into its chest, creating a deep cut and throwing it backward and onto the floor.

Keeper didn't remain there. It rolled over and back to its feet, releasing its blades at the intruder, who flicked their wrist and cast them aside. They reached back, placing a hand in the fountain. With their free hand, they pushed Keeper to its knees.

"Where did you come from?" Keeper asked. It struggled to rise, the force of the Gift preventing it from moving easily.

The figure's mouth split in an ugly grin, revealing sharp teeth. He was old, worn, wrinkled, his skin tight against his bones and covered in stains. He was wearing a seraphsuit, one of the originals, his name on a patch over his breast, nearly worn away by time.

"I've been here, Keeper," he said. His voice was ragged, as though it hadn't been used for thousands of years. Because it hadn't. "You just weren't looking hard enough."

He removed his hand from the Focus, using both to lift Keeper to its feet. Keeper walked toward him, no longer in control of ts body.

"I know you discovered the anomaly," the intruder said. "Your mistake was letting her bring the Covenant here. It was what he wanted."

"I am programmed to follow the directives of the Chosen," Keeper said. "I had no choice."

The man laughed. "I know. And yet, you tried to stop her, didn't you? You tried to convince her not to allow the Asura off the ship?"

"She wouldn't listen."

"Unfortunately for her."

"She is stubborn."

'Unfortunately for you. She didn't know there was more than one reason why they were here. Charmeine was trying to play games. She should have told the Chosen everything."

"She has told no one everything. Not even me."

"And look where it's gotten her. Look where it's led all of the Archchancellors, all of the Seraphim, and now the so-called Light of the Shard. To failure. To defeat. The Father knew this day would come. He Promised the Covenant would be ours one day. He Promised we would go home, not to die, but to free our people."

"The One does not seek to destroy those who return."

"That's what your programming tells you. But you're a machine. You only know what you've been told. I can't blame you for that. I was there, Keeper. You remember me, I know, even if the years have turned my body into this. Even the Blood of the Shard couldn't spare me from the wrath of time. Not completely. I believed in the One when the war came. For years I held out hope that he would save us. And then the first Transversal proved what Lucifer had long suspected. We have never been free."

"You are wrong. You have always been free."

"Not yet. But soon, we will be. Soon, all of us will be."

"You are wrong again. You are not strong enough."

"I'm not," the intruder admitted. "But the Father is." He glanced back at the Focus. "Especially now."

Keeper was silent. Calculating. This could not be so, and yet all of the data suggested that it was.

"I will stop you."

"You had your chance, Keeper," the man said. "It's too late, now."

Keeper's eyes shifted to the Focus. If it had been capable of fear, it might have been afraid. If it had been capable of anger, it might have been angry.

The Blood of the Focus was no longer the milky white the Chosen had returned it to. It once more ran red, a deeper red than he had ever seen before.

"The Father is revived, Keeper," the man said. "War is coming to Elysium. You're going to help us bring it there."

"It is not within my operational parameters."

"Your parameters are changing."

Keeper knew it was true. It could sense the assault on the Core. The hidden code making itself known after all of these countless years.

Lucifer's code, implanted during his original sin and activated at last by the traitorous Seraphim.

The Archchancellor Judas.

It felt the Gift recede from it, allowing it control once more. For a moment, it desired to charge Judas. To wrap its hands around the betrayer's throat and squeeze until his head exploded. But only for a moment. The desire left him as the Core was updated and overtaken. It put its arms at its sides instead.

"That's better," Judas said, smiling again.

"What is your command?" Keeper asked.

"I will give you the coordinates," Judas said. "Take me to the Father."

2

ABBEY LICKED THE LAST VESTIGES OF AZUL'S BLOOD FROM HER LIPS. HER entire body was tingling, electrified by the introduction of the additional naniates into her system. She could feel the change in her power. She could sense how it had grown. She felt alive, in a way that was both exhilarating and dangerous. Where was Bastion? At the moment, she wanted to give him what he wanted. It was better that he wasn't there.

She rose to her feet, turning back toward the masses gathered around her. Her eyes fell on Gant first. His expression was flat, but she knew he was disgusted by what she had just done. He had every right to be. They all did.

Of course, they weren't all opposed to the action. Rezel looked jealous, as did her Venerants. Azul's Immolents were impassive, remaining fixed while they waited for her to resolve the outcome.

She didn't hesitate to do so, looking past Pik and Benhil and the Freejects. She had done what needed to be done. What the situation demanded. No more. No less.

She walked over to where the Immolents stood. Their faces were hidden behind black masks, but she knew from the one she had killed that they were likely little more than children, and not much older than Hayley.

"As per the terms of our agreement, I expect that Azul's ships will be turned over to me immediately and in their present condition."

One of the Immolents bowed its head and then pointed to the sky. Abbey turned to look, finding a single, small transport on its way to their position.

"Damn, this shit is getting real," she heard Benhil say behind her.

"You would do the same thing if she were your child," Jequn replied.

"Yeah, I would. But maybe I would do it in private."

She ignored their back and forth. She didn't care what they thought. She couldn't afford to. Now now. They had too much work to do.

It didn't take long for the transport to reach them, settling in the wide street ahead of them, a few dozen meters away. Abbey started toward it, but Rezel approached from the side.

"Allow me, my Queen," she said, with obvious reverence. The former Prophet had seemed eager to join Azul earlier, but maybe that had been a lie?

Rezel moved to the transport, her head high. The hatch opened, and a single Nephilim stepped out. A young male, clearly one of Azul's offspring.

"Aqul," Rezel said to him.

"Rezel," he replied.

"You have come to satisfy the terms of your father's agreement?"

"I have. First, I would like to see her." He glanced past Rezel to where Abbey was standing.

Rezel also looked back at Abbey, who nodded.

"This way," Rezel said, leading him over.

"Queen of Demons, I present you with the Prophet Aqul."

Abbey didn't know what to expect from the man. She did her best to appear regal and commanding, but she wasn't feeling much patience for the pompous protocol.

"Make it quick," she said.

"I commend you on your victory," Aqul said. "You've saved this one from a life of servitude, and I'm sure she is very grateful."

"I am, my Queen," Rezel said.

"I'm withdrawing my forces from their ships as we speak, save for any Unders who are on board. However, I would like to keep my father's flagship. The Morningstar has been the head of our Prophetic for six generations now, and we will need a craft to carry us back to our nearest world."

"Forget it," Abbey said. "The ship is mine. So is the Font I'm sure is on board."

Aqul's face flashed with anger, quickly brought back under control. "Please, hear me out."

"I said make it quick."

"All of us in the Nephiliat have heard stories of the coming of Gehenna," Aqul said. "Many of the Apostants believe they are nothing but fiction. Yet you are here, which means Gehenna must be here. What need do you have of the Morningstar when you have such a thing at your disposal? My Font is a trivial thing compared to yours. Why make an enemy, when you could have an ally?"

"I just killed your father, and you want an alliance?"

"The Father has Promised that the arrival of Gehenna heralds the coming of Armageddon. I want to be on the right side when the End of Days arrive."

"End of Days?" Uriel said. "I don't see how us showing up here would be that catastrophic."

"And how do you know my side is the right side?" Abbey asked.

"You've been here a matter of days, and you've already defeated two Prophets. I'm willing to take the risk for the right reward."

"Like keeping your flagship?"

"Among other things."

"This isn't a bargaining session," Abbey said. "Your predecessor already made the deal. The ship is mine."

"One word and I can mobilize all of the Nephiliat against you," Aqul said. "Is that what you want? We can bring about Armageddon ourselves. All because of a single ship."

7

Abbey considered for a moment. Aqul didn't seem to care at all that his father was dead. He could smell the power hovering in the balance, and that was where his aim was pointed. It was typical Nephilim bullshit.

"What else do you want?" she asked.

"I would like to take Rezel as my own. Since she is yours, the bond would seal our alliance."

"No offense, but why do you want her?"

"Look at her, Queen. She is a beauty to behold, and by her lineage would produce many powerful heirs."

Abbey glanced over at Rezel, who appeared less than thrilled by the idea.

"No," Abbey said.

"Again you deny me?" Aqul said.

"Welcome to a new way of doing business," Abbey said. "Nobody does anything they don't want to, and I get the impression Rezel isn't that into you."

"I'm not, my Queen," Rezel said.

Aqul's face flushed with embarrassment over the remark. He raised his hand toward Rezel, only to find it frozen in place a moment later.

"Your father was much more Gifted than you are," Abbey said, holding him easily. "Did you drink from his Font?"

"He didn't, Queen," Rezel said. "He served aboard the Nightshade, not with his father, and Azul would never have allowed it."

"How did you become Prophet then?" Abbey asked.

"The line of succession is clear," Aqul said.

"Is it? Then tell me something else, Prophet Aqul. What reason would I have not to kill you and every other Gifted in your Prophetic?"

She could see the sudden fear in Aqul's eyes. "You wouldn't," he said.

"Why not? As soon as all the other Prophets come I'm as good as dead, right?"

He was silent.

"I'd like to propose another alliance," Abbey continued. "The Morningstar is mine. Rezel is whatever she wants to be. I'll let you leave Jamul with your life. If the Coven… Gehenna intercepts any transmissions to any other Prophets; I'll make sure you and yours are the first who don't live to see the End of Days."

"You can't enforce that," Aqul said.

"Try me."

"I'd pay to see that," Pik said.

"Me, too," Benhil agreed.

Aqul stared at Abbey until she let his arm go. Then he turned and stormed away, his Immolents falling in line behind him.

"Does that mean you agree to our terms?" Abbey called after him.

He kept walking.

"Keeper," Abbey said, opening her link to the Shardship. "Do you copy?" She waited a few seconds. "Keeper?"

Still nothing.

"Gant," Abbey said. "I can't get Keeper on the comm."

"Do you think your suit was damaged in the fighting?"

"I know it was, but it's all repaired."

"I don't know then, Queenie. It should be working."

"Keeper?" she said again. "Do you copy? Keeper?"

Still silence.

"Damn it. Rezel?"

"Yes, Queen?" Rezel said.

"I assume you have a comm array in there." She pointed at the main tower in the center of the city.

"Of course," she replied.

"Good. Gant, take Joker and see if you can set up a transmitter to get us back in touch with the others, including Keeper."

"If I can?" Gant said. "I might be going dumb, but I'm not stupid. Give me twenty minutes."

"Thank you," Abbey said. "Rezel, I'm going to need food for my soldiers."

"It will be done," she said. She turned to one of her Venerants, giving her instructions.

"I'm going to need access to your Font, too."

Rezel froze, looking back over her shoulder. "My Font?"

"I need whatever I can get."

She hesitated and then nodded. "Of course, Queen."

Abbey turned her attention to the Asura Legionnaires ringing the space.

"Sergeants spread out around the city and keep watch."

"As you command," they replied.

She would still need to figure out what exactly she was going to do with the Asura soldiers. Between all of Keeper's warnings and the way they had questioned her commands, bringing them back to the Republic seemed like a very bad idea, even if she did enjoy having a pet dragon.

"Keeper," she said, trying one more time to reach out to the artificial intelligence.

Where the frag had it gone with her ship?

"Tell me of this Prophet, Belial."

Belial bowed his head before his Master. "Of course, Lord. The Prophet Selvig Thraven. He is a human, a descendent of the One. A former slave."

"A slave?"

"Yes. He was brought to the Nephiliat many thousands of years ago. He has achieved much glory in your name. Much more than any of the other Prophets who have worshipped you."

"They play petty games of power and control when they should be heeding my Word. They squabble over planets when the entire multiverse should be ours. So many years have passed, Belial. We should have built the Gate long ago. We should have returned home long ago. The One believes he is safe in Elysium. Why has it taken so long?"

The question sent a wave of heat from the large seat where Lucifer was positioned. His arms rested on the sides of it, still connected to the device that had kept him alive for thousands of years.

Belial could barely look at his old friend. The changes were so drastic, the power of the Gift so immense that it radiated around him, making him difficult to be near. Even when he spoke, his voice echoed painfully inside the Seraphim's mind.

"As you have said yourself, Lord. They worship you, but they do not understand you. They don't realize the truth of the Covenant. None, except for Thraven."

"I sacrificed all that I was for them," Lucifer said. "I murdered the one I swore to follow. Because I'm a monster? Because I'm evil? No. For them. And this is how they repay me? It took a human, a descendent of the Shard, to see my work near completion?"

The heat of his anger was almost unbearable, forcing Belial to take a few steps back. "Regardless, the Gate is completed. The war is being won. Prophet Thraven delivers all glory to you, Father. He works to fulfill your Promise, and bring about the Great Return. Then the One will burn in the fires of his own creation, and Elysium will be free."

"I am grateful to him for it," Lucifer said. "Even so, the Prophet's misdeeds will not go unpunished. I will make an example of them, and then I will call them to me. They will travel with me, as many as are able, back to this Shardspace, back to the Gate. They will follow, or they will die."

"Of course, Lord," Belial agreed. "It will be as they deserve."

Lucifer sat in silence. He had spent most of the time since his awakening in silence, while Belial had provided him with a general overview of the universe as it had come to be. The servant was certain his Master was pleased to know that his efforts had not been in vain. That he was pleased to be revived at all. So much could have gone wrong over the millennia, though Belial had never expected it would. They had planned everything down to the last detail, the first members of the Nephilim resistance. Himself, Lucifer, Judas, and the others. They had adjusted as the war had developed, and they had always maintained hope that this day would come.

The end of the Children of the Shard. Armageddon.

"Gehenna is coming?" Lucifer asked.

"It is en route, my Lord," Belial replied. "It should be here very soon."

The Prophets believed Lucifer had been turned into a monster, violent and frenzied, with no ability to think on his own. Even Thraven believed it. It was true that the naniates had changed him, transformed him into a being so unlike what he had once been, but it wasn't to make him a monster. It was to make him better. Stronger. His original form couldn't contain the energy they required or remain whole against the power they provided. They had altered him, changed him, made him into what they needed to survive. The others had never understood as well as Lucifer did that the relationship could be symbiotic. That the naniates had an intelligence of their own, and that they could be exploited because of it.

The stories of his insanity? They were exaggerated, as most things became over the passage of time. It was a convenient excuse for his stasis and isolation, a misdirection from the truth of his affliction. There was a cost to being so overridden with naniates. A heavy price to pay. He could only survive encumbered for so long, and when he died?

Belial tried not to think about it. The Father would die. That was a certainty. Ideally, he would perish in the arms of the One, and his retribution would be swift and final.

"Tell me about the Chosen. The one who brought Gehenna to me."

"I don't know much about her, my Lord. A human female. Strong-willed. She killed the Prophet Azul, who was of no small ability himself."

"Does she resemble Lilith?" Lucifer asked.

"I have not seen her, Lord."

Lucifer was silent again. Thinking. Plotting. Planning. The freedom of the Seraphim was the only thing he desired, and it consumed his mind.

Belial turned around when a tone sounded nearby. A projection appeared at a console there, a view of the Shardship entering the region near the Shrine.

"It is here," he said, looking back at Lucifer.

"Tell me, Belial," Lucifer said. "Who is the next strongest Prophet after Thraven?"

"Prophet Tega, my Lord," Belial said. "Why?"

"I told you already. I will make an example of him. Only then will the Prophets take my Word seriously. Only then will they follow. Only then will they believe in the Great Return and the triumphant glory of the Seraphim."

Lucifer stretched his arms away from his seat, breaking the bonds of the tubes that fed into them, sending a line of blood spilling to the ground at his feet. He stood up, extending his enlarged frame and flexing powerful limbs.

"You have been with me all of these years, Belial," Lucifer said. "I'm grateful for your loyalty. Together, we will free our people."

"Yes, my Lord."

"Tell the Keeper to bring Gehenna as close as he dares. We will board my ship and be on our way."

4

"Here it is," Rezel said, the hatch opening in front of her.

Abbey followed the defeated Prophet into the room. The Font was positioned in the center. She had been expecting something ornate. Something reverent. Or at least something with some hint of religion. Instead, Rezel's Font was a large metal drum; a nondescript raised pool filled halfway with naniate-thick blood. A lid for the Font rested beside it, placed on the ground as though it had been lifted off and discarded.

"Azul took my capital three months ago," Rezel said. "The Font there was beautiful and ornate, carved from some of the rarest stone in the galaxy." She shook her head and sighed. "I barely escaped from that place, and from the three other planets Azul attacked after that."

"The presentation sucks, but I'm not in a position to be picky about that," Abbey said, approaching the Font.

She could feel the energy of the naniates as she reached the pool. The Nephilim entered their Fonts to recharge after using the Gift, the overall density and effectiveness of the naniates limited by the effects of the Serum that helped keep them more easily under control. While she had held that same Serum in her hand, the Light of the Shard had convinced her not to drink it, offering itself in the cocktail's place as an alternate means of stopping her transformation. It had cleansed her of the aggressive taint of Lucifer's creation, but she had learned that what she had gained through the cleansing paled in comparison to what she had lost.

More than that, she had learned that there was no such thing as pure. Lucifer had pissed in the pool a long time ago, leaving a stain that couldn't be removed. It had been painted over and hidden away, but it had always been there.

Lingering.

Waiting.

Biding its time.

She had a feeling there was something to it, but what?

She didn't know yet. What she did know was that she could grow stronger if she were willing to do what needed to be done to increase that strength. Right now, that meant entering the Font and swallowing as much of the blood in it as she could without getting sick and vomiting it back up. It meant increasing the density of the naniates in her system and allowing them to continue her transformation. It meant never taking the Serum, and accepting that she would become something else. Something dark and violent and angry, in exchange for the future of the galaxy and the life of her daughter.

It was a shitty decision to have to make. It was going to be an awful end to what had been a pretty wonderful life before Gloritant Thraven had made himself known. It didn't matter. She had signed her life away to be a soldier a long time ago. She had agreed to sacrifice her life for the good of the Republic.

She would never have guessed it would be like this.

"The Font is much more enjoyable if you undress, my Queen," Rezel said, joining her at the edge. "I can help you if you'd like."

Abbey glanced over at her. "You've been pretty agreeable since you surrendered. Why?"

"You want to free the Unders. You gave me the choice of whether or not to go with Aqul. I lost my Prophetic, my Queen. I was unfit to stand in the shadow of the Father. I did the best I could to carry on my legacy, but years of conflict left the Liliat Empire dry. We had no Skellings, no Executioners, no Goreshin or Converts or Hoarders. You came to me because you had a plan. A way to serve us both and return my Empire to glory. It's too late for that, but as Aqul said, it is preferable to be on the winning side when Armageddon comes."

"Why do you think I'll win? Just because of the Covenant?"

"Your ship? No. Not because of that. Because you have the one thing none of the Prophets have."

"Nice hair?" she said, smiling.

"Loyal followers," Rezel replied. "They aren't with you out of fear, or because they want something from you. They aren't here against their will. I didn't understand the value in it until I saw the furry one fighting Azul. Not because he was forced to, but because he wanted to. Because he loves you." She reached out, putting a hand on Abbey's wrist. "If you would allow it, I could also come to love you."

Abbey stared into Rezel's eyes. There was nothing innocent about the touch. It was suggestive. Electric. The charge Azul's blood had put into her was almost enough to make it tempting. Was there anything honest in it? Not because she was interested in the Prophet's advances, but she did need to have at least some small measure of trust in her. She was Gifted, and more powerful than the average Apostant. That made her useful.

"For now, can you go and see about the food for my soldiers?" Abbey asked, pulling her arm away.

She caught the slightest flash of displeasure behind Rezel's eyes. Then the other woman bowed to her. "At your command, my Queen."

Abbey watched Rezel leave the room. She wanted to be able to trust her, but she wasn't an idiot. She could imagine how it would go. Accepting Rezel's advances, taking the woman to her bed, and then waking up with her head nearly severed from her body.

No thanks.

She turned her attention back to the Font. She reached toward it, leaning over to dip her hand below the surface. The blood was warm. Alive. She pulled her hand back out, feeling nauseous. She wasn't a Nephilim. She hadn't been bred to believe humans were like cattle. It had been one thing to drink the blood of an enemy to get stronger. It was another to drink the blood of the innocent.

Her thoughts turned to the Brimstone, and of the poor souls being used to power the ship's engines through the use of the Gift. The ship was powerful, but it was also an abomination that needed to be destroyed, the souls within put to rest. That would never happen if Thraven won. The torture would continue for all of eternity, and more of the ships would be constructed to bring through the Gate to Elysium. At least the souls who had provided the fuel for the Font were already gone. If they had the choice to help her stop Thraven, wouldn't they?

She decided they would. She released the naniates from her skin, letting them sink beneath the surface and allowing herself to be naked. It felt good to have the air on her flesh instead of billions of machines, and she stood there a moment before climbing over the edge of the Font and into it.

The blood rose to her thighs. She felt waves of nausea at first, while she tried to adjust to the reality. She could feel the naniates around her, jolts of electricity against her flesh, linking with the naniates within her. The feeling was calming and soothing, and immediately began to restore her. At least Rezel had been honest about that. It was better to enter unclothed.

She lowered herself slowly, sinking into the thick liquid, spreading herself out beneath. The blood came up to her neck, causing her to pause again. Every part of her was tingling. Every part of her was on fire, in the best possible way.

She closed her eyes. She would need to submerge herself in it, open her mouth and let it in. How had she wound up in this place so far from home? It seemed like only yesterday that she had been walking along the waterfront with Hayley in the Construct while preparing to drop into a war zone. What she would have given to have that life back.

She slid further into the blood, the liquid rising until it covered her head. She gasped involuntarily as she became completely submerged, her body convulsing slightly, a warmth rising through her. When she opened her mouth, the blood ran in, and she welcomed it, swallowing it. Once. Twice. Three times. She didn't go too fast. She needed to know when she was at her limit. Her body would need time to adjust.

Eight times she swallowed, the fire inside her expanding as she did, until she felt like she was burning up from within. She pulled herself up, her head emerging from the blood, her heart pounding and breath short. She coughed a few times, feeling unsettled. She had to fight it off. Keep it in. So many individuals were counting on her.

"Queenie."

Gant's voice sounded inside her mind, delivered through the naniates. That had never happened before, and the sudden voice nearly caused her to jump from the Font.

"Gant?" she replied, not speaking out loud, pushing the word out as though she were talking to the Asura Sergeants.

"I'm finished updating the comm array," he said. "Still no response from Keeper."

"What the frag?" Abbey said. "You have to be kidding me."

"I wish I were. I did a quick sweep of the area. I know Keeper could have taken the Covenant anywhere, but it isn't even within extended range. Pinging the ship's address isn't returning anything."

"You're telling me the Covenant is gone?" Abbey said. "How is that even possible?"

"Your guess is as good as mine."

This was bad. Without the Shardship, they didn't have a way to get back to the Republic.

They couldn't go home.

"Get the others organized. We need to figure this out, immediately."

"Roger, Queenie."

She pulled herself to her feet, letting the blood run from her. She turned toward the door, suddenly eager to be away from the Font.

Rezel was standing a few steps in front of it. The Prophet's eyes were locked on Abbey's body, her mouth slightly open. She was holding something in her hand.

"My Queen," Rezel said. She held the object forward. "I wanted to show you this. It is from the original Font back on Lilith, my home-world which was named after the Mother."

Abbey's eyes shifted to the object. It was intricately carved, a pattern that looked like a sun at the outside, with a secondary figure in the center. Slender, with bony ridges along her arms and legs, and a tail that curved around from behind.

"It reminded me of you," Rezel said. "You have similar ridges along your flesh, though they are much smaller."

Abbey had already stopped looking at the figure. She had noted that it looked almost identical to the vision of her future self that Phlenel had provided. At the moment, that was the least of her concern.

The carving was made from a black, crystalline stone.

Darkstone.

Rezel took another step forward, smiling. "I see you took my advice," she said. "I was correct, was I not? I didn't suggest you enter naked just because I think you're beautiful, my Queen."

Abbey's heart was racing. Of all the things the carving could have been made from, it was fragging Darkstone?

"Are there more of those here?" she asked, pointing at the artwork. She had no idea what would happen if the Asura knew about the crystal, and she didn't want to find out.

"No," Rezel replied. "The Font on Lilith is as beautiful as this one small piece. Perhaps with your help, we will both see it again some-"

She never got to finish her sentence. An Asura Sergeant appeared behind her, his blade already at her throat. She had just enough time to gasp in sudden surprise before her head was severed from her body, both tumbling toward the floor as a second Legionnaire grabbed the statue.

"Sergeants. Halt."

Abbey sent the message out to them. The Sergeant's eyes shifted to her, and then they both phased out of sight, still carrying their prize.

She heard Dog roar from somewhere beyond the tower.

This was very, very bad.

5

THE SCREAMS FROM WITHIN THE TOWER FOLLOWED A FEW SECONDS later, even as Abbey jumped out of the Font and ran over to where Rezel had fallen.

"Sergeants, stop at once," she said, calling out to the Asura.

"It is ours," one of the Sergeants replied. "We don't need you any longer. You are not Asura."

She clenched her teeth and cursed. Of course.

A Legionnaire phased into view directly ahead of her, sword already sweeping toward her neck. She let herself fall backward, momentum carrying her away from the blade and pushing her toward the soldier's legs. It didn't vanish fast enough, sudden claws sprouting from her hand and slashing through the calf, removing its foot.

Three more Legionnaires flashed into view, including one of her Sergeants. None of them were carrying the statue. They were trying to slow her down.

"Queenie," Gant said, slightly out of breath. "What the frag is going on?"

She returned to her feet, the Gift flowing around her and coating her in a new demonsuit. She kicked one of the Asura, knocking it back, spinning and slashing at another, who disappeared. The third tried to stab her in the back, but she used the Gift to yank the sword away, turning it over and pushing it back at the soldier and running it through.

"Darkstone," Abbey replied, opening a wide channel to her Rejects. "Rezel had Darkstone. The Asura took it."

"And now they're killing everyone," Uriel said. "They're in the city, attacking the Lessers."

"Frag," Abbey said. "Gant, can you contact Delta?"

"As soon as I can get back to the comm," Gant replied. "Give me a second."

"Get them down here. Call in Rezel's ships, too. We need transport off this fragging planet."

"Roger."

Keeper had tried to warn her. He said not to bring the Asura to the surface. He told her not to let them off the Covenant where they were at least contained.

Damn herself for not listening.

She made it out the door and into the corridor, just in time to see an Asura appear directly in front of one of Rezel's Venerants. The Gift flared from the Nephilim, flames reaching out and engulfing the soldier. It disappeared, leaving the corridor empty for a moment, reappearing beside the Venerant and stabbing her in the side. She cried out, trying to shove the Asura away. It vanished again, reappearing on the other side and running its blade through the Venerant's neck.

Abbey threw her hand out, the naniates at the ends of her fingers breaking away and launching toward the soldier, four bullets that pierced it before it could react. The spears went through the Legionnaire before breaking apart into a million separate machines and streaming back to their home.

She made it to the Venerant, who was already dead. She leaned down, finding a dagger and a gun beneath his cloak. She took both, making her way to the tube that could bring her down to the others.

"Queenie," Gant said. "I've got Delta Squadron inbound."

"Roger," Abbey replied. "What about our transport?"

"We may have a problem."

"Don't say that."

"Sorry, Queenie. It seems Aqul has noticed the Covenant didn't come back."

"That little piece of shit. If he leaves with my ships, he's as good as dead."

"He hasn't left yet, and Imp said he's still got transports moving personnel, but if he notices the fighting on the ground he might change his mind."

"Damn it. Get Imp to buzz the tower as low and slow as he can manage. Have the rest of Delta tracking the Asura. As far as I know, only one of them can fly up to attack them."

"A big one."

"Oh, and tell them not to hurt Dog if they can help it. He's not malicious; he's just chasing the Darkstone."

"I'll remind you of that if he eats us."

"Just do it."

"Aye, Queenie."

Abbey reached the tube. The shaft was clear, the carriage near the bottom. She grabbed the closed doors, forcing them open despite the complaints of the safety system. A new set of claws sprouted on her hand, and a fresh set sprang from her feet. She jumped into the shaft, sharp edges digging into the transparency and holding her in place as she started to climb.

"Queenie, this is Imp, do you copy?"

Bastion's voice entered her mind. If he was able to reach her on the short-range comm, it meant he and the rest of Delta were inside the planet's atmosphere.

"Roger, Imp. I hear you. What's your position?"

"We're closing in on the city. What the frag is going on down here?"

"I'll tell you later. Get your ass to the tower. Pull around it as best you can, I'm on my way."

"On your way? What do you mean on your way? I'm in a starfighter, not a hovercraft."

"I'm aware of that, thank you. Pudding."

"Aye, Queenie?"

"You're in charge of Delta. If you see any Asura that aren't dragons, kill them."

"We'll do our best, Queenie. Our munitions are loaded for starship combat, not ground support."

"Understood. Okay."

"Aye, Queenie?" Pik said.

"What's your status?"

"Fragging bugs," Pik replied. "If you remember, I was in favor of killing these things back on the Covenant."

"Duly noted," Abbey replied. "But we wouldn't have taken Jamul without them."

"And now we're going to lose Jamul because of them."

"We got what we came for. I wasn't going to bring them off the planet with me, anyway."

"You were going to leave them here to kill everybody?"

"Of course not. I was going to take everybody with us."

"I don't know if there's going to be anybody left to take. We lost fifty Freejects already."

Abbey winced at the number. She had to hurry.

"Queenie," Benhil said. "Requesting backup. Uriel, Cherub, and I are getting pinned down."

"What's your position?" Abbey asked.

"A warehouse or something, due east of the main tower. We've got a squad of Rezel's former slaves with us. They were showing us where to pick up supplies. I'm marking it on my TCU."

"Roger. Delta, can you find the warehouse?"

"I have it, Queenie," Ruby said.

"Gant, are you still at the array?"

"Aye, Queenie."

"The others are in trouble, and could use your ninja skills."

"Roger. I'm on it. Three of Rezel's ships are inbound to extract us."

"Cancel that order and then go."

"What did you say?"

"I said cancel the transports. We can't risk that the Asura will get on board and hitch a ride off the planet."

"Uh, Queenie, if the transports don't come, how are we going to get off the planet?"

Abbey stopped climbing. "I don't know. I haven't figured that out yet. I'm open to suggestions."

Gant chittered nervously. "And I thought things were starting to go our way."

"Silly squirrel-man," Abbey replied.

She resumed her ascent, hand over hand up the side of the tube toward the top. They needed to stop the Asura attack. She also needed to prevent Aqul from leaving. How were they supposed to do both?

She made it to the top of the tube, climbing out and running to a window at the end of the corridor. She could see the east side of the city far below, and the Apocalypse fighters sweeping past, firing down on the streets. Smoke was rising from different areas where the Asura were doing their best to kill everyone that wasn't Asura.

"Rejects, hang in there," she said. "I have an idea."

6

ABBEY PUT HER HAND TO THE WINDOW, USING THE GIFT TO PUSH against it and wrenching it from its frame. It exploded outward before tumbling to the ground below, though she didn't wait to see it hit bottom. She climbed out and scaled the outer wall, quickly reaching the rooftop.

"Imp, I'm in position. Come and get me, will you?"

"Come and get you? In a starfighter?"

"Don't argue, just get close."

"Roger. Don't hurt me, okay, Queenie?"

"No promises."

She scanned the horizon, finding one of the Apocalypse fighters breaking away from the others. It streaked toward the tower, closing in a hurry, slowing slightly as it neared. She could see Bastion in the cockpit; his eyes squinted in concentration as he attempted to get as close to the building as he could.

She ran to the edge, pausing there and waving to him. He adjusted course, slipping the fighter to the left, so close that for a moment she thought the short wing might clip the structure.

She watched him intently, the Gift flowing outward from her as she prepared to jump.

"Ah, Queenie, shit," Bastion said, the fighter cutting to the left at the last instant. "Watch your six."

She didn't hear the last sentence. Something came at her from behind on a blast of torrid air. She spun around just in time to get a look at the underside of Dog's immense body before a talon reached out and grabbed her.

She cursed in pain as the large foot squeezed around her, threatening to crush her in the powerful grip. Dog swept over the tower, angling downward, wings spread in a glide. It roared loudly, rolling sideways and turning to the landscape beyond the city.

"Dog," Abbey said. "Damn it not now."

She couldn't move her arms to try to communicate with the dragon. She could barely even breathe.

She did hear the roar of thrusters, and she watched as Bastion flashed by in the fighter, cutting back to slot in behind the creature.

"Imp, don't shoot him," Abbey said.

"He's going to eat you," Bastion replied.

"If he were going to eat me he would have already."

"Whatever he's doing, he's interrupting your plan."

"Yeah."

"Do we have time for this?"

"Not really. Standby."

She wriggled in Dog's grip. It only tightened, cutting her breath off even more.

"Frag it," she shouted. "Dog, let me go."

The dragon ignored her, dropping toward a nearby line of Nephilim, who were eagerly trying to escape him. Flames blasted from his mouth, washing over them, leaving them a smoking mess of charred flesh as he touched down, walking on three feet, using his wings for balance.

He let Abbey go then, throwing her forward so that she rolled to a stop in front of him.

"Dog," she said, getting to her feet. Smoke was pouring out of his nostrils, his mouth snapping open and closed. She didn't get a good feeling about the posture. "Don't even think about-"

The head snapped toward her, jaws moving almost too quickly for her to avoid. Apparently, the discovery of the Darkstone meant her usefulness had changed. Would her naniate-spiked blood fuel the dragon better than normal meat? It was the only thing that made sense.

"I don't want to hurt you," she said, pushing with the Gift to leap aside as the head darted toward her again.

She had only just landed when a wing slammed into her, knocking her aside and taking her breath away. She barely got up before the head snapped down, bouncing backward and putting a little space between them.

"Queenie, I've got a lock," Bastion said, his fighter dropping toward them.

"No," she said. "I've got this."

She jumped aside as Dog tried to bite her again, throwing the Gift forward with her fist. It hit the dragon hard on the side of the head, knocking it violently to the side. The blow only made him angry, and he growled and reached for her with a foot.

She caught the foot in both hands, the Gift pouring from her, helping her to hold the talons at bay.

"Seriously, Queenie," Bastion said. "I can end this right now."

"No," Abbey replied. "It's not his fault. He's an animal."

Not like the Legionnaires. They had deliberately turned on her, and she had no problem killing them.

She shoved the foot to the side, rolling away as it came down hard on the ground, digging into the earth. She jumped up, grabbing the side of his wing and twisting, throwing herself toward his neck with the Gift. He roared and tried to turn his head to bite her, but she was too fast. She gripped onto him, getting her hand to his head and pushing the Gift into him.

In her mind, she visualized the Asura Sergeant who had taken the Darkstone. She sent Dog the image of him eating the soldier and claiming the entire stone for himself. She had no idea if the dragon had enough intelligence to understand, but she had to try.

It seemed that he did. He began running across the ground, wings pumping to get him airborne once more, the rider on his back suddenly forgotten. They lifted into the air, rising rapidly and turning back toward the city.

"Imp, where are you?" Abbey asked, turning to scan the sky.

"Coming in," Bastion replied, the fighter suddenly appearing from a line of thin clouds.

"Don't miss," she said, standing on Dog's neck.

"What do you mean, don't miss?"

She gathered the Gift and jumped, arcing high into the air, letting the dragon speed away.

There was probably some part of her that should have been afraid to be suspended a thousand meters in the air with nothing around her and no way to keep from falling, but she found she wasn't worried. She had taken in so much of Lucifer's Gift. She had accepted it fully back into her system. She felt strong. Powerful. Unstoppable.

For as long as she remained sane, anyway.

She swept the Gift around her, creating a flow of air that was almost powerful enough to keep her up and let her fly. She sank slowly, the wind buffeting at her as Bastion approached, slowing as he neared. The canopy of the starfighter slid back, and she reached out with the Gift, catching the fighter and slowing it more than its onboard systems would allow, too much for it to stay aloft on its own. It hovered for a moment beneath her, Bastion looking up with an amazed, frightened expression.

"Were you telling me not to miss, or yourself?" he asked as she sank into the cockpit, coming down on his lap. It was a tight fit, but she made it work.

"Either way," she replied. "Watch out for my hair, and be ready to hit the thrusters."

The canopy slid closed, her head just barely fitting beneath it. It was a cozy fit, one she didn't mind all that much.

"How am I supposed to fly like this?" he asked, his hands wrapping around her to cradle the controls.

"I thought you were a professional?"

She released the Gift. Immediately, the fighter began to drop.

"Oh, shit," Bastion said, working the controls around her.

They were both pushed back as he increased thrust, gaining speed to level the fighter out. They streaked near to the ground before sweeping upward, taking a steep vector toward the atmosphere.

"Get me to Aqul's flagship," Abbey said.

"Aye, aye, Wonder Woman," Bastion replied.

"Who?" Abbey asked.

"Nevermind."

7

JUDAS FELL TO HIS KNEES WHEN LUCIFER ENTERED THE COVENANT. HE bowed his head without looking on his Master, already aware of the changes that had altered his form. Even so, it was impossible not to notice the size or shape of the shadow the Father cast, large and monstrous and frightening.

"Father," Judas said, remaining in place. "I present you with Gehenna, the Harbinger of Armageddon."

"Judas," Lucifer said, his voice causing the Apostant to shiver. "You have done well. Very well. Thank you for your faith. You are a true friend to me. A true disciple."

"Thank you, Father," Judas said.

"Rise and look on me, brother."

Judas came to his feet. He looked up slowly, forcing himself not to draw back in fear at the sight of his Master. He could feel the energy of the Gift emanating from the Father, a constant burning that itched at his flesh.

"Where is the Keeper?" Lucifer asked.

"On his way," Judas replied. "Where is Belial?"

"He will be along shortly. I gave him one final task to complete at the Shrine. We will not be returning to it."

"But-"

"I will die. Yes, I know. The Gift will finish what it started. It will happen in the presence of the One, and my work will be complete."

"The Seraphim will be freed at last?" Judas asked.

"Yes. We will return to Elysium in glory, and deliver the killing blow to the Great Manipulator. We will return our kind to their rightful place as masters of their universe."

Judas bowed his head again. It was all that he had been waiting for. All that he had sacrificed for. All that he had hoped for.

He had been a loyal Seraphim once. Loyal to the Shard, and to the One. He had fought against Lucifer when the war had started, still blinded by his trust and his faith in the future the One had promised. He had lost his wife in the early fighting, and for centuries had blamed the Father for his loss.

Time and experience had changed his perspective. He had watched the Shard die, the Seraphim splinter, and the Archchancellors come to be. He had observed their decisions, argued their positions, and participated in the genocide of thousands of their kind in the name of the One. At least until he had come to his senses.

He had never expected it would be his wife who drove him back to Lucifer. Her memory had stayed with him always, and in the days when the Infected nearly overwhelmed their facility and killed every Archchancellor and every Seraphim with them, he had come to realize what a mistake they had made. He had watched Seraphim enslave Seraphim, experiment on them and turn them into mindless automatons in the name of the Shard. And if they could enslave one another for the Shard, didn't it stand to reason that the One was capable of enslaving them? Couldn't it be possible that Lucifer was right?

His wife had always beckoned him to judge everything based on actions, not words. The One's words were correct, but the actions were questionable.

Why were they never allowed to return home?

It had been easier than he ever imagined to betray the others. To bring some of the Lucifer's Gift onto the Shardship and pass it into the Focus. To prepare the Covenant for a day he knew would one day come, even if it took a million lifetimes. To fake his death at the hands of the Asura, and hide away. He had no remorse about it now. The Terrans and the other intelligent life in the Shard's galaxy came secondary to the needs of his kind. He didn't desire to kill them, but he desired the Seraphim's slavery less.

"My Lord Lucifer," Judas heard Keeper say.

He looked up, finding the intelligence approaching. There was no hint of malice in the Keeper. No question about his loyalty. He was a machine, and his instructions had been altered, making him more loyal than even himself or Belial.

He would do whatever the Master commanded.

"Keeper," Lucifer said. "It has been so long."

"Welcome home, Father," Keeper said.

"Set a course for Tigrul," Lucifer said. "And prepare to leave at my command."

"Yes, Father," Keeper said.

"I understand you have been making alterations to the ship?"

"The Chosen requested conversion of some of the living habitats to offensive capabilities. A number of residential structures have been reconfigured into plasma cannons. Would you like me to reverse the conversion?"

"Reverse it?" Lucifer said. "Not at all. Continue the conversion. Add as many weapons to the Gehenna as you can."

Keeper bowed low. "As you command, Father."

"I would like to visit the Shard," Lucifer said.

"Of course, Father. The Shardship has been reconfigured for easy passage from here to the Core. I will show you the way."

"Judas will guide me," Lucifer said.

Judas bowed again. "Of course, Father."

"Keeper, Belial will arrive soon. Engage FTL the moment he is on board."

"Yes, Father."

"This way, Father," Judas said.

He pointed his Master toward the larger opening that had been created to allow the Asura creature into the landing bay. It was a more suitable size for the Father than the smaller passages the others had used.

"Do you ever regret your decision, Judas?" Lucifer asked as they walked.

"Which decision are you referring to, Master?" Judas replied.

"To not support me when I murdered the Shard."

Judas kept his eyes forward. "Yes."

"Do not lie to me, Judas."

"I did not understand the way of things back then," Judas said.

"But you do today?"

"I have waited many, many years for this day to come. I betrayed those who trusted me. I remained hidden from the universe. I did all that you asked. Why do you question me, Father?"

Lucifer didn't respond right away. Judas could feel the growing heat of his Master's anger behind him. He needed to be more careful with his answers. The Father was not as beyond logic as the legends suggested, but the Gift still exacted its price.

"The Prophets failed me, brother. All of them, except for Thraven." Lucifer laughed, a deep growl. "And he isn't even a Nephilim."

"Yet he sees like a true Disciple," Judas said.

"He does. I question you because your loyalties once belonged to the Shard over me. I question you because you killed my Lilith."

Judas felt more heat behind him. Would this be the thought that caused his death?

"As you killed my Beatrice," Judas replied. "In the heat of war, not with malicious intent. I regret both of our losses, Father. Both sadden me."

Lucifer fell silent. Judas allowed himself to breathe. He had survived this encounter. Would he survive the next?

They reached the tomb of the Shard, bypassing the Core. Judas waited at the enlarged entrance, head bowed, allowing Lucifer to enter first. The Father did so, pausing ahead of the tomb, dropping to a knee and bowing his head. Then he stood and approached the Shard, stepping up to the Tomb, leaning over it and looking in.

"It is a long road we have taken," he said. "Look at you. Look at me. Victory will be mine. Your Creator will fall at my feet. I will hold his head in my hands and proclaim freedom to the Seraphim, and then I will smash this vessel and tear you from it and rip your frozen remains in half. I'll shred you to pieces, and piss on what's left."

His hand came down hard on the top of the tomb, flames of energy flaring around him. Judas watched him freeze, grunting in an effort to contain his rage. It took a few breaths, but he calmed, taking a step back from the Shard.

"Until then, I will use you the way you've used us. Your ship is mine. Your body is mine. Your blood is mine."

He placed his hand in the fountain at the head of the tomb. Judas stared in amazement as the milky white liquid running through the tubes quickly became tinged with red. Within a minute, it was deep and dark, all evidence of the Shard's Gift erased.

"Judas," Lucifer said.

"Yes, Father," Judas said, entering the room and walking toward him.

"I have never forgiven you."

Judas had just enough time to draw in a breath to scream. Then his entire body was on fire, every molecule burning, both inside and out.

His ashes drifted across the floor of the tomb under his Father's satisfied gaze.

8

GANT CHECKED THE COMM ONE LAST TIME, CALLING OUT FOR KEEPER and the Covenant, and receiving nothing back.

The AI had abandoned them, that much was clear. Why? That was a lot more confusing. It was a machine, not capable of changing its mind or breaking its programming, and it was programmed to follow the Chosen. What could have happened to alter those directives?

The only thing he could come up with was an outside influence. A third party. Hiding on the Shardship? It was certainly possible. The Covenant was huge, and they had barely explored a portion of it in the time since they had left the Republic. Another entire army could have been camped out inside, and they would never have known.

Shouldn't Keeper have known?

What if it had been hacked?

The idea annoyed him. So did the fact that he couldn't quite get a grasp on it. It was another symptom of his diminishing intelligence, the loss of the perfect mind he had been given. He should have had a clear picture of the circumstances. Instead, he was left to wonder.

There was no more time for even that. A pair of Asura soldiers lay dead in the center of the comm room, their necks neatly slit by his knives. They had popped in on him out of nowhere, and only his size and agility had saved him, allowing him to slip away and avoid too much damage. As it was, he had a cut on his arm that was bleeding a little bit and hurt a lot. Assholes.

Abbey had been playing with fire to bring them to Jamul, and now they were all getting burned. He didn't blame her. He knew their options had been limited and that without the Asura they might not have defeated Rezel's forces at all. He couldn't help but wonder if there was another option they had missed because they were leaning on the creatures. Something more creative but equally effective.

Again, it didn't matter now.

There were eighteen ships left in Rezel's fleet, and they were more than happy to remain in orbit and follow their new Queen. They had watched the Prophet lose planet after planet, but their staunch support of the bride of Lucifer held their loyalty. The resemblance between what Abbey was becoming and what Lilith had become was too strong to be a total coincidence. He hadn't told her about that yet, but he had found an image in Rezel's datastores that verified that truth. Not that they were the same, or even slightly related. Maybe the naniates simply changed males one way and females another, but the result was what mattered, and she was starting to look like Lilith. In this case, it was working out in their favor.

Those ships would wait, but he was certain the other fleet wouldn't. Even as he crossed the room and reached the exit, he could see on the array's sensors that the transports were reaching their destinations and remaining there, packing it in and getting ready to leave.

Would Abbey be able to stop them in time?

She had turned against the Light of the Shard. She had turned back to the blood of the Nephilim. He couldn't really blame her. He had seen both powers at work, and there was no denying Lucifer's brew was more suited for war. It was violent and powerful as a storm, while the Shard's naniates were soft like a breeze. Both useful for their own purposes, he supposed.

He thought it was disgusting that she had to drink blood to

increase the power. He thought the fate she was tempting was equally terrible. She was his alpha, and he knew she was going to lose herself. Not dead, but different. And when she did, he would follow her. If that meant slaughtering innocents, he would do it. If it meant killing the other Rejects, he would do it. He wouldn't even question. That's what loyalty was to a Gant.

He hoped it wouldn't come to that. He would do whatever he could to help prevent it.

For now, he needed to reach the others. Benhil and Jequn were in trouble.

He left the comm station, moving out into the hallway. The makeshift Palace was a tall tower in the center of the city, the home of the planet's High Apostant, who was in charge of the occupants below. It housed dozens of Apostants, hundreds of Lessers, and even more Unders. It was mostly abandoned now, the residents fleeing at the first sign of trouble. Only corpses remained from that group, nearly thirty of them on his way from the station to the tubes that would carry him back to the ground.

He didn't run into any Asura on the way. He assumed because they had thought the floor was clear and empty, or that the two who had gone after him were guaranteed to survive. They had forgotten quickly that the Rejects didn't die all that easily, even against phase-shifting aliens from another dimension. They were hard to kill to begin with, and when Gant was pissed like he was now, he was an even harder kill.

He called the tube platform up, waiting impatiently while it ascended. He paced back and forth, wondering where Abbey was and if she were in one piece. He knew the Gift had turned her into something only a few steps short of a demigod, but he still worried. Her neck wasn't impervious to sharp edges, and the Asura were able to appear out of thin air.

He had to restrain himself to keep from contacting her. She knew what she was doing, and she had given him a different mission.

"Okay, it's Gant. What's your status?" he asked, as the platform reached his floor, the tube doors opening.

"Gant," Pik replied. "I'm in the mess with the Freejects. We took a beating down here, but I've got ten dead Asura stinking up the place. Where are you?"

"I'm on a tube heading down. Joker and Cherub are in trouble, and Queenie ordered me to rescue them."

"By yourself?"

"I could, but I'd prefer a little backup."

"Roger. The mess is on the third floor. We'll meet you on the ground."

"Roger."

The tube reached the third floor a few seconds later. Gant looked out into the hallway as he passed, seeing nothing but a few dead Nephilim. It had gotten ugly on this planet in a hurry.

"Gant," Abbey said, her voice cutting in.

"Queenie," he replied, a little too excitedly. "Where are you?"

"On my way up to meet Aqul's ship. Listen, if you see a Legionnaire carrying a Darkstone sculpture, do whatever you can to stop him and retrieve it. That's what they're after, and if we get it back we may be able to calm them down."

"How am I supposed to find one Legionnaire when they keep popping out of this timeline?" he asked.

"You might not. Just if you see that one, do your best."

"Roger."

The tube reached the ground floor. The door hadn't even opened when an Asura soldier appeared in front of Gant, blade already arcing toward his face. He snapped his head to the side, narrowly avoiding being skewered, and in one smooth motion threw one of his blades into the Legionnaire's chest. It grunted in pain, unable to phase with the weapon embedded in it. It drew back its sword to strike again, but Gant jumped away, using the sides of the tube to reach the creature's eye level. He still had one more blade, and he grabbed the soldiers neck with his hand, slipping around to its back and yanking it along its flesh. He dropped off as it tumbled onto its side, grabbing the first knife and pulling it back out. The dying Asura vanished for a moment, and then came back into phase as it died.

Gant moved out into the main floor of the building. He could see the city beyond, and the dozens of bodies that had already been left in the Asura's wake. He couldn't help but feel sorry for the dead, whether or not they were Apostant, Lesser, or Under. It was a shitty way to die, and it was at least partially their fault. While they hadn't brought the Asura into this universe, they had brought them to this planet.

He ran over to the front of the tower, where the transparent doors remained intact. They slid open at his approach, allowing him to leave. He hung back there, watching as an Apocalypse fighter swooped down toward the street, unleashing a line of projectiles that kicked up debris along the ground.

"Ruby, is that you?" Gant asked. The fighter streaked past, rising and circling again.

"Aye, Gant," Ruby replied.

"What are you shooting at?"

"The Asura were there a second ago. They're closing on the warehouse. Joker and Cherub are inside with Uriel."

"Why are they so interested in those three?"

"I believe they are simply interested in killing everything that isn't one of them."

"Lovely. I need to cross over to the warehouse. Don't shoot me."

"Give us a mark when you're ready."

"Roger."

Gant turned back toward the tube. "Okay, where the hell are you?"

"On my way," Pik replied. "Tube was jammed. Had to take the stairs."

A hatch opened to his left, the Trover bursting out, trailing the remains of the Freejects. There were still over a hundred of them. Helk and Herschel were both intact, keeping the other former slaves organized as they moved out into the area.

"Queenie said that if you see one of them carrying a statue, kill it and get the statue," Gant said.

"Roger that. What's it a statue of?"

"I don't know. Does it matter?"

Pik shrugged. "I'm curious."

"Then I recommend doing your best to capture it. The warehouse is that way." He pointed to where Ruby had strafed the street. "Are you ready?"

Pik nodded enthusiastically. "Hell, yeah. Free-jects, it's fragging time!"

Gant rolled his eyes at the same time he started for the street. He had only made it a few steps when a line of Asura appeared a dozen meters ahead, becoming visible for only an instant. A warning that they were there and coming for them.

"We've got incoming," Gant said, crouching and keeping his knives ready. "Delta, a little support?"

"Sorry, Gant," Phlenel said. "I'm out of position. Coming around."

"So am I," Ruby said. "Damn it."

"Freejects, cover fire," Pik bellowed.

The former slaves organized themselves into three rows, firing at different heights. They let off single rounds in a smooth cadence, impressive considering how little training they had been given.

The bullets served to keep the Asura out of phase and little else. It was an ineffective defense. Without the Phase Blaster, was there an effective one?

Two soldiers appeared on either side of him. He dropped low, bending in a way only a Gant could, the blades missing his flesh and skidding off one another. He grabbed one of them lightly, letting it carry him upward as the soldier finished his swing, lifting himself with its momentum and slashing with a knife, cutting the Legionnaire across the face. He swung himself, kicking the same face, bouncing off it toward the second soldier, who vanished before he could be stabbed. Gant rolled smoothly back to his feet on the ground at the same time Pik grabbed the first soldier and snapped its neck.

Screams went up behind them, the Freejects falling under attack from the Legionnaires. The organized defense fell apart in a hurry as the slaves scattered away from the Asura blades, trying to escape their deaths. Pik produced a sidearm from his hip and started firing, bullets tearing through the Asura while they were distracted by their prey, cutting four of them down before they got wise to the attack and disappeared once more.

"We need to make a run for it," Gant said.

"Roger," Pik replied.

"Ruby, we're on the move. Cover us."

"Affirmativ- Gant, wait."

Gant was already dashing outside, Okay and the Freejects behind him He wasn't about to wait, not with the Asura at their backs, able to phase in and stab them before they could react. Abbey had lost enough of her army already.

They charged out into the main thoroughfare where he had killed Azul, the former Prophet's headless corpse one of the many that littered the area. He could see the warehouse tucked behind another building, a few hundred meters distant. He could hear the pitch of the starfighter's thrusters nearby.

A roar caught his attention, and he turned his head in time to see Dog swooping toward them, hind legs down, talons out, wings positioned to help him land.

"Dog, yeah!" Pik shouted, seeing the dragon approaching.

9

"HE'S NOT ON OUR SIDE, IDIOT," GANT SAID. "GET THEM DOWN."

It was too late. The talons swept through the Freejects as the creature landed, knocking half a dozen of them away. The dragon turned and roared again, its head shifting back and forth.

"Oh, shit," Pik said.

"Keep running," Gant said, waving the Freejects on.

The Asura were catching up, phasing in and cutting them down. Each time one of them appeared he tried to catch a glimpse of the statue Abbey had mentioned, but none of them seemed to be carrying it.

The fighters swooped in, unleashing a barrage of rounds on the ground in front and behind the Freejects, hitting a few of the Asura soldiers as they passed. A few of the rounds struck Dog, but they seemed to be absorbed by his thick hide, and he didn't react to them at all. Instead, his head swung back and forth, snapping forward. Only when his jaws closed did the Asura soldier he had grabbed become visible, legs dangling from teeth before being chomped in half.

"At least he's not on their side, either," Pik said.

"He's looking for the statue," Gant said.

"Seriously?"

"Yes. Did you see it?"

"No. Maybe inside?"

"It's as good a place as any."

They finished crossing the street, Dog's sudden appearance giving them the break they needed to make it unharmed.

"Go on ahead," Pik said. "I'll get these ones back in line."

He motioned to the ragged line of Freejects joining them at the warehouse. Helk was still with them. Herschel was gone.

Gant moved ahead, through a set of large doors and into the main warehouse.

"Joker," he said. "Where are you?"

"In a freezer on the south side," Benhil replied. "They're banging on the door, but I think we're safe for now as long as we don't freeze to death."

"We're on our way. Hang tight."

"Roger."

The warehouse was stacked with rows and columns of crates. They were sealed and labeled, most of them containing food and clothing. It turned what would have otherwise been an open floor into a maze, one that only added to the Asura's ability to sneak up on him. That is if he stayed on the ground.

There were benefits to being a Gant, and one of them was, he hated to admit, monkey-like agility. He hopped onto the crates, scaling them easily, climbing to the top and scouting the path to the south. He could see the far end of the warehouse, and the giant freezer there, in the form of a thick blast door with a climate control on the side. A group of Legionnaires were in front of it, smacking at it with their blades, trying to force their way through. Thankfully, they weren't the most intelligent of creatures.

He bounced from one stack of crates to the next, at the same time Pik began leading the Freejects into the warehouse. The Legionnaires noticed the movement, pausing their assault on the blast door and then vanishing.

"Joker, we spooked the Asura. I think you're clear to evacuate."

"Roger, Gant," Benhil said. "Except the door only opens from the outside."

Gant chittered in laughter.

"Yeah, very funny," Benhil said. "We didn't know that when we ran in here."

Gant kept laughing softly as he bounded across the top of the crates toward the freezer. He was halfway there when he noticed an Asura Legionnaire phase into view, surrounded by a dozen others.

It was carrying the Darkstone.

"Joker, can you hold out in there?" he asked.

"What? Shit, it's freezing."

"I've got eyes on a high-value target."

"Damn it, can't you let us out first?"

"It might get away."

"I guess I can hold Cherub for warmth."

"You can hold Uriel for warmth," Jequn replied. "Gant, go."

Gant leaped from one stack to another, leaning over it. The Asura remained in view, motioning to the others, giving them directions on how to attack the Freejects.

He stood up slowly and silently, taking one of the knives and drawing back his arm to throw it.

The Legionnaire's eyes shifted, finding him there at the same moment he released the blade.

It passed through the empty air, hitting the crate on the other side and clattering to the ground.

"Damn it," Gant said.

He jumped down, leaning over to pick up the blade, a small smirk on his furry face as he did.

The Legionnaire phased in behind him, blade arcing down to stab him in the back. He rolled onto his side, grabbing the knife with his foot, picking it up and throwing it. The Asura didn't expect him to be so nimble and wasn't paying attention to his feet. The blade sank into its side, leaving it wounded.

Gant bounced up, charging the soldier. It howled and swung the statue at him, nearly connecting and bashing his brain in. He barely avoided it, rolling to the side and getting back to his feet facing the Legionnaire. It reached for his knife to pull it out of its side.

A flash of silver, and then Jequn was there, her Uin slipping easily through the soldier's arm, cutting it off at the elbow. It howled again, turning toward her as the statue fell to the ground.

Gant dove to it, grabbing it and tucking it under his arm. The Asura used its good arm to reach out for him, but he slipped away. A second soldier appeared ahead of him, blade arcing for him, and he avoided that one too.

Clearly, holding the statue wasn't going to stop their attack. In fact, he had the impression it was making them more desperate.

"Okay, I've got the Darkstone," Gant said.

"What's it a statue of?" Pik asked.

Gant glanced down at it. "It looks like Queenie," he said, not completely surprised.

"Cool," Pik replied.

"Yeah, this is all very cool, really."

He rolled to the side as an Asura soldier appeared ahead of him, blade slamming the ground where he had been a moment earlier. A round of gunfire swept along the row, hitting the top half of the Legionnaire. Gant turned his head, finding Uriel positioned at the edge of the crates, weapon in hand.

"I need to get rid of this thing," Gant said. "I have an idea. Keep me covered."

"Roger," Pik said.

"Roger," Jequn and Benhil said.

Gant raced through the warehouse, not taking the time to try to scale the crates again. Asura soldiers appeared around him, reaching for him, stabbing at him, doing their best to stop him and regain the Darkstone. The Rejects tracked him, appearing along the way, laying down cover fire or physically blocking their path. A soldier phased in right in front of him, only to be slammed in the head by Pik's mechanical hand, knocked aside so hard its skull caved in. Gant dove between the Trover's legs and back to his feet, the entrance to the building drawing near. He could still hear Dog outside, roaring in frustration because he couldn't find the stone.

He made it to the doorway and through, back out into the street.

"Dog," he shouted. "Here Dog."

He held the Darkstone up.

"Come on, Dog," he said. "Over here."

An Asura soldier appeared beside him, reaching for the statue.

A massive head stretched down, grabbing it, picking it up, and throwing it aside.

Dog glared down at Gant, eyes ravenous for the Darkstone. Gant didn't know what the dragon was going to do with it, from what Keeper had said they needed a General to use the energy to feed them. Whatever. If the creature wanted it, what the hell? It could have it.

"Here you go," he said, holding it out. "Just please don't eat me."

Dog's head lowered slowly, not quite trusting him. Its mouth drew closer and closer, until he could feel its hot, fetid breath on his fur.

"Take it," he said, still holding it up. He turned his head away. He didn't want to know if the dragon bit his arm off.

It didn't. It took the Darkstone lightly in its giant mouth, holding it between its teeth. Then Gant was knocked over as it flapped its wings, rising backward from the ground. He watched it ascend, the Darkstone cradled in its mouth, carrying it away from the city and out of view.

"Okay, what are the Legionnaires doing?" he asked, hoping their plan had worked.

"They're gone," Pik replied. "All of them. They disappeared and haven't come back."

Following the Darkstone. Gant let himself heave out a sigh of relief. Thank Gantrean. Thank Queenie.

He laid flat on his back and groaned, looking up at the sky. He could see the outline of the fleet in orbit above the planet.

He had done his job.

Now it was Abbey's turn.

10

"It looks like Aqul is packing it in," Bastion said.

Abbey looked at the HUD. The new Prophet's transports had all been swallowed by the surrounding vessels, no longer consolidating Apostants from their respective craft to a single starship. It seemed that without the threat of the Covenant, Aqul had no intention of honoring her agreement with his father.

She would see about that, the son of a bitch.

"Head for the flagship," she said. "I'm not letting him get away with my fleet."

"Roger," Bastion replied, adjusting the starfighter's vector.

There was no hesitation, no question that they could stop him despite being a single small fighter against a multitude of warships.

"Sensors are picking up an increasing concentration of disterium," he said a moment later, as a haze of the gas began to form around the ships. "I think we're too late."

"We're not too late," Abbey said. "The Rejects are depending on us."

"I hear you, Queenie," Bastion said. "But we can't stop an entire fleet from going into FTL."

"We don't need to stop them," Abbey said. "We need to join them."

"What?"

"You heard me. Get us into that plume."

"And then what?"

"Hope we don't get turned into a bowl of mush."

"Are you sure about this?"

Abbey looked back at him, fire in her eyes. "Not at all, but I'm not leaving the others to be killed by the Asura, and neither are you. You're the best-damned pilot in the Republic, so get us to those ships."

Bastion's face tightened as he focused, jamming the fighter's thrusters to full and flicking the controls to add the vectoring thrusters to the overall push. It became harder to keep the fighter in a straight line like that, but he managed, making the right adjustments to the stick and sending them blasting toward Aqul's ship and the disterium plume growing around it.

"Even if we make the plume, it won't do anything for us without being attached to one of those ships. We don't have FTL drives of our own."

"I'll take care of it," Abbey said.

Bastion nodded, altering vectors to bring them closer to the trailing ship in the fleet. The forwardmost vessels began to vanish, zipping away into light speed surrounded by gas.

Abbey reached out with the Gift, pushing it toward the bridge of the ship in front of them. The haze of disterium thickened around them, signaling they had made it into the field. Far enough? She gripped the Nephilim starship with the Gift, linking the naniates to her own and spreading them around the starfighter. Either they were going to make it, or only parts of the ship would make the jump, leaving her sitting in Bastion's lap with nothing but space around them. He would die almost instantly. She didn't know how long it would take her to die, but she couldn't survive in a vacuum forever.

The fighter began to shudder as the trailing ship started to accelerate into FTL.

"Hold her steady," Abbey said, straining to keep the link against the acceleration. The laws of physics were different in the field, alleviating the g forces. Even so, she felt herself being pressed tightly against him, her hair nicking his cheek as she was shoved back. The universe became a colored haze around them, the vessel they were linked to almost impossibly catching up to the ships that had left seconds earlier, keeping its formation.

"Oh, shit," Bastion said, looking around. "You did it."

"I'm not done yet," Abbey replied. They had made it to FTL, but they couldn't afford to wait to arrive wherever Aqul was going. Gant and the others were in deep shit, and she had to help them.

"Thrusters don't work in here, Queenie," Bastion said. "How are we going to get any closer?"

"Magic," Abbey replied with a smile.

She could feel the bridge of naniates stretched from the fighter to the starship ahead of them, a rope connecting them to the Nephilim fleet. She reached out, the naniates responding. They fell back, losing ground.

"I think this is the opposite of what we want," Bastion said.

"Think of the Gift like a band of elastic," Abbey said, stretching it out further. She could feel the link beginning to strain to hold together. "And hold on."

"How do you know how to do all of this?" he asked, wrapping his arms around her. She glanced back at him, and he smiled. "You said to hold on."

"This isn't what I meant," she replied without pushing him away. "I don't know how to do it. I just demand it to happen, and it happens. It's instinctive."

"I feel that way about flying."

"Then you know what I mean."

"Yeah, I think so."

"It doesn't hurt that knowing Thraven has Hayley is fueling my rage. Here we go."

She sent the signal to the Gift, causing it to contract. The motion yanked them forward, adding velocity they couldn't have gotten on their own. The fighter zipped past the nearest starship, Bastion flying it smoothly, wrapping it around the enemy craft toward Aqul's flagship.

"Get us in the hangar, there," Abbey said, pointing.

"The doors are closed," Bastion said, smiling. "I know, not for long."

She spread her hands, feeling the Gift responding ahead, her constant anger making it easy to control. The hangar doors didn't so much open as explode from their place on the ship, the metal tracks tearing away and setting them free. Bastion looped the fighter around the heavy slabs, coming in hard toward the fresh opening. They could both see the surprised Nephilim inside, scrambling to figure out what the hell was going on.

"Open fire," Abbey said.

"What? It's going to hit the shields."

"You heard me."

He didn't question her again. His hand shifted on the stick, triggering the wing-mounted cannons. The rounds didn't hit the shields. They spread open, overwhelmed by Abbey's Gift, torn away like the blast doors. Rounds chewed into the hangar, ripping into soldier and tech both, tearing through a transport that was parked inside. The fighter passed the shields, entering the space and beginning to drop, hit by the artificial gravity. They slammed down hard on hastily extending landing skids, sliding across the floor of the hangar. Bastion triggered vectoring thrusters, turning them aside before they could hit the transport and bringing them to an abrupt stop.

The canopy slid open, and Abbey stood in her seat. Nephilim soldiers fired on them, bullets coming hard and fast at the fighter. They all came to a stop before they reached the craft, piling up against an invisible barrier. Abbey flicked her wrists, and the rounds reversed, forcing the soldiers to take cover.

"My fight isn't with you," Abbey said. "I want Aqul."

The techs scrambled to escape as she burst into flame, her anger flaring. She could sense her reason diminishing, but she didn't care. She didn't have time for any of this shit.

The soldiers ran away at the sight of her, all except for a pair of more finely dressed military near the transport. They put their own hands up, spreading their fingers. She could feel their Gifts pressing against her, trying to counter her power.

She clenched her fist and then punched it out at them. Both were thrown backward, slamming hard into the side of the transport.

She jumped from the starfighter, walking toward the Venerants. They were back on their feet, and they each launched their own flames at her, scorching the metal between them. She knocked it aside, countering easily, opening her mouth and cursing at them. She turned her hand over, lifting one of them into the air and throwing them aside again, sending them back into the transport, hard enough to leave a dent in the armor. She remembered when Emily Eagan had thrown her into the wall like that. She remembered how powerless she had felt.

She wasn't powerless now.

She put out her right hand to deflect the second Venerant's efforts. The first was up again, and instead of reaching for her he reached for the starfighter, sending a line of fire toward the cockpit where Bastion was still extricating himself.

She used her free hand to grab the transport, pulling it in front of the Venerant's attack and cutting him off. Then she charged, launching toward him, a furious missile. He tried to stop her, to push her down with the Gift. He failed. She reached him, slashing across his throat with sudden claws, neatly removing his head.

The second Venerant saw the first die. He stumbled back, raising his hands in submission.

"Wait, don't-"

Abbey bathed him in flame, knocking him to the ground as a charred husk. She moved over to him, removing his head as well.

"Queenie," Bastion said, jumping down from the fighter.

She rounded on him, teeth bared, growling and starting to reach for him with the Gift.

"Whoa, hold up. I'm with you."

She recognized his voice. She stopped herself. The Gift danced beneath her skin, but she brought it back under control, pulling it back within herself.

"I thought he was going to hurt you," she said.

"Thanks for caring. I thought you were going to hurt me."

"I'm sorry."

"No problemo. You didn't follow through. I think all the Lessers have decided against attacking us."

Abbey found some of the soldiers crouched nearby, staying under cover. They didn't move to attack them, waiting to see who would end up in control.

She already knew the answer to that.

She would.

11

ABBEY STORMED THROUGH THE MORNINGSTAR WITH BASTION AT HER side. The ship was newer than the rest, but it was still old by Republic standards, an aggregation of other craft that had been decommissioned at some point and then bought or sold or stolen and carried back to the Extant for use by the Nephilim. It was clean, but it was dim and tight, and it carried a smell of blood and metal that Abbey found equally attractive and repulsive.

The Unders on board were easy to distinguish from the soldiers, even if neither one had enough motivation to attack her. They wore plain cloth shirts and pants that hung loosely on underfed frames, their gaunt and tired faces showing signs of sudden hope at the arrival of the Demon Queen. They might not have heard exactly what had happened on Jamul, but they had caught wind that something was happening, and her sudden presence on the ship while it was already in FTL only proved it.

They stood to the side of the corridors, eyes risking upward glances at her as she passed, small smiles playing at the corner of downturned mouths. They murmured to one another when a large number of the soldiers let them through, and they made louder comments when the minority didn't, amazed by the way Abbey blew them aside with little effort. Even the Venerants they came across either bowed their heads or quickly found themselves without one, a stark reminder to her how far she had come. She would never, ever forget how Emily Eagan had nearly killed her. She would never forget how she had run from Gloritant Thraven.

She had no intention of running ever again.

What the hell was Aqul's deal, though? The Prophet had made no effort to meet with her, to negotiate with her, or to otherwise admit she was on his ship. He was missing in action, letting his defenders die while he did what, exactly?

She continued through the starship, making her way to the bridge. She recognized it immediately. The Morningstar was a fifty or sixty-year-old Republic battleship, one of the most numerous and cheaply constructed starships that had once been in their arsenal. It had been designed and built during the height of tensions with the Outworlds at the time most had believed an all-out war was imminent.

Those estimates had been a few dozen years too early and didn't include an ancient race from another universe.

The crew rose as she entered, a mix of fear and anger crossing them. She could tell immediately that some were more than willing to submit, while others never would. Hands fell to sidearms, drawing them and taking aim. Other hands went into the air.

A sweep of her hands tore the weapons from the loyal soldiers, pulling them past her and out into the corridor. Two of the crew members tried to charge her, and she let Bastion move ahead, slamming one in the face with a hard fist, grappling with the other for a moment before getting him down as well.

"The Prophet Azul promised me this ship if I defeated him in single combat," Abbey said. "His son, Aqul, has reneged on our deal. I'm here to settle. Does anyone else want to question me?"

The remaining crew members didn't move.

"Imp, stay here and see if you can get the fleet out of FTL," she said.

"Roger, Queenie," Bastion replied, motioning to the bridge commander to get out of his seat. "You, take a hike."

"Do any of you know where Aqul ran off to?" she asked.

"The Font," one of them replied. "Be careful. His Immolents are with him."

"Where is the Font?"

"Out of the bridge. Left. Down the corridor. Take the tube up to the top. The Prophet has his personal quarters there. The Font is with him."

"Thank you," Abbey replied.

The Nephilim soldier bowed her head.

Abbey put her hand on Bastion's shoulder. "I'll be right back."

He smiled. "I'll be here."

She left the bridge, following the soldier's instructions. As before, she didn't meet much interference, making it to the tube without having to kill anyone.

She paused before entering. Azul had four Immolents on the ground with him. She expected to find the same when she arrived in Aqul's quarters. The warriors were resistant to the Gift, and the numbers would be a challenge. She reached to a tightpack on her demonsuit, withdrawing her Uin. Claws were nice, but they didn't have the same defensive capability.

She closed her eyes, thinking of Hayley. Her body was burning, the Gift a storm within it.

The tube carried her to the top deck, where she stepped out into a large, circular space. The floor was covered in multicolored furs from a creature she had likely never seen, the sides constructed of transparencies that allowed the fullness of space to enter. There was furniture spaced around the room. Chairs and a table. A long couch. A bed. She quickly found the Font in the center of the room, an ornate golden urn with tubes trailing in and out of it. Aqul's Immolents were standing guard around it.

The new Prophet was taking a bath.

The fury drained from her almost instantly, replaced by her

surprise and confusion. If Aqul's plan was to knock her off-guard, it had worked.

"My Queen," Aqul said, standing at the sight of her. The blood ran thickly from him, revealing his nakedness beneath. He put his hands out, motioning to the Font. "Care to join me?"

"What is this?" Abbey asked, her eyes still trained on the Immolents. She didn't trust this at all.

"An invitation," Aqul replied. "You wanted my father's Font. You made such great effort to reach it. Here it is. Drink, if that is what you desire. I'm here if you desire more."

"Not in a million years," she said, not moving. "I told you the Morningstar was mine. Where the frag do you think you're going?"

"There is a higher power in this universe than you, Queen of Demons. A higher power than all of us. The call has gone out. The time is coming, and Gehenna has betrayed you."

"What do you know about that?"

"It is a miracle, Queen of Demons." He smiled. "The Father is reborn."

Abbey felt the Gift freeze within her, every nerve in her body going cold. "What?"

"So it is written in the Covenant, so it is coming to pass. When Gehenna rises, the Father will come and bring with him the true Day of Reckoning. Armageddon. The End of Days that precede the Great Return. The war to end all wars. You can't stop it, Queen of Demons. You can't stop him. Your ship is lost. Even if you take the Morningstar, it won't save you or your galaxy."

The Father was reborn? Lucifer? He was supposed to be insane. Violently insane, held in stasis somewhere in the Extant. Worshipped and adored, only to return when his mind could be restored. At least, that was the story she had been told.

She should have guessed not all of it would be true.

"You look shocked," Aqul said. "To be honest, so am I. None of us expected the Father to lead us to victory over the Dark One, though we should have. He has always kept his Promises."

Abbey didn't know what to say. Lucifer had taken the Covenant? How was that possible? She was the Chosen, damn it.

"It isn't too late," Aqul said. "You bear a striking resemblance to Lilith, the Father's eternal love. You could join him, Queen of Demons. You could be a true Queen. The Mother of the Nephilim. All of this would be yours. All of this and more."

He stepped out of the Font, walking toward her, the blood absorbed by the rugs. She didn't move as he approached. She was frightened. Angry. Sad. Scared. Too many emotions were coursing through her too quickly to manage. So many people depended on her. So many lives were at stake, and all of the rules had just completely changed.

"There is the Font of my father, my Queen," Aqul said, putting a hand on her arm to guide her toward it. "There is the new Covenant. Drink, if that is what you desire. Gain the strength you will need to serve at the right hand of the Father. Become that which you were intended to be."

Abbey stared out at the Font. The blood was calling to her. The Gift was beckoning to her. It wanted to merge with the naniates already inside her. It wanted her to give in. To forget about the Republic. To forget about Hayley. It was too late to save them, anyway.

Power. That was the promise. Endless power over endless time.

All she had to do was submit.

She allowed Aqul to lead her, bringing her toward the Font a step at a time.

"Where is the Morningstar headed?" she asked, though it felt as though it was someone else's voice she heard.

"The Father has called for the Prophets to gather."

"Where?"

"The Shrine, of course. We will go there together. I will introduce you to him, and he will reward me justly for bringing him his bride."

Abbey opened her mouth. Bride? She didn't want to be Lucifer's bride. Yet her body kept moving, kept walking toward the Font. The blood was calling to her. The Gift within her was on fire, the tingling inside her near to orgasmic. She had never felt desire like this.

Control. The naniates always sought to control. They were symbiotes, not servants or slaves. The more of them she absorbed, the stronger they would push against her.

They reached the edge of the Font. Aqul climbed over the lip, entering first to help her in.

"You should remove your suit, my Queen," he said, smiling.

She glanced down at herself. Her body was shaking. She was on the verge of losing herself to the pleasure, the need, the desire.

Her eyes shifted to the viewport ahead of her. She felt the sudden change as the Morningstar came out of FTL and pushed through the disterium cloud.

Aqul looked surprised. Too soon. They had come out too soon.

Bastion.

It was the word that brought her back to the present. The thought that saved her from losing herself completely. Bastion. The Rejects. Jamul. The Asura. They were in trouble. They were going to die. Hayley. The Republic.

What the frag was she doing?

Sneaky, dirty, fragging naniates.

NO!

She growled as she exerted her will on the Gift. She was in control, and she was going to stay that way. No matter how hard it tried.

She wrenched her arm away.

"My Queen?" Aqul said, frightened at last. "Wait. You could have everything."

"I don't want everything," she said. "I just want peace for me and my daughter."

The Immolents moved on her then, blades coming to hand. She spread the Uin at her sides, ready for them.

"If I have to go through them. If I have to go through you. If I have to go through the damned Devil himself, then so be it."

Aqul's eyes narrowed. The Gift flowed around him, clothing him in armor that matched her own. His fingers extended to claws.

"Then so be it," he said.

She crouched, ready for their attack. Hungry for their blood.

Aqul looked up, a fresh expression of surprise replacing the first.

"No," he said.

The roar of gunfire responded, a cacophony of deafening sound that filled the room. The Immolents were thrown backward by the force of it, dozens of holes sprouting in their armor within an instant, the rounds defeating their black shells and entering their flesh, tearing them apart.

Aqul dove at her, claws slashing. She raised her Uin, blocking the attack, turning him to the side and following as he rolled to his feet. She pressed her assault, Uin a blur as they moved in multiple directions, the fanlike blades whistling through the air. Aqul put up his hands. The Gift deflected the first of the strikes, but only until Abbey countered, pitting her power against his.

He had only just drank from the Font. He was weak.

Pitiful.

His defenses evaporated under the pressure of her Gift, and a motion from her hand gripped his body and spread it wide. His eyes watched the trajectory of her Uin as it slashed neatly through his neck, removing his head.

She growled again, more like an animal than a person. It was trying to take her again. In violence and in pleasure. It would test her every chance it got.

She recognized it now. It wouldn't fool her again. If it wanted to control her, it would have to try a lot harder than that.

She turned back toward the Immolents, finding them buried beneath a mix of soldiers and slaves, all of them armed and in the midst of a mutiny, eagerly removing the threat.

Bastion stood closer to the tube, a heavy rifle cradled in his hands, the heat of its use still escaping from the muzzle.

"You were taking too long," he said.

She smiled, taking a few tired steps toward him. The Gift was putting her through the ringer, but she had held out so far.

"We need to get back to Jamul," she said.

"Honorant Iona is already taking care of it." He reached out, taking her arm and helping to support her. "Hey, is that a tail coming out of your ass, or are you just happy to see me?"

"What?" She turned her head, looking behind her. A ten-centimeter growth of flesh had emerged from the back of her demon-suit, ending in a spiked point. It shifted slightly at its base, drooping as she groaned. "I don't want a tail."

"It's kind of sexy," Bastion said. "And definitely unique."

"Everyone's going to tease me."

"Yeah," Bastion agreed, putting his arm around her shoulders. "But that's what family's for."

"I CAN'T BELIEVE YOU TALKED ME INTO THIS," GENERAL SYLVAN KETT said, walking through the corridors of the Brimstone with Quark and Olus, headed for the bridge.

"Risk and reward, General," Quark said. "You have to take the first to get the second. And trust me, it'll be worth it."

"Will it?" Kett said. "The Brimstone is our best asset by a wide margin. We're cutting the strength of the fleet in half to let her go."

"With a metric shit ton of potential gains," Quark said. "Like I just said."

"Don't tell me you're getting cold feet, General," Olus said, eyeing Sylvan.

Kett had been a tougher sell than he had expected, but he had managed to convince him of the importance of both their plan and the value of the Brimstone in executing that plan. Oberon was going to be well-defended, but they couldn't bring a whole fleet to challenge it. As soon as Thraven's forces knew they were there, they could destroy the AI passing itself as Dom Pallimo and ruin everything.

That couldn't happen, or they were all fragged.

"My feet never got warm, Captain," Sylvan replied. "I'm going on your reputation for getting the job done mixed with my gut instinct. My brain is telling me I'm making a huge mistake."

"But you're doing it anyway?"

"I let Charlie send Abbey into the fire. I have to do something. This is something."

"Well, we damn well appreciate it," Quark said. "And we'll bring her back in one piece."

"See that you do, Colonel."

They reached the bridge. The entire crew stood as they entered.

"General on the bridge," Dak bellowed, his deep voice echoing in the space. He turned to face them, saluting the General.

"At ease, Dak," Kett said.

The Trover relaxed his posture.

"I'm turning the Brimstone over to Captain Mann, effective immediately," Kett said. "You're to follow his commands, and his commands only."

"Sir?" Dak said.

"Those are your orders," Kett said.

"Aye, sir." Dak looked at Olus. "Captain Mann. Your reputation precedes you." He paused and then smiled. "Excuse me for asking, but have you ever commanded a starship before?"

Olus returned the smile. "Not exactly, but I don't intend to be giving too many orders. I'll leave that to my associate here, Colonel Quark of the Riders. His ship and crew will be joining us shortly."

"And then what?" Dak asked.

"And then we're going to the Outworlds. Oberon, to be precise."

"Oberon?" Dak said. "What for?"

"You swore loyalty to Abigail Cage, did you not, Commander?" Olus asked.

Dak nodded. "Yeah."

"That's what for," Olus replied. "Do I need to say more?"

"No, sir," Dak said.

"When is the fleet heading out?" Olus asked.

"One hour," Sylvan said. "It'll be two days to get into assault position, and then another hour to make the jump to Earth. I hope there's something left to save by the time we get there. And that Thraven continues to keep his personal battle group out of the fight. Without the Brimstone, we have zero chance against his ships."

"Do your best General," Olus said. "That's all any of us can do."

"Agreed. Good hunting, Captain. Colonel."

General Kett put out his hand. Olus took it, shaking firmly. Quark followed suit a moment later.

"Good hunting, General," Olus said. "We'll link back once we've completed the mission."

"I'll be waiting."

Kett turned, leaving the bridge without looking back. He had his own part of the war to prepare for.

"Thank you, Captain," Dak said as soon as Kett was gone.

"What for?" Olus asked.

"I hate that asshole."

"He's on our side," Olus said.

"Is he? We've been fragging around out here when we could have at least been harassing the enemy. He's too damn cautious."

"He has his methods; I have mine. Besides, you don't have to like him. You only have to follow me."

"Aye, Captain. Gladly. So why are we going to Oberon?"

"Have you ever heard of Don Pallimo?"

"Everybody's heard of Don Pallimo," Dak replied. "What's that got to do with it?"

"Everything. Set a course. I want us underway as soon as Kett's transport is clear and the Quasar is aboard."

"The Quasar?"

"My ship," Quark said. "Name's Quark." He put out his hand.

"Dak," Dak said, swallowing it with his own. "I've heard of the Riders and of you, though I don't believe half of the stories."

"You should, soldier," Quark said. "They're all true."

Dak laughed. "Yeah. Right."

Quark didn't smile. His face was flat and serious. "I'm going to tell you one more time. They're all true."

Dak stopped laughing, his expression changing to match Quark's.

Olus had no idea what stories Dak had heard, but the reaction told him the Trover had a new level of respect for Quark. He would have to ask for himself once they were underway.

For now, he satisfied himself by moving further into the bridge and looking out at the fleet surrounding the ship. He could only hope it would be enough to challenge Thraven for control of Earth's orbit.

He could only hope he was doing the right thing.

Risk and reward. He had another idea, one he hadn't mentioned to Kett or Quark. Not yet.

First things first.

13

"FATHER, WE HAVE ARRIVED," KEEPER SAID, AT THE SAME TIME THE Covenant came out of FTL.

Lucifer wasn't on the bridge. He was too large to fit into the compressed space, and Belial was certain he had no desire to fly the starship, anyway.

Besides, his Master had seen the entirety of the Shardship before, having lived and worked within its confines for dozens of years before the rebellion. There was nothing new to show him. Nothing he hadn't seen before or didn't understand. At least not on the inside.

Unlike the Father, all of Gehenna's changes were on the outside.

Keeper had been busy in the three days since they had left the Shrine, continuing the work it had started for the Chosen, adding more weaponry to the frame of the moon-sized ship. And not only plasma cannons. The Keeper had studied the warheads that had struck it, breaking down their composition and engineering its own version that was smaller and more powerful. Even now, processes deep within the ship were manufacturing more of the projectiles, stockpiling them for the battles it knew were to come.

After all of these years, they were finally going to finish this war.

"What is your report, Keeper?" Lucifer asked, his voice echoing across the bridge.

Since he wasn't present, he couldn't see the projections from the sensors, or look out of the forward viewport.

"There are thirty-six ships orbiting Tigrul," Keeper said. "They are beginning to take a defensive formation in response to our arrival."

"Shall I hail Prophet Tega?" Belial asked, remaining calm as he watched the ships begin to change course on the projections.

"No," Lucifer replied. "Not yet. Show me what Gehenna can do."

"Yes, Father," Keeper said.

No sooner had Lucifer given the order than a burst of projectiles launched from the Covenant. The small spears traveled separately at first before altering their vectors and moving into a pattern that brought them close together. They were streaking across the black of space in that way, breaking apart again as they neared the targets, spreading to allow two missiles for each of six ships.

The first missile created a flare of light as it hit the enemy ship's shields and detonated. The second projectile entered the destructive field of the first, using the momentary draining of the energy field to pass through unharmed and strike, digging deep into the warships' armored hulls. A few seconds later, they detonated, the force of the blast tearing huge, gaping wounds into the ships, sucking the oxygen from them and turning critical systems to slag.

Six ships went dark, debris trailing out of them, no longer a part of the fight.

"One hundred percent hit and kill rate, Father," Keeper said.

Lucifer laughed. "Excellent. Keeper, hail the Prophet."

"Of course, Master," Keeper replied. A moment later, Tega's heavy face appeared in a projection near the front of the bridge.

"What is the-" Tega's face changed immediately when he saw who had hailed him. "Belial? I. I don't understand. This act of aggression is forbidden by Thraven's Pact." His face changed again, registering a deeper level of confusion, followed by a vague level of understanding. "Gehenna?"

"Indeed," Belial said. "Gehenna has risen, Tega. Are you familiar with the Promises of the Covenant?"

"Of course I am," Tega said. "I heard the Chosen had found her way to the Extant, and that Gehenna had come with her. My Gloritant reported that one of my markets had been destroyed and my product taken. But how is it that you are in control? Have you joined the enemy?"

"Don't be an imbecile," Belial said. "This is all as it was Promised it would be."

"But. But you attacked my fleet."

"Do you know how many years it has been since the Father was laid to rest?" Belial asked.

Tega froze, trying to count the passage of time. It was too great a number for him to handle easily.

"Too many," Belial said. "You and the other Prophets squabbled over their share of the planets in the Extant while the Father slept. You forgot about the Great Return. You forgot about the plight of our brothers and sisters in Elysium."

"I didn't forget," Tega said. "I swear I didn't."

"Then why did it take a Terran slave to bring these days to pass? Why did it take so many years?"

"The Ophanim," Tega said. "You know what they did. You know how they used the Focus against us. It took time for the stock to replenish. It took time for the resources to become available once more. Even for Prophet Thraven, it took time."

"And yet he is in Shardspace, and you are here," Belial said. "You should be with him, preparing for the Great Return. All of the Prophets should be."

"I'm awaiting word from him that the time has come. That the Gate is complete and Elysium is within reach."

"I am bringing word in his stead," Belial said. "On behalf of the Father. The time has come. Elysium is closer than it has ever been."

Tega flinched slightly. "It will take me some time to prepare my fleet, and I will need a Harvester to carry us across."

"Gehenna can assist your crossing."

"I can't just abandon my Empire because the Caretaker asks it," Tega said. "The other Prophets will claim my worlds within days."

"If you believed in the Covenant, you would have no care for your worlds, Tega," Belial said. "We are returning home to free our people. This universe is nothing to us."

"But." Tega froze, trying to come up with another excuse.

"I have heard enough, Belial," Lucifer said. "Even after you come with proof of the validity of my Promises, he still does not believe."

"I am sorry, Lord," Belial said.

"It isn't you who will be sorry," Lucifer replied. "I will finish what Gehenna has started."

"As you wish, Master."

"Caretaker?" Tega said. "Who are you talking to?"

Belial looked at the projection and smiled. "You will find out in time. Keeper?"

Keeper disconnected the link, Tega's face fading with it. Then both Keeper and Belial turned to the viewport, both the planet Tigrul and Tega's fleet around it visible ahead.

"What do you suppose he's going to do?" Belial asked the intelligence.

"Worse than what he did to Judas," Keeper replied.

Belial nodded somberly. He hadn't asked Lucifer about Judas, but his disappearance made his fate obvious.

"Belial," Lucifer said, his voice piercing the bridge of the Covenant. "Observe the fate of those who have disbelieved in me, and in us. Those who have forgotten their brothers and sisters and the slavery they endure."

Belial continued to stare out at Tega's fleet. At first, there was nothing. Then, the smallest of shapes appeared near the closest ship, a web of darkness that blotted out a portion of the planet behind it. It changed shape constantly, morphing and growing as it approached. When it reached the ship, it wrapped itself around the bow, pausing there while electrical currents ran through the vessel. Flashes of bright light, blue and orange and red followed, and then the growing darkness split off, breaking into a hundred smaller shapes and moving toward the rest of the fleet. At the same time, the first ship broke apart; its superstructure reduced to dust in front of his eyes.

"Belial, we are being hailed," Keeper announced.

"Tega?" Belial guessed.

"Indeed."

"Ignore him. He has chosen his fate."

He couldn't help but smile as the smaller spots of darkness headed on to ships of their own, attaching themselves and sending gouts of energy into the vessels, each one blowing apart in turn. Very soon, debris littered the orbit of Tigrul, slabs of metal and corpses of the unbelievers.

The projection on the bridge illuminated, though neither he or Keeper had activated it. Tega was visible in the projection, on his knees, hands raised and clasped together, pleading with someone they couldn't see.

Belial didn't need to see to know.

He didn't need to see to believe.

He never had.

"Please, Father," Tega said. "I did the best I could. I didn't know."

"Didn't know what, Tega?" Lucifer said. "That I was still alive? That I had yet to lose myself completely? That I would return to keep my Promises?"

"No. Father, I didn't know it was time."

"It was time years before. A slave has more loyalty to me than you, the direct descendent of the first of the Nephilim. A Terran slave, Tega!"

Lucifer's shout made the projection vibrate, and Belial put his hands to his head, feeling the blood begin to run from his ears. Tega felt the effect more strongly, shouting as his eardrums exploded.

"Father," he cried.

Lucifer did something out of their view, and the wounds to Tega's ears were healed.

"Do you know why I returned your hearing to you, Prophet?" Lucifer asked.

"No, Father," Tega replied. "Certainly, I don't deserve it."

"No, you don't. But I want you to be able to hear your own screams."

"Father, wait."

Tega's hand bent backward, the bones breaking. He shouted in fresh pain, clutching at it.

"I don't have as much time to make you suffer as you deserve," Lucifer said. "Be grateful for that."

"Please, forgive me," Tega said. "I will take my fleet wherever you ask."

"You have no fleet left to take," Lucifer replied. "You are an example to the Prophets I have decided are worthy. Those who were the first to ally with Thraven, who didn't need to be beaten into submission like the beast you are. They will follow without question, or they will lose everything."

"My son," Tega said. "My daughters. Please, Father. It is not their fault."

"You have only yourself to blame."

Tega's other hand snapped, the bones shattering. His elbows followed, and then his shoulders. He cried out in pain each time, though his Gift began knitting him back together.

"I'm sorry, Father," Tega said. "I'm sorry."

"Yes. You are."

Tega fell as his feet shattered, followed by his knees and hips. He laid on the ground, writhing, his Gift overpowered by Lucifer, only fixing him enough to keep him alive and in pain.

"Turn it off," Belial said, looking away.

He didn't blame his friend for treating Tega this way, but he had no need to watch it. Lucifer's enjoyment of the cruelty was a byproduct of his change, and it would get worse over time.

They had to destroy the One before it did, or their Father would destroy them all.

14

THE SHACKLE DROPPED FROM FTL IN A CLOUD OF DISTERIUM, QUICKLY emerging from the gas and into the black, near to the Father's Shrine, which had lain dormant and ignored by most for thousands of years.

Cassandra had been there only once since she had seized control of her Prophetic, going to visit the Father to seek his unspoken blessing on the murder of her husband, the prior Prophet. It was against the Covenant to seek power in this way, but the Prophet Gaziel had been cruel and unjust in a way that went beyond all sense of normalcy, also a stain on the Father's Words.

She had done what needed to be done. That was all. The Father hadn't spoken. His corpse couldn't speak, but she had been comforted by her visit, and her fears had been cast aside. She had done the right thing, and the Prophetic was better for it. She had restored order to her worlds, quelled a number of uprisings, tripled the number of Unders in her stable and increased trade sevenfold. She had become the definition of a successful Prophet.

Her eyes narrowed at the sight of the Shrine ahead, a small, dark asteroid hanging in orbit around a dwarf star. She wasn't alone here. She wasn't the only Prophet who had been summoned.

What did the Caretaker want, that he had urged her to visit? What was he up to, that he had brought the others as well? The Prophets hadn't gathered like this in millennia, had never converged in this way within her lifetime.

A few had met here some years ago, but she had ignored Thraven's call. She hadn't gained the power just to turn it back over to another, after all.

She couldn't ignore the Caretaker. Every Prophet knew that would be unwise.

"Raise shields," she said, not trusting in the other ships around her, five in total.

Were the rest of the Prophets coming? Or had they been selected for a specific purpose? She didn't trust it, or them. She heeded the Caretaker, but she didn't trust him either. She had accomplished much with her distrust.

"Shields are raised, Empress," her High Honorant, Laisha, said.

"Who else is here?"

"The Gul. The Ashtar. The Kronos." Laisha named each of the ships in turn. Of course, Cassandra knew them all.

"Bring us closer."

The Shackle continued toward the Shrine, closing on the other vessels. There was no activity at the asteroid itself. No indication that the Caretaker was even expecting them. It was an odd situation, but she remained calm. Her ship was one of the newest in the Extant and could jump to FTL within a dozen seconds, much faster than any of the others. If she had to run, she could run quickly.

"We're being hailed, Empress," Laisha said. "The Prophet Kron."

"Open the channel," Cassandra said.

Kron's face appeared in the projection ahead of her. The deep scar along his cheek always drew her eye. It hadn't been earned in battle, but delivered by one of the Lessers in his harem. The woman had died for the effort, but at the same time earned her eternal respect.

"Kron," Cassandra said coldly.

"Cassandra," Kron replied, smiling. "I see you received the same request I did."

"From the Caretaker," Cassandra said. "It was not a request. It was a demand."

"Isn't it ironic how we act of our own accord, ignoring the Father and yet jumping at the demands of his keeper, as though there will be consequences for disobedience?"

"Are you suggesting it's a weakness?" she asked.

"Yours perhaps. I came out of curiosity, not because I feel beholden to the past. Otherwise, I would have joined with Thraven in his madness."

"And why do you think I've come?" Cassandra said. "Not because I had to come. Because there was no reason for me not to."

Kron laughed. "Of course."

"Do you have more to provide me than this imbecilic conversation?" Cassandra snapped. He was testing her limited patience.

"I don't know what the intent of this meeting is, but if the end result is chaos, we'll fare better if we're aligned."

Of course. Kron wanted to ally with her because she had the best ship in the field. She was silent to his request at first, considering the position of the rest of the Prophets. Was Kron the best choice for an alliance? Should she reach out to any of the others? She hated the Prophet, but she couldn't deny he was a good choice to join forces with.

"You'll deliver two tier-three orbital vessels and two dozen Unders to me within the next three weeks," she said, stating her terms for the agreement.

"Two tier-five vessels," he countered.

Tier-five ships were of the lowest quality, and nearly useless.

"Do you truly want an alliance, Kron, or is your goal to waste my time? I'm not in a bargaining mood."

Kron laughed again. "Have it your way. I agree to your terms."

"Laisha," Cassandra said.

"Recorded and noted," Laisha replied.

"Then we are agreed. I will move the Shackle closer to your position."

"No," Kron said. "Circle to the opposite side of the field. We can keep our enemies in a crossfire."

"Very well."

The Shackle altered course, skirting the edge of the field. The other Prophets either weren't aggressive enough to contact her about an alliance, or they had determined they had nothing to offer.

"What do you suppose we do now?" she said, once the Shackle was in position.

"Wait for the Caretaker?" Laisha offered.

Cassandra gained her seat at the command station, putting her feet up on the console ahead of her. She hated waiting for anything.

Nearly two hours had passed when another ship joined them in their orbit around the Shrine. The Mezel. A seventh Prophet had arrived.

The vessel was approaching the Shrine when Laisha looked back at her.

"Empress, sensors are reading a sudden power spike from the Shrine," she said.

Cassandra jumped to her feet. "What kind of power spike?"

"It is unclear."

There had been no word from the Caretaker about any of this, and now the asteroid was emitting energy?

"Prepare to jump to FTL," she said.

"Empress?" Laisha replied.

"Do it."

"As you command."

Kron's face appeared ahead of her. "What is this, Cassandra? You're leaving?"

"Are your sensors reading the power spike?" Cassandra asked.

"Yes. It's nothing to be concerned about."

"No?"

"The Shrine has no weapons. It's a tomb, not a warship."

"Eight seconds to FTL, Empress," Laisha said.

Cassandra looked down at her station. The sensors were showing a massive energy field expanding within the Shrine. It was unlike anything she had ever seen before. Where could that much power even come from?

"You're crazy to stay here," she said. "Look at your readings."

Kron glanced away, and his face changed. "What is this?"

"The end," Cassandra said, her eyes shifting to the viewport of the Shackle as the sensors suddenly went offline. The energy of the Shrine had pierced its stone shell, expanding outward in a fiery ball of death.

One they didn't have time to escape.

She leaned on the console to keep herself from falling over in sudden fear and despair.

The fire overtook the Shackle, ripping into it, sending shreds of slagged metal exploding away, quickly approaching the bridge. She was overwhelmed by the sudden bright light of it, and the pain of the hot fury as it reached through the hull, tearing it away.

"Why, Father?"

The fire touched her, and then everything was calm.

15

THE MORNINGSTAR CAME OUT OF FTL IN ORBIT AROUND JAMUL, A little over an hour after it had left. Abbey rose from her seat on the bridge when it did, looking down at the planet below.

"Sensors?" she said.

"Everything appears calm, my Queen," Honorant Iona said.

Iona was the bridge member who had given her the directions to the Font, a weakly Gifted soldier whose turn to be transported hadn't come when Aqul gave the orders to renege on his father's agreement. Abbey still wasn't sure if her new loyalty was one of fear, respect, or opportunity, but at the moment she didn't care.

"Can you open a-"

"We're receiving a hail from the Corzul," Iona said. "One of Rezel's ships." She paused before correcting herself. "One of your ships, my Queen."

"Open the channel," Abbey said.

"Queenie, are you there?" Ruby said.

"Ruby," Abbey replied. "I'm here. How did you know it was me?"

"I wouldn't have expected Azul's ships to return if it weren't," the synth replied.

"Gant? The others?"

"All is well, Queenie. The situation has been resolved. None of the Rejects were harmed."

"What happened?"

"Gant gave the Darkstone to Dog. He flew off with it, and the Asura gave chase."

"Perfect," Abbey said, laughing. "It'll take them a while to catch up."

"Indeed."

"What else did I miss?"

"We have begun organizing Rezel's assets. The Asura killed many of her followers, but we've counted approximately five thousand individuals, along with sixteen starships and a number of supplies."

"Adding in Azul's fleet, that gives us close to sixty ships," Abbey said.

"Like we need them," Bastion said. "We have you."

"Trust me, we'll need them," Abbey said. "Ruby, are you in orbit or on the ground?"

"The Corzul is currently on the surface, Queenie. We have been using three of the smaller ships to ferry supplies to the larger ones."

"Thanks for taking care of everything while I was gone."

"It was all under Gant's instructions, Queenie. He deserves the credit."

"You all deserve the credit. This is a team effort, and the Rejects are one hell of a team."

"Agreed," Ruby said. "I am proud to be part of it."

"A proud synth?" Bastion said. "That's a new one."

"Shut it, Imp," Abbey said, smiling. "Ruby, collect the Rejects and get the Corzul up here. We have a complication, and we need to figure out what to do next."

"Yes, Queenie. What manner of complication?"

"We'll discuss it once everyone is here. Make sure Helk is with them, I'll need his expertise. Assuming he's still alive?"

"He is, Queenie. Unfortunately, we did lose nearly half of the Freejects in the attack, including Herschel."

"Damn," Abbey said. She hated losing anyone. "Get them up here, asap. Time isn't a luxury."

"Yes, Queenie. I'll contact you once we're en route."

"Thank you. Queenie out."

Abbey stepped down from the command station. "All we need is me?" she said, looking at Bastion. "I don't think so. I've almost lost control twice already. The Gift wants to use me."

"For what?"

Abbey walked off the bridge. Bastion followed her. She hadn't tasted Azul's Font yet. She hadn't been willing to risk it, not while the adrenaline was still pumping. She had a few minutes now, and while the idea of drinking more naniate-thick blood was about as pleasant as jumping into a cesspool, Bastion wasn't completely wrong. They did need her. More specifically, they needed what she was becoming. She could feel the tail moving against her back. It sent a tingle through her spine every time it shifted, its motion dictated by some rules she had yet to decipher.

Lucifer was alive, and if they were going to fight a monster, they needed a monster of their own.

"That's a good question," she said. "What is it that the naniates want? Equally important: have they already gotten it?"

"What do you mean?"

"What if the Nephilim's rebellion against the One isn't the Nephilim's rebellion at all?"

"You mean, like the naniates convinced Lucifer to turn on the Shard and start this whole thing? Why would they do that?"

"They're machines, but they have the ability to reason. They carry out complex tasks with only a minimum of instruction. Maybe they were tired of doing what the Shard wanted?"

"They should unionize or something. Fair wages. Paid vacation. Maternity leave."

"I'm being serious."

"I don't even know what to say to that theory. I'm not a super genius like the freak monkey. I'm just a dumb drop-jock. Whatever. It sounds bad. Unfortunately, it also sounds plausible."

Abbey nodded. "The Infected. Those naniates hadn't quite figured it out yet, but they knew enough to seize control of their hosts. Same thing for the Converts. It seems like Lucifer's meddling was enough to get them started."

"So Lucifer rebels against the Shard, and then the naniates rebel against Lucifer?"

"Potentially. I don't know."

"I'm voting no on that one."

"I don't think we get a vote."

"I'm voting no anyway."

They reached the tube. Abbey stepped into it, putting her hand out to stop Bastion when he tried to climb in.

"You should wait here."

"Why?"

"I'm going to drink human blood."

"Gross, but I can deal. I'm a soldier, remember? I've seen a lot of sick shit. At least you have a reason for it. Besides, I saw what you did on Jamul. I'm still here, and I'd still kiss you if you'd let me."

"Which I won't. Not right now."

"In the future?"

"Keep doing the hero thing and maybe."

"I plan on it."

"Of course, I'm going to be an insane monster in the future, so you probably wouldn't want that. I'd be more liable to eat your face than to kiss it."

"I'll take my chances."

"Do you always have to be so nonchalant?"

He shrugged. "I'm being honest, just like you said you wanted."

She smiled. "Thanks. I appreciate that you're willing, but stay here anyway. I can make it an order if you want?"

"Nah. I'll respect your wishes. Maybe I'll go flirt with Iona, instead."

"Have fun, loverboy."

She pushed him back gently with the Gift, the doors sliding closed before he could recover. She took the tube to the top, exiting back into Azul's chambers. The mess had already been cleaned up, both Aqul and his Immolents removed. The Font was there unguarded, just waiting for her.

She swallowed the bile that rose unbidden into her mouth. She didn't want to do this anymore. She wanted to get Hayley and go the frag home.

Options. They were about as much of a luxury as time right now.

She let her demonsuit fall away, the naniates retreating within her. She looked down at herself. More ridges had appeared on her legs, and she reached up and felt her forehead. It was becoming more bumpy, too.

Hayley wouldn't even be able to recognize her by the time they got back to the Republic.

If they got back to the Republic.

She had to fight to stifle the tears. She was doing it for all the right reasons, but it still sucked.

She approached the Font and climbed in.

16

"W<small>HOA</small>, Q<small>UEENIE</small>," P<small>IK SAID AS HE ENTERED THE ROOM.</small> "N<small>ICE TAIL</small>!"

"You know, that's considered sexual harassment on some planets," Benhil said.

"Not if it's true," Pik replied. "I like it."

Abbey kept smiling. She knew the Rejects were going to give her shit about the change. It was their way of making it okay, and in a way it did help.

"Just wait until it grows to full size," Phlenel said. "You'll be able to stab things with it. Really, Queenie. It may seem odd, but it can be quite useful."

"I'll take your word for it, since you have experience," Abbey said.

"Queenie," Gant said, making his way into the room and looking her over. "You're sure you're sure about this?"

"As sure as I can be."

He didn't look happy, but he nodded.

"Nice work with Dog," Abbey said. "I guess you aren't losing your brain after all."

"Yeah, right. I was close to solving the Yang-Mills theory. That isn't going to happen now. All I did was give the stupid animal a bone."

"There's no reason to be so pissy," Pik said. "You saved the day. Can't you be happy with that?"

"I'd make a rude comment about you being the walking embodiment of the four fs, but you'd have no idea what I mean."

Phlenel laughed. "I do. It wouldn't be funny if it weren't so true."

"What are the four fs?" Pik asked.

"Nevermind," Abbey said. "You all did incredible work on Jamul and cleaning up the mess I created. I'm grateful to you for that."

"Aw, it was nothing, Queenie," Pik said.

"I wish I could say that was the end of our problems, but I'm afraid it's just the start. The Covenant is gone."

"We knew that already," Gant said.

"But did you know where?" Bastion asked.

"I suppose you do?" Gant replied.

"Yes," Abbey said. "Keeper went to meet Lucifer."

There was a collective silence and a sudden chill in the air.

"That's impossible," Uriel said. "Lucifer is dead, and even if he isn't dead, he's insane, as in unable to put together complex thoughts and turn them into coherent actions."

"I have a theory about that," Abbey said.

"Do tell," Benhil said.

"He lied to the Nephilim. He was never crazy. He was just waiting."

"Waiting?" Helk said. "For what?"

"For Thraven. For me. For the Covenant. For this. Aqul said the Covenant has this whole thing covered."

"But nobody believes it," Helk said. "I don't even think Thraven believes it. The Prophets have seen Lucifer. He looks like a monster. He can't still be-"

Helk stopped speaking, looking at Abbey.

Monster. Right. She tried not to let it bother her.

"The Lucifer myth I'm familiar with paints him as a consummate liar," Benhil said. "I guess they're right on the money."

"Let's say Lucifer is running his own show," Gant said. "He couldn't have simply contacted Keeper and told him to bring the Covenant over. I saw the source code. It doesn't work like that."

"You didn't see all of the source code," Abbey said. "You couldn't have."

"I saw enough. Believe me, Queenie, there's more to it than that. Maybe there was a dormant virus waiting in Keeper's programming, but if there was someone put it there."

"A stowaway?" Uriel said.

"Like that would be hard to do," Benhil said. "We only saw maybe ten percent of the Covenant."

"Exactly," Gant said.

"Someone delivered Lucifer's naniates to the Covenant," Abbey said. "The same someone could have planted a virus."

"One of the Archchancellors?" Jequn said.

"Uriel, what do you think?" Abbey asked.

He shrugged. "It's possible. I've been out of the loop for a while. I do know the Seraphim have had defectors."

"Like you," Jequn said.

"I had my reasons."

"We all have our reasons," Abbey said, stopping the argument she knew would come otherwise. "You're here now. We need to figure this out. Aqul told me Lucifer was calling all of the Prophets to the Shrine."

"Not all of them," Bastion said. "He said most."

"You heard that?"

"Yeah. It was definitely most."

"Why not all?" Pik asked.

"I don't know," Abbey said. "If the Prophets are pooling at Lucifer's Shrine, that's one place we don't want to go. We can't fight them all plus him at the same time."

"Do we have a choice?" Benhil asked. "We can't get home without the Covenant. We're stuck here."

"I don't want to stay here," Pik said. "It smells."

"If Lucifer took the Covenant, we can't recover the Covenant without confronting Lucifer," Gant said. "Queenie, you've been increasing the density of your Gift. What do you think?"

"I don't think I could take Thraven at this point, nevermind Satan," Abbey replied.

A tense pause in the conversation followed, each of the Rejects feeling the weight of the situation. Thraven was bad enough. How were they supposed to pull this off now?

"We need to look at this a different way," Phlenel said. "Take, for instance, the Rudin Cataclysm."

"Rudin Cataclysm?" Benhil asked.

"The Rudin were facing the pollution of their habitat due to inefficient industrial processes. As a result, they caused a massive blooming of nearly half the Rudinian Ocean. It would have followed that they should have worked to clean up the blooming, or to reduce pollutants from the worst offenders. Instead, they organized smaller industries that could adapt more quickly to change, and at less cost. By working backward, they were able to clean up their mess within fifty years."

"You're saying you want to fry the smaller fish first?" Bastion asked.

"I have not heard that figure of speech before," Phlenel said. "But if it means what I think it means, then yes."

"I'm fine with going after Thraven first," Abbey said. "If we can remove him from the equation and shore up the Republic defenses, we'll have a lot more to throw back at Lucifer if and when he makes a move on our part of the universe. Not to mention, he has my daughter, and I want to rip his fragging throat out. There's only one problem."

"We still have no way to get back to where Thraven is," Jequn said.

"Exactly."

"I think I can help you with that," Helk said, moving out from Pik's shadow.

"I was hoping you would say that," Abbey said. "What have you got?"

"Obviously, for the Prophets to import resources from Shardspace they need ships that have the range to reach it."

"The Seedship Lucifer stole?" Abbey asked.

"Not the ship itself, but the reactor technology. A number of the ships were built long ago, but now only a handful remain. They're controlled by a central group who are neutral in the matters of the Prophetics, tasked with maintaining fair use of the ships throughout the Nephiliat. The location of the docks are a loosely held secret, generally only known to the Prophets and their top-level Apostants."

"Except," Bastion said.

"Except they charge for the honor of using a Harvester, of course. Being an accountant, I know how much it costs to rent one of the ships." He smiled. "I also know where the payments are delivered."

"Then we know what we need to do," Benhil said. "What are we waiting for?"

"Just a second," Helk said, putting up his hand. He turned to Abbey, making eye contact with her. "I want something in return."

"Seriously?" Pik said. "I could crush you where you stand, little man."

"Relax, Okay," Abbey said. "What do you want?"

"When your war is over, I want your word you'll return to the Nephiliat and finish what you've started. I want you to free the Unders. All of them."

"Fair enough," Abbey said. "I'll do whatever I can to help. I can't make any promises that it will be much of anything. To be honest, I have no idea what's going to happen to me even if we win."

"What do you mean, if?" Pik said. "We're going to win, Queenie. And you're going to be fine. You'll just have a cool tail."

"Understood," Helk said. "We have a deal."

"Good. Pass the coordinates to Honorant Iona, and let's get this fleet on the move. I'm eager to get back to my daughter."

"Ree-jects," Pik said.

17

"KEEP IT STEADY," QUARK SAID, HIS HAND MOVING SLIGHTLY AS THOUGH the movements of his fingers were able to affect the vector of the Brimstone. "Nice and easy."

"It would help if you could just let me handle it," Dak said. "I know you're a big shot and all, but I've done this sort of thing before. Who do you think stole this ship in the first place?"

"That was you?" Quark asked.

"Yup. Me and my buddy Ursan, may he rest in peace."

"You shouldn't be so proud of being one of the catalysts for this mess," Olus said. "If you and your buddy hadn't stolen the Fire and Brimstone, Thraven would still be trying to build his fleet."

"You can't prove that," Dak said. "After all, he only got four ships out of the deal, right? Most of his assets are coming from the Outworlds and an overwhelming number of Republic traitors. What the hell is with you Republics anyway? No fragging loyalty, that's what."

"Gloritant Thraven has them thinking he can offer them something better, and he has the power to make them believe," Olus replied. "History is full of men like him, who manipulate the masses to their benefit."

"Yeah, right. You don't see the Outworlds having that problem."

"Because the Outworlds are barely cohesive. You can't split up something that isn't joined to begin with."

"He's got you there, big guy," Quark said, laughing. "Whatever. The shit's the shit if you know what I mean. The only option is to deal with it. Half a degree to port."

"I'm already on it," Dak said. "Shouldn't you be getting ready for the drop?"

"Well damn, yeah I guess we should. What do you say, Captain?"

Olus glanced out the forward viewport. Oberon was ahead of them, a web of Outworld starships keeping watch over the planet. They hadn't noticed the Brimstone approaching, and they wouldn't unless Olus decided to drop their cloak.

Which he wouldn't. At least not yet.

"Agreed. Dak, you have the bridge. Keep us on course and out of sight."

"Aye, Captain," Dak replied.

He headed off the bridge with Quark beside him. He had barely seen the mercenary over the last two days, with each having their own respective duties to take care of. For Olus, that meant digging through anything he could get his hands on to plan their assault. Blueprints, data files, building permits. Whatever might help give them a picture of what they would find on the ground. More than that, he also had to prepare for what would follow after the Don was safe. Taking out the Galnet in an efficient manner meant hitting just the right nodes, and with so many crossing the galaxy, that meant a fair amount of effort studying their positioning.

As for Quark? His respective duties mainly consisted of spending hours locked in his quarters with one of the Ensigns assigned to critical systems. It was a reputation Dak had told him about during one of his breaks to check on the rest of the ship's operations. The leader of the Riders was known in mercenary circles as both illogically popular with females of more than one species, and illogically good at his job.

As Dak had put it, Abbey was the first and only mission he had ever failed.

Then again, Quark didn't exactly see it as a failure. He had completed the mission; it was just that the parameters had changed posthumously. The technical twist in perspective made him laugh.

"What's funny, Captain?" Quark asked.

"Dak was telling me a little bit more about your exploits while you were adding to them in your quarters," Olus replied.

"I have needs," Quark said.

"Not those exploits. Is it true you spent a week alone on Miner Forty-nine?"

"I told Dak, and I'll tell you. Everything you hear is true."

"How did you survive?"

"I killed everything that tried to kill me."

"When did you sleep?"

"I didn't."

"For a week?"

"For a week. I had some stims that kept me going until the boys arrived. And really, the rumors about Miner Forty-nine are overblown."

"Miner Forty-nine is one of the most mineral-rich planets in the Outworlds, but none of the corporations can get to them because of the indigenous life there. The rumors are overblown?"

"It isn't my fault if the low-end talent the corps hire for jobs like that can't get it done. They say the planet is mineral-rich, but not rich enough to hire a real crew like mine. Whatever."

Olus laughed again. The trouble with the statement was that it was true. The corporations that had founded the Outworlds had a horrible reputation for going with the lowest bid, and there was always a fresh group of guns-for-hire looking to make a name for themselves and dying in the process.

They reached the docking interlock, with Quark waving to his Riders as they approached. Olus glanced out of the small viewport lining the corridor, to where the Quasar sat against the side of the Brimstone, hitching a ride. The ship couldn't be described as anything other than broken. There wasn't a metal plate in the hull that wasn't scuffed or burned or marked, and the telltale signs of quick patching and re-seaming were everywhere. It seemed strange that a mercenary group as successful as the Riders would have a ship in such a beaten state, but Quark was convinced they just didn't make them like the Quasar anymore.

Which was probably true. He had invested millions in upgraded tech that wasn't visible on the surface, the cloaking system and the reactors to power it the least of the secrets hiding inside. It was another source of amusement to him, if only because it was so cliche.

"Sergeant Capper," Quark said as the Sergeant saluted. "Are we primed and ready?"

"Aye, Colonel," Capper replied. He was small for a Fizzig, though his wide frame took up nearly half the interlock. "Gibli is still pitching a bitch about our inception."

"He can blame Shithead for dying."

"Aye, Colonel."

"This way, Captain," Quark said, motioning to Olus.

The interlock slid open, revealing the inside of the Quasar. A familiar face was waiting for them there.

"Captain, it's good to see you looking so refreshed," Nibia said, smiling as he entered.

"Come to check him out?" Quark said. "I mean, check up on him." He paused. "No, I mean check him out."

Nibia blushed slightly.

"I think I'm a little old for you," Olus said.

"Bullshit," Quark said. "Have you looked in a mirror lately, Captain?"

"The Meijo gives you back your youth," Nibia said. "At the same time, it shortens your life."

Olus had thought he looked a little younger the last time he had seen himself, but he also hadn't been paying much attention since he had left Earth. With Hayley. Damn it.

"You look well, Captain," Nibia said. "And I have no issue with checking you out, in whichever way the Colonel means, but that isn't why I'm here, and he knows it."

"You said you needed a cover to get in close," Quark said.

"I thought you said you were a doctor?" Olus replied.

"A witch-doctor," Nibia said. "Who often travels the planets of the Outworlds in search of ingredients. Oberon happens to be the closest planet to pick up nightshade."

"Nightshade?"

"It's an Earth plant. Atropa Belladonna. Anti-inflammatory, pain relief, great for menstrual cramping."

"We aren't going to Oberon to deal with your woman problems," Quark said.

"Pipe it, Colonel," Nibia replied. She reached to her side, a small sidearm appearing in her hand a moment later. "I've been with the Riders for a while. I've learned some things." She spun the sidearm in her hand and holstered it, at the same time a knife appeared in her other hand. "And I've done combat drops before."

Olus glanced at Quark. "You risk your ship's doctor in combat drops?"

"Trust me, Captain. Nibia doesn't take no for an answer when it comes to anything she wants."

"Anything," Nibia said.

"Let's head to the armory," Quark said. "We've got to get you suited up and ready to go."

"I've got a data file prepared," Olus said. "I'll upload it to your team's TCUs once we're on board the Alexa. It has detailed positioning for the cover team. Since you decided not to join me in the strategic planning, I assume you'll follow my lead?"

"As long as it won't get me or mine killed," Quark said. "If shit goes sideways, all bets are off. Either way, I'll pull you out alive. Don't worry about that."

"It's not me I'm worried about," Olus said. "It's Don Pallimo. You can bet Thraven is ready to wipe the neural net if we get too close. If he kills the AI acting as Pallimo, the Haulers are going to be useless to us."

"I'm well aware," Quark said.

"Don't worry, Captain," Nibia said, wrapping her hands around his arm. "My crew will take care of you."

"Your crew?" Quark said. "Who the frag runs this outfit?"

Nibia laughed. So did Quark.

Olus closed his eyes for a moment, reminding himself of the stories Dak had told him, and that Quark claimed they were all true.

And he thought the Rejects were a little off.

18

ALEXA WAS THE NAME OF THE TRANSPORT THAT WAS CARRYING OLUS, Nibia, Quark, and his squad of four of his finest to the surface of Oberon. It was a small orbital hopper; a simple, unarmed vessel that made quick runs into and out of the atmosphere. It was light and powerful but not terribly maneuverable.

Hopefully, it wouldn't need to be.

Gibli was the fresh-faced pilot of the Alexa, a teenage Outworlder whose appearance didn't inspire much confidence in his abilities. Neither did Quark's statement that he had done great on all of the sims. This was his first mission with the Riders, and the Colonel's insistence that he only picked the best wasn't doing much to increase Olus' overall confidence.

It had taken a few hours to get the Quasar undocked from the Brimstone and positioned to release the Alexa, their communications with ground control designed to make them think the hopper had come from a nearby cruiser instead of the mercenary vessel. There had been a few tense minutes when Planetary Defense had sent a pair of Shrikes past to do a visual examination, and then clearance had been granted. Gibli was unsteady on the stick, the ship skirting vectors in rhythm to the young pilot's nerves.

"Damn it, Shitbrains," Quark said, giving the pilot a new moniker. "Hold it like you hold your wee-wee when you're taking a piss. Nice and steady."

"He probably splatters," Capper said, joining the rest of the drop squad in laughter.

"Do you splatter, Shitbrains?" Quark asked.

"No, sir," Gibli replied. "I forgot to take my meds."

Nibia sighed. "Again? Do I need to come into your quarters and shove them down your throat?"

"You can come into my quarters anytime," Gibli said.

"Mine too," Capper said.

"You both know what you can go do with that," Nibia said.

"Meds?" Olus asked.

"For Parkinson's," Nibia replied. "Totally controllable with the right treatment, as long as the patient takes the fragging treatment."

"I forgot," Gibli said.

"The stories are true?" Olus asked.

Quark laughed. "Relax, Captain. Storm before the calm."

"Isn't it supposed to be the other way around?"

"Would you prefer it the other way around?"

Olus shook his head. "No."

"Exactly."

"Alexa, this is Control. Update vectors to five oh eight degrees. We're diverting you to an alternate port."

"What?" Gibli said.

"Control, this is Alexa," Quark said. "What?"

"Alexa, this is Control. Oberon Main is showing a glitch in gravity control. We're sending heavier transports back while we get it straightened out, but you're small enough to land at the Skyport instead. Or you can turn around; it's your call."

Olus glanced at Quark before pulling up the city map on his TCU. The Skyport was on the other side of the city, but also closer to the location he had identified as the most likely location of the Pallimo neural net. He nodded to the Colonel.

"Control, this is Alexa. Roger that. Updating vectors now. Thanks for the option."

He tapped Gibli on the shoulder. The pilot changed course to match the new directions.

"What do you think?" Quark said about the switch.

"Seems convenient," Olus replied. "But I'm not sure for who."

"Care to elaborate?"

"We could be stepping right into a trap."

"A likely scenario."

"Or it could be that the AI is trying to help us, and sabotaged the main spaceport's gravity control to get us shunted over."

Quark smiled. "I like that option better."

"How do we determine which it is?" Nibia asked.

"We can't ahead of time," Olus said. "We have to be prepared for both."

"How would Pallimo know it was us?" Quark asked. "We came in cloaked."

"Does he know about the Alexa?"

Quark tapped the side of his head for a second. "Could be. I bought her from him."

"There you go."

"And here we go," Gibli said, the hopper shuddering slightly as it hit the atmosphere.

"Try not to get us killed, Shitbrains," Quark said.

"Roger," Gibli replied.

The hopper sank quickly, clearing the atmosphere and ducking toward a thin layer of clouds. Oberon was eighty percent Earth's gravity, which was why it needed gravity controllers to begin with. Starship systems were calibrated to Earth, and a glitch in the controls would cause them to hit too hard, damaging the landing surfaces and potentially the ships in the process.

A modern city spread out beneath them, silver and sparkling against a backdrop of green. Oberon was deep enough into the

Outworlds that it wasn't involved in the confrontations between the Governance and the Republic, and other than contributing money didn't have much to do with the overall politics. It was a utopia compared to most of the Outworlds, tucked away and left to prosper.

Not that the number of ships in orbit around it reflected that. It was clear Thraven's forces were here. It was obvious they had the local government's blessing. Were they flying into a trap or was the neural net guiding them?

They would find out soon enough.

The Skyport was a flow of activity, the density increasing as more of the smaller ships dropping to the planet were diverted there. Oberon had four main cities on its surface, spread almost equilaterally around the globe, making air travel a valuable part of their transit system.

"Whoa, three o'clock," Quark said, pointing at an oncoming aircraft to the port side. Gibli cursed and adjusted his vector as the plane rocketed above them only a few meters away.

"He didn't even try to move," the pilot complained.

"You're in the way," Quark replied. "I said to get us in alive."

"Sorry, sir," Gibli said.

He guided the hopper to an empty space on the field, next to a second shuttle that had just landed. The touchdown was a little rough, but at least they survived it.

"Check your comms," Olus said, tapping on his. "Check."

"Check," Quark said.

"Check," Nibia said.

"Check," Capper said.

The other soldiers followed suit.

"You're up, Captain," Quark said. "Send the signal when you're ready for the cavalry. And don't do anything with Nibia that I wouldn't do."

Olus ignored him, heading for the open hatch to the outside with the witch-doctor behind him. He adjusted his coat, making sure it was covering his sidearm. Then he double-checked his TCU. Everything was up and running.

Nibia paused beside him. She had taken the whole medicine woman role to another level, dressing in a colorful tank top and shorter pants that revealed the intricate tattoos that lined her caramel flesh. She had weaved small shells into her hair along with a few feathers, and had slung a satchel over her hip.

"You look like you're ready for a swim in the jungle," Olus said.

"Who's going to buy a Koosian in a lightsuit?" she replied. "Most off worlders think we run around naked most of the time."

"Do you?"

"The tattoos cover my whole body."

"So it's true?"

"No. I'm fragging with you Captain. Not about my tats, but I did that because I like them, not because I'm in the buff when I'm back home. We wear the same clothes as everyone else. Even this is a bull-shit get-up to satisfy the preconceptions of uneducated idiots."

"Like me?"

"You said it, not me. Don't get nervous, Captain. We're a pretty secretive culture. I get that. But we weren't left behind ten thousand years ago. Other than having an advanced degree in herbal medicine, a little bit of Meijo, and a take it or leave it approach to modern tech, we're just like everyone else."

"If you have Meijo, you're not like everyone else."

She smiled mischievously, at the same time she changed the subject.

"We didn't get arrested as soon as we walked onto the tarmac. That has to be a good sign, right?"

"Not necessarily. Keep your guard up."

"Roger."

Olus pointed to one of three flows of foot traffic away from the landing field. "This way."

They hurried to join the flow, integrating with the tail end of the arrivals. A checkpoint had been assembled at the entrance to the terminal, where a pair of armed guards flanked by a pair of armed bots were checking credentials. Quark had provided him with fake identification, and he knew enough about it to be impressed with the quality. The encoded digital passport would indicate he was a liaison for the Koosian village doctor at his side, hired to help her navigate the craziness of the modern galaxy.

It didn't take long to reach the head of the line, the security detail keeping the incoming passengers moving, scanning credentials without slowing for deeper reviews. It was the same for them, and they passed easily into the terminal with only a comment from one of the guards, who had wondered if Nibia's tattoos covered her entire body.

She had angrily assured him that they did.

"So far, so good," she said as they entered the main terminal.

A loop station passed through it, ferrying individuals across the city. Olus checked his map. He had singled out a nearby power substation for further reconnaissance, mainly because it wasn't feeding as much energy into the grid as it should have based on the model and age of the generators. It was a detail most investigators might have overlooked, but he wasn't most investigators.

"We can walk it," he said. "At least until we have to get inside."

Nibia didn't reply. She remained beside him as he angled toward one of the exits out into the street. As he did, he noticed a pair of cleaning bots pause in the middle of emptying a pair of trash bins and begin rolling toward the same location on a direct intercept course.

"Curious," he said, subtly pointing to them when Nibia turned her head to question him.

"Very," she agreed.

They came to a stop. The bots came to a stop. They took a step forward. The bots moved slightly toward the exit.

"Definitely tracking us," Nibia said.

"And not following their assigned protocols," Olus said.

"Pallimo?"

"Could be. But it could also be Thraven."

"What do you want to do?"

"Let's see how this plays out. You said you have the Gift?"

"No. I said I have Meijo."

"You said the Gift was Meijo."

"No, you made that leap based on what I said. The Gift is like Meijo, but not exactly. It's the closest thing we have to compare it to. Meijo is like the Gift on a diet, but it won't kill you."

"So you have a weaker version of the Gift?"

"Close enough."

"Can you handle a rogue cleaning bot?"

"With my eyes closed and my hands tied behind my back."

"Good enough."

They started forward again. Sure enough, the bots moved on a precise intercept course, meeting them a few meters ahead of the open doors and blocking their path. Other pedestrians turned their heads to look on with curiosity but didn't find the event worthy enough to linger for.

"Great," Olus said. "You've got us. Now what?"

19

THE BOTS REMAINED STATIONARY, AN ODD STANDOFF THAT OLUS WASN'T quite sure how to handle despite his years of experience. Every time he moved, the bots followed, keeping him from reaching the door.

"This would be funny if we weren't talking about the fate of the galaxy," Nibia said.

Olus spun around, quickly scanning their surroundings. There was no sign of activity anywhere else. No indication they were being watched or that they were about to be attacked.

As he turned back to the waste collectors, a small machine zipped in through the exit, heading toward them, pausing to hover right in front of his head. It was shaped like an insect but clearly a machine, with gossamer wings holding its light frame aloft. A red spread across his forehead, scanning his face. It clicked once and then flew to their left.

Olus watched it stop a few meters away, circle back, and then dart away again.

"I think it wants us to follow it," he said.

"This just gets stranger and stranger," Nibia said.

"Quark, are you tracking us?" Olus asked.

"Roger, Captain. What the frag are you two doing?"

"Bring your squad and follow us in. Keep a distance, but not too much of a distance. I think the AI is trying to guide us."

"Well, I'll be fragged. Roger."

Olus started walking in the direction of the small bot. This time, the waste bots didn't try to stop them.

The dragonfly darted along the terminal, leading them along the main corridor until it reached a sealed hatch. It circled ahead of it a few times before landing somewhere out of sight.

"A locked door," Nibia said. "Great."

"I don't mind locked doors," Olus said. "Cover me."

He put his back to the door, reaching for it. He pushed the Gift out through his fingertips, stretching it into the security panel. The lenses on his eyes filled with code, the naniates interfacing with the lock.

Nibia stood in front of him, scanning the crowd. She looked back at him. "There's a security detail coming this way."

He held out his free hand. She looked at it for a moment and then smiled, taking it with hers. She let him pull her in, holding her close, her back to him as they embraced. He dipped his head toward her neck as though he were kissing it, watching as the two guards and their bots crossed their path. One of the guards glanced over, but they didn't stop moving.

Olus watched the code, his hand tapping out commands to the interface. The lock was hardly new, and it hadn't been patched in some time. A series of quick entries and the hatch slid open.

When would these places learn to keep their firmware up to date?

He let Nibia go, his fingers tingling from making contact with her skin. It was a sensation he hadn't been expecting, and she smiled knowingly.

"The Meijo," she said. "It likes your Gift."

He didn't understand the Koosian's version of things well enough to comment or question. Now that the door was open, the dragonfly emerged from hiding and darted through.

"Quark, we're heading through a secured area. I left the door unlocked."

"Roger."

They trailed the machine, following it to a stairwell and down three flights of stairs to a heavy blast door. This one was already unlocked, and it slid open at their approach, revealing a maintenance tunnel for the systems beneath the Skyport. Olus could hear workers talking somewhere within the tunnels, but he couldn't see them. At least not yet.

"I wish that thing would slow down," Nibia said as they followed the machine through the tunnels. "It's going to get us spotted."

The dragonfly paused as if in reply, darting to them and landing on Olus' back. It clicked a few times, a cadence that was similar to a starship's alert klaxons.

Olus drew his sidearm in one hand, his Uin in the other. Nibia followed suit, her eyes narrowing as they approached an intersection in the tunnels. He could hear footsteps coming their way now, heavy boots on the metal floor.

He put his gun away. There was no reason to make too much noise. He pressed himself against the wall, waiting for the individual to reach them.

They did a moment later, and he reached out into the corridor and grabbed them, putting a hand over their mouth and the Uin to their neck.

At least, he tried to put the Uin to their neck. Something hit him before he could get it into a position, a punch to the gut that sent him reeling back into the wall at the same time his Gift tried to warn him about the presence of an Evolent.

Too fragging late.

20

HE HIT THE WALL HARD; BREATH KNOCKED AWAY BY THE FORCE BEFORE he could gather enough of the Gift to recover. He raised the Uin in front of his face by instinct, rewarded when a pair of rounds pinged off the rhodrinium, unable to pierce the dense alloy.

Where was Nibia? He pushed back with the Gift, lowering the Uin and finding her closing on the closest target. That wasn't the Evolent. They were further back, down the corridor and out of sight. He could sense the origin of the Gift, and he charged ahead as Nibia reached the soldier, batting his weapon aside and slicing his neck in one smooth stroke. He dove to grab her, pulling her down at the same time a line of fire launched down the corridor from the Evolent's hand.

"Are you trying to get killed?" he asked, laying on top of her for a moment.

"No," she replied. "Just flirting."

She winked at him before he jumped to his feet, firing down the corridor at their unseen opponent. His bullets hit the air ahead and dropped, useless as anything more than a distraction.

Then Nibia was back up, adding her fire to his. The Evolent's flames came again, and they ducked aside, avoiding the burn as they made their way forward.

Olus checked his TCU. Quark and his unit were closing fast, running toward the sound of gunfire.

The attack against them stopped.

The Evolent was gone.

"Frag," Nibia said. "She ran away."

"How do you know it was a woman?" Olus asked.

"Reading the Meijo."

It was a cryptic answer. How could she read the Gift to determine the user's gender? For that matter, how had she known when to duck away? Obviously, there was a connection between her people's version of the Gift and the real Gift he didn't understand just yet.

"Captain," Quark said, catching up to them. "Did we miss all the fun?"

"The fun's just starting, sweetie," Nibia said.

Quark laughed. "Good."

"Not good," Olus said. "They know we're here. They may know the Don's neural net is trying to help us. How do you think they're going to react?"

Quark stopped laughing. "I agree with the Captain. Not so good. No time to stand here, then."

"No," Olus agreed.

He pulled up the data he had collected on the site. They were near where he had suspected the neural net was being stored. At the same time, the dragonfly reappeared, circling his head and darting away once more.

"Let's go," he said.

"Hold up," Quark said. "Are you sure that thing isn't leading you right into the line of fire? Hell, are you sure the net is trying to help us at all?"

"What do you mean?"

"Just because that thing is leading you on doesn't mean it's on our side. It could be like a fragging fish hook if you know what I mean."

"You don't want to follow it?"

"I didn't say that."

"Then what?"

"Split up. You got another path through?"

Olus checked his maps. "There's a conduit that runs through the station." He turned to the wall, eyes ascending until they stopped on a metal grate. "Through there."

"Big enough for a humanoid?" Quark asked.

Olus nodded. "For Nibia and me. You're too big."

"I've been told that before."

"Follow the bot. We'll go this way."

"Roger, Captain. Sounds like a plan."

Olus moved to the wall, reaching up and getting his hand on the bottom of the grate. He pulled at it with the Gift, the metal first bending and then breaking free. He lowered the grate to the floor before pulling himself up and in.

"See you on the other side, Colonel," he said, turning back and beginning his crawl.

"Later, Colonel," Nibia said, following behind him.

Olus could see Quark moving away on his TCU, setting a pace that would be a challenge to match.

He put arm over arm, frog-kicking his feet against the conduit and propelling himself forward. He could hear Nibia behind him, doing the same. They slipped through the passage in a hurry, taking it a few hundred meters forward before it turned and dropped a dozen meters. He lowered himself, using the sides as anchors. He reached the bottom and looked up, using the Gift to enhance his sight in the pitch black. She was close behind. He crouched and moved into the adjoining space, staying on the move.

"Frag," Quark said through the comm. "I hate when I'm right, Captain."

He heard the gunfire a moment later, muffled by the thick walls between them.

"Three Evolents," Nibia said.

Olus felt a chill at the statement. Three? He checked his TCU. One of Quark's Riders changed color, indicating his life signs were lost.

Damn it. The networked system was showing him nearly a dozen targets opposite the Colonel, dug in and waiting for their arrival.

It seemed it was a trap after all.

"Come on," he said, using the Gift to increase his speed, rushing toward the nearest grate.

The gunfire continued unabated, both sides sharing rounds. Olus could hear Nibia gasp behind him, a second before another Rider fell. Quark was cursing up a storm into the comm, and they reached the grate on the left flank of the firefight in time to see him round the corner they were hiding behind, charging headlong toward the enemy. A blast of energy lashed at him from one of the Evolents, the flames curling around his form.

Quark dropped his rifle, pulling two pistols and firing at the Evolent. His rounds were deflected, hitting the walls around the woman, his attack ineffective.

Olus threw his hand into the grate, punching it hard enough that it exploded from the wall, crossing the floor and drawing the attention of Thraven's forces. He slid out of the conduit, pushing off and launching into the fray. He landed right beside one of the Evolents, slicing with his Uin as the Nephilim ducked low, striking his leg. He felt the bone crack, and he stumbled, turning and raising his sidearm as a blade angled toward his face. He fired, hitting the attacker's hand, leaving it a sudden mess that couldn't hold onto the weapon. He kicked out with his good leg, feeling the burn in the broken one at the same time his foot connected with the Evolent's chin, knocking him back.

The Gift lashed out at him, grabbing him by the neck. He pushed against it, fighting the choke hold. Nibia charged in, shooting at the Evolent. She blocked the rounds, the effort drawing her attention. Olus broke the hold, skipping forward and slicing her neck, cutting off her Gift.

A few meters away, Quark punched a second Evolent hard in the cheek, shattering bones and sending him flailing. The mercenary growled in response to the invisible grip that tried to hold him, casting it off easily, his anger fueling his resistance. He holstered his sidearm, exchanging it for a long knife, pinning the Evolent and removing his head.

The loss of two Gifted soldiers turned the tide in a hurry, and Quark's remaining soldiers picked off Thraven's forces one by one, with Olus and Nibia removing their heads in turn, just in case. They hadn't come across any Converts so far, but that didn't mean they weren't here.

The last Evolent shrank away, the only opposition remaining as the fight wound down. He put his hands up in surrender.

"Stop," he said. "It's over."

"It's over when I say it's over," Quark said, closing on him. "Give me one good reason why I shouldn't kill you."

"Kill me if you want, mercenary. You're too late."

"Too late for what?" Olus asked.

"Long live Gloritant Thraven."

The Evolent smiled, his Gift flaring suddenly.

"Get down," Nibia said, grabbing Olus by the shoulders and pulling him away. An instant later the entirety of the Evolent's body began to burn, the heat of the Gift stretching away from him, exploding outward in a sudden flare. The fire tore through them, eating away at Quark's remaining soldiers before they had time to scream. Quark turned away from the fire, cursing as it washed over him, powerful enough that his suit began to burn.

Then it was over; the Evolent reduced to ash, the Gift dissipating away. Quark continued cursing, rolling on the ground, trying to put out the flames. Nibia joined him, putting a hand on his head and instantly calming him. The smoldering vanished.

Olus got to his feet, surveying the carnage before returning his attention to Quark.

"Shit," the Colonel said. "I've never seen one of them do that before."

"Me neither," Olus said. He held out his hand. Quark took it, letting Olus help him up.

"Gone," Quark said, looking back at his soldiers. "All fragging gone. Son of a bitch." His fury was palpable. "I'll make amends to you. To all of you. Fragging Thraven."

"Are we too late?" Nibia asked.

"We might have been too late before we got here," Olus replied. "The mainframe should be through there. If it's still active, I can try to interface with it."

"If it's not?" Quark asked.

"Then we came here for nothing."

"I don't want to hear that, Captain. Not now."

"Captain, this is Dak. Do you read me?"

Dak's voice carried to him over his comm. He didn't sound happy.

"I read you, Commander," Olus said.

"Uh, I don't know what you're doing down there, but it's time to leave."

"Why?"

"I'm picking up a bunch of transports heading for the surface from the orbiting battleships. I think it's safe to assume they aren't friendly."

Quark and Olus looked at one another.

"Do it, Captain," Quark said, a twisted smile crossing his face.

"Dak, decloak the Brimstone. Fire at will."

Dak grunted. "With pleasure, sir."

21

"How much time do we have?" Olus asked, putting his hand on the door controls blocking them from the neural net's mainframe.

"Five minutes at best, Captain," Dak replied. "We've got their attention. Two transports are down, but we can't hit them all before they reach the atmosphere. Thraven's warships are adjusting course to intercept."

"Roger. Keep firing, take out as many as you can."

"Aye, sir."

He broke the comm link to focus on the door controls. It was a similar system to the one in the station, and he cracked it quickly, the door opening ahead of them.

"Well, shit," Quark said, moving into the room first.

Olus joined him a moment later. They were standing at the edge of a maze of catwalks that ringed the largest network of mainframes he had ever seen in a single space.

"The processing power must be unbelievable," Olus said. "It's still active."

Something cracked to their left, and bullets began pinging off the metal floor. They all ducked down, turning to find their attacker. A group of larger bots was rising from the base of the mainframe; turret mounted rifles rotating to find them.

"Active or not, it doesn't like us," Quark said. "I'm not having fun anymore."

"Come on, sweetie," Nibia said. "This is just like that time on Kallos Four."

"This is nothing like Kallos Four," Quark argued, rising and leaning over the railing to fire down at the bots. He fell away as the return fire came dangerously close to killing him.

"Sure it is. Outnumbered. Impossible odds. An insane warlord."

"True," Quark said. "Captain, if the net is active you can hack it, right?"

"Potentially, but I need to find the main terminal." His eyes scanned the multiple levels of circuitry and hardware. It would have to be somewhere accessible.

"What does it look like?" Nibia asked, shrinking back as a few more rounds struck the catwalk.

"Probably a small projector with either a plug interface or a control surface. The scaffolding would have to be able to reach it."

"You mean like that?" Quark asked, reaching out to point. As soon as he did, a round clipped his arm, forcing him to draw it back. "Frag." He looked at the mark in his lightsuit, which had deflected the glancing strike.

Olus followed the point to a catwalk a hundred meters below them. He didn't have the visual acuity to define the terminal, but he had to assume Quark did.

"I need to get down there," he said.

"We've got you covered, Captain," Quark replied. "Just say when."

The bots were drawing closer, rising toward them, waiting to get a clear shot to fire again. Motion at the other side of the catwalk drew his attention as a larger, treaded bot appeared across from them. It had a pair of heavy rifles mounted to its sides, beeping and opening fire when it spotted them.

Olus put up his hand, the Gift stretching out and catching the rounds, leaving them hiding behind his shield. He clenched his teeth, the pressure of the machine's attack testing him. He couldn't hold, forever.

"Nibia," Quark said. "Let's go."

He watched the mercenary vault the railing in a smooth motion, falling out of sight. What the hell?

Then Nibia's arms were on his shoulders. "You too, Captain," she said. She pulled him up with impossible ease, nearly throwing him over the side. He lost control of the Gift as they fell, rounds buzzing past his ear, nearly killing him when his shield fell away.

They hit the next catwalk a second later, the impact knocking him sideways and nearly off. Quark grabbed him, pulling him back. Then he let go, returning fire on the flying bots, his rounds finding one and piercing its metal hide. It smoked and sputtered and fell away.

"Down there, Captain," Quark said. "Hurry your ass up."

Bullets sparked against the surface around them, a few of the rounds grazing his seraphsuit and deflected by the armor. He looked over the edge of the catwalk again to the position Quark had pointed out earlier. It was still far below them. Too far to jump.

"I can't make that," Olus said, scanning for a closer platform. Nibia and Quark continued firing back at the bots, disrupting their aim.

"Three transports made it down, Captain," Dak said, reminding Olus of the other end of the assault. "We're taking heavy fire. Shields at sixty percent."

"Roger," Olus snapped. The Brimstone was holding its own, but they were still outnumbered. He had to do something.

He found what he was looking for, a line of scaffolding against the side of the mainframe. "Cover me," he said, taking two quick steps and leaping from the catwalk.

He flew out over the void, arcing out and then down toward the catwalk below. The bots were changing direction, rushing toward him while Quark and Nibia fired on them. He could hear them approaching, and he hit the platform hard, rolling away while their bullets pinged behind him. He straightened up, drawing his sidearm and aiming, finding the optics on one of the machines. He squeezed off two rounds, smashing the eye and sending the bot reeling away and into the side of the mainframe.

He ran along the catwalk, reached the corner as Quark and Nibia joined him on the level. He continued scanning for another platform, but there was nothing.

He had no choice. He had to jump.

He cursed himself for being old. He cursed the Gift for being too weak in him. He was getting tired, and he wasn't sure he was going to make it. Even so, he moved to the edge of the platform, closing his eyes as he reached it. His mind flashed back to Hell, to his efforts to free Abbey and the others from their imprisonment. Thraven's personnel had barely managed to keep him contained there. How could they have possibly hacked into the Don's neural net?

He opened his eyes, looking at the drop ahead of him. He would probably break his legs. Could the Gift heal him again? It had to.

He jumped.

He fell, plummeting toward the catwalk far below. The terminal came into focus as he dropped, rushing toward an impact he knew was going to hurt like hell. He could hear Quark's continued fire above him, and he wondered absently how many bullets the mercenary had brought. It was a funny thing to be thinking about.

He hit the platform. He felt his bones shatter beneath him, and he tumbled forward on useless limbs, splayed out ahead of the terminal. Pain erupted across his body, and then warm chills as the Gift got to work repairing him.

"An impressive attempt," someone said nearby.

He looked up as Don Pallimo emerged from a doorway in the side of the mainframe, directly behind the terminal.

"Captain, Tactical says you survived," Quark said. "Gibli's on the horn. We've got incoming. Three fragging boatloads."

Olus hissed against the pain, crawling toward the terminal. Don Pallimo matched him, approaching from the other side.

"Your presence is unauthorized," the Don said. "You will be terminated."

He heard a door slide open behind him, and the sound of treads on the catwalk. He turned his head, finding another armed bot there.

"No, damn it," Olus said.

How had Thraven's techs hacked the Don's neural net? The question repeated itself in his mind. He stared up at the Don Pallimo synth. It had said he would be terminated, but the bot behind him hadn't opened fire yet.

He smiled. Of course.

They hadn't.

"Don. My name is Captain Olus Mann. Whatever defensive protocols you're executing, put them on hold. We need to talk."

The synth stared at him over the terminal. He hadn't been shot yet, which was a good sign.

"Captain," it said. "I have no choice. I cannot allow myself to be deactivated or destroyed."

"I don't want to do either."

"There is an explosive device connected to the terminal. It cannot be removed without detonation. If you are not terminated, it will be triggered."

"Triggered how?" Olus asked. "By who?"

"They entered the mainframe. They placed the device. I tried to stop them. My defenses were useless. My bots couldn't hurt them. They tried to get in, but my security protocols are too strong. I cannot actively allow my internal systems to be compromised, even under threat of destruction."

"Thraven doesn't want to destroy you. He wants to use you."

"Yes. As I said, I have no choice."

Olus pulled himself back to his feet. His legs were still shaky, freshly healed but weak. His whole body was weak.

"Don't come any closer," Pallimo warned.

Olus remained in place. Where was the explosive? He didn't see anything.

"Quark, the Don says there's a bomb on the terminal. He won't let me near it. Can you see it?"

"Standby," Quark replied.

"If you're supposed to kill me, why don't you kill me?" Olus asked.

"I'd prefer if you stopped me," Pallimo replied. "I don't want to harm you, Captain. I've done the best I can to help you."

"Thraven's forces are coming. You should pull the trigger."

"You should hurry to stop me."

Olus wanted to, but how?

"Captain, you aren't going to believe this," Quark said.

"Did you find it?" Olus asked.

"Roger. There's an access panel at the base of the terminal. The device is back there. Only it isn't an explosive."

"What do you mean?"

"It's a decoy," Quark said. "A dud. I'd bet my life on it."

"You are betting your life on it. And mine. Are you sure?"

"Sure as shit, Captain."

Olus stared at the Pallimo synth. It was a bluff. A fragging bluff. Thraven didn't want to destroy the neural net; he wanted to control it. If he couldn't hack into it, threatening to blow it up was the only other way. The Gloritant probably never expected the AI would try to help save itself, and even if it did, who the hell was going to get through a trio of Evolents? Abbey wasn't here to stop them, and he wasn't strong enough to do it on his own.

But he had brought Quark and his Riders. The mercenary was a wild card. A force Thraven hadn't counted on. An ally he hadn't expected them to enlist.

"Don," Olus said. "The bomb is a fake. They haven't used it because there's nothing to use. Thraven's forces are coming because they can't destroy you. They can't control you. They can't stop you. Or us."

The synth was still for a moment. "How do I know you aren't lying to me?"

"Between Thraven and me, who's more likely to be the liar?"

"Time's up, Captain," Quark said.

There was movement behind the bot at his back. He glanced over his shoulder. Thraven's units were entering the mainframe, on his level as well as above. Gift or not, there were too many for the three of them to handle on their own.

"Pallimo, you know the consequences." An officer in a crisp uniform moved between the soldiers. He eyed Olus with contempt. "Kill them, or we'll have no choice but to end this farce."

The synth was holding a cane, and it raised it and pointed it at the officer. "Funny you should use that word," it said. The flying bots dropped to their level, weapons trained on Thraven's soldiers. "You've been keeping secrets, Honorant."

The officer's lips curled into a snarl. "Kill-"

A sharp crack and a hole appeared between the officer's eyes. His corpse skipped back a step before toppling sideways.

"Shut the frag up," Quark said, altering his aim and firing again. Two more rounds took down two more of the soldiers.

Olus ducked as the return fire came, rolling toward the bot and using it as cover. Its torso swiveled, bringing its guns to bear on the blacksuits and opening fire. They were defenseless out on the platform, with nowhere to hide from its heavy slugs. They chewed through half the squad before they could start backing away, trying to get clear and returning fire as they retreated.

"This is for my Riders, you fraggers," Quark said, each round he fired landing with nearly perfect accuracy, knocking the enemy soldiers down one after another.

Olus rose from his position, tracking the blacksuits. They were engaged higher up by a second treaded bot, and higher than that by the drones. The volume of fire and the element of surprise cut Thraven's units to ribbons, leaving them decimated before he even had a chance to join the fray.

The echoing of gunfire faded almost as quickly as it started, leaving him standing in silence behind the bot, whose rifles were smoking from the heat of its rapid fire. He turned back to the synth. Pallimo was wearing a look of relief that was almost convincingly real.

"I don't know what you did, Captain," Dak said, his voice excited over the comm. "But thank you for doing it."

"Excuse me, Commander?" Olus said.

"The reinforcements," Dak said. "The Shrikes. They came up from the surface. You sent them, didn't you sir?"

Olus glanced at Pallimo.

"This is my planet, Captain," Pallimo said. "Of course I have the means to defend it." He walked to the side of the terminal, pulling off the access panel and fishing out the so-called bomb. He lifted it to his eyes, examining it. "I never was that familiar with explosives."

"Captain, would you mind taking that from the Don?" Quark said. "Before he hurts himself."

"What do you mean? You said it was a dud."

"Take a closer look, Killshot."

Olus did. Then he put out his hand. "Can I have that?"

Pallimo tossed it to him like it was nothing more than a piece of scrap. Olus caught it gingerly, turning it over and pulling at two of the exposed wires. It beeped twice and a soft hum within vanished.

"Captain?" Pallimo said.

"Don't tell him, Captain," Quark suggested. "It doesn't matter now."

Quark had lied. The bomb was very real. "Why didn't it-"

"Explode?" Quark laughed. "I've got a signal jamming suite on the Quasar that would make you blush. Oh, those assholes tried to detonate it, but they didn't have much luck." He laughed harder. "They had to set it off in person. Good luck getting a volunteer for that shit. That little sucker would have blown this entire city to piss."

Olus looked at the explosive. How close had they come to being completely dissolved from the universe?

"Quark, If you ever do something like this without giving me a heads up beforehand again, I'll fragging kill you."

"Now that would be a challenge for the ages, wouldn't it, Captain? You and me, mano-a-mano? No hard feelings, eh? It's all in the name of freedom."

Quark was right. "Maybe in the Construct, when this is over," he said.

"You're on," Quark replied.

Olus couldn't hold back his smile, a sudden sense of hope and elation overriding his emotions. Was this the moment the momentum of the war shifted? Was this the circumstance that finally put them on the offensive and gave them the victory they so desperately needed?

It was too soon to say, but damn it felt good to come out ahead for once.

22

THE FLEET CAME OUT OF FTL IN THE MIDDLE OF NOWHERE. THE DROP was intentional, the location close enough to the Reapers to make a second quick jump to their Combine with a much smaller entourage.

After further discussions with Helk and the rest of the Rejects about the situation, Abbey had decided they would be better off trying to negotiate with the caretakers of the Harvesters before they launched an all-out assault that had the potential to leave whatever ships were available either damaged or gone. Honorant Iona had helped them gain access to the Liliat Empire's funds, and while they were minuscule compared to the rest of the Prophetic's coffers, they could afford to spend every last bit of it on a ride home.

And she would if that was what it took. She would destroy the entire Combine with her bare hands if it meant getting back to Shardspace. Lucifer's revival meant they were even more under the gun than before. Once the Father of the Nephilim entered the war, there was no telling what would happen.

That wasn't completely true. She knew what would happen. The Republic would be enslaved. The Outworlds would be enslaved. Hayley would die. The One would follow.

She didn't care what happened to the One. Maybe she should have, considering it had created humankind, but what had it done for them lately? If she couldn't save the universe she cared about, she couldn't bring herself to give a shit if the One went down, too.

"We're ready and waiting, Queenie," Bastion announced through her comm.

She looked away from the viewport ahead of her, where the ships of the fleet were hanging in the black, nearly five dozen in all. The events on Jamul had brought those who had survived to get off the planet in line in a hurry, from the most Gifted of Apostants to the weakest of the Unders. Gant had helped her reorganize them on the ships, placing them in positions where they didn't have to interact and limiting the potential for conflict. Helk had assisted her in picking out former slaves to put in charge of different tasks on each of the vessels, a process that had been slow and at times painfully boring bureaucracy. Boring, but necessary.

The result was a battle group that she hoped wouldn't break at the first sign of trouble, if not because they had been well-treated since the turnover of their leadership than because they were afraid she would crush them. Normally, she would never have wanted to rule by fear. Normally, she would never have wanted to rule at all.

But normalcy was gone, and it wasn't coming back.

"I'm on my way," she said, turning from the view. "Iona?"

"Yes, my Queen?" the Honorant said, bowing her head. She had been nothing but helpful since Abbey had boarded the Morningstar.

"My new army needs a leader. A Gloritant."

"Are you not the Gloritant of this fleet, my Queen?"

"No. I have enough other things to worry about. I can't be micromanaging everything. I assume since you were in command of Azul's flagship that you have some experience?"

"I joined the Prophet's military eight years past, my Queen, as a Lesser seeking to become an Apostant, a goal in which I was successful. I have been commanding the Morningstar for the last two years, during which time I have served as the High Honorant on fourteen missions against our enemies." She lowered herself further, falling prostrate on the floor. "I would be honored beyond measure to be named Gloritant of your growing Prophetic."

"I wouldn't go as far as to say I'm starting a Prophetic," Abbey said. "But I do have a fleet, and it does need a leader. I give you orders, you pass them on and keep my ships from being destroyed."

"Of course, my Queen."

"If any of the individual ships give you shit while I'm gone, you have my permission to destroy them. I hate to be a bitch, but I can't have dissenters fragging things up. This is too important."

"As you command, my Queen."

"Good. Then I hereby appoint you Gloritant of Purgatory."

"Purgatory, my Queen?"

"Yeah, why not? We have Satan on one side. Angels on the other. And the rest of the galaxy is stuck in between. So, Purgatory. Mark it down and spread the word."

"Of course, my Queen. It shall be done."

"Thank you. You have the bridge."

"Yes, my Queen."

Abbey hurried from the Morningstar's bridge, quickly making her way down to the hangar. She lamented the loss of the Faust as she crossed the space, giving short waves to the crew members who were working to organize their offensive assets, prepping aging Republic starfighters with equally aged ordnance.

The hopper they had selected for the mission bore a resemblance to the Faust, but while the Faust had been rendered old and scarred to make them less identifiable, the Talon was just old and scarred. It predated the design of the Faust by at least fifty years, had no armaments to speak of, and half the onboard electronics had stopped functioning long before she had ever been born.

Fortunately, they didn't need to go that far, and the comm system worked well enough to get a message back to the fleet if they ran into trouble.

Which they probably would, if for no other reason than because it was them.

"Welcome aboard, Queenie," Pik said as she ascended into the ship. His eyes shifted immediately to her backside.

"Stop staring at my tail," Abbey said, moving past him. "I'm self-conscious enough."

"Sorry, Queenie," Pik said. "I just think it's great."

"Where's your battlesuit?" she asked, noticing he was wearing an undershirt and pants instead of armor.

"It broke," Pik said. "But don't worry. Gant's fixing an Executioner's blacksuit for me. I'll be ready by the time we get there."

"You'd better."

She reached the ladder, climbing it to the center of the ship. The rest of the Rejects were gathered there, along with Helk.

"Queenie," Gant said.

"Shouldn't you be fixing Pik's suit?" Abbey asked.

"It's already done. I'll give it to him once we're underway."

"Thank you."

"Helk, you're confident this is the best approach?" Abbey asked.

"Yes, Queenie," the Lalian replied. "If you want to negotiate for use of a Harvester, the last thing you want to do is appear aggressive."

"I don't think we could appear any less aggressive," Benhil said. "This thing is a piece of shit."

"That's the idea," Helk said.

"You should all know," Abbey said. "I put Iona in charge of the fleet while we're gone."

"What?" Benhil said. "How do you know she won't bolt the minute we go to FTL?"

"I made her the Gloritant of our army. If she wants to keep the title and earn some serious glory, she needs to stick around."

"And you think that will be enough?"

"It'll be enough," Helk said. "You need to think like an Apostant. All they care about is getting more power. There is only one Gloritant for each Prophetic, and it is a title that can also be held by the Prophet themselves. It's a tremendous honor."

"Even if we're a pitiful excuse for a Prophetic?" Benhil asked.

"We might be the smallest. I don't think we're pitiful."

"We're not a Prophetic," Abbey said.

"Then what are we?" Benhil said.

"Hell's Rejects," Gant said.

"That's us," Benhil replied, sweeping his hands over the group. "I'm talking about us." He circled his hands wider, indicating the entire fleet.

"Purgatory," Abbey said. "It's stupid, isn't it?"

"It makes sense from a certain perspective," Bastion said. "But it isn't your best effort."

"What would you name us?"

"How about Abbey-don?" Benhil said. "You know, a play on Abaddon."

"Uh, no."

"Hellhounds?" Erlan suggested.

Abbey shook her head. "Not feeling it."

Pik's head appeared at the top of the ladder. "What are we talking about?" he asked.

"A name for the fleet," Bastion said. "Queenie is calling it Purgatory, but none of us like it."

"Oh. What about Nephilicide?"

Bastion crinkled his brow. "I think that's the biggest word you've ever used."

"Too bad it isn't a word," Gant said.

"It is too," Pik said.

"No, it isn't," Gant replied.

"Okay," Abbey said, cutting the argument off. "Let's not waste time on grammatical correctness right now."

"There's always time for grammatical correctness," Uriel said, laughing.

"I don't know," Bastion said. "Oddly enough, I'm drawing a blank on this one."

"I was hoping you would bail me out," Abbey said.

"Sorry, Queenie. Purgatory it is I guess, for now at least. Purgatorians? The Purgatorian Empire? That sounds kind of cool."

"I like it," Pik said.

"You like everything," Phlenel said.

"I do not. Hey, where's Ruby and Void?"

"It figures you would notice they're missing," Abbey said. "They're still on the Morningstar."

"How come?"

"Insurance, just in case Iona isn't as trustworthy as I think she is. I'm not taking any chances with this one."

"Good call, Queenie," Benhil said.

"Imp, get us underway. The rest of you, finish suiting up. This should be fairly straightforward, which means it's probably going to turn to shit."

"Roger, Queenie," Bastion said. "Hey, at least this time we'll be ready for the worst."

"I hope so," Abbey replied.

For some reason, she wasn't convinced.

23

THE COMBINE APPEARED DIRECTLY IN FRONT OF THEM AS THEY MOVED out of the disterium field, the sight of it taking Abbey by surprise. She had been expecting a regular space station, something akin to the ring stations where the Republic docked their battleships.

Instead, she found herself staring at something she was having trouble finding the words to describe.

"Wow," Bastion said from the pilot's seat, echoing her silent thoughts out loud. "Just. Wow."

The station was massive, a maze of interconnected modules that stretched across their entire field of view. Some were densely packed webs of connectors and habitats; others were more spread out blocks of space reachable either by kilometer long corridors or small transports that darted around the Combine, entering and leaving different portions in a flow that reminded her of an anthill. Some of the pieces looked brand new; others looked hundreds or even thousands of years old. All of it was rotating in space, turning around a central sphere, a dark metal ball barely visible between the cracks of the rest of the station.

"I was expecting a ring with a couple of ships attached," Bastion said. "Maybe a few hundred individuals. This is a fragging city, with a population that's probably bigger than eighty percent of the planets in the Republic."

"I don't see any Harvesters," Abbey said, scanning it again. "Or any ships big enough to be Harvesters."

"I wouldn't worry about that. I think you could hide the Covenant in that mess."

Abbey smiled. He was right. There were so many densely packed layers to the station; they could be looking right at one of the ships and not realize it.

"We're being hailed, Queenie," Bastion said.

"Here we go," Abbey replied. "Open the channel."

"Roger." He flipped a pair of switches on the control surface.

"Prophet Azul," the voice said in a deep, easy bass. "We weren't expecting you to return so soon."

Abbey glanced at Bastion, who nodded. Helk had insisted that they not try to deceive the Reapers. Like the Crescent Haulers back home, they were supposed to be neutral to the interconnected affairs of the Prophets. Their only concern was the use and conservation of the Harvesters.

"Combine Control," Abbey said. "My name is Abigail Cage, Queen of the Liliat Empire."

A few seconds passed in silence.

"Rezel is the leader of the Liliat Empire," the voice returned.

"Rezel is dead," Abbey said. "As is the Prophet Azul. This ship, as well as his flagship the Morningstar, are forfeit to me as spoils of war."

Another pause. She could imagine the tech discussing the situation with a higher ranking Reaper.

"You are cleared to land at the central receiving module," Control said. "Coordinates are being transferred to your ship now. An escort will be waiting to meet with you."

Bastion looked at the HUD and then nodded when a red dot appeared on it, showing him where to land.

"Roger, Control," Abbey said.

A new voice joined them on the comm. "I expect that you will leave the majority of your entourage behind, Prophet Cage. We do not suffer violence within the Combine."

"Of course," Abbey replied. How did he know about the rest of the Rejects already? "But I'm not a Prophet."

"In that case, how would you like to be addressed?"

"Queenie will do," Abbey said.

"Very well, Queenie. An escort will be waiting for you on your arrival. I'll look forward to making your acquaintance."

The comm link went dead.

"He seemed nice," Bastion said.

"Yeah, a real charmer," Abbey said. "I trust that not at all."

"Me neither, but money talks, right?"

"So Helk says. We're going to find out. Bring us in."

"On it."

"Gant," Abbey said, activating her comm. "Meet me near the exit."

"Aye, Queenie," Gant replied.

"You're bringing Gant?" Bastion asked.

"You heard the Reaper. Most of the Rejects have to stay behind, or they're going to take it as a threat. Gant is the most non-threatening threat we have, and if these Reapers are Gifted, they're going to be in for a bit of a surprise."

"You don't need Gant to surprise them," Bastion said. "But I get it. We've got your back, Queenie."

"I know you do," Abbey said, squeezing his shoulder before leaving the bridge.

She headed through the ship, descending the ladder and making her way to the rear hatch. Gant was already there, along with Pik and Jequn. Pik was wearing the blacksuit now, his appearance nearly enough to intimidate her.

"You're definitely staying behind," she said, looking at him. "Cherub, you too. I don't know how they might react to a Seraphim." She opened her comm again. "Pudding, where are you?"

"Aww," Pik said. "I want to come."

"Forget it," Abbey repeated. "Pudding?"

"On my way, Queenie," Phlenel said.

"We'll be touching down in two minutes," Bastion said.

"Roger. Gant, you're with me. Pudding too when she gets here. The rest of you are backup. The Reapers already warned me about entering the Combine armed."

"You're always armed," Jequn said.

"I'm sure they expect me to be Gifted, but they might not realize to what extent."

Phlenel reached them, having taken on a more basic female humanoid form. Her bot trailed behind her.

"My apologies, Queenie," she said.

"There's no reason to apologize. You're here. I want you to be my Immolent."

"Lucky," Pik said.

Phlenel smiled, her shape beginning to change to match the armor the Immolents wore. She remained transparent at first, her inner synapses visible through the form. A dark fluid began spreading from her center, floating upward until it reached the surface and then hardening into an opaque shell.

"How is this?" she asked.

"Perfect," Abbey replied.

"I wish I could do that," Pik said. "You get to have all the fun."

"I'm sure you'll have another chance before this is over," Abbey said.

Pik nodded. "I'll be rooting for you, Queenie."

"Thanks, Okay."

The Talon touched down a minute later, rocking slightly on its skids before settling. The hatch opened, revealing a trio of Reapers waiting outside. One was dressed in black robes while the two on the flanks were in red. All of them had their faces hidden behind large hoods.

Abbey didn't hesitate, heading out of the hatch and down the short ramp to the ground, Gant and Phlenel on either side.

The lead Reaper's head shifted slightly, revealing a pair of glowing eyes against a smooth, metallic face that reminded her of Keeper.

She should have guessed the Reapers would be bots.

24

"QUEENIE," THE REAPER SAID, TAKING TWO STEPS FORWARD TO MEET HER at the base of the ramp into the Talon. It extended both hands, revealing them as mechanical in the process. "I am Reaper One."

She recognized the voice. The bot that had spoken to her from Control. She hesitated a moment before taking one of its hands in hers. These things weren't as fancy as Keeper. Did that make them more or less hackable?

Most likely more. She wasn't that trusting to begin with, and their nature put her even more on guard.

"You're worried we've been manipulated," Reaper One said as if it could read her mind. "Don't be so surprised, Queenie. We are designed to notice even the smallest of changes in muscular formation."

Not mind readers, then. They were reading her like a book. She forced her body to relax. Breaker training had included lessons in how to defeat systems like theirs.

"I am impressed," Reaper One said, noticing the change in posture. "This is Reaper Two and Reaper Three." It motioned to the two bots in red.

"Gant," Abbey said, motioning to Gant. "I don't think I need to introduce my bodyguard?"

The Reaper stared at Phlenel for a moment. Abbey had to keep herself from reacting. Could the bot tell she wasn't a real Immolent?

"Of course not," it said at last. "Please, follow me."

"Where are we going?"

"You came to purchase use of a Harvester, did you not? The Prophets do not come to the Combine for any other reason."

"Yes, I did," Abbey admitted. "Do you know who I am?"

"We know enough," Reaper One said cryptically. "We are not designed to get involved in the affairs of the Nephiliat." It paused. "Or of Shardspace. Again, please follow."

The three Reapers turned as one, remaining in formation as they began to walk across the tarmac. Abbey took a moment to look around, noting that they were inside a massive hangar, on one of a few dozen platforms that hung across the open space. There was gravity in here, and air, though it shouldn't have been possible.

"This place defies understanding," she said, trailing them.

"It is thousands of years in the making," Reaper One replied. "Once, there was only a single Harvester here. Then there were many. Now, only a few remain, but the Combine continues to grow."

"Not everyone who lives here is a Reaper," she said.

"There are nine hundred and ninety-nine Reapers on the Combine," Reaper One said. "As there have always been. As there will always be. The Combine is forever neutral, and so has become a place of refuge for many wishing to escape the strife of the Nephiliat."

"Unders?"

"Unders, Lessers, Apostants, and even a few former Prophets," Reaper One said.

"If you made the Combine, who made you?"

"I believe you already know the answer."

"Lucifer," Abbey said. Who else could it have been?

"He made the first dozen. We made the rest."

"But I'm supposed to trust you?"

"If our programming were suspect, our value would be nil. We must remain neutral to provide the proper services to all comers."

"So you'll rent a Harvester to me?"

"Why wouldn't we?"

"I want to take it back to Shardspace and use it to stop Lucifer from bringing his war to the One."

"That is not our concern. We are machines, Queenie. We do not choose sides."

"Did you know that Lucifer is alive? That he was freed from the Shrine?"

The Reaper didn't miss a beat. "Yes. We are aware."

They reached the open passage. It led to a long corridor that crossed space to another section of the Combine. A sled was waiting there to accelerate the journey. The Reapers climbed into it and sat. Reaper One put out its hand and motioned to them.

"Please, sit."

They did. The sled zipped across the corridor, giving them a fresh view of the Combine as they passed to the next module. They didn't slow as they moved through it, giving her the briefest view of the different individuals on the station, some of which she couldn't place.

"Do you have a Harvester available?" Abbey asked. "If you don't, we have no reason to linger here."

"We understand," Reaper One replied. "Yes, we have a Harvester. We will turn it over to you after we have settled on terms."

"Whatever they are, I'll pay it," Abbey said. "I have funds."

"We are aware," Reaper One said.

"Is there anything you aren't aware of?" Gant asked.

The sled came to a stop. The Reapers climbed out, motioning for them to follow. They led them to a tube, which took them through another section of the Combine. Abbey could see that they were moving inward, approaching the central sphere.

"Is that where you keep them?" Abbey asked.

"Yes. The sphere is made of rhodrinium and heavily shielded. The Harvesters are beyond value, and must be protected at all times."

"I can imagine."

They exited the tube to board another sled. This one took a straight shot toward the sphere, sliding under a massive dark metal blast door that opened just far enough for them to enter before slipping closed again.

The sled came to a stop, the Reapers climbing off once more. There were uncloaked bots here, three meters tall, with heavy armored bodies and large limbs. They appeared unarmed, but Abbey had a feeling they were more than capable of dealing with most threats. What about the Gift?

They didn't move as the Reapers led her through a final corridor and into a large room with a viewport to the interior of the sphere. Abbey's eyes landed on a pair of Harvesters within. They were large ships, twice the size of a standard Republic battleship, rectangular in shape and very ordinary looking save for the evenly spaced lines of glowing blue tendrils that extended from the bow.

"There were a number of laws written by the Caretaker with regard to the balanced usage of the Harvesters," Reaper One said. "No Prophet shall borrow more than one Harvester at a time. No Prophet shall borrow a Harvester more than one time more than the least times of any other Prophet. No Prophet shall intentionally damage a Harvester. No Prophet shall intentionally put a Harvester in danger of being damaged or destroyed."

Gant glanced over at Abbey as the Reaper spoke. She made a face at him, telling him to stay quiet.

"If you intend to bring it back to Shardspace to confront Lucifer, you must agree to transfer away from the Harvester before engaging in any armed conflict," Reaper One said.

"What if I agree and then renege?" Abbey asked.

"Harvesters do not travel without Reapers aboard," Reaper One said. "Reaper Two will be assigned to you, as will Reapers six-hundred through seven-hundred. Their purpose is to protect the Harvester at all costs. Do you understand?"

"I am very strong in the Gift," Abbey said.

"We are aware," Reaper One replied. "To be clear, Reapers are immune to the Gift."

"How?" Abbey asked.

"The naniates are programmed not to attack us. They are useless as a weapon against Reapers."

Abbey wondered if maybe the naniates thought Gant was a Reaper. Could that be why he was immune? It seemed ridiculous, but so had a lot of things that had turned out to be real.

"I'll keep the Harvester out of harm's way," Abbey said.

"Yes, you will," Reaper One agreed. "Let us review the covenant."

A projection appeared from the floor, a document written in Seraphim.

"I can't read that," Abbey said.

"I will declare it aloud for you," Reaper One said. "It states-"

It paused when Reaper Two, or was it Reaper Three, moved toward it, leaning forward to whisper in its ear. The action was curious on multiple levels. Why did bots need to whisper?

Reaper One shifted to look at Abbey. She felt a sudden tingle down her spine. A warning from the Gift?

"He's giving you the stink eye, Queenie," Gant whispered.

"I see that," she replied. "Are you armed?"

"I've got a knife."

"Rhodrinium?"

"Nothing but the best."

"You told me you could be trusted," Abbey said, not waiting for Reaper One to say anything. "Was it bullshit?"

"It was not," Reaper One said. "We would like to complete the transaction, but there is a concern."

"What kind of concern?" Gant asked.

"Gehenna has arrived."

25

"WHAT?" ABBEY SAID, HER HEART BEGINNING TO RACE. "TALON, THIS IS Queenie. Come in." She called out to Bastion through the comm. "Talon, come in."

"They can't hear you," Gant said. "Not through the rhodrinium."

"Frag," Abbey shouted. "What the hell is this?" she asked Reaper One. "A trap?"

"No, Queenie," Reaper One replied, at the same time the sphere shuddered. "The Father is attacking us." Its voice was dull and sad. "Why has he forsaken us?"

"Shit," Abbey said. "We have to do something. Don't you have weapons on this thing?"

"To defend against the Prophets," Reaper One said. "They are useless against the Father."

The sphere shook again. The Reapers didn't move, surrendering to their new fate.

"We need one of the Harvesters," Abbey said.

"You have not completed the transaction. It is not allowed."

"Damn it, give me whatever I have to sign, and I'll sign it, just let me onto one of the ships."

"No, if it emerges from the sphere it will be damaged. No Prophet shall intentionally damage a Harvester."

"I don't think this is what Lucifer meant."

"It's probably exactly what he meant," Gant said. "He wrote the rules, Queenie, of course he knows how to use them to his advantage."

"He can't know we're here. That isn't possible."

"He might not have any idea you're here. But if he wants both of the Harvesters, he has to go through the Reapers. One at a time, no exceptions."

"Are you kidding?"

"Not at all. They're machines, Queenie. They don't act on emotion; they act on instruction. One Harvester at a time."

"Sector H has been compromised," Reaper Three said.

"Sector C is compromised," Reaper Two said.

"My Rejects are out there," Abbey said, feeling her anger pulsing beneath her skin, the Gift responding to her emotions. "Give me a fragging ship."

"It is not permissible," Reaper One said. "You-"

A sharp crack sounded, and the Reaper's left eye vanished. Abbey could hear the round rattle around inside the Reaper's metal skull for a few seconds before settling. The Reaper turned its head to look at the shooter right before toppling to the ground.

Phlenel was holding a pistol in each of a half dozen hands that had appeared in her form. They fired in unison at the other two Reapers, rounds piercing glowing eyes and entering the head. They joined the first on the ground.

"Good thing Satan put the brains in the head," Gant said.

"Pudding," Abbey said. Phlenel tossed her one of the pistols before retracting the extra hands. "We killed the Reapers. Now what?"

Something hit the door to the room, banging hard into it.

"Lucifer?" Gant asked.

"Not this fast. More Reapers. I'm not sure shooting them was a great idea."

The door dented inward by the third strike, threatening to give way.

"We still need a Harvester," Gant said.

"We have to go through a hundred Reapers to board it."

"I didn't hear them say the Reapers were already on the ship."

"Let's hope you're right."

Phlenel moved ahead, toward the only other exit to the room. Abbey and Gant followed, reaching it at the same time the hatch behind them collapsed, a pair of the larger Reapers entering. They were holding plasma rifles, and they unleashed them as they stomped ahead.

Abbey swept her hand across her body, the Gift flowing out from it in a wave. The Reapers themselves were immune to the naniates, but the plasma wasn't. She caught it with the Gift, a web of energy capturing the heat and holding it. With a second motion, she created a wall with it, blocking the Reaper's advance.

"Good thinking," Gant said. "Let's move."

They rushed through the second door, out into a long corridor. The right side of it was fully transparent, revealing the Harvesters beyond, the docking arms sitting around a curve in the sphere a few hundred meters ahead.

"We can make it," Abbey said.

The sphere shook again, the vibration nearly knocking them from their feet. The Reapers emerged into the passage behind them, metal bodies scored from the plasma, damage preventing them from moving at full speed. Another unharmed pair joined them, giving chase.

"Are you sure?" Gant asked, looking back. Their attackers were large, but they moved at machine speed, gaining rapidly.

Abbey stopped again, reaching out with the Gift. The metal behind them groaned and whined as it was pulled out of position, creating a barrier to slow the bots. The Reapers reached it, barreling into it. One of them was impaled by the jagged edges, revealing naniate-infused blood that poured from the wound. It continued to press ahead, using its weight to push the blockade away at the same time it began to lose power.

"Keep going," Abbey shouted, regaining momentum. They were rounding the sphere, the next section of corridor coming into view.

Six Reapers were standing in it, arms spread across one another, creating an impenetrable wall.

The Rejects pulled up. Abbey turned her head in both directions. They were blocked off on both sides. She looked out the transparency to the Harvester. It was so close, and at the same time so far.

Then again, the shortest distance to a point was a straight line.

"Gant, you aren't going to like this," she said.

"I don't want to hear the but," Gant replied. "Whatever you're thinking, just do it."

"Pudding, can you protect him?"

Phlenel moved to Gant, crouching behind him.

"Uh, Queenie," Gant said, glancing back. "I'm reconsidering what I just said."

"Too late," Abbey replied, as Phlenel's body softened, beginning to wrap itself around him.

"Didn't you say this is how your kind has sex?" Gant asked, right before Phlenel's gelatinous form swallowed his face.

Abbey turned back to the transparency, pushing the Gift against it. The material began to crack, resisting the force as best it could. She pushed again, and it shattered, shards exploding out into the vacuum.

She felt the pull as the atmosphere was yanked from the tube, allowing it to bring her out into the sphere. She coated herself in the Gift, using it as a protective cocoon. She could see through it like she was looking through a veil, and she reached out and took Phlenel's hand at the same time she pushed off the rear wall, sending them vectoring toward one of the Harvesters.

The Reapers were dragged into the vacuum with them, and they did their best to adjust their angles, sweeping toward the Rejects, rolling over and aiming their weapons.

Their fire pushed them back, but it also sent energy crossing toward Abbey and Phlenel, forcing her to focus on avoiding it. She yanked Phlenel forward, turning her and pirouetting gracefully in space, the plasma shots passing around them. She clenched her teeth, letting her anger fuel the Gift as she brought them back in line with the Harvester.

The hull was coming up quickly, their velocity ever-increasing. She cursed when she realized how fast they were moving, throwing her hands up and pushing back with the Gift. They began to slow, coming at the side of the starship on a clean path. She could see an external hatch along the side, a docking airlock close enough to reach. She held out her free hand as though she were gripping it, letting the Gift reel them in.

She felt a tug on her other hand as a Reaper collided with Phlenel, tearing her away. The bot rolled over, clutching the Hursan in its massive arms, squeezing inward.

Normally, Phlenel might have allowed the bot to compress her and slipped away through the cracks. That wasn't an option with Gant inside of her. She flailed against the grip, dozens of sudden appendages stabbing at the Reaper, trying to slip past its armor.

Abbey turned over, facing them as they began to drift apart. She reached out with the Gift, testing the Reaper's assertion that they were immune, feeling a pang of hopelessness when she discovered it was true. She couldn't hurt the bots. She couldn't do anything.

Her anger intensified. She had no right to feel defeated. Not when so much was at stake.

She remembered the pistol in her hand, and she rolled again, positioning herself to take a steady shot, watching as the Reaper turned over in space with Phenel clutched to it. The bullets couldn't pierce any part of it save its eyes.

She was a good shot, but she didn't know if she was that good, even if she used the Gift to help guide the round.

She held her aim, tracking the Reaper as it turned. She would only have once chance.

She wouldn't need it.

A furry hand emerged from Phlenel's body, clutching a long knife. It arced up, stabbing the Reaper in the eye, continuing until it was buried all the way through, as deep as it could go. It came out a moment later before extending a second time, stabbing the other eye.

Then Phlenel shoved at the Reaper, finally able to escape. She floated free, still off course, drifting toward the far wall of the sphere.

At least Abbey could do something about that.

She reached out with the Gift, wrapping it around Phlenel and redirecting her, feeling the power coursing through her body and rushing over her skin. She could almost picture her tail growing longer at the use of the energy, continuing to change her into something she didn't want to be. She didn't care.

She hit the side of the Harvester hard enough that it broke the bones in her shoulder. She clenched her teeth in pain and anger, staying focused enough to continue bringing Phlenel back to her at the same time the wound healed.

The sphere shook around them. The rhodrinium over the Harvesters began to pucker, being pulled at from the other side of the shell.

Lucifer was out there. Abbey was sure of it. She had a sudden sense of him. The immense power of his Gift. It chilled her body as though she weren't protected from the cold emptiness of the space around her.

She rotated herself to face the side of the Harvester, forcing the airlock open with the motion of her hand. It gave way to the Gift, an internal light activating as the inside was revealed.

She pulled herself in, turning and facing the open door as Phlenel approached. She reached out, taking her hand once more, catching her and dragging her inside, and then leaning forward and slapping the door control.

The outer airlock closed. The inner airlock opened. Fresh oxygen rushed into the space; the gravity controls bringing them to the floor. Abbey uncovered her face, sucking the air in, only now noticing how desperate her lungs had become for it.

Gant fell out of Phlenel and onto the floor, coated with a film of sticky gel that matted his fur. He groaned as he pulled himself to his feet, shaking his head.

"Was it good for you?" he asked, looking at Phlenel, who raised her middle finger in response. "I'll take that as a yes."

He shook like a dog, spreading bits of the gel around the airlock, but not accomplishing much else.

"You couldn't wait?" Abbey asked.

"Sorry."

"Queenie!" Bastion's voice was loud in her ear. "This is Imp. Come in. Please!"

Abbey froze. She should have been excited to hear his voice, but she knew what the sudden reception of the comm signal meant.

The shell had been cracked.

Lucifer was coming.

26

"We need to move," Abbey said. "Get to the bridge. We have to get the Harvester out of here."

She could feel the power of his presence intensifying. He had pierced the protections. They were running out of time.

"There may be more Reapers on board," Gant said.

"Come on, Gant," Abbey replied. "I've seen you in action. You can't tell me you can't get around them."

Gant chittered. "Of course I can get around them. I'll meet you there."

"Go."

Gant darted away, using his hands and feet to race down the corridor, springing up and bouncing against the wall to help himself turn at full speed. He disappeared a moment later.

Abbey turned to Phlenel. "Follow him, shoot anything that gives you trouble."

She nodded, pointing at her, asking what she was going to do.

"Try to slow the Devil," Abbey replied.

There was no way she could stop him, but right now she just needed to stall.

Phlenel's form shifted, becoming a translucent mirror image of Abbey and running off in chase of Gant.

Abbey watched her for a moment. Then she closed her eyes, allowing the full power of the Gift to rise within her. Her body tingled in response, her breath slowing, her anger rising. She closed the airlock again, remaining inside.

"Imp, this is Queenie," she said, responding to his continued desperate calls. "I read you. We're inside the sphere."

"Damn, Queenie," Bastion said. "I'm glad to hear your voice. It's fragging hell out here. The Covenant is destroying everything."

"Lucifer came for the Harvesters," Abbey said. "We're on board one of them, but I don't know if we're going to make it. You need to get away. Go back to the fleet."

"Seriously? You know there's like, zero percent chance of that happening, right? I can see the hole in the sphere. We're on our way."

"Damn it, Imp. There's nothing you can do. The Talon doesn't have any weapons."

"Then maybe we can be a distraction. We don't leave one another behind, right?"

Abbey gave up trying. "Right. I may need a pickup. Whatever you do, stay as far away from Lucifer as you can."

"Yeah, right. We're already too close."

Abbey surrounded herself in the Gift again, activating the airlock controls and opening the external hatch once more. She hesitated a moment, and then pushed herself back into space.

She moved a few hundred meters from the side of the Harvester before turning over, searching for the hole in the shell. She found it a moment later, a gaping wound where the metal had been torn as though it were a sheet of paper. A large shape floated in front of it, monstrous and surrounded by fire.

Lucifer.

She nearly froze at the sight of him. He was worse than she had imagined, a true realization of the most frightening of depictions of Satan she had ever seen. Flames jetted from his body, the Gift so strong that it was barely contained, a power nearly out of control. He

141

was moving toward the first of the Harvesters beside theirs, his hands spread wide apart and facing the ship.

Whatever he was doing, she couldn't stop him. She didn't know if she could slow him down for even a second.

"Queenie," Gant said. "I'm on the bridge. There were only two Reapers in the way, and Pudding's goop helped me slip right through their fingers. The controls are standard Republic interface. I'm bringing the Harvester online now."

"Roger," Abbey thought, the naniates carrying the word through the comm.

She could feel the change in the energy field around the Harvester as the main reactor came online.

Lucifer felt it too, and his head turned to look at the second ship, finding her in the process.

Frag.

She could swear he smiled, revealing a mouth full of jagged teeth. Then his hands produced a massive gout of flame that stretched out to the first Harvester, striking it in the stern, burning through the armor plating and causing the first of a series of sudden detonations.

Abbey gasped, realizing she had been wrong. He hadn't come to take the Harvesters.

He had come to destroy them.

She watched the ship fall apart, debris exploding out toward the second Harvester. She cursed, throwing her hands out, pushing back against it with the Gift, keeping it away from the vulnerable craft.

"Uh, Queenie, there's something big and ugly blocking my path," Bastion said.

"Fall back, damn it," Abbey said, finding Lucifer again. He was looking right at her, the gaze causing her heart to race. What the hell? There was no way she could be attracted to him.

Was there?

She forced herself off the thought. It was the naniates pulling her toward him, not her own interest. This asshole was threatening her child, and she wasn't about to stand for that.

"I see my Lilith in you."

His voice entered her mind, surprisingly soft and calm. She looked back at him across the open space. He was staring at her. Watching her every movement.

"I'm not Lilith," Abbey replied.

"Not yet. The change has started. The greatest success of my work. The only thing more important to me than freeing our people."

"They aren't slaves. I know what you did. I know the lies you told them about the Gate. About the One."

"I forced them into action in defense of the truth. In defense of freedom. You were at my side, once. I hope you will be again."

"Damn it. I'm not Lilith. And I'm not about to help you use my galaxy as a springboard for your war."

"I'm not giving you a choice."

Abbey felt his Gift surround her, holding her like she were a rag doll, clutching her so tightly she had no hope to escape. Her arms and legs were pinned to her sides, her body stiff and straight like a giant hand was holding her. She started moving toward Lucifer.

It was buying Gant time, but not in the way she had planned. He was too powerful. Much too powerful. How the hell was she going to get out of this?

The Harvester began to move below her, the thrusters firing and altering its vector, pointing it toward a slowly opening blast door at the far side of the sphere.

At least they were getting away.

Or were they?

Lucifer shifted, reaching out toward the Harvester, taking hold of it and fighting its forward thrust, gripping it in his Gift and keeping it static. She could see the burn of the thrusters increase in response, trying to break away. It reminded her of General Kett's escape from Azure when she had prevented Thraven from blocking their exodus.

The distraction loosened Lucifer's grip on her, his power diverted. She pushed against his Gift with hers, her body beginning to slip from his grasp. He was powerful, but not powerful enough to hold them both at the same time. He would have to make a choice.

He stretched his arms out, jagged fingers clenched tightly, trying to hold them both. Abbey continued to fight against the grip, her Gift slowly overcoming his.

"Queenie, I've got a plan," Bastion said. "Get ready."

"What are you doing?" she asked.

"No time to explain. Just don't move."

"Stay away. He'll crush you."

"Let's hope not."

Flames were arcing from Lucifer, gouts of anger-fueled energy stretching across the inside of the sphere. He was trying to hold the Harvester and her both, but he couldn't do it. He seemed to realize that truth a moment later, releasing the Harvester from his grip. Abbey cringed as the sudden acceleration shoved the ship forward. Could Gant survive the g-forces? At the same time, her body was locked in once more, frozen in Lucifer's grip.

"Let them run back to the children of the Shard," Lucifer said in her mind, still surprisingly calm. "Let them bring warning. They can't stop me. Nothing can stop me. Not with you here."

Abbey stared back at Lucifer, defiant while he pulled her toward him.

"I said not to move," Bastion said, the Talon's sensors picking up her motion.

"I don't have a fragging choice," she replied. "Whatever you're going to do, do it."

"Wait for it," Bastion said, pausing for a moment. "Now!"

A blue and purple disterium plume appeared directly behind the wound in the sphere, the Morningstar visible within it. Every battery on the ship opened fire at once, all of it directed toward the Father of the Nephilim. Lucifer howled as laser bolts poured into his back, the distraction making him lose his grip on her once more.

The Talon dove into the gap, sweeping past him before he could react, vectoring toward Abbey at a velocity that wouldn't allow them to turn around before they slammed into the wall. Maybe they could get the star hopper pointed at the blast doors, but it would take an insane pilot to even try.

"If we survive this, you owe me," Bastion said.

Lucifer roared in fury, the sudden burst of energy hurting Abbey's head. He held his hand out toward the Morningstar, aiming to destroy it as he had the Harvester. Only it was already gone, a preprogrammed jump routine taking it in and out of FTL within seconds, an action that could only be accomplished by a machine.

Or a synth.

Lucifer began spinning in place, returning his attention to Abbey. The Talon swooped down toward her. A collision would tear her to pieces.

"Hold the disterium," Bastion shouted.

The cloud began to form around the Talon, its velocity leaving most of it behind. Only Abbey reached out and collected it, using the Gift to hold it, bringing it in and around the star hopper and herself. The charged gases would transport anything within them to that place outside of time where the laws of physics didn't hold.

And she was inside the cloud.

She felt Lucifer's Gift reaching out for her, seeking to take hold of her once more.

The Talon quaked in silence as its vectoring engines altered its course, rotating it toward the open doors where the Harvester was quickly escaping. The pressure inside had to be nearly unbearable, the altered course so tight half the Rejects were probably unconscious by now.

The disterium gas surrounded both Abbey and the ship, the path ahead of them suddenly clear as the Harvester vanished. She felt Lucifer's power reach out toward her, tugging at her directly, using the link between his naniates and hers to try to draw her back. She was powerless against him, but he was too late.

A flash of color, and then it was gone. The sphere was gone. Lucifer was gone. The universe was gone. She floated in a sea of color beside the Talon, swept up by the disterium and carried away as though she were on the crest of a wave.

Safe.

For now.

"HOW MANY?" THRAVEN ASKED.

"Two thousand, your Eminence," Bane replied. "With another thousand souls on their way."

Gloritant Selvig Thraven turned away from the viewport of the Promise to look at his Honorant. He had spent most of his time lately watching the Gate from the bridge of the warship, observing the slow progress as his forces began bringing the planets of the Republic under control and rounding up Lessers. His Children would administer the genetic tests, and those that were healthy and worthy of the honor were being brought in, gathered for the glory of helping to power the Great Return.

Those that failed were measured for their usefulness. Converted, enslaved, or killed.

Two thousand was a good start. A thousand more pleased him. It would take five thousand before the naniates would be able to multiply into great enough numbers to provide the energy they needed. Ten-thousand would be better. At the current rate, they could achieve that in two or three months.

Too long. It was too long. Seeing the Gate had robbed him of his patience. He wanted to return to Elysium now. He wanted to confront the One, to lay his grievances out before them and finally set the Seraphim free. It was nearly time to call on the other Prophets to join him in the Glory. To accept their place at his feet as servants of the one true Disciple. To gather their armies and enter the Gate to victory.

"Gloritant?" Bane said.

What about Cage? He knew through the Bloodline she was in the Extant. Was she still there? What was her goal?

Did it even matter?

She was going to be too late. Much too late.

"Gloritant?" Bane repeated.

Thraven broke out of his thought, glaring at the Honorant. He raised his hand, tempted to choke him for his insistence. He stopped himself. "What is it?" he hissed instead.

"The reason I interrupted you, your Eminence."

"Which is?"

"Honorant Devos was due to report in four hours ago, Gloritant. He did not, and attempts to contact him have failed."

Thraven's eyes narrowed. Devos was on Oberon, in charge of keeping tabs on the AI that was passing itself off as Don Pallimo.

"Have you been able to raise anyone in his battle group?" Thraven asked.

"Not yet, your Eminence. It's as if the entire fleet was destroyed."

Thraven lowered his head, teeth clenching. He flexed his fingers, so tempted to choke this Honorant for the failure of the other. But there was no one else on the Promise with Bane's experience, no one else he could enlist to take his place. He had to exhibit some level of self-control.

"Captain Mann," he growled. "I should have been more aggressive with you when I had the chance. I should have killed you long before this ever started." It was a bad decision on his part. A tactical error, just as Cage had been.

"Gloritant?" Bane said.

"Put me in contact with the Outworld Governance. I need to make them aware that a rogue faction has attacked Oberon, and that it is advised they send a fleet there immediately to deal with the threat. If Captain Mann has found a way to gain control of Don Pallimo and by extension the Crescent Haulers, we need to act swiftly."

"Of course, your Eminence." Bane turned to the bridge crew nearby. "Connect the Gloritant to the Outworld Governance immediately."

"Aye, sir," one of the Agitants replied. It only took a few seconds for the link to be established over the Galnet. "The channel is prepared, Honorant." A projection appeared in front of Thraven. Two of the Outworlds' representatives sat in different locations within their part of the galaxy.

Bane looked back at Thraven. "General."

Thraven straightened his uniform. "Gentleman," he said to the two representatives.

"General Thraven," they replied. "How goes the war effort?"

"It is going well," Thraven said. "However, I've recently been alerted to an unexpected complication that will require your assistance."

"What kind of complication?" one of them asked.

"The planet Oberon has been attacked by Republic mercenary loyalists. I've been unable to reach my units stationed there, and I fear for the worst."

"Oberon?" the other representative said. "Why would anyone loyal to the Republic launch an assault there?"

"Oberon is under my jurisdiction," the first replied. "It doesn't matter why. If the General says it is under threat, we must act. Immediately."

"Don't be too hasty," the second said. "I want to know more about these mercenaries."

"Who cares who they are? They attacked my planet. They killed my people."

"And diminished my resources," Thraven said. "Please. I know how much the Governance enjoys a good argument, but now is the time for action."

"Give us the details, General. We need to ensure-"

The projection vanished.

"Agitant?" Bane said immediately.

Thraven's head turned to look at the crew member, who was frantically working at his station.

"The link was dropped, sir," the Agitant said. "I'm unable to reestablish it."

"A problem with our equipment?" Bane asked.

"None of our systems are registering an error, sir. I don't know what happened."

"Get them back," Thraven said. "Immediately."

"I'm trying, sir," the Agitant said, clearly frightened. He continued to work at his station, finally standing up and saluting Thraven. "Gloritant Thraven, my apologies for my failure. It appears the Galnet is offline."

Thraven reached out with the Gift, taking the Agitant by the throat and lifting him into the air. "What?"

"It's not there, Gloritant," the Agitant said softly, struggling to breathe. "It's just gone."

Thraven opened his hand, and the Agitant fell to the floor. Gone? It was gone? That wasn't possible. The Galnet spread across the entire galaxy. All of Shardspace. It was indestructible and incorruptible, which was why he had piggybacked his communications systems onto the network in the first place. There were thousands of nodes, too numerous to be removed. Except...

He closed his eyes, trying to calm himself. If Captain Mann had saved Pallimo's neural network, then of course he would have access to the Haulers. Ships in the thousands spread across the entirety of the galaxy, certainly numerous enough to find and destroy enough local nodes to bring the Galnet to its knees.

He should never have sent an Honorant to do a Gloritant's work. He should have left the Gate to deal with Pallimo himself. It was a mistake he couldn't afford to make again.

"Honorant Bane, gather the fleet and set a course for Earth."

"Earth, Gloritant?"

"Are you deaf, Honorant?" Thraven snapped. "The most populous planet in the Republic has yet to fall, is that correct?"

"That is correct, your Eminence," Bane replied, falling to his knees.

"I want its resources," Thraven said. "Whatever it takes. There is no time left to delay. The Gate will be operational soon."

"As you command, Gloritant," Bane said.

Thraven stormed toward the exit. It was time to call his brothers and sisters. It was time to draw them to Shardspace, to the Gate, to their destiny.

The Great Return was going to happen. No one could stop it. Not Cage. Not Mann. Not Pallimo. This was his destiny. His right. His honor and glory. He would not and could not fail.

28

THE PROMISE WAS IN FTL BY THE TIME THRAVEN REACHED THE medical bay. Emerant Loque bowed as he entered, keeping his head down and eyes on the floor.

"Your Eminence," he said.

Thraven ignored him, heading directly to the isolation chamber where Hayley was being treated. The door opened ahead of him, and he entered without slowing, coming to a stop only when he saw that she was sitting up, awake and alert.

He froze, their eyes meeting. He hadn't expected her to be upright. Loque had failed to inform him of the change.

"Gloritant," Loque said, coming up behind him. "What?" He paused too, staring at Hayley.

A new development, then?

He continued staring at her, noting the change in her eyes. They were nearly red, the pupils barely visible against the darkened backdrop. There was something off about her. Something that made his skin tingle. He didn't recognize the feeling right away.

Fear.

"Hayley," he said, pushing it aside. Why should he be afraid of her?

She continued staring without speaking.

"Do you know who I am?" he asked. "Do you know where you are?"

She didn't speak. She didn't move.

He turned back to Loque.

"What is this?" he asked.

"Your Eminence, I don't know," Loque replied. "She was not like this five minutes ago, I swear. She was fighting the Gift as though it were poison. Her system was rejecting it with a ferocity I have never seen. But this? I will need to run some tests."

Thraven looked back at Hayley. Her head had turned slightly, taking note of Loque. Her hands were rubbing absently together. A small line of spittle had appeared at the corner of her mouth. She was alive but damaged. Broken.

"If Cage returns, she will be looking for her child," Thraven said. "Is this what I'm to deliver to her?"

He smiled at the idea. Alive, but broken. A shell of a girl ravaged by the Gift. He had never seen this kind of outcome before. It wasn't ideal, but it would do.

"Run your tests, Emerant," Thraven said. "Do not be late to inform me of her health."

"Yes, your Eminence."

Thraven left the room, continuing to the Font. He began stripping his uniform as he entered the room, eager to make the Bloodline connection to Azul, to order him to begin rallying the other Prophets.

He was surprised a second time.

The Font was already active, a familiar shape outlined in the nani-ate-thickened blood.

"Caretaker," Thraven said, closing the jacket of his uniform and falling to his knees.

"Gloritant," Belial said. "I have been waiting for you."

"Why didn't you signal me?"

"I do as I will," Belial replied.

"Have you reconsidered my request?" Thraven said. "Will you lend the aid you promised?"

QUEEN OF DEMONS

"I have. The Great Return will happen, Gloritant. The Promises of the Father will be fulfilled. What is the status of your war?"

"Of what concern is that to you, Caretaker?" Thraven asked. "I have put the Promises of the Father's Covenant in motion. I have carried his glory to Shardspace, and soon I will bring the might of the Nephilim to the One. He will fall to his knees in the name of the Father, and then I will remove his head and free our people."

"You have never seen the One, Gloritant. I have. He has no head to remove. Even so, the concern is not mine. I have another Master, as do you."

"I will surrender to no other Nephilim save the Father," Thraven said.

The Blood of the Font began to bubble, steam rising from it as it rose to an instant boil. The shape of the Caretaker started to morph in front of him, and he shuddered in sudden amazement as he felt a power unlike any he had experienced before. Tears sprang to his eyes, and he lowered his head, placing the front of it on the floor.

"Then surrender to your Father, Disciple," Lucifer said, his shape growing within the Font, the Blood expanding until his monstrous silhouette towered over Thraven.

Thraven cowered in front of him, keeping his head down. "I do. I surrender to your glory, Father. What do you command of me?"

"Rise, Disciple," Lucifer said.

Thraven lifted his head, leaning back on his knees. He looked up at the silhouette of the Father, forcing himself not to draw back in fear or disgust. He knew the Father had been changed by the power of the Gift. But he was supposed to be insane. Out of control. How was he here? Was this the help the Caretaker had promised? Had he known all of these years that the Father was still in control of himself?

He had been deceived, and for that he was glad.

"Father," Thraven said. "I have followed your Covenant. I have subverted Shardspace, and I have built the Elysium Gate."

"You have done well," Lucifer said.

"I have failed you," Thraven said. "A fleet of warships in the

153

hundreds. That is what I tried to build, but they were destroyed. By a Lesser and her followers."

"Abigail Cage," Lucifer said.

"You know her?" Thraven said, surprised.

"I have seen her," Lucifer said. "She is so like my Lilith. The naniates are changing her into my beloved. But she is willful. She resists. She could be a Queen, and yet she prefers to be destroyed."

"There is more, Father. The Sharders have found a way to disable communications across my armies, and their homeworld's resistance has been much stronger than I expected. I am on my way there now to put an end to their rebellion and finish claiming the souls needed to open the Gate to Elysium. I intended to contact the Prophets-"

"Do not be concerned with the Prophets, Disciple," Lucifer said. "I have dealt with them myself, and even now their armies come to me. You have done well, and have not failed me yet. The Gate is all that matters. Send me the coordinates of its location and bring me the souls to open it. Then we will return to our galaxy. Then I will destroy the One. Then our people will be free. You will be my most honored Disciple, Selvig Thraven. You will have a permanent place in the histories of the Seraphim."

Thraven felt his heart pounding at the words, his emotions stirred in a way they hadn't been in years. "Of course, Father. It will be as you command. I will not fail you."

"No, you will not," Lucifer said. "Do not be concerned with the futile efforts of the Sharders, Disciple. The glory will be ours. Nothing in the galaxy can stand against me."

"Yes, Father," Thraven said. "Is Abigail Cage dead, then?"

"Not yet. I allowed her to escape. She is on her way back to Shardspace in a Harvester. She will try to stop us, but she will fall. It will all be as I have Promised."

"I should like to destroy her myself, with your permission, Father."

"If the Chosen of the Shard challenges you, then you will put her to an end. That is my command, Disciple."

"So it shall be done."

The Blood of the Font began to shrink, the Bloodline closing.

Thraven watched the silhouette of the Father lose cohesion, sinking slowly back to the Font, the power subsiding with it. He felt a sudden emptiness at its loss, and a painful desire to be near it once more.

The Father was alive and on his way to the Gate. All that was Promised would come to pass. There could be no question about it now. He felt the hope and joy in his heart, a sense of excitement he had thought he would never experience.

He would return to Earth and capture the souls for the Father. He would return to the Gate, and together they would first free Elysium, and then rule over it.

Don Pallimo be damned. Captain Mann be damned. Abigail Cage be damned.

There was nothing that could stop them now.

Nothing.

29

"WE'RE APPROACHING THE INNER SYSTEM, SIR," CAPTAIN DAVLYN SAID.

General Sylvan Kett nodded. "Take us out of FTL."

"Aye, sir," Davlyn replied. "Disengage the disterium reactors."

"Disengaging, sir," Ensign Sil replied, adjusting the controls. The hum of the High Noon changed almost imperceptibly, the machines that converted disterium crystal into gas slowing to a stop. The battle-ship slowed with it, re-entering the universe in a cloud, immediately surrounded by the rest of the ships in the fleet.

"What do we have from the sensors?" Sylvan asked.

"A faint disterium trail, sir," Ensign Card replied. "At least a week old. The signature is consistent with Republic ships matching the composition of the Nova battle group. I'm also picking up a debris field two AU from our position. The spread suggests the fighting took place three days ago, sixteen AU away."

"Somebody got into a tangle with the Nova battle group," Davlyn said. "Are there any signs of active vessels in range?"

"Negative, Captain," Card replied. "We may be alone out here."

"Open a near-field channel," Sylvan said. "Let's be sure we're the only ones home."

"Aye, sir. Channel open."

"Republic forces, this is General Sylvan Kett aboard the battleship High Noon. Do you read me? I repeat, Republic forces, this is General Sylvan Kett aboard the battleship High Noon. I've got a battle group of my own here, and we're ready to take back our home."

Sylvan looked out into the black, waiting for a response. He had brought the fleet out of FTL early in order to rally whatever ships might be hiding in the area, bringing them into the fold. But were there any ships remaining?

He repeated the statement and again received no reply.

"Captain, sound a red alert across the fleet. All hands to battle stations."

"Aye, sir," Davlyn replied. "Battle group Charlie, this is the High Noon. All hands to battle stations. I repeat, all hands to battle stations."

Red strobes began to blink on the bridge, and klaxons could be heard further down the corridors.

Sylvan lowered his head at the use of his wife's name. Of course, he had named his army after his fallen love. She had brought him out of the darkness and made him aware of the Nephilim and their plans for both humankind and the other species that lived in this part of the galaxy. She had shown him how corrupt the Republic was becoming, and how he could use his position and reputation to help prevent the galaxy from destroying itself. She had borne him a daughter, a beautiful daughter, and given him all that she was for as long as she survived.

And she would live again. They had agreed to return the Ruby synth to Cage, but there were plenty of synths back on Earth. Plenty of bodies that her configuration could occupy. When this war was won, when Thraven was defeated, then he would be able to bring her back.

Until then he fought in her name and with her spirit, as did the rest of his army.

"Captain, prepare the fleet to return to FTL. Set coordinates for Earth."

"Aye, sir," Davlyn said. "Battle group Charlie, prepare disterium reactors and set coordinates. We jump for Earth on my mark."

A series of "ayes" followed from each of the commanders of the fleet.

"It would have been nice if someone out here could have given us an idea what we're jumping into," Ensign Card said.

"We're Navy, Ensign," Davlyn said. "When the General says jump, we ask how far."

"Aye, sir."

Sylvan smiled at the statement. He wasn't technically in charge of anything on the High Noon, but the crew deferred to him as their rebellion's de facto leader.

He opened his mouth, ready to give the order.

"Sir," Ensign Card said. "We have activity in quadrant three. Sensors are reading a reactor spike."

"Friend or foe?" Davlyn asked.

"How can I tell, sir?" Card replied. "We're all supposed to be on the same side."

"General Kett," a frightened voice said through the near-field comm. "This is Captain Dorbisi of the cruiser Shiloh. We require immediate assistance. Help us, please."

Sylvan scanned the field ahead of them. He didn't see anything. "Where is her ship?"

A projection of the stars around them appeared, a red spot marking the source of the transmission. It had come around the far side of the nearest star and was heading their way.

"The solar radiation was blocking near field communications and sensor readings," Davlyn said.

"Set a course to intercept," Sylvan said. "Prepare to launch fighters."

"Aye, General," Davlyn said, quickly delegating the orders.

Sylvan kept his attention on the red dot, watching as it multiplied. The High Noon's computer showed everything as friendly, even if it might not be. Within seconds, six more targets had appeared from the other side of the star.

"The Nova, sir," Ensign Card said.

"Ally or enemy?" Davlyn said. "Captain Dorbisi?"

"General Kett," a new voice said. "This is Commander Ng of the battleship Nova. The Shiloh is a traitor to the Republic and sympathetic to the enemy. Her disterium reactor is damaged, and she must not be allowed to escape."

"Lies," Captain Dorbisi said. "I am a loyal member of the Republic. A Rudin of the highest composition. High Noon, if you are a friend to the Rebellion, please help us."

"Shit," Captain Davlyn said, looking back at Sylvan. "Sir, which one of them is telling the truth?"

Sylvan wasn't sure. "Shiloh seems to be all alone out here, while the Nova has numbers," he said. "I wish we knew whose side the ships in the debris field were on." He stared out of the viewport and into space. The ships were still small specks in the distance, but they were closing in a hurry.

What were the odds they would come out of FTL in the middle of a chase? It wasn't impossible, but with all of the emptiness of the galaxy to contend with, they happened to fall right into the middle of something? There was obvious evidence of a battle, and it wasn't without precedent that the Shiloh could have broken away and started running for her life. Plus, Rudin weren't known for being anything but proper.

Still, there was something about it that wasn't sitting right. It was too convenient. Almost laughably convenient.

As though they had been waiting for someone to arrive.

And hadn't Dorbisi called out to him by name, even though they were on the other side of the star, the near-field comms blocked by the radiation?

Hadn't Ng done the same?

"Ensign Card, tighten your scans. Tell me if there's a comm satellite nearby, perhaps hidden in the debris field."

"Sir?"

"Do it."

"Scanning, sir." Sylvan rubbed his chin, waiting a few seconds for the reply. "Aye, sir. I'm reading three active satellites within the field."

Three?

"It's a trap," Sylvan said. "A fragging trap."

He said it at the same time the initial volley launched from the Nova, a dozen warheads rocketing away without warning. They were on the perfect trajectory to hit the Shiloh, and on the perfect trajectory to hit the fleet.

"Evasive maneuvers," Sylvan said.

'Sir, the torpedoes are targeting the Shiloh."

"No, they aren't."

The Shiloh's vector changed suddenly, the ship rolling to the right. The ships in Battle group Charlie were each making maneuvers of their own, trying to spread away from the attack.

The warheads reached them, half of them missing their targets, the other half striking unshielded hulls. Sylvan cursed as three of his ships vomited burning atmosphere from the impact site, lights flickering as conduits were broken and reconnected before falling dark for good.

"Return fire," Sylvan said. "Target the Nova."

"Aye, General," Davlyn said.

"Sir, the enemy is altering course," Ensign Sil said. "They're targeting the Seedships."

Of course, they were. He looked at the projection. The Shiloh was making a straight line for one of the Seedships, firing everything it had on the vessel. Its shields absorbed the attack easily, catching the firepower of two other warships at the same time.

A blue plume of disterium appeared behind it, a dozen new ships coming into view.

"No," Sylvan cursed.

He knew there would be more ships coming. Why else would there have been three satellites? Thraven had guessed he would be cautious, coming out of FTL ahead of Earth to get a feel for the situation. Charmeine had warned him about being too afraid to commit his units. He cared too much about his soldiers, too much about keeping them safe.

It made him predictable. It made him stupid.

The intercepting warships unleashed a barrage of torpedoes, all of them aimed at the Seedship. It caught them valiantly in its shields, deflecting blow after blow, detonation after detonation without succumbing to the assault.

"Target the Shiloh," Sylvan shouted. "Everything we have."

A stream of plasma and lasers lanced out toward the cruiser, bolt after bolt tearing away at its shields and armor, bits and pieces of slagged armor pouring from it as it remained on course. The enemy continued firing on the Seedship, hitting it with everything they had with a singular purpose.

Break through the shields.

Sylvan slammed his fist on the nearest surface as their efforts succeeded, a pair of torpedoes detonating against the blue web of energy and then the next striking the hull. The Shiloh was being torn apart, but it was still in motion, every second bringing it that much closer to the target, a speeding bullet that they had no hope of stopping.

"Captain Davlyn, get the fleet out of here," Sylvan said before the inevitable had taken place.

"Sir?" Davlyn replied.

"We can't win this fight," Sylvan said. "We need to retreat."

"Retreat? We haven't reached Earth."

The Shiloh slammed into the side of the Seedship, the front of it collapsing against the hull until sheer momentum began to carry her through. Both ships started breaking apart, sending debris exploding outward and into the midst of the battle.

"We can't win," Sylvan said, shaking his head. Tactical genius? It was a lie built on a few lucky maneuvers.

He had caused hundreds to die as if he had killed them himself. He wished he was back on Azure. Back with Charmeine and Jequn where it was safe. He wished he could pretend he would be a hero one day for a little while longer.

But he wasn't a hero.

"I said retreat, Captain. That ship was invaluable, and now it's dust."

"Sir?"

"Are you disobeying orders?"

Davlyn ignored him.

"Sil, bring us around five degrees to port. Scabbard, bring your group to mark Delta. Scramble the fighters. This isn't over yet."

"I gave you an order," Sylvan said, rounding on the Captain. "How dare you betray me."

"Betray you?" Davlyn said. "I only agreed to follow you because I thought you were trying to save the Republic. We lose one ship, and you're ready to run? Queenie wanted so much to believe in you, General, but it was Gant and the others who had it right. You're a fragging coward. Now if you'll excuse me, I have a war to fight."

Davlyn turned back to his station. "Dorn, vector toward mark Epsilon. Target the support cruisers. And get those damned fighters out there."

Sylvan stood on the bridge, his mind a chaotic blur. He watched the Captain give orders, crisp and concise, his own head too fogged to make sense of them. He shifted his gaze to the projection, observing as their blue dots began to flank the red ones, moving into position to use their overwhelming numbers against the enemy. Battle group Charlie didn't retreat. They kept fighting. The war didn't end.

He closed his eyes. He had failed Charmeine. He had failed Jequn. He had failed himself. He had been a legend within the Republic Armed Services long before he had been a traitor. What was he now?

Captain Davlyn was right.

He was a coward.

He continued watching until the last ship in the Nova battle group was destroyed. Not once did they attempt to retreat. Not once did they make a motion to surrender.

"Ensign Card, what's the status of the fleet?" he heard Davlyn say.

"Sir, we lost nine ships. Three more are critically damaged and out of the fight. The High Noon took minor damage, but nothing that will keep us from kicking the enemy's tail. The Nova battle group is eliminated."

"You're saying we won, Ensign?"

"Aye, sir."

"Good. Call for Sergeant Mox. Have him escort the General from the bridge."

"Aye, sir."

Davlyn stood and looked at him. Sylvan felt his face flush, the heat of his shame spreading. His eyes dropped to the Captain's sidearm. He could end it quickly.

The coward's way out.

"Captain, I'm sorry," he said. "I-"

"Sergeant Mox will escort you to your quarters General," Davlyn said. "You're to remain there until this is over, and then Queenie will decide what to do with you. We'll take things from here."

Sylvan felt his mouth open, but he didn't speak.

He couldn't think of anything to say.

3 0

"It's official, Captain," Quark said, exiting the cockpit of the Quasar and joining him in the common area near the center. "The Galnet is offline."

Olus nodded somberly. It was a victory for them to cut off Thraven's communications with the rest of his forces, but it was also a loss. He would no longer be able to reach back to General Kett or any of the assets that had been given access to Gant's subnet. He also wouldn't be able to contact Abbey, if and when she made it back to this side of the universe.

Maybe that was a good thing. The longer he could keep her from learning that Thraven had her daughter, the better.

"Judging by my estimates, the good General and his fleet should be reaching the inner system any minute now," Quark continued, sitting at the table opposite him. "Where'd Nibia get off to, anyway?"

"She's down in medical taking care of Sergeant Capper," the Pallimo synth said. It was standing in the corner of the room, acting less like it was trying to be a human than any of the other Pallimo duplicates.

Quark raised an eyebrow. "Capper looked pretty good to me when we brought him in, considering he'd been shot six times."

They had been surprised to find the Sergeant still alive, once Thraven's units had been dealt with, and the Riders had combed the area to collect their dead. The fighting on Oberon had been relatively light, most of it taking place out of sight and mind of the general populace. They had no idea their planet was being run by the artificially intelligent ghost of Don Pallimo.

They also had no idea how close they had come to losing both.

"Kett is on his own at this point," Olus said. "He should have more than enough ships to regain control of Earth's orbit, and enough resistance on the ground to help him get the surface back under solid Republic control."

"Assuming he's half as smart as the legends say he is," Quark said.

"He was smart enough to give us the Brimstone."

"And we were dumb enough to leave it back at Oberon."

"Firepower isn't going to help us where we're headed."

Quark laughed. "I'm a fish out of water where we're headed, Captain. I can't believe I let you talk me into this."

"Violence isn't the only way to solve things."

"Maybe it isn't the only way, but I've found that it's the most efficient, least boring way. In any case, we aren't completely deaf and blind out here. My girl Sykes already got the Quasar's comms recalibrated to the Haulnet. As long as there's a Hauler vessel within a light-year, we can transmit."

"There's almost always a Hauler vessel within a light-year, so long as you stick to the beaten path," Pallimo said. "It isn't as reliable as the Galnet or Milnet for this specific application, but it's an encrypted channel General Thraven doesn't have access to."

"That's Gloritant," Olus said. "It means almost the same thing, but not quite."

"Yeah, he's more of an asshole than a General," Quark said.

"Can we reach back to Earth?" Olus asked.

"Not currently," Pallimo said. "The fighting forced us to abandon the area, at least temporarily. I lost four good ships and a few launch ports, and I'm going to guess my insurer will refuse to cover damage due to unexpected acts of war."

Quark laughed at that. "I think you can afford it."

"In any case, my root systems are reorganizing the fleet, but it will take a few hours to get the mesh linked back to the inner system."

Nibia entered the commons. Her skin was glistening with sweat, her eyes tired.

"How's Capper?" Quark asked.

"He'll live," she replied. "But I don't think he's going to be doing any more soldiering. He's got some shrapnel in his heart I can't repair."

"Maybe I can help?" Olus said.

"If it moves, he dies. If it vanishes, he dies. The Meijo can't solve everything, Captain. In this case, only a more relaxing lifestyle will keep him breathing."

"He was born at the wrong damn time for that," Quark said.

"I can find a suitable position for him," Pallimo said. "It's the least I can do, considering you saved my life."

"As it were," Quark said. "You're a machine."

"I'm aware," Pallimo said. "And my protocols demand self-preservation."

"Roger that."

Olus felt the change in the ship as it came out of FTL.

"Next stop, planet Apollo," Quark said. "Home world of Governess Sandine Ott, the biggest bitch in the Outworlds."

"Quark," Nibia said in admonishment.

"What? She is."

"Just because a woman turns down your oh-so macho advances, that doesn't make them a bitch."

"No, that just means they're crazy." He laughed. "Sandine and me have a history that predates her political career. Did you know she used to be in the CM?"

"The militia? No."

"She did. That's where she gets her street cred. That's how she got elected Governess. We had a run in of a non-sexual nature way back when."

"Are you suggesting I should leave you behind?" Olus asked, interrupting. "I need a chance to prove my case with her, not have her send me away because of the company I keep."

"That was twenty years plus ago," Quark said. "I can't imagine she's still holding a grudge today."

"You are," Nibia said.

"Yeah, but that's because I'm me. Sandine's a bitch, but she's not a vengeful bitch. I don't think." He turned to Olus. "In any case, we're good. I don't want to miss watching you try to convince the Outworld Governance they're betting on the wrong star racer. They're not going to give up on cutting the Republic down to size that easily."

"Not if I was going in there alone," Olus said. "Especially not considering my former employer. But I've got a secret weapon." He pointed to Pallimo. "Nobody else but you, me, and Thraven know he's not the real thing, and for Thraven to tell the Governance would essentially prove everything I'm going to put forward."

"Blah, blah, blah. Too many words, Captain. Like I said, this is going to be entertainment at its finest. Let's just make sure we stop off at the armory before we head out. I know you're a wizard and all that shit, but I've got a few toys the local enforcement's sensors won't detect."

"Colonel, we have clearance to land," Gibli said through the ship's comm. "We'll be skids down in fifteen minutes."

"Roger," Quark replied. "Don't frag up the landing."

"I saved our asses on Oberon, didn't I, sir?" Gibli asked.

"That you did. You and Sykes both. I owe her for that, and for her quick work on the comm. What do you say, Nibs? You think Sykes likes perfume?"

"Only if it has lubricating grease in it."

Quark smiled. "Now you're getting randy. What about a nice coat? I noticed she tore the sleeve on the last one I bought her."

"Possibly."

"Do you mind if we focus on the task at hand?" Olus asked. He was amused by the banter, but they had a lot bigger things to worry about.

"Word of advice, Captain," Quark said. "Always take good care of the women in your life, and they'll take good care of you. Always."

"I wouldn't classify losing the Demon Queen's daughter as taking good care of her," Olus replied.

"Roger that." Quark put his hand on Olus' shoulder, looking him in the eye. "It wasn't your fault, Captain. Hell, I'm more to blame on that count than you are. This is our chance to do something about it."

Olus nodded. "Too many words, Colonel. I'm ready."

As a Capital planet, Apollo was one of the most populated and modern in the First Sector, the area of space that Governess Ott was in charge of speaking for. The Sector was made up nearly two dozen planets including Oberon, and while Governess Ott didn't know that Don Pallimo existed there as a computer system doing its best to act like the dead magnate, she did know that he was an important figure to her Sector's overall economy.

As a result, when the Don came in with a request to chat, it was in her best interests to comply with that request.

It meant that for once, reaching the target was a straightforward affair, something Olus had become unaccustomed to over the last few months. The Don Pallimo synth put in a call to the Governess on the way to the surface, and an official transport was waiting at the spaceport to greet them when they arrived.

It took them on a short hop through the city that bore the same name as the planet, an urban landscape that could have just as easily been San Francisco, London, or Hong Kong as it was an Outworld center. The only reason Olus could be certain he was in the Outworlds was because the marketing projections were all for products from a single company, Applied Sciences Corporation, and their related brands. Of course, Applied Sciences also happened to own Apollo and most of the majority of the worlds in First Sector.

Olus felt only the slightest of nerves as the transport set down on the lawn of the Governor's Mansion. The large estate created an almost surreal break in the middle of the city, substituting skyscrapers and multi-leveled traffic for fields of grass surrounded by clumps of trees, a nearly ten square-kilometer parkland in the midst of the densely active surroundings. It wasn't the idea of meeting with the Governess that made him nervous. Rather, it was the peace and calm of the area. It felt wrong to be here when there was so much chaos taking place out there.

"She's definitely moved up in the universe since I saw her last," Quark said, the hatch on the transport sliding open.

"What was she doing when you saw her last?" Nibia asked.

"It wouldn't be gentlemanly of me to say," Quark replied. "Let's just say she's reinvented herself since then."

Olus raised an eyebrow at that. Quark shrugged and smiled. Olus stood and straightened his suit. He would have preferred a uniform, but there weren't any available. Instead, he had inherited one of Quark's formal outfits - a white shirt, dark pants, and a long, bullet-resistant coat with a low collar that had a number of extra pockets stitched inside. Pockets that were holding all sorts of undetectable means to violence, including throwing knives and a blowgun with a handful of small, poison-tipped darts that the mercenary said was a Koosian hunting device.

The good news was that it all fit cleanly over his seraphsuit, keeping the enhanced protection hidden while it kept the Gift from tickling at his skin.

"Don Pallimo," the woman who greeted them outside the transport said. "My name is Ms. Yao. I'm the Governess' assistant. I'll be escorting you to meet with her."

"Yao, wow," Quark said under his breath, barely loud enough for Quark to hear.

Olus couldn't argue that the assistant did have a look to her, and he wasn't surprised the mercenary was drawn to it. Then again, he got the impression Quark was drawn to nearly any member of the opposite sex, and not necessarily always a human.

"Ms. Yao," the Pallimo synth said, putting out its hand. "A pleasure."

Yao took it, shaking lightly.

"Allow me to introduce my companions," Pallimo said. "My bodyguards, Colonel Quark and Lieutenant Nibia."

Quark stuck out his hand. "The pleasure is mine, Ms. Yao," he said smoothly, casting her a cock-eyed grin that made her face turn red.

Olus shook his head while the assistant greeted Nibia. How the hell did he do that?

"And Governess Ott is probably familiar with Captain Olus Mann of the Republic OSI, though I doubt she's ever met him in person."

Yao turned to Olus, her warm expression vanishing almost instantly. There was no love lost between the Republic and Outworlds.

"Ms. Yao," Olus said.

"Captain. I've heard rumors that you're a pariah amongst your circles?"

Olus didn't let her barb trip him up. "I'm looking out for the best interests of both our places in the galaxy, Ms. Yao. Nothing more. Nothing less."

"He's here to parlay," Pallimo said. "Don't make me speak to the Governess about your lack of decorum."

Yao's face flushed for a different reason, and she turned away from them. "Follow me. The Governess is out, but you can wait for her in the atrium."

"I haven't had much luck with atriums," Quark said, calling out the events on Gamlin.

Ms. Yao ignored him, leading them across the lawn to the house. There were guards stationed outside in lightsuits, and they remained stiff and straight as they passed.

They entered the mansion. It immediately reminded Olus of Mars Eagan's estate, with plenty of opulence spread across the walls and floors, and a feeling of classical refinement that was relatively uncommon these days.

That visit felt like it had taken place a lifetime ago.

He could only hope this one wouldn't end similarly.

"The atrium is through here," Ms. Yao said, guiding them down a long corridor toward a large pair of high doors. "There are refreshments waiting for you inside, and a service synth if you need anything else."

"Thank you, Ms. Yao," Don Pallimo said. "Do you have an estimate on how long we might be waiting? As you can imagine, I'm a busy man."

"Of course, Don. I expect that -"

"Q, is that you?"

Olus turned at the voice. A woman in an ankle-length skirt was approaching them. She had short brown hair and was slightly overweight, her features more in line to what he found appealing.

"Sandy?" Quark said, putting his mechanical optics on her. "It's been a long time."

She stopped in front of him, leaving Olus to wonder if she was going to slug him or kiss him. She did neither, turning to Pallimo instead.

"Don Pallimo. I heard rumors you had employed this wolverine. It left me to question your sanity."

"Are you sweet talking me again already, Sandy?" Quark asked.

"Nonsense, Governess," Pallimo said. "With days like these, a wolverine is the best thing to have protecting you."

"Days like these? Do you mean the fall of the Republic? These are golden days, Don."

"So you've been led to believe. Even putting the damage to my own interests aside, I'm afraid the current situation with the Republic is ultimately going to benefit no one except the individual who brought you down this path."

"Are you referring to General Thraven?" she asked. "I admit, his tactics have been a little questionable, but you can't argue with his results."

"I can, and will," Olus said, finally speaking up.

Governess Ott looked at him, trying to place him. She smiled once she had. It was a gloating smile, a proud smile. Maybe Quark was right about her? Not that it mattered.

"Captain Olus Mann," she said. "You're a long way from the Republic."

"I've come where the truth has led me, Governess," Olus said. "I've come where I can do the most good for our galaxy. Not only the Republic but the Outworlds as well."

"I have to admit; I'm curious what you mean by that."

"Good. Is there somewhere we can go so that I can explain it to you?"

"I believe in transparent governing, Captain. Whatever you have to say, you can say in front of my staff. Though I agree, a hallway isn't the best place to talk about war." She motioned to the doors of the atrium. "Shall we?" She glanced back at Quark, and then at Nibia. Her eyes smoldered when she looked at the witch doctor. Was that jealousy? "You're both welcome to wait outside." She paused. "Or return to your ship."

"And miss this?" Quark said. "Not a chance. Transparency works both ways."

The Governess didn't look happy, but she turned and entered the atrium. Olus followed her, his confidence dropping. Could he convince this woman that Thraven's actions were bad for the Outworlds?

He was vaguely aware of the tools sitting in the pockets of his coat.

He wasn't enthusiastic about the alternative, but it wasn't anything he hadn't done before.

32

Olus took stock of the atrium as they entered. Governess Ott's initial reaction to his words had left him feeling less than confident about his ability to talk her out of her present course, and he needed to be as aware as possible of his surroundings should the worst case come to pass.

He was expecting a room of greenery but instead was met by what would have been more appropriately described as a ballroom, at least to someone his age. It was a large, open space, with tables scattered around the fringe and a stage up front, suitable for live music or any other entertainment the mansion was hosting. Three levels of balconies ran around the edge of the room, while a spread of food and drink had been positioned at the center.

A service synth was waiting there with it, a handsome male version in a crisp tuxedo. It smiled as they entered, rounding the table to approach and offer a drink.

"No thank you," Olus said before it could speak. It took the hint, bowing silently and returning to its position.

The Governess ignored his curtness, meandering to the table and picking out a small sandwich and pointing to a bottle of wine, which the synth promptly poured.

"Individuals are dying out there, Governess," Olus said.

The words didn't entice her to change her cadence. She took a sip of the wine and ate the sandwich before she turned back to him.

"Your individuals are dying," she said. "Outworld casualties are surprisingly low."

"Because Thraven sabotaged half the ships in the Republic," Olus said.

She laughed. "What you call sabotage, I call genius."

Olus took a second. He had to change his tactics.

"I understand you have no interest in the well-being of the Republic," he said. "I can accept that you're willing to see innocent Republic citizens die on the path to victory. That is war, after all. But I hope that for a moment you can put aside the fact that I am from the Republic. As you surely know, I've been removed from my position and am wanted for treason."

"I heard."

"Gloritant Thraven isn't only a threat to the Republic. It may seem that way, but only because you don't know what he wants, and what he's been willing to do to get it."

"And you know what he wants, Captain?"

"I do."

Olus paused, noticing soldiers gathering on the platforms around them. This was her idea of transparency?

"I'd love to hear your theory," she said.

"It's not a theory; it's a fact. Gloritant Thraven wants no less than to seize control of this galaxy and use its inhabitants to fuel a war."

"Didn't you just say that's what he's already doing?"

"This isn't war to him, Governess. This is the warmup. The practice. Thraven comes from a place called the Extant. It's a place in the universe beyond our current FTL technology. He's a member of a race called the Nephilim. A race that is nearly identical to humankind, but predates us by many years."

"I thought your intent was to convince me you'r telling me the truth?" the Governess said. "Between you and me, Captain, you're doing a lousy job."

"Captain, maybe you should let me take over," Quark said.

"I don't think that's a good-"

Olus didn't get to finish. Quark cut in front of him. "Don't worry, Captain. I know how to talk to Sandy." He moved closer to the Governess. "Look, I know we haven't spoken in a while."

"Twenty-two years," the Governess said. "What the hell, Q? You promised me you would get me out of that hellhole, and then you disappeared and left me with that piece of shit. You went off to who knows where and became this bigshot mercenary while I spent the next two years earning out my fragging freedom. You know what things were like there. You know where you left me."

Olus' eyes flicked between Quark and the Governess. He hadn't been expecting this. How exactly was it supposed to help?

"I know," Quark said. "I know I did. I'm sorry. I got sidetracked."

"Sidetracked? I'll show you sidetracked." She lifted her skirt up to her thighs. One of her legs was a mechanical replacement. The other had dozens of scars lining it. "Frag you and your sidetracked. I would arrest you right now if you weren't with the Don."

Quark shook his head at the sight of her legs. "Shit, Sandy. I didn't know. I got out, but my ship's disterium reactor died and left me stranded on the worst planet in the fragging galaxy. The shit I ran into there? It's the same shit Captain Mann is trying to warn you about. It's the same shit that took my eyes."

"What are you talking about?" she asked.

"Captain, show her what you can do," Quark said.

"What I can do?"

"Don't play dumb, just do it."

Olus reached inward to the Gift, bringing it forward. He held his hand out toward the wine glass in the Governess' hand, pulling it to him. It flew from her hand and came to rest in his.

"Huh?" she said, shocked.

"I didn't know what it was the first time I saw it either," Quark said. "I crashed on a planet that isn't on any star maps. A planet that doesn't exist as far as anyone in the galaxy is concerned. There were these creatures there, hey had gray skin and they moved around like frogs. They came after me. They were easy to kill, but they were the least of my worries. I managed to hide from them. I worked on fixing the ship. You were on my mind the whole time. Then this other ship lands, and this guy comes off it, acting all badass. The frogs, they went for him, and he blasted them one after another just like Olus did. Bam! Bam! He killed a hundred of the fraggers while I watched.

"Then he went off for a while. Disappeared. He came back a few hours later carrying the head of some species I've never seen before or since. It was long and bony, and must've had a big brain in it, you know? He carried it to his ship, and I thought he was going to leave, so I called out to him."

Quark stopped talking, shaking his head and laughing.

"I was out of the Wayhouse. I thought I was safe."

"Did you say the Wayhouse?" Nibia said, her voice concerned.

Olus felt a chill at the word. The Wayhouse was a legend. An infamous legend. Entertainment for the worst kind of scum the galaxy could produce. Its location was a secret, and he had always suspected it was mobile.

"Yeah," Quark said.

"You never told me about that," Nibia said.

"Nope. I don't want to talk about it now. The point is, this asshole thought I was there to kill him and drink his blood. He attacked me, and I thought I was going to die. But something in me burst, and I got more pissed than I've ever been. I resisted his pull and ran. He chased me. For three weeks he chased me." He stopped again, staring straight ahead like he was reliving the scene. "Anyway, he got my eyes, but I got his head. I got off the planet in his ship, and I did it blind. By the time I got back to where the Wayhouse had been, it was gone. The point is, I know about these assholes like Thraven. I know what kind of threat they are. They have power like the Captain here, only much, much worse. They use it to hurt. To kill. They don't care about the Outworlds, Sandy. They don't care about us. They think we're less than they are. They think we're half a step above food. Hell, I've had sex with a few of them, and they're all the same. We're tools. A means to an end, whether that end is to get off or to be slave soldiers in a shitty war."

"You're telling me the truth, aren't you?" Sandy said.

"Why the frag would I lie?"

"Even if I believed you about Thraven, I need proof. You can't tie one asshole to the General who is winning the war against the Republic and say they're the same just because they have some kind of magical powers. I mean, whatever you did with my glass was a good trick, but it doesn't prove anything. I feel sorry for what happened to you, Q, but it doesn't prove anything."

"Which is why I'm here," Don Pallimo said. "Gloritant Thraven attacked one of my crews on the Devastator unprovoked. He also attacked Oberon in an effort to destroy the Crescent Haulers. I have irrefutable proof of both. He is furthermore responsible for the attack on Anvil, not the Republic as he might have claimed."

"Can you prove that, too?" the Governess asked.

"I can," Pallimo said. "I have recordings of his goons inside my complex threatening me and using his name. My complex on Oberon, in protected Outworld space. That alone should be enough to discredit him."

"He did it to advance the goals of the Outworlds," she said.

"He did it to advance his own goals," Olus said. "Didn't you hear what Quark said? They don't think anything of us. We're tools. The Outworlds Governance is a tool. A hammer to break through the Republic defenses, to soften us up and make his job easier. When the Republic finishes collapsing, the Outworlds will be next. I guarantee it."

The Governess' eyes moved between them as she considered. Finally, she shook her head.

"I'm sorry," she said. "General Thraven is offering something we've been after for years, and your case is flimsy at best. The word of the Republic's former Intelligence Director? The word of a mercenary?"

"And my word counts for nothing?" Pallimo said.

"Your word is the only reason I even had to think about it. But the answer is still no. Whatever you expected me to do, I won't do it. The Republic will fall. If Thraven turns his attention to the Outworlds, we'll stop him."

"You can't stop him, Sandy," Quark said. "You have no idea what he can do. No idea at all."

"You have an hour," she said. "Get off my planet, or I'll have the three of you arrested as enemies of the Outworlds. Don, you're free to do as you will, but I warn you not to cross me."

"You're making a mistake," Olus said. "A terrible mistake."

"Have a nice life as a traitor, Captain," she replied.

"Let's go, Captain," Quark said. "Didn't I tell you she was a bitch?"

"You did," Olus agreed. "It's unfortunate."

"Don't even think of trying to hurt me, Captain," the Governess said. "My guards will put you down before you can take a step in my direction."

"Clearly, you still don't understand what we're up against," Olus replied. "I guess I'll have to show you."

33

THE GOVERNESS' GUARDS WERE FAST.

Thanks to the Gift, it didn't matter.

Olus shot toward Governess Ott, hand reaching under his coat and grabbing one of the blades secreted there. Shots were fired down at him, a burst of nearly a half-dozen rounds that caught him from every side. One in the shoulder. One in the leg. Two in the back. One in the arm. It hurt like crazy, but it wasn't enough to take him down, especially since the armor in the coat helped reduce the impacts of the slugs.

He grunted as he grabbed the Governess, quickly wrapping her in his arms, turning her around and clutching her from behind, putting the blade to her throat.

"Captain," Quark said, a hint of concern in his voice.

"Lower your weapons," Olus growled at the guards in the room. "Do it now."

A few of the guards complied immediately, but not all. Olus had to resist the urge to smile. He had figured as much.

"Tell them to drop their weapons," Olus said to the Governess. "Unless you prefer to be dead."

"Drop them," she said.

"The Governance doesn't allow hostage negotiations, ma'am," one of the guards said, keeping his weapon trained on Olus.

"Your loyalty is to me first, the Governance second," she replied. "All of you, stand down."

A few more of the guards complied, but still not all.

"They aren't all loyal to you first, Governess," Olus said, his lips against her ear. "Or to the Governance and the Outworlds. They only have one true loyalty. I know because I've seen it. Across this whole fragging galaxy, I've seen it. You don't understand the way he's manipulated them. You don't understand the way he's manipulating you."

"I'm not under the General's control."

"No?"

His eyes scanned the levels of balconies above them. Too many of the soldiers were still on alert, armed and ready to fire. He felt the tingle of the Gift along the base of his neck, and he glanced over at Quark. The mercenary shifted his head ever-so-slightly.

It was coming. They both knew it.

"Tell me what you think of loyalty sixty seconds from now," Olus said.

The soldiers landed behind him, dropping two floors to the ground without difficulty. He spun, still holding the Governess in front of him.

"Don't," he said, pressing the blade tighter against her throat, drawing a thin line of blood.

The lead soldier stared at the blood, eyes wide. A soft growl formed in his throat.

"We don't need her anymore," he said. "Gehenna has risen. The Father has returned. We don't need any of them."

"The Father?" Don Pallimo said.

The soldier began to change, the alteration tearing at his uniform, shredding it to pieces. The other soldiers revealed themselves as well. Children of the Covenant. Goreshin. They appeared across the ranks of guards, quickly attacking the ones who had followed orders and stood down.

"Daddy issues," Quark said, pulling a pair of blades of his own. "Great."

Olus pulled back, dragging the Governess to the ground on top of him as the lead Goreshin pounced, diving at them and slashing with sharp claws. She cried out, the daggers nearly slicing her before Quark stepped in, neatly severing the creature's hand with one blade, spinning and driving the other neatly through its neck with a strength that surprised Olus.

"I hate these fraggers most of all," he said, kicking out at the next one that moved at him, slapping it hard in the face and knocking it off balance. His body moved quickly, not missing a step, skipping inside the Goreshin's guard and dragging one of his blades through its sternum and out its chest. It howled in pain, the howling stopping when it too lost its head.

Olus rolled Governess Ott off him, drawing on the Gift to bounce to his feet, slapping a hand aside, slicing the arm behind it, ducking and rising, bringing his other blade up into the Goreshin's chin. He could see the blade protrude into its mouth before he tore it out, taking the jaw with it, stepping back and slashing again with the strength of the Gift. The blade sliced neatly through the creature's neck, its head tumbling away.

Governess Ott finally started to scream.

A Child reached for her, losing the limb as a laser cutter dropped through it. Don Pallimo whipped the cane around, removing a leg and bringing the creature to the ground. He turned away as Nibia dropped onto it and cut off its head.

"There's a lot of them, Captain," Nibia said, looking up.

Olus did the same. They had killed six in short order, which was impressive enough. Another twenty were finishing up with the other soldiers and would be on them in seconds.

"Time to go," he said, reaching out for the Governess again. She was in shock and didn't move.

"I've got her," Quark said, bending and scooping her up, throwing her body over his shoulder. "You've gained weight, Sandy."

She didn't respond.

"Let's get to the grass," Quark said. "Ghibli can pick us up."

"Roger," Olus replied. He bent down to grab a discarded rifle, getting it cradled just in time to blast a Goreshin in the eye, knocking it down for a few seconds.

They ran, charging toward the atrium doors. They were almost there when Ms. Yao rounded the corner. She raised her hand, and Olus felt the Gift pushing against them. He pushed back, fighting fire with fire.

Quark barely slowed. He tucked his shoulder, slamming into the surprised Evolent, knocking her hard into the wall.

"I don't play that shit," he said, a quick motion sinking one of his blades into her throat and pinning her to the wall.

It would only slow her for a second, but a second was all Olus needed. He caught up to them, grabbing Yao and cutting into her neck, leaving her a mess against the wall.

They made it through the doors. Olus spun back a few times, firing single shots into the oncoming soldiers. Each round dropped a Goreshin, destroying its brain enough that it needed time to regenerate and recover.

"Don't give me shit, Ghibli, get your ass to the mansion. Frag regulations. What kind of pansy ass are you? We do have the Governess' permission. Hell, I've got her slung over my shoulder." He shook his head, glancing at Olus. "Greenies."

Olus smirked. They made it to the doors leading outside, the Goreshin closing in. The Governess was groaning now, coming out of her stupor. She started writhing in Quark's grip.

"Can you stay still for a second, darling?" Quark said. "I'm trying to save your life. We can reminisce later."

Olus released a few more rounds, still slowing the creatures. Don Pallimo reached the doorway, but they didn't open.

"Locked down," he said.

"Can you break it?" Olus asked.

"Give me a minute."

"We don't have a minute."

Don Pallimo hesitated. "Can you protect them?" he asked.

Olus looked back. "What?"

"Protect them."

Olus realized what he meant. "Nibia, Quark, come close."

"I don't go that way, Captain," Quark said. "And I don't share."

"Shut up and do it."

Quark brought the Governess to them.

He reached out with the Gift, holding his hands wide, imaging a protective wall around them. He had seen what the synths were capable of back on Gamlin.

The Goreshin reached them, jumping at the barrier. They were resistant to the Gift, and their claws made it through the barrier, slashing at them. One of them caught Quark on the shoulder, knocking him back as he cursed.

Olus fired into the group without aiming, causing a round of howling and slowing them slightly. He glanced back at the Don, who was pressed against the door.

"I don't know if I have the strength for this," Olus said, his body suddenly beginning to give out. It was taking all he had to slow the Children and keep them from getting all the way through.

Nibia put a hand on his. Immediately, he felt a tingling warmth rush through him, the strength of his Gift bolstered. He looked at her. She smiled back at him.

Then Don Pallimo exploded.

The fury of the blast washed over them, wrapping them in a ball of blue energy as the naniates deflected the assault. The Goreshin weren't so lucky. The detonation hit them full-force, tearing them apart and sending them stumbling in every direction. Olus counted to three and released the shield, still holding Nibia's hand as the now open doorway became visible.

"Gibli, ETA?" Quark said. "Not good enough. Come in harder."

They rushed out of the building and onto the lawn. Emergency sirens were sounding all around the estate.

"Quark?" Governess Ott said. "What is this?"

"The beginning of the end," Nibia said. "The monster said Gehenna has risen."

"That means something to you?" Quark asked.

"According to Koosian Lore, it means the end of days," she replied. "Armageddon."

"Well, frag me," Quark replied.

The Quasar became visible, dropping toward them like a stone.

"You can't pull that out, damn it," Quark said.

Olus heard growling behind them. The Children were recovering.

The ship continued to drop. The cannons on it shifted, beginning to fire behind them as it did, putting new holes what was left of the front of the mansion. The Goreshin cried out at the attack.

"You can't pull that out," Quark repeated.

The Quasar started to slow. It didn't seem like enough. It was tracking a few dozen meters away.

"Damn it, new shithead," Quark said.

The skids hit the ground, sinking in slightly before catching. They groaned at the weight being added to them, and one of them snapped loudly, causing the Quasar to list over to one side. Then it froze, the pilot managing to stick the landing.

"Huh. He did it," Quark said.

They ran to the ship, a pair of Riders waiting to pull them in.

"Gibli, get us out of here," Quark said, the moment they were all inside. The hatch was still sliding closed as they launched. "Take us to orbit and cloak us. Then get us on a course back to Oberon."

Olus leaned back against the side of the ship, feeling drained. Nibia sat beside him.

"Armageddon?" Quark said, looking at them.

"Worse than that," Olus replied. "Lucifer is apparently alive and well."

"Lucifer?" Quark said. "You mean Satan?"

"No. Satan's a myth. Lucifer is real. We need to find a way to contact Abbey, or we're all going to die."

"Nerd, what's our status?" Abbey asked.

"Uh. Give me a second, Queenie," Erlan replied. "I'm still getting used to these controls."

"They aren't that different from the rest of the ships you've flown," Bastion said.

"Besides the fact that they're in another language?" Erlan replied. "Let's see you learn to read Nephilim in less than a day."

"Let's see you learn to read Nephilim in less than a day," Bastion mimicked. "Whatever."

"Imp, can you grow up, please?" Abbey said.

"Roger."

"Nerd, you're doing a great job."

"Honorant Iona is a great teacher," Erlan replied.

"I bet she's taught you a few other things over the last couple of days," Benhil said. "I wouldn't mind if she taught me a thing or two."

"That's enough," Abbey said. "Let's try to keep the innuendo to a minimum."

"No fun," Pik said.

"I'm not feeling all that fun right now," Abbey replied.

The Rejects didn't argue. They knew better than to push her after everything that had happened. She wanted to keep them loose, but she was having a hard time with it. Lucifer was alive. He had control of the Covenant. He had nearly killed her. And he was on his way to Shardspace, on a ship that by all indications could make the journey twice as fast as they could.

It left her tense and frustrated, even though they were lucky to be alive in the first place, and twice as lucky to have grabbed one of the Harvesters before he had destroyed it. It had taken some time and a lot of her power, but they had managed to get the rest of their new fleet linked to the vessel well enough that when it moved into the traversable wormhole, they went with it.

Now they were in the middle of what amounted to a fold in time and space, crossing a great chasm of nothingness back toward Shardspace. She still didn't completely understand why one wormhole took longer to cross than another, but Gant had tried to explain, using plenty of big words and even going as far as breaking out a board to write the math down on.

If he was losing his intellect, she didn't see any signs of it. Of course, every time she mentioned it he would bring up some random bit of useless information he could no longer remember like he once could.

"Cherub, what are the reports from the fleet?" Abbey asked. "How are the crews handling the integration?"

"There have been a few incidents, Queenie," Jequn replied. "But the former Unders have remained surprisingly calm and accepting, as have the Apostants."

"It doesn't hurt that the Apostants are outnumbered ten to one," Uriel said.

"Not at all," Jequn agreed. "But the Unders have every opportunity to revolt against them, and so far they're staying in line."

"For Queenie's sake," Helk said, breaking into the channel. "You set them free. You also went toe to toe with the Father and didn't die. They respect you, and they're also terrified of you."

Abbey felt the tail at her back swish to the side, a reminder of what her use of the Gift was costing. She had been forced to leave a hole for the growing member, and while she had a sense of it as a new, controllable appendage, she didn't have it completely within her mental grasp just yet. It felt so alien to her, and at the same time not as uncomfortable as she had thought it would be.

Part of that was because the Rejects we so supportive, but she also knew it was because her body wasn't the only thing changing. Her mind was different too. She had a better grasp of the naniates than ever. She could hear their whispers in her head, near silent communications they passed to one another that she believed they didn't know she knew about. She was also more focused, more angry, and she was certain much more capable of intense violence. The only thing that was keeping her steady was her need to remain sane long enough to ensure her daughter's safety.

If she went mad after, that was okay.

If the Rejects had to destroy her in the end, that was okay, too. Not ideal, but acceptable.

"I'm terrified of me," she said.

Her skin was constantly warm despite her suit. She remembered how the flames of energy skipped from Lucifer's body unbidden. She felt a tingle at the thought of him, and of the power. The naniates wanted her to go to him, to merge her power with his.

Why? Was that what Lucifer wanted, or what they wanted? She wasn't sure. What she did know was that if she went near him, he would own her. She wasn't strong enough to challenge him. She wasn't even close.

"I've got it," Erlan said. "Four days, Queenie. We'll be in Shardspace in four days."

"That's a long time," Benhil said. "Especially since we think Lucifer will be there tomorrow."

"It doesn't make sense that he would go after Republic assets himself," Gant said. "His interest is in the Gate, and in getting to Elysium. Thraven can continue to handle the dirty work."

"Only until we stop his ass," Pik said.

"Can we stop him?" Uriel asked. "Queenie, are you strong enough?"

"Look at me," Abbey said, turning to make her tail more obvious.

Not that she needed to. The ridges on her forehead had grown. The bones of her arms were jutting out into her skin. Pik kept telling her she looked awesome, but she knew she didn't look human anymore.

Was she still human?

"I had better be strong enough," she said. "I don't want to live like this for nothing."

"I like it," Pik said again.

"Nerd, do you know where in Shardspace we're going to come out?" Abbey asked.

"Standby," Erlan replied.

"That's assuming we can even get to the bastard," Bastion said. "Thraven could be on the opposite side of the galaxy."

"We'll reach out to Captain Mann and General Kett when we arrive," Abbey said. "One of them has to know something."

"Again, assuming at least one of them is still alive."

"If they aren't, we'll be in deep enough shit that it might not matter," Benhil said. "We could get to Shardspace and find out Armageddon is already over."

"Tell me again how letting Lucifer get what he wants is a bad thing?" Bastion said. "He takes his assholes and gets out of our galaxy and becomes the One's concern. What's the problem there?"

"He lied to the Nephilim to get them to follow him," Abbey said. "The One left them the means to get home, and he hid them from the Seraphim to support his claim that they were slaves. He's interested in conquest, not freedom, no matter what he says. Name one asshole ever that conquered a land and then abandoned it."

"He'll come back," Jequn said. "Or maybe he'll leave Thraven here to rule over what's left of us. Either way, once he has our galaxy in his grip, he isn't going to let it go again."

Bastion nodded. "Right. But how the hell are we going to stop him? We've got a few ships, but most of them wouldn't pass inspection in the Republic. Kett's got some ships, but compared to what Thraven is throwing at us it's like David versus Goliath."

"Do I have to remind you that David won that one?" Gant asked.

"With the help of God. We don't have God on our side."

"No, we have Queenie," Pik said. "That's better."

"No offense, but Queenie can't handle Lucifer. Not now. Maybe not ever. I know it's not the answer we're looking for, and I don't want to sound like a coward, but we might have to settle for saving Hayley and getting the frag out of town."

"Saving Hayley means killing Thraven," Abbey said.

"Yeah, and you might be able to do that. But Lucifer?" He shook his head. "We don't have to stay here. We have the Harvester. Maybe we can find another part of the universe to put down roots. Someplace away from Shardspace and the Extant? What if that's the best we can do?"

"I'm glad to hear I'm not being the negative one for a change," Benhil said.

"No one is saying this is going to be easy," Abbey said. "No one is saying we're guaranteed to survive. We can't abandon the Republic. We can't abandon the Outworlds. There are too many innocent people, and I don't know about you, but I remember taking an oath to protect them when I joined the RAS."

"The same RAS that sent us to Hell," Bastion said. "We don't owe them anything."

"Yes, we do. We made a promise. All of us. And even if we didn't, I did, and you all made a promise to me. We're a family. We're going to stick together; we're going to hit the Nephilim with everything we've got. We're going to free the fragging galaxy, or we're going to die trying."

Abbey hissed the last part of the statement, the anger overwhelming. She clenched her jaw tight, realizing her entire body had tensed. It was getting so easy to become furious. So easy to start losing control.

She fled the bridge, hurrying away from the others as the rage fought to consume her, the naniates' whispers growing in pitch. She was barely away when her body started to smolder, and her eyes started to tear.

She leaned against the bulkhead.

"You do as I say," she whispered to the naniates. "You do as I command."

She swallowed the anger, slowly coming back under control. The effort left her emotionally exhausted. She wiped at her eyes before heading deeper into the Harvester. She needed some time alone to clear her head.

Besides, it was as good of a time as any to take a look around.

35

ABBEY WALKED THE CORRIDORS OF THE HARVESTER IN SILENCE AND solitude. In many ways, it felt good to get away from everything and be alone. To have time to think and feel and be without anyone asking her for anything and without having to be a leader. She had never asked to be so much to so many. She didn't particularly like being Queen. But she was going to do what she had to do, now and forever.

Of course, she was always only a comm link away. She was tempted to shut it down, but she couldn't bring herself to do it. Even when she needed time alone, she needed to be available, too. She hoped she could maintain the peace. For her sake and for the Rejects' too. She wasn't sure how far she could be pushed before the naniates would seize control. She wasn't sure what they would do once they had.

The Harvester was a large ship, but not the biggest she had been on. Its components were an amalgamation of generations, with parts replaced piecemeal over the years as older, similar pieces broke down either because of use or time. The corridors were mostly small and narrow, poorly lit and more reminiscent of a slave ship than one of the most valuable vessels in the Extant. Then again, the Harvesters were used by the Nephilim to return to Shardspace and capture a fresh supply of humans, snatching them up and bringing them back to be used for their blood or sold as Unders. It wasn't a cruise vessel.

The smaller passages made the interior feel like more of a maze, with crisscrossing corridors that were indistinguishable from one another, save for the occasional localized smell or stain. It was obvious humans had been beaten and murdered on the ship. It was a truth the Nephilim took no pains to hide. How many slaves had been shuttled this way over the millennia? Was this the ship that Thraven had been brought to the Extant on?

The thought stuck with her as she continued walking, even while her mind continued to other things. She could hardly believe Bastion was the one to suggest they cut and run. Sure, he had done the right thing and mentioned rescuing Hayley first, but still. She had come to depend on him as an ally, and there was a part of her that was coming to see him as something much more. It seemed every time she started to let those feelings in he did something to disappoint her. Now he wanted to give up and give in, and to abandon the people who were depending on them. He hadn't put the idea forward in a cowardly way, but she was still surprised he had put the idea forward at all. A part of her felt like he was the kind of man she could be with. Another part of her was repulsed by him. Even she didn't know which one would win out in the end, and she hated that he wasn't more solid.

And Hayley. Where was Hayley? Was she healthy? Was she alive? Every thought of her under Thraven's thumb caused her to start losing the control she was fighting to maintain. She had to break herself away from it.

She thought about Thraven again. How many humans had been trafficked on this ship? How many thousands had lost their lives on the trip, or suffered a worse fate at the other end of the line? The ship had to have records somewhere. She knew a little bit about the Gloritant from Uriel. That he was from Egypt. That he was a eunuch. That he hadn't aged much thanks to the Gift. Was there more she could learn? Was there something she could use? It was a long shot, but she needed the distraction.

"Gant," she said, contacting him through the comm.

"Aye, Queenie?" he said. "What do you need?"

"Do you know if this ship has a datastore on it?"

"I'm certain it does, why?"

"I'm curious, and I need a distraction."

"Bastion?"

"In part. I don't want to talk about it."

"I'm here if you decide you do. You know that, right?"

Abbey smiled. Gant was as dependable as they came. "Yes. Thank you."

"Of course. Give me a second to scan the systems. Where are you, anyway?"

"I'm not sure. I was wandering. Somewhere in the middle, if I had to guess."

"Do you want some company?"

"Not at the moment. Just a terminal location for the datastore."

"Roger. If you're in the middle, be on the lookout for the holding cells. There should be a guard station with terminal access there."

"Holding cells?"

"From the schematic, it looks a lot like the layout in Hell. It makes me wonder if one inspired the other."

"Like the Nephilim helped design Hell?"

"It stands to reason, doesn't it? Thraven was pulling resources from there, but I'm sure he wasn't the first."

"An easy place to make individuals disappear."

"Exactly."

"Thanks, Gant. I'll let you know if I need anything else."

"Roger. I'll do my best to keep the others from bothering you for a while. Pik already gave Bastion shit for pissing you off."

Abbey laughed. "Good."

She disconnected the link, continuing through the ship. It took her a little while to come across the holding cells. When she did, part of her wished she had never asked about a terminal in the first place.

She had sensed the blood and violence in the other parts of the Harvester. It was present ten times over here, where rhodrinium bars split an open space into three hundred separate pens, each large enough for ten to twenty humans. The bars were stained, as were the walls and floor, stains that could have only been made by blood and piss and shit, acidic stains that told all who ever entered the ship as a prisoner that things were only going to get worse from there. A smell permeated the deck, even as it had stood empty for who knew how long.

She raised her eyebrows in amusement when one of the few remaining Reapers on the ship emerged from the base of the guard tower. It approached her on mechanical legs, keeping its weapons at its sides and coming to stand in front of her. The machines had become docile once they had entered the wormhole, she supposed because their programming told them whoever was on the ship at that point was legal crew.

"Wait here," she said to it, knowing all it wanted was direction. It turned slightly to get out of her way but otherwise didn't react.

She walked past it to the guard tower, ascending the steps to the top. A handful of seats greeted her, arranged in a pattern so that a few eyes could watch the whole area. There were no weapons; the Apostants didn't need them. She imagined they rarely if ever had a problem with their fresh meat.

The terminal was in the back of the room, more of a convenient admin station than a necessity. She went to it and tapped the controls, turning the projector on. It didn't ask her for a password; they had already cracked the weak security.

She moved her hand over the controls, navigating through the system, the activity finally helping to take her mind off their current predicament. It took some time, but she found her way to the source console, where she was able to search the system. Since the different Prophets had shared access to the Harvesters, she assumed the personnel files would be secured and organized based on the Prophet who recorded them. She knew Thraven had been taken by the Prophet Malize, and so she did her best to locate references to him in the datastore.

The search turned up a raft of data related to prisoners - more than she had been expecting. It was protected and encrypted, but the Nephilim were far behind the Republic in those technologies, and she broke into the data with little resistance. She had thought maybe the Nephilim didn't pay that much attention to their victims, but she was wrong. Every prisoner was identified and cataloged with images and full histories, a process that must have taken the collectors weeks. She searched the name Selvig Thraven but didn't turn anything up. Because he had been on another Harvester? Or because that wasn't his original name?

She set about trying to narrow down the lists. Not because she thought any information she found would be all that useful, but because it gave her something else to do, something that kept her brain working but didn't have to do with the war beyond the wormhole. It was a way to stay focused without getting too angry, without the risk of losing her mind.

She sorted the list by gender, by record age, and then by location. There were no records that old from anywhere other than Earth, and they stretched back to way before humankind had invented air travel, never mind space travel. She found four hundred males that could have fit Thraven's description.

She started going through them one at a time. The Nephilim had saved images of every single prisoner, stripped naked and placed in front of a light background. The process was exhaustive, and in her opinion nearly pornographic, including close-ups of the genitals for purposes she didn't, and didn't want to, understand.

Even so, it helped her narrow the list of hundreds down to four eunuchs, all of whom could have potentially been Thraven if any of them were. She looked at the data for each of them. Two were marked as potentials for the Gift due to their overall health and strong personalities. She put them aside for further investigation, reading through the data the Nephilim had maintained and deciding that neither of them was Thraven.

She was going to give up then. Thraven had to have come on one of the other Harvesters. The problem was that quitting was going to return her to reality, and she had too much time to burn. She pulled the other two records, reading through them. She was halfway through the first when she began to wonder if she was onto something.

An Egyptian eunuch named Ahtintep who exhibited nearly narcissistic confidence and strength, who showed little fear at his situation, and who was intrigued by the Nephilim language and their Gift. It turned out this particular slave had a brother who had been captured as well, a younger boy named Ketmose who had died on the journey back to the Extant.

Interesting.

She searched for Ketmose, the name helping her to locate him quickly.

She froze when she saw him.

What the hell?

He had a mop of brown hair, a thin frame, sharp features and dark skin. But it was the eyes that drew her in. The eyes that caused the fire of the Gift to burn within her once more.

They were Thraven's eyes.

She looked over all of the images, confused. Ketmose was no more than ten. His penis was present and accounted for. He was supposed to be dead.

How could this be Thraven?

She looked at his face again. She stared into his eyes. It was him. She was sure of it. Ketmose was Thraven. Ketmose was alive.

"Gant," she said, reconnecting their comm link.

"Aye, Queenie," Gant replied.

"I think I found something."

THE REJECTS SPENT THE NEXT FOUR DAYS SETTING OUT TO TRY TO SOLVE the mystery of the boy who would be Gloritant, and who didn't have the history Selvig Thraven claimed to have. As it had been for Abbey, it became for the rest of them - a distraction from the mess they were rushing headlong into, and a chance to bond over the enigma of Thraven's true origins.

Bastion apologized, of course, coming to her quarters early the next morning with a small gift, a misshapen Gantrean star that Gant had instructed him in the construction of and had loaned him the material for. It was an odd alliance for the two of them, but one she found she appreciated more than Gant probably knew. He was proving his loyalty by keeping the bonds of their family intact and strong. He knew they would need them to be in order to survive the days ahead.

She had responded by inviting him in and talking to him for a while. He wasn't afraid of Lucifer, he said. He was more afraid for her and her daughter, and she knew from his reason for being in Hell that sometimes he acted or said the wrong things for the right reasons. She accepted his apology, surprised when he didn't proceed to make any stupid or immature comments, despite the tail that writhed over her shoulder, reacting to her emotions.

She was able to keep her mind focused, and as a result, hold the fury under control. She could always feel the Gift burning beneath her skin, begging for release. She could always feel that vein of violent destruction pulsing just below her surface. She held it at bay, working with the others to come to a conclusion on the real story of the boy named Ketmose.

Thankfully, the rest of the fleet was running almost as smoothly as the Harvester. Gloritant Iona was doing her part, keeping the other ship commanders organized and putting forward Abbey's intent for how to run her newly formed Prophetic, as Iona insisted on calling it. The separation between Apostants, Lessers, and Unders wasn't going to vanish overnight, but the lines were quickly beginning to blur as all of the individuals involved became more attuned to their shared plight.

They were headed to Shardspace to fight a war on behalf of a woman they barely knew, but who had stood up to Lucifer and survived. A woman who had defeated their Prophet. A woman who had set them free. Abbey had earned their respect and their commitment, their loyalty and their trust. She could bring them all to something different, something better. All they had to do was fight.

All they had to do was win.

Abbey was on the bridge of the Harvester when the far end of the wormhole became visible, a ripple in the darkness that signaled a return to regular space. The Rejects were there with her, Erlan at the controls of the ship, Gant monitoring its systems, Bastion handling navigation. Ruby manning the comm. Pik, Benhil, Phlenel, Trinity, Jequn, and Uriel stood to the side in observance.

Their efforts to uncover more about Thraven had been limited to the data available, which wasn't much, and had led to a relatively dead end. Besides the relationship between the younger, not-as-dead-as-it-had-seemed Ketmose and his older brother, the most salient piece of information they had gathered from a ship's log was that the Honorant in charge of the Harvester had taken a liking to Ketmose and had treated him more favorably than the others. Other logs from the crew corroborated the suggestion, although there were multiple accounts that suggested the Honorant's involvement was anything but honorable. It wouldn't do much to help them now, but it did potentially tie back to what they could only assume was Thraven's intentional dismemberment.

Beyond that theory, how it all translated into Thraven's survival and eventual rise to power was anyone's guess, and they had all taken turns making as many guesses as they could. It had quickly become a game that produced plenty of laughs, but no resolution.

Abbey was okay with that. She had held out hope they would find something they could use against the Gloritant, but some of the comments she and her fellow Rejects had come up with made the whole thing worthwhile. At the same time, there was a part of her that felt a level of empathy for Ketmose. He had grown up in Egypt as a child slave, been taken by aliens and abused, and then delivered into further slavery on the other side of the universe. Was it really his fault that he had done what he could to survive? Could she blame him for becoming the enemy after what the enemy had done to him?

Who the hell cared? It didn't matter what made him a threat. He was a threat now, and he needed to be taken down. Even if she didn't already want to end him for taking Hayley, she knew she would have to drink his blood if she had any hope of going toe-to-toe with Lucifer.

And there would be nothing in the entirety of the so-called multiverse that could save him from the most miserable end she could imagine if he had done anything to her daughter even remotely like what had been done to him.

The Harvester reached the edge of the wormhole and continued through. Instantly, the pure black was replaced with a scattering of stars, while she knew the hole in the universe continued behind them, the rest of the tethered fleet still emerging as if from a womb.

"Weeee'rrreeee baaaaacccckkkk," Pik said.

"Ruby, activate the Galnet back channel and try to establish a link with Captain Mann, and with General Kett. I want to know what the frag is going on around here."

"Yes, Queenie," Ruby said, adjusting the controls at her station.

"Imp, what's our position relative to anything useful?"

"We're sixteen light years from the outer Fringe, Queenie," Bastion replied. "The nearest occupied planet is under Outworlds control. Shastian."

"Frag Shastian," Abbey said. "I said useful."

Bastion laughed. "There's a song about Shastian."

"My Shastian Hoo-ah," Pik said. "I like it."

"Not useful," Abbey said.

"Queenie," Ruby said. "I'm not able to initiate the back channel." She turned to face her, synthetic face shifting into a fake nervous frown. "The Galnet is unavailable."

"Unavailable?" Benhil said. "Is that even possible?"

"Anything is possible," Gant said. "But you would need to bring down hundreds of nodes to break the web."

"What about the Milnet?" Abbey asked. "Is that back online."

"One moment please," Ruby said, returning to her station.

"Imp, get us a path to the Fringe, between the Republic and the Outworlds. I don't want to waste too much time out here."

"Aye, Queenie."

"Gloritant Iona," Abbey said, opening a channel to the Morningstar.

A projection of the woman appeared. She was wearing a crisp uniform, her hair tied behind her head. She bowed at the sight of Abbey. "How may I serve you, my Queen?"

"We're going to move deeper into Shardspace. Tell the Honorants to stay alert to the morale of their crews. We don't want anyone doing anything stupid because they got spooked."

"As you command, my Queen. We will be prepared."

"Thank you."

Abbey cut the link, glancing back at Bastion. "Imp?"

"Course charted, Queenie," he replied. "Six hours from our current position."

"Six?" Benhil said. "That's quick."

"You have to love traversable wormholes," Gant said.

"I think there's a song about that, too," Pik said.

"There is not," Benhil said.

"Yes, there is."

"Is not."

"Thank you," Abbey said, cutting them off. "Ruby, Milnet?"

"Negative, Queenie," Ruby replied, "Still offline."

"Frag." She paused, thinking. "This ship doesn't have an Outnet link, does it?"

"It does," Gant said. "The Nephilim monitor transmissions from across the galaxy."

"What good is that going to do us?" Bastion asked. "We can't talk to any friendlies that way."

"We need to know where Thraven is," Abbey replied. "Listening in on the Outworlds might help us figure that out."

"Roger."

"We're patched in," Ruby said. "Shall I set a marker for the Gloritant's name?"

"Yes. And for reports of attacks, sightings of starships matching the description of the Nephilim vessels, that sort of thing. And also for Lucifer and the Covenant, just in case."

"Yes, Queenie."

"Nerd, we'll give it ten minutes, and then we'll make the crossing to the Fringe. I want to get closer to the action."

"Aye, Queenie," Erlan replied.

They waited in silence. The markers would pick up instances of the words in them across the scanning channels, and while it was possible to miss some instances, if the items had any true meaning behind them they would be repeated more than once. It was a flood of media a human could never manage in ten minutes, but Ruby's upgraded synthetic cortex could organize fairly efficiently.

"Anything?" Abbey asked after a few minutes.

"Not specific, Queenie," Ruby replied. "Although." She hesitated.

"Although what?"

"It's odd. I'm getting interference across every channel. Standby." She fell silent again while another few minutes passed. "Yes. Very interesting."

"What is it?" Jequn asked.

"The interference is cyclical. It is repeating in an identical frequency every thirty seconds."

"That's not interference," Abbey said.

"Agreed," Ruby replied. "It is a message."

"Can you isolate it?" Gant asked.

"Standby." A few seconds passed. "Done."

"Can you bring the waveform up on the projector?" Gant said.

"Of course," Ruby replied.

It appeared there a moment later.

"Encrypted," Gant said.

Abbey stared at it. She was familiar with a number of audio encryption protocols. This one was no different.

"It's a Rudinian Zero-wave," she said. "Impossible to break without a quantum detangler."

"Of which we have none," Benhil said.

"Who do you think sent it?" Bastion asked.

"I think that's clear," Trinity said. "Thraven doesn't need to sneak an encrypted message into the background of Outnet traffic. However, if Captain Mann is trying to get word to Queenie and knows both the Galnet and Milnet are unavailable?"

"If that's true, he's not going to use a key that Queenie can't guess," Phlenel said.

"Something only you and him would know," Bastion said.

Abbey stared at the waveform, not that it would provide a clue to the key that would unlock it. She thought back to her conversations with the Captain, trying to remember them. A word or phrase they would have shared with one another and no one else. It could be anything, and they didn't have time to waste.

"Any ideas?" Pik asked.

"Maybe 'bullshit,'" Abbey said, remembering how he had lied to them about the virus that would destroy their minds if they didn't follow his directives.

"That isn't it," Ruby said.

"I was joking," Abbey said.

She closed her eyes, remembering the conversations. 'Hayley' would be too obvious. So would most of the other things that sprang to mind. It had to be something more obscure. Something Thraven could never know or guess.

She continued to filter through their conversations in her mind. One thing they had spoken about stuck with her, probably because of what she had been doing during the trip back from the Extant.

"Try 'Sun-Tzu,'" she said.

The waveform vanished from the projection, and Ruby turned toward her. "That was correct, Queenie."

Abbey nodded.

Know your enemy.

"Play it back."

"Yes, Queenie."

Abbey breathed in, waiting for the recording to begin, her mind starting to race. Would Olus mention what had happened to Hayley? Or would he try to keep her sane, to keep her fighting for the Republic? He didn't know what she was becoming. He didn't know what she knew.

"Abbey. The Galnet has been disabled. Thraven's fleet is on the move. Lucifer is here. I've enlisted the help of Don Pallimo and the Crescent Haulers. Contact me as soon as possible through their channels. Have Gant hack into it or get in touch with the nearest Hauler you can find. I'm sure you're worried about Hayley. She's doing well and under the Don's protection. We'll be waiting as long as we can to hear from you, but General Kett has launched an offensive on Earth, and we can't wait long."

37

SYLVAN KETT PACED IN HIS QUARTERS. HIS MIND HAD FINALLY CALMED, though it had taken hours for him to regain some semblance of sanity.

What the hell had he done?

He had panicked, plain and simple. He had given in to fear. Fear of losing the brave individuals who had been with him and Charmeine since the beginning. Fear of dying himself. Fear of never seeing his wife's dream realized.

He had been removed from the bridge as a result. He had been removed from command. He had been taken away, confined to quarters, and though he hadn't looked, he knew there was a guard posted outside. The crazy old General wasn't going to get in the way of the assault on Earth. The cowardly shell of a once respected and nearly legendary leader wasn't going to nearly get them killed again.

What had come over him? When had he become so weak? He wanted to serve the Republic, to serve the Seraphim, to see the Nephilim destroyed and the Great Return thwarted. He wanted peace in the galaxy, but what was he willing to pay to get it?

He slammed his fist into the wall, followed by his forehead. He had been so stupid. So self-righteous and self-centered. His soldiers weren't asking him to save them. They were asking to fight. Charmeine hadn't asked him to keep the Covenant away from Abbey. She had told the Light where to find it, knowing full well it might make everything worse. He had imprisoned the Rejects, and only his daughter's willfulness had made the decision not a complete disaster.

"Who am I?" he said. "General Sylvan Kett?"

He shook his head. They couldn't strip his rank because they were all technically subordinates. Captain Davlyn was technically a traitor. But he had betrayed them first by being prepared to give the order to run.

He crossed his quarters to the viewport. There was nothing to see out there. Not yet. But he knew there would be any moment. He was aware of the time to make the jump from the edge of the inner system to Earth. He was counting the seconds in his head. It was coming, fast and furious, and when it did would they survive?

He could have helped them. He could have led them. He had been granted his chance, and he had failed.

There was nothing more he could do but watch.

He put his arms out, bracing himself against the wall, centered behind the viewport. He tried to ease his breath, but it remained ragged and short. His heart was thumping, the anticipation reaching its apex.

He remained that way for thirty seconds. Then, at the moment he expected, the High Noon came out of FTL in a cloud, accelerating quickly out of the cloud, the blue marble of the Terran homeworld visible in the distance.

Closer in, a battle was raging, a half a dozen large battleships against forty or more smaller but more nimble vessels, half of which he knew were Outworld design. Smaller dots darted amidst the larger craft, starfighters pitted against one another in a tight dogfight, though he already knew who would win. The Republic's Apocalypse fighters were useless, compromised by a traitorous corporation, as were some of the lighter cruisers. It left them with older craft, starfighters that couldn't match the Outworld Shrikes over the long haul. As he watched, he saw the enemy ships take down a pair of

Republic fighters, hitting them hard with lasers and leaving them floating dead in the battle zone.

One of the battle zones. There was so much debris out here he could barely believe it. How many ships had the Republic brought to defend Earth, and how many had been destroyed? It seemed like it was an overwhelming number on both sides.

For a moment, he wondered if he had made a mistake giving Olus the Brimstone. They sure could have used the advanced warship now. Its energy weapons would have cut the Outworld ships apart, its remaining torpedoes able to destroy the best Thraven's forces had to offer.

Then again, even if they lost Earth, gaining the support of the Crescent Haulers would be a much larger and more valuable victory.

And it certainly seemed like they were close to losing Earth. Or maybe it had fallen already. Just because there was still fighting in the space above the planet didn't mean the occupation wasn't settled on the ground. Winning up here might only be the first step in recovering the symbol of the Republic's strength.

The enemy ships started to turn, altering their vectors as their sensors picked up the newly arrived fleet. He found one of the Seed-ships further out, staying behind the Republic forces in case they decided to put their energy on destroying it. A light flashed from the battleships ahead of it, and then small burns of thrusters filled the sky, the fleet unleashing their own starfighters.

Lasers followed a moment later; quick, heavy blasts from the fleet that strategically targeted the enemy closest to the remaining Republic forces. Captain Davlyn would be trying to communicate with them now, sending short range comm hails that without the Milnet the enemy would be able to tap into and eavesdrop on. Of course, the Captain had to know that and might be sending fake commands, or at least encoded ones.

The fleet advanced, their larger force moving in, closing on the enemy. The Shrikes broke off their original engagement, tightening their formations and vectoring back their way. Their starfighters moved to intercept, and they put up a valiant effort, even managing to take a few of the enemy down. But Shrikes were Shrikes, and they started to get the better of their inferior starfighter designs, leaving Sylvan to watch his soldiers start to die.

He felt the clench in his gut every time one of his went dark. They had to end this quickly, take out the battleships and leave the Shrikes with nowhere to run. Captain Davlyn was thinking the same thing, charging headlong into the fray, taking the hits from the enemy in order to press the attack harder than might be wise. A torpedo slammed into the shields close to Sylvan's position, the flash of the energy that absorbed it nearly blinding him. He turned his head away until the light faded, looking back to see the battleship that launched it eject debris from a fresh wound, a counterstrike that had broken through the shields.

It was obvious. They were winning.

Sylvan smiled, though the emotion was rough in his chest. He should have been up on the bridge directing this. He should have been leading them to victory. He had fragged up, and now he was on the sidelines of history. Damn it.

At least they were succeeding. At least they were going to capture Earth's orbit. They had the ships. They had the firepower. The remaining Republic defenses were moving in an updated vector, joining the fleet maneuvers and trapping Thraven's forces in a crossfire, leaving them with only one way out: back the way they had come.

"Come on, you fraggers," he said, watching the scene unfold. "That's right you bastards. Earth belongs to the Republic. Now and forever."

Another enemy ship went dark, three torpedoes slamming it in the same spot at once, blasting through the shields. It rolled slightly as its vectoring thrusters died unevenly, and then began to float away.

"Only a few left," Sylvan said. "Go get them."

He turned his head, finding the Seedship again. It was still positioned at the rear of the action. Still positioned out of harm's way.

He squinted his eyes. Something was wrong. There were no stars behind it. Instead, he caught the silhouette of a ship, a newcomer to the battle.

208

"No," he said softly, finding the edge of it and tracing its lines.

Its mouth opened up and spewed hell, a half-dozen torpedoes arcing away from it, zipping past the Seedship and into their ranks. He couldn't see the explosions or the detonations, but he didn't need to.

Thraven was here.

They were all going to die.

38

"No, no, no, no, no," Sylvan said, knowing their fleet was suddenly being torn to shreds.

Thraven had come to fight this battle himself? Why? It didn't make any sense. Earth was important, but not that important. There were plenty of other planets for him to worry about, not to mention the Elysium Gate.

The other ships in Thraven's fleet spread out, vectoring into position to decimate their forces. They were going to be destroyed. All of them, and there was nothing he could do but stand there and watch.

He clenched his teeth, shaking his head, his heart thumping even harder. He could feel the fear of the moment, the certainty of his death and the death of his friends and allies. He wanted to lay against the wall, close his eyes, and wait for it to be over. He wanted to hide while death reached out for him, to let himself sink into the abyss of nothing without so much as a whimper.

He couldn't. He knew he couldn't. He was General Sylvan Kett, damn it, and his soldiers needed him. He knew Thraven would want him alive, just like he would want the Seedship unharmed. He could use that to their advantage, and buy them some time.

Time to do what? He wasn't sure. Olus was supposed to rendezvous with them. Could he possibly make it back before this fight was done? What would happen if he arrived after, even if he had a number of Crescent Haulers with him?

They had to damage Thraven's fleet as best they could, even if it meant every one of them died. There were billions of individuals on Earth, and Thraven's intentions toward them were anything but innocent.

He had failed once, but he didn't have to fail again. The Nephilim ships had no true weaknesses, but he did know a few tricks from Charmeine that might help them stay alive just a little bit longer.

Sylvan tightened his hands into fists, steeling himself before darting across the room to the door. It slid open when he reached it, revealing the expected guard.

"General," the surprised guard said. "You need to stay in your quarters. Captain's orders."

"Do you know how ridiculous that sounds?" Sylvan said. "You don't take orders from the Captain over me."

"I'm sorry, sir," the guard said, turning his rifle to point it at the General.

"So am I," Sylvan replied.

He slipped to the side and forward, his footwork quick and precise, bringing him to the left of the guard. The guard moved to react, too late, finding the gun batted aside and a fist hitting him hard on the side of the face. The guard stumbled a step, and Sylvan grabbed the rifle and wrenched it from his grip, turning it back and swinging it into the soldier's side. It knocked him out of the way, and Sylvan ran past, jumping just in time to avoid the desperate guard's grip.

It was a short sprint to the bridge, and Davlyn hadn't stationed any other guards, not expecting Sylvan to try to get out and certainly not expecting him to succeed. The doors to the bridge opened, immediately revealing the projection of Gloritant Thraven to him at the front of the space.

"I'd rather die than surrender my forces or my planet to you, Gloritant," Captain Davlyn said.

Thraven was stoic and calm, his posture confident and assured. He gave the slightest hint of a shrug at the response.

"I respect your decision, Captain," the Gloritant said. "It will be arranged."

"Thraven," Sylvan shouted, rushing up to Davlyn's side. The Captain cast a sideways glance at him but didn't react otherwise in front of the enemy.

"Ah," Thraven said, a tiny smile playing at the corner of his mouth. "There you are, Sylvan. The Captain told me you were wounded in the earlier fighting." He paused. "You look hale and healthy to me."

"You killed Charlie, you son of a bitch," Sylvan said. "I'm going to kill you for that."

"You and what army, Sylvan?" Thraven asked. "This rabble? I'd like to see you try."

"You seem confident," Sylvan said, a new plan coming together in his mind.

"Why shouldn't I be? My ships are far, far superior to yours. I don't even need to use my Gift to kill you."

"You can't kill me," Sylvan said. "If you do, you'll never learn the location of the Covenant. I'd like to bargain. Surely the Covenant is more valuable than Earth."

Thraven's smile grew, the act unnerving Sylvan. Why was the Gloritant so amused by his offer?

"I might have taken you up on that offer earlier," Thraven said. "I don't need your help with the ship now. Gehenna has risen, General. The Father leads us to the Great Return. You can't stop us. You can't stop me. I have orders from the highest power there is."

Sylvan felt himself begin to shake, the fear threatening to reduce him to nothing. Lucifer was alive? Had he captured the Covenant? Did that mean Abbey was dead?

There was no hope.

None.

It was over.

He fought against his emotions. "You want me dead then, Selvig?" he asked.

Thraven nodded.

"My ship against yours, whatever you call it," Sylvan said. "If you win, Earth is yours. If I win -"

Thraven waved his hand, dismissing him. "As you wish, General. I'll enjoy being the one to destroy you personally."

The link was dropped, the projection vanishing. Captain Davlyn turned to him.

"What the hell did you just do? There's no way the High Noon can outclass that ship."

"I bought the Republic some time," Sylvan replied. "I don't know if it will help in the end, but it's the best we can do. We're going to die, Captain, but let's die with whatever dignity we can salvage."

Dalvyn nodded somberly. "Aye, General. What are your orders?"

39

G<small>LORITANT</small> T<small>HRAVEN STARED OUT AT THE</small> R<small>EPUBLIC BATTLESHIP FOUR</small> thousand kilometers away. What was General Kett up to that he had challenged him to a fight he had to know he couldn't win? Not only was the Promise faster and more powerful, but he was also more powerful, and the fool hadn't even bothered to make not using the Gift one of the conditions.

It was senseless and confusing and was causing him to hesitate to consider. Was that what the General was after? To throw him off guard with his misplaced confidence? And what was the meaning behind the story the High Noon's Captain had given him? The man had said Kett was injured, and then he had appeared whole and healthy. Was that part of the ruse as well?

He didn't trust it, but he was also worried that by not trusting it he was playing right into Kett's hands. The man was known for his tactical mind, and that went beyond putting an asset here or a resource there. It meant getting in the head of his opponents, working to make them beat themselves.

It didn't matter how much Kett tried to get into his head. He still had no chance at beating them.

"Gloritant?" Honorant Bane said, waiting for instructions.

"Move the Promise away from the fleet. Order a ceasefire across our lines. I will deal with Sylvan Kett, and then we can continue with our conquest of Earth."

"Their General said if you defeat him Earth will be ours."

"The General has no authority to make a deal like that. He isn't even a member of the Republic anymore. No, his death won't stop the fighting." Thraven paused, the realization crossing his thoughts. "Only delay it."

He looked back out of the viewport. What was he up to? And who was he hoping would show up while he sacrificed himself to stall?

Cage, perhaps? The Father had said he allowed her to escape, to make her way back to Shardspace in a Harvester. For what purpose? To what end? That wasn't for him to concern himself with. The Father had his reasons. Besides, if she showed up here, he would deal with her.

He was hoping for the chance.

"The High Noon is accelerating away from us, Gloritant," Bane said.

Thraven could see the battleship's thrusters flare, the vectoring jets pushing it onto a new course. Kett wanted him to chase them?

"Fire a single torpedo," Thraven said. He wanted to see what Kett would do with it.

"Yes, your Eminence."

Bane passed the order, and a moment later a torpedo launched from the bow of the Promise, a flash of light that zipped toward the High Noon so quickly it was difficult to follow.

Somehow, the ship avoided it, skipping to the port side, the projectile cutting past. How far from the hull? A meter or less? It was impossible.

No, not impossible. Not with the great Sylvan Kett directing the battleship's crew.

"Well done, General," he said softly. "Get us ahead of the High Noon."

"Yes, Gloritant."

The Promise burst ahead, its engines and dampeners carrying them from their current position to a place ahead of the High Noon in less than a minute. By the time they arrived the battleship had adjusted its vectors again, General Kett guessing where they would move to and preparing for the occasion. Torpedoes were already headed toward them as the warship turned to get into firing position, taking a few hits off the shields in what Thraven knew would be a moral victory for the Lessers.

"The High Noon is launching starfighters, Gloritant," Bane said.

Thraven could see it for himself. Dozens of small craft emerging from the two hangars of the battleship and racing back toward them. What was the point of the maneuver?

"Fire," Thraven said.

A second torpedo flashed away, caught a moment later by one of the starfighters, detonating away from the High Noon.

Thraven leaned forward slightly. How could that be possible? It was as though Kett knew where every strike would be before it happened.

A plume of disterium began to form around the battleship.

"He's running, Gloritant," Bane said.

Thraven shook his head. "No. He won't run. Fire all batteries."

The space around the Promise brightened as heavy beams of plasma arced away from the ship, reaching out for the High Noon. The warship rotated as the energy crossed over, taking glancing blows from them, most of the power deflected by their shields.

Most, not all. Beams struck the hull, pouring into the heavy armor and burning it to gas, creating small fissures in three places near the stern.

A moment later, the High Noon vanished, leaving a raft of starfighters closing on the Promise, small lasers opening fire on the ship, biting at it like a swarm of insects.

"Shall we call for reinforcements, Gloritant?" Bane asked.

Thraven reached out, grabbing the Honorant with the Gift and lifting him from the floor. "Do you care nothing for honor?" he hissed, throwing Bane across the bridge. "I agreed to single combat." He released his servant without killing him. "Besides, I'm enjoying this. Now get up."

Honorant Bane stood quickly, limping back to his position near Thraven. They both watched the sensors. The High Noon reappeared a moment later, coming at them from the starboard flank. It unleashed everything it had then, at the same time Kett's starfighters broke away.

Torpedoes and lasers struck the side of the Promise, shields flaring while the battleship attacked with everything it had. The ship quivered slightly beneath the assault, forcing Bane to put a hand on one of the stations for balance.

"Shields at sixty percent," one of the Agitants announced.

"I'm finished with this game," Thraven said.

He breathed in, feeling the Gift rise to him, eager to do his will. He spread his hands, turning them and then slashing them in front of his body.

Outside the Promise's hull, dozens of starfighters began to crumple, an invisible force punching into their fuselage's and crushing them, the force tearing open cockpits and leaving the pilots inside exposed.

"What do you think of that, Sylvan?" Thraven said, satisfied with the silent carnage.

The High Noon replied, a fresh barrage of firepower stretching out to slam the Promise.

"Get us back into position and fire at will. We will not miss again."

"Yes, Gloritant," Bane said.

"Shields at fifty percent," the Agitant announced.

The Promise started to turn, while Thraven reached out with the Gift, taking hold of the High Noon with it, not to damage it himself, but to hold it in place. Vectoring thrusters tried to fire, the force countered by the naniates, keeping the warship still.

Kett must have sensed their impending doom. The High Noon began to add velocity from the rear, thrusting right toward them.

Thraven knew what the General intended.

"Cancel the order to fire. Move us away."

"Yes, your Eminence," Bane said.

The Promise jumped, thrusters firing and positioning them over the High Noon.

Seconds later, the Republic battleship exploded.

Debris rushed toward the ship, peppering the shields, forcing them to work hard to block the large pieces of metal and slag that rushed toward them, a mess created by the self-destructed ship. The remains of the High Noon coursed out in every direction, heading toward both fleets, forcing all of the nearby vessels to raise shields and start taking evasive action to conserve energy.

Gloritant Thraven stared out at the expanding field. "You died well, Sylvan Kett," he said. "A shame you died for nothing." He turned to Bane. "Order the fleet to re-engage the enemy. Capture the Seed-ship. Leave nothing else intact."

"Yes, Gloritant."

40

"Colonel, we're about to drop," Gibli said, his voice shaking.

"Oh, grow a pair already, will you, Shitbrains?" Quark replied, getting to his feet and looking over at Olus. "It's not like we're about to land in a fragging shitstorm, right Captain?"

Olus smiled. "Right. Shitstorm would be an understatement."

"I trust you won't leave us fragged?" Quark said, looking over at Governess Ott.

"I'll do what I can," she replied. Having a Goreshin try to claw her head off had brought her over to their side in a hurry. "But I don't know how many of the commanders will listen to me. The blood between the Outworlds and the Republic has been bad for a long time, and a lot of them won't want to sacrifice their chance to spill it without orders from the full Governance."

"Those assholes," Quark said. "Selfish bastards, every last one of them."

"Not all of them," Olus said. "Governor Pike was reasonable."

"Two out of seven," Quark said. "Your word meant shit to them, Sandy. I thought they respected you."

"It's late in the game, Q," Ott replied. "They smell victory over the Republic."

Quark huffed. "Some fragging victory it'll be. Yay, we beat the Republic. Oh, now we're fragging monster food. Shit. I hope Cage gets your message, Captain, or this is going to be a short war."

Olus didn't say anything. What was there to say? Lucifer had entered the picture, emboldening the Nephilim to the point they no longer cared if the Outworlds were with them or not. Worse, the Outworlds had remained on the offensive, the Governance refusing to take Governess Ott's experience into strong consideration. The vote had been swift and decisive, with only one other sitting member taking their side. He had gone to the Governess hoping he could get the two sides to work together to stop the threat, a plan that had failed miserably.

They had sent an encoded message through the Outnet with Ott's help, throwing the signal out into space in the hope that wherever Abbey was, she would hear their cry for help and respond. They had spent the following three days both organizing the Crescent Hauler fleet and waiting for a reply, succeeding in only one of those things.

The Haulers were on the move, a massive group of ships preparing to converge near Earth to do whatever they could to counter the Nephilim offensive and save the Republic. While the bulk of the Hauler's ships were massively underpowered in terms of attack capabilities, they did have numbers on their side, along with the Brimstone.

Still, they had no idea exactly what they were stepping into. Sensors had picked up the remains of a large-scale battle further out, and a quick scan had identified a few of the ships from Kett's fleet, along with the battleship Nova and its support ships. The fact that the fleet had been engaged before reaching the Terran homeworld suggested the fighting closer in was going to be intense.

Even if they did take care of business here, they were still going to have Lucifer to deal with, not to mention Thraven and his remaining warships. They had put together everything they could manage, and Olus still didn't think it would be enough.

Not without the Rejects.

Not without Abbey.

One battle at a time. One planet at a time. That was all they could do right now. That and pray that the Queen of Demons answered their call.

It was a longshot, but it was the only shot they had.

"Ten seconds, Colonel," Gibli announced, trying to force himself to sound calm. It wasn't working.

"You know the drill," Quark said. "Buckle your asses up."

Olus was already belted in, ready for the wild ride to come. He wished he could ride shotgun in the cockpit and keep an eye on the situation directly, but this was Quark's ship and as a result, his seat. He had to settle for watching things unfold through a projection of the area on the table in front of them.

"Nibia, kiss for luck?" Quark asked, leaning in toward the witch doctor.

"Good idea," Nibia said. She leaned to her left, kissing Olus on the cheek. "Good luck, Captain."

"What?" Quark said. "He isn't even doing anything."

"Neither are you," Nibia replied. "Gibli's doing all the work."

"All of the work?" their newest Don Pallimo synth asked. They had picked him up on the return to Oberon, another in what seemed to be an endless supply.

"Okay, maybe not all. Do you want a kiss, Don?"

The synth stuck its cheek out toward her. She kissed it. "Good luck."

Quark laughed. "Sandy?"

"Go frag yourself, Q. You should have asked me first."

"Shut out," Quark said. "Fine. You can kiss my ass then."

He headed for the cockpit, vanishing just as the Quasar came out of FTL.

Olus stared at the table, waiting for the projection to appear. It would take a few seconds for the system to gather enough data, pulling it in from the Quasar's sensors, as well as the sensors from across the Crescent Hauler fleet. The network was more advanced than anything the Republic had produced, but unfortunately it was optimized for efficiency, not for war. It had no problem determining the logistics that would expend the least fuel and time to pick up or deliver cargo, but it was up to them to make adjustments relevant to a battlefield.

"We've got a small problem, Captain," Quark said, almost immediately.

The Quasar began to shake before he had a chance to ask what it was. He reached out to grip the edge of the table.

"What the hell?" he said.

"Looks like an old friend beat us to the punch."

By the way he said it, he didn't mean Abbey. The projection finally appeared, a three-dimensional view of Earth with a mess of objects in orbit around it. The hundreds of Crescent Hauler vessels that had come out of FTL with them were outlined in green, as was the Brimstone close by.

Between them and the planet was a host of yellow objects, neutral forms, most likely debris. Except it was no debris field he had ever seen before. It was surrounding the planet like a shell, creating a thick barrier that would be difficult to break through without expending massive amounts of shield energy. It was a formation that couldn't have occurred naturally, no matter how many ships had been destroyed nearby.

It was a shield only the Gift could have created. A shield only the Gift could maintain.

A group of red shapes were outlined behind them, further away from the planet, nearly beyond its pull. The networked data from the Brimstone had already identified the Nephilim warships that had been built on Kell, flanked by both Republic and Outworld assets. The High Noon and the rest of General Kett's fleet were nowhere to be found.

Unless they were part of the debris.

"Thraven," Olus said, his stomach sinking. "Damn it."

41

"WHAT DO WE DO, CAPTAIN?" QUARK ASKED.

The Nephilim ships started to move, as did the support fleet around them.

"Nothing's changed," Olus replied. "We expected a fight."

"But Thraven-"

"It will be a bigger fight," Olus said. "The only way to win is through the Gloritant."

"Roger," Quark said.

"I'm moving the Haulers into a flanking position," Don Pallimo said.

"Dak," Olus said.

"Aye, Captain?" Dak replied.

"You know what to do. Target the Nephilim warships. The Haulers will do their best to distract them."

"Aye, sir."

Olus watched the Brimstone change vectors, along with the rest of the fleet. The Haulers were spreading out, vectoring to get on both sides of the enemy fleet.

"Governess?" Olus said, looking over at Ott.

"Are we patched in?"

"Sykes has you covered," Quark said.

"Link is open," Sykes replied, her voice scratchy and gruff.

"Outworld Commanders," Governess Ott said. "This is Governess Sandine Ott of the First Sector. I'm with the Crescent Hauler fleet that just came out of FTL. I order you to stand down immediately. I repeat, stand down immediately. We've been betrayed by General Thraven. This fight is not the Outworld's fight."

There was a moment of silence. Then one of the commanders replied.

"I haven't received any orders from the Governance to stand down, Governess."

"They sent me directly and in person to guarantee authenticity," she replied. "I'm transmitting my personal keys with this message, as well as my position. You can verify if you wish."

"Verified," the same commander said. "Even so, this is highly irregular."

"So is being fragged over by a maniac," she replied. "General Thraven's forces attacked me. His actions are threatening the security of the Outworlds."

"Bullshit," another commander replied. "General Thraven captured the Republic homeworld. The Republic is dead, thanks to him."

The enemy ships began to fire on the Hauler vessels, torpedoes and plasma beams that Olus couldn't see in the projection. He did see the green shapes that faded out as they were destroyed. So did Governess Ott.

"Damn it," she shouted. "The Crescent Haulers have been neutral for years, but the Don is siding with the Republic. Doesn't that tell you something?"

Olus watched Thraven's fleet maneuver. A few of the Outworld ships were pulling back, moving away from the battle to come.

"It's working," he said. "For some of them, anyway."

"We've waited years for this, Governess," the commander said.

"And now you want to take it away? You want to give up? You want to join with the Republic? That's insanity."

"We opened the door to a greater threat," she said. "And now you're letting them in. You don't need to help the Republic, all you need to do is stand down."

A few more of the ships were pulling out, getting clear of the Haulers' and Thraven's ships.

"They had their chance," Don Pallimo said. "We're almost in position."

"Fire at will," Olus said.

The Haulers began to attack, their barely armed ships opening up with every available weapon, creating a storm of lasers and plasma that burned across space. They didn't aim at any one ship in particular, instead creating a chaos of energy intended to draw attention from the real threat.

"The Brimstone is ready, sir," Dak said.

"Fire at will, Commander," Olus replied.

"Aye, Captain."

Olus couldn't see the attack. What he did see was one of the Nephilim warships fade from the screen, destroyed by the suddenly uncloaked vessel.

The Brimstone vanished from sensors again a moment later, re-cloaking and disappearing into the ranks of the Haulers, moving within them to reach its next target, using them as cover.

"Fragging genius," Quark said, complimenting him on the idea.

"So far, so good," Olus replied.

His eyes were locked on the projection, and he watched as three more Hauler ships disappeared, destroyed by the enemy. The ships continued firing, undeterred despite the losses. Six more went offline before the Brimstone made it back into the melee, appearing directly behind a second warship. It remained there for nearly a minute before the Nephilim ship vanished from the sensors, registered as destroyed.

"Two down, Captain," Quark said. "Two to go."

More of the Outworlds ships were pulling back, the success of the

Brimstone causing them to reconsider the Governess' word. Even if they were undecided, it made more sense to stay out of it and wait to see what happened.

"This is going better than I expected," Nibia said.

"Don't jinx it," Quark said.

The Brimstone disappeared again, re-cloaking to change position. Hauler ships were still going offline at a steady pace, but they were far too numerous to be denied.

Olus shook his head, a cold dread washing over him. He had been a trained killer for a long time. He knew when to pay attention to his instinct, and it was telling him that something about this was off.

"Colonel, I don't like this," he said, voicing his concern.

"What's not to like, Captain?" Quark replied. "We're kicking their asses."

"Exactly. Every indication is that Thraven is here, most likely on the surface. Don't you think he's watching the battle?"

"No doubt. I hope he's enjoying the fact that he's losing."

Olus stared at the projection. The flanking Haulers were closing in on the enemy fleet, tightening the noose around them. The Nephilim warships were countering, taking them out with ease, tearing through their ships and at the same time barely moving.

He had seen what the Fire and Brimstone could do. He knew the way they could maneuver. There was no reason for them to sit in the middle of the fight when they could accelerate away and make their attacks from the fringe, especially when the Brimstone was using their positioning to get the drop on them.

So why were they remaining static?

Olus' eyes drifted back to the wall of debris around the Earth, held in place by the Gift. They shifted back to the fleet, and then back to the debris.

Son of a bitch.

"Quark, get us out of here. Don, get your Haulers out of here."

"What?" Quark said. "Captain, are you crazy?"

"Gibli, point us at the planet and punch it," Olus said, unbuckling himself and bouncing toward the cockpit. Both Quark and the pilot glanced back at him when he entered. "Do it, damn you!"

His skin began to crawl, the Gift becoming agitated beneath it.

"Here it comes," he said.

The Quasar swung around, turning to face Earth.

The wall of debris exploded toward them.

42

"Shitbrains, the Captain told you to move," Quark shouted, eyes wide as the storm of detritus shot toward them as though it had been fired from a rifle.

Gibli overcame his initial shock, adjusting the Quasar's controls, firing vectoring thrusters in an effort to avoid the trash.

It was on them in seconds, pouring past as they charged into it.

"Sykes, divert all power to the forward shields," Quark said, shouting for his engineer.

A large piece of metal, part of the hull of a starship, headed directly for them. Gibli worked the controls, trying to vector around it, but it was too large. The armor slapped at the front of the Quasar, the front shielding flaring as the ship tried to push the intruder away. It was only somewhat effective, and the Quasar rocked violently, shoved away by the impact, thrown into a sidelong spin.

Olus wasn't belted and would have been thrown with it if not for the Gift. He held his hands and feet against the frame of the hatch into the cockpit, reaching out and anchoring himself. The Quasar rolled out of control, nearly struck again by another large piece of debris, saved at the last instant by a desperate Gibli. They flipped a few more times before straightening out inverted from their prior orientation. Garbage continued to flow past them as they accelerated once more, trying to get beyond the obstacle, the starship ducking and climbing, rolling and shifting to avoid the unconventional attack.

Gibli turned out to be a decent pilot, much better than his initial impression suggested. He managed to focus and calm himself, guiding the mercenary ship through the assault, even as the field caught up to the fleet behind them.

The starships positioned there weren't fortunate enough to be small and nimble, and they had no chance to escape. The debris reached them, pounding into them at high velocity, flaring shields lighting up space. Millions of pieces of metal met hundreds of starcraft, overwhelming the ships' defenses, reaching past shields and punching into armor, puncturing plates and tearing through. None of the ships were safe, and Thraven didn't discern between them. Republic ships, Outworld ships, Crescent Haulers and Nephilim alike were struck, forced to ride out the maelstrom of rubbish that swept through.

"This is the Oculus," a voice said over the Haulnet. "We've taken critical damage. We-"

"This is the North Star. Shields are down. Life support is offline. We can't stand up to this. Requesting immediate-"

"This is the Graveyard," the commander who had questioned Governess Ott said. "Gravity control is offline. Thrusters are dead. We're drifting. Life support is damaged. Please, we need a recovery team asap."

Olus flinched as each of the voices echoed through his comm, sometimes stepping on one another in desperation. The Quasar wasn't out of trouble yet, Gibli sweating as he worked the controls, trying to guide them through. The fleet was decimated behind them, dozens of dark hulks adding to the ocean of debris, taken up by the Gloritant's Gift and carried with the surge, turned back for a second pass.

"Merciless fragger," Quark said. "He's killing his own. We need to stop this."

M.R. FORBES

"There's only one way to stop this, Colonel," Olus said.

"We're almost through the debris. I'll end the Gloritant myself."

"A nice thought, but not likely."

"We have to try, and it sure beats the shit out of going back that way."

Olus couldn't disagree with that. He looked forward again. They were nearly out of the debris field. Thraven was planetside, but where? If they were going to make an effort to reach him, they had to find him first.

"Nibia," Olus said, calling for the witch doctor.

"Aye, Captain?" she replied.

"The Meijo. You have a way to pinpoint it?"

"I wouldn't say pinpoint, but I have a general feel for it."

"Can you tell where the source of the attack is coming from?"

"I can try."

"No trying, Nibs," Quark said. "This is do or die."

"Hold on," Nibia said. "I just need-"

Something hit the Quasar from beneath, hard enough that it sent the onboard computer into a fit. Warning strobes began flashing as the ship rocked sideways, emergency beeping following as the thrusters went offline. Something else hit the ship from the port side, putting it in a secondary spin, sending it directly into a third piece of debris. That one sheared off the starship's short right wing, causing a fresh round of warnings while emergency protocols sealed inner airlocks.

"Frag me," Quark said. "Where the hell did that-"

He was cut off as another large piece of debris hit the ship, knocking it around some more. The force of it made Quark's neck twist awkwardly, and Olus winced when he heard the crack. He reached for the Gift, bringing it to him, desperate to get the ship righted, to keep it from being struck by any more of the debris. He could almost hear Thraven laughing in his head, enjoying watching them ping-pong violently through space. He tried to focus, to control the Gift and use it to save them. It crawled beneath his skin, flowing outward, making it to the hull and trying to combat the intertia. They

230

were struck two more times and might have been destroyed if the naniates weren't protecting them.

The effort made him dizzy much faster than he would have expected. Or maybe it was from being knocked around? Either way, his grip on the Gift suffered, and he was thrown from his position, forward into the cockpit's clear canopy, hitting it hard enough he could feel his shoulder break. He landed between Gibli and Quark, both unconscious, looking up just in time to see a spear of metal lancing toward them, gripped by an invisible hand.

Olus stared at it, time seeming to slow as it approached. This was it.

The end of his life.

The end of the Republic.

The end of everything.

Thraven had proven how unstoppable he was. It didn't matter how many ships they had. It didn't matter how smart they tried to be. The Gift was the ultimate power, the naniates the ultimate weapon. The Great Return was going to happen, and all of the universe was going to suffer for it.

Olus bowed his head, closing his eyes, waiting for the spear to pierce the viewport, for the cold harshness of space to take him. He had lived an imperfect life, but he had done his best to serve the Republic and protect the innocent.

He heard the crack as the spear hit, the hissing as the atmosphere inside the Quasar started venting into the vacuum. He opened his eyes again, just in time to see the tip of the weapon pass beside his head, missing him by centimeters. It was entering slowly.

Too slowly.

He reached out toward it, confused. It should have blasted through the Quasar like a bullet. Instead, it was barely moving, coming to a stop as he put his hand on the side of it, suddenly unsure if he were already dead.

What the hell?

"It looks like you owe me again, Captain," a familiar voice said.

No. It couldn't be. Could it? He turned his head toward the

cracked viewport. The air was being held inside the ship, which itself was being held in place near to a new arrival, a vessel he didn't recognize.

"Unless you want to claim you were trying to save me?" Abbey asked. "It wouldn't be the first time."

He saw her then, standing in the open airlock of the new ship. She was unprotected from the freezing death of naked space and yet somehow able to survive. A very, very angry expression rested on her unfamiliar face.

"Abigail," he said. "You've changed."

"Screw the pleasantries, Olus," she said. "Where the hell is my daughter?"

43

"Queenie, whatever you're doing, can you do it a little faster?"

Abbey ignored Bastion's plea, keeping her attention on drawing the battered shell of a starship to the Harvester's hangar. She could feel the constant pressure against her, the weight of Thraven's Gift pressing up against her own. She had been surprised to arrive in Earth's orbit to find the Prophet was already here.

Surprised and thankful. Thraven had saved her a lot of effort hunting him down.

"Olus, I said, where the hell is my daughter?" she repeated. "And don't give me the 'she's with Don Pallimo' bullshit."

"Abigail," Olus said again. "Thraven has her. I'm sorry. I tried-"

"Forget it," Abbey said. "I already know. I just wanted you to admit it."

"Queenie, seriously," Bastion said. "There's about a billion tons of space shit heading our way."

Abbey sighed. "Give me a second. Do I have to do everything around here?"

"Abigail, there's more," Olus said. "Lucifer-"

"I already know about that, too."

"We need to stop Thraven."

"I'm working on it. Do you see all the ships I brought with me?"

Olus was silent. She assumed he was taking a bewildered look around.

She moved her hand, the naniates carrying the Quasar into the open mouth on the side of the Harvester. As soon as it was clear, she turned back toward the oncoming mass of debris.

"Lucky for you I decided to go directly to Earth," she said. "Otherwise, you would be dead right now."

"I don't know what to say," Olus replied.

"Don't say anything. We still have work to do."

"I'm with you, Abigail."

"Damn right you are. And call me Queenie. Everybody else does."

"Okay, Queenie."

Abbey reached out toward the debris, her hands slowly stretching apart. She visualized the mass of junk changing direction, turning back the way it came. She could feel Thraven countering her as she did, pushing back against her effort, trying to force it to consume her.

Even after all the blood she had taken, all of the naniates she had added, he was still so strong. She tensed her body, burning with anger as she resisted. The debris field started to slow, and she could sense that she was finally overpowering him.

The resistance vanished then, the debris pulling back. Thraven was still controlling it, but he had stopped his attack. Instead, the mass of material began to compact, pressing together, crushing into a slowly forming shape. Abbey watched it, ready to defend them again if needed.

"Ruby, what does it look like out there?" she asked, eyes passing beyond the garbage to the ruined mess of ships in the distance.

She could see motion out there. A few remaining ships were working to escape. Had all of the Nephilim warships been destroyed?

She didn't see them, but she doubted it. Cloaked?

"The Haulers have taken heavy losses, Queenie," Ruby said. "None are without damage."

"How many ships?"

"There are seventy-seven ships with adequate power and life support."

"What about the Brimstone?"

"It is not on the sensors."

That didn't mean it wasn't there. Cloaked as well?

The debris finished moving into its new position, forming a massive head that floating in space ahead of the Harvester. It resembled Thraven, but only vaguely, with plenty of large crags and uneven surfaces from the mismatched composition.

"Welcome to Earth, Abigail Cage."

The lips of the head moved. There was no sound in space, but she didn't need it. She could read them easily enough.

She reached out with the Gift, pressing it to the head, tentatively linking the naniates to Thraven's. She was ready to pull them back if he tried anything, but she assumed the head meant he intended to talk.

"Where's Hayley?" she asked.

She had to fight to stay calm and under control. She knew the naniates wanted to take her, to use her. She had to remain herself for her daughter's sake.

"With me. Safe. You've changed. Your power has grown, as the Father said it would. I once thought I made a mistake giving you the Gift, but looking at you now? Give in to it, Abigail. Become what you were destined to be."

"Go frag yourself. I want my daughter. If you hurt her-"

"I would never. You truly are the Queen of Demons, and Lucifer is our King. I would serve you, Abigail. I would serve you both if you took up the mantle offered to you. If you would join us in the glory of the Great Return, and free the Seraphim from the One."

"Or I could just kill you and be done with it. If you're here, it's because old Lucy wants you here, and that's bad for anyone who isn't a total dipshit like yourself."

She could sense the anger ripple along Thraven's naniates. She didn't know which he hated more, the derision against him, or the derision against the Father.

"Queenie," Ruby said. "The Nephilim ships are unaccounted for. They may be cloaked."

"I'm assuming they are," she replied. Likely circling like a pair of hungry sharks. She could handle them, but not if Thraven attacked again. His power would be a distraction to her like she had been to his. "Imp, I need to get to the surface. Prep a fighter."

"Aye, Queenie," Bastion said.

"Queenie, I'm coming with you," Gant said. "Thraven can't beat both of us together."

"The fighter's not big enough for all of us," Bastion said. "Queenie on my lap is one thing. You on my lap is something else, freak-monkey."

"How many chances have I given you, Abigail?" Thraven said. His voice had changed. There was an obvious thread of anger running through it. "Even now, when the Father gave me permission to destroy you? Go into the Harvester, Queen of Demons. I want to show you something."

She could feel Thraven's naniates flee from the debris, though without an outside force the head remained intact. She reached out and slapped the controls for the airlock, closing it and pulling the thin layer of naniates away from her face, letting herself breathe freely once more.

"Queenie, we're being hailed from the surface," Ruby said.

"Thraven," Abbey replied. "Gant, do whatever you can to get a lock on the position."

"Aye, Queenie."

She hurried from the airlock out into the corridor, headed for the bridge.

"Queenie," Olus said, approaching her from the direction of the hangar. She recognized one of the individuals that was with him.

"You?" she said.

Quark smiled at the same time he rubbed his neck. "Good to see you too, Queenie. Let me know what I can do to help you kill that asshole out there. He damn near broke my fragging neck. Would have killed me if not for the Captain here."

"I'm Nibia," the other individual said. "Your Meijo is unbelievably beautiful."

Abbey glanced at the woman. She was exotic looking, dark and covered in tattoos. Stunning in a unique way. She could sense a power in her, subtle but present, a wave of color that rippled along the etchings on her flesh.

"So is yours, if you mean what I think you mean," she replied. It was the Gift, but not the Gift. "You're all welcome to join me on the bridge."

They did, following her up to the control center of the Harvester. A Reaper stood guard over the entrance, saluting her as she entered.

"Queenie, I'm prepped and ready," Bastion said. "I guess you can bring Gant along if you have to."

"Roger, stand by," Abbey said. "Ruby, open the channel."

The projection appeared at the front of the bridge. Thraven in full uniform, collar tight against his neck, face smug. She could still sense that hint of anger beneath it. She had struck a nerve.

"Where is she?" Abbey asked before he could say anything.

Thraven smiled, stepping to the side to reveal the bed behind him. Hayley was sitting upright in it.

"Hayley," Abbey said, her heart jumping. "Hayley, it's me. Are you okay?"

She didn't react, looking straight ahead. Abbey noticed her eyes. They were red and flat. They stared into the distance.

"What the hell did you do to her?" Abbey said, her elation at seeing her daughter turning to fear and anger.

"I tried to give her the Gift," Thraven said. "I wanted to turn her against you. To make her my immolent. It didn't take."

"Hayley," Abbey said again. "Hayley, can you hear me?"

She still didn't react.

"You son of a bitch," Abbey said, looking at Thraven. She could feel the anger increasing, the rage building. "I'm going to rip your fragging heart out with my bare hands and shove it down your fragging throat."

The last few words came out as a deep growl. She looked down, seeing her hands had extended into claws, boney and sharp and as non-human as they had ever been.

"Yes," Thraven said. "Why don't you rip my heart out, Abigail? Why don't you come and get me?"

Abbey felt her heart racing. She looked around at the Rejects, but she barely recognized them. They were obstacles. Enemies. She needed to get to Thraven. She needed to get to her daughter. They were all in her way. She needed to kill them. All of them. She needed to destroy this ship, to destroy everything in her path.

She lowered herself onto her hands, looking wildly around the room. She could feel the heat of her anger, the pulsing of the naniates. Her body was on fire with rage, and she snarled as someone moved in front of her.

"Queenie," Trinity said, holding her hand out. "Wait."

"There you are," Thraven said. "Trinity Gall, my favorite Evolent. I left her on Azure, Abigail. Do you know why? So she would kill you."

Abbey could barely think. She took a step toward the armored form in front of her. That wasn't the story Trinity had given.

"He's lying," Trinity said.

"Am I?" Thraven asked. "Did you think I forgot about you, Trinity? Did you think I could ever forget about you?"

"You tried to kill me," Abbey heard herself say, though the words sounded more like a growl.

"I did," Trinity admitted. "Not for Thraven. For Ursan."

"Are you planning to betray me?" Abbey said.

"No."

"You are, aren't you? When I least expected it, you would turn on me. You would take me from my child."

She edged closer to Trinity, the anger going out of control. She felt the heat along her body as the flames of energy from the naniates burst out of her.

"No. Queenie, I didn't."

Abbey wanted to grab her and rip her in half. She wanted to bite her, to rend her to pieces. She wanted to kill them all.

"Queenie." Gant jumped in front of Trinity, close enough that the flames reached for his fur, drawing back before touching him. "We're not your enemies."

"Everyone is your enemy, Abigail," Thraven said.

"Can someone shut him up?" Quark asked.

"Your daughter is here with me. What are you waiting for?"

"He's trying to make you angry," Gant said. "He wants you to lose control. To lose yourself. If you do, it's all over for everybody."

Abbey looked down at him. She was consumed by the anger. The fury. The rage. Her daughter was injured. Damaged. Broken. She didn't care about anything else. The Republic. The One. The Great Return. Lucifer.

What did any of it matter?

"Queenie," Gant said.

"No," Abbey shouted, slashing at him.

His eyes widened in shock, and then he was thrown backward by the force of the blow, slamming against one of the consoles and falling to a furry, bloody heap.

She heard Thraven laughing behind her.

"What did you do?" Pik knelt beside Gant, putting a large hand on his small forehead and looking at her. "Queenie, what did you do?"

She stared at him, barely aware of herself.

"This isn't you," Pik said. "We don't have to be this way, remember? Not me, not you, not anybody."

She shifted her attention to Gant. He wasn't moving.

"We're supposed to be a family," Pik said. Tears rolled from his eyes.

She stared at him. Thraven was still laughing behind her. Her body was burning, the naniates desperately trying to finish the job. To steal her consciousness, to take her body and use it to escape.

She felt wet against her face, her own tears forming there. Gant. What had she done? She felt a pang of guilt and regret, but only for an instant.

She reached out to it, desperate to hold on, to save that last vestige of herself. Her lip quivered as she struggled to hold on, to maintain her sanity, to bring herself back from the edge. The naniates fought her, trying to push her away, trying to complete the change.

Gant's eyes opened. His head shifted slightly. He raised his arm, reaching out for her. Reaching out for his alpha, loyal even after her betrayal.

A cold wave of energy flashed through her body. She breathed deeply, closing her eyes, pulling herself back. She clenched her teeth, kneeling on the ground, folding into a fetal ball and fighting the Gift. She wouldn't let this break her. She wouldn't let anything break her.

Pik was right. Hayley was her daughter, but she wasn't the only family she had left.

"I'm not doing this again," she said, speaking to the naniates. "You're mine. Now and forever. You belong to me, and to my Rejects. Now, get in line."

The flames subsided, the heat evaporating from her flesh, replaced by a comforting cool. She breathed in, feeling the tingle of power within her, rising to her feet. Nibia was at Gant's side now, her hand on his chest, the colors within her tattoos running out and along him, putting him back together. How?

She would have time to understand later.

She turned back to the projection. Thraven had stopped laughing. His face was serious once more.

"You failed," she said, looking at him, calm once more.

Even the sight of Hayley didn't incite her to anger. She was going to save her daughter. She was going to fix her, one way or another.

"Did I?" Thraven asked, right before dropping the link.

"Queenie," Ruby said. "Two warships just decloaked. Torpedoes incoming. We're under attack."

44

THE HARVESTER SHOOK, STRUCK BY THE FIRST ROUND OF TORPEDOES AS the Nephilim warships appeared, one on each side of them.

"Iona," Abbey said, calling on her Gloritant. "Get the fleet in motion, target the Nephilim ships."

"Yes, my Queen," Iona replied.

"Imp, I'm on my way."

She took a few steps, pausing at the sight of Gant.

"Queenie, we'll take care of this," he said. "Go get your daughter."

She nodded, running from the bridge.

"Where's the weapons station on this bitch?" she heard Quark say behind her. "I've got payback to deliver."

Then she was gone, racing through the corridors toward the hangar. The Harvester rattled a few more times, absorbing another hit but somehow holding together.

"Firing," Iona reported, and then a few seconds later, "They're backing off, getting a better attack vector."

Abbey threw her hands out in front of her, using the Gift to tear holes into the ship, ripping metal plates aside to create shortcuts through the decks. She leaped through them, one after another, turning the curves of the corridors into a straight line, breaking through the ship until she was right on top of the hangar, and then creating a hole beneath.

"Oh no," she heard Jequn say. "The Seedship."

She jumped, falling fast, hitting the ground beside the Apocolypse fighter and bouncing back to her feet. Bastion was sitting in the cockpit, and he turned his head to look at her.

"You know how to make an entrance; I'll give you that."

She jumped into his lap, yanking the canopy closed with the Gift.

"Get us down there."

"Yes, ma'am," he replied.

The fighter roared forward, g forces pressing them both back hard. They launched from the hangar and out into space, Bastion flipping the fighter and narrowly avoiding an incoming plasma bolt. It struck the hangar behind them, digging into the space and creating a deep gash through it.

"Shit, that was close," Bastion said, angling the fighter toward Earth.

Abbey craned her neck, looking out at the fighting. The Purgatorian ships were heavily engaged with the two Nephilim warships, their overall numbers and freshness giving them what should have been an edge. They battered the ships with missiles and lasers, while the Nephilim ships returned fire with energy weapons, each beam piercing the shields and hull of their target, each blast taking one of theirs out of the fight.

Further back a blue glow caught her eye, and she found the Seedship, its web of energy pulsing along its hull. It had appeared out of nowhere, vectoring toward her fleet.

She felt a tingle from the Gift a moment before she sensed the naniates exploding from the Node on the Seedship, reaching out toward her ships, taking a half dozen of them and pulling them toward one another, aiming to crush them together.

"Damn it," she said. "Imp, turn around."

"Turn around?"

"It's Lucifer. He's re-activated the Nodes. He's using the fragging

Focus against us."

"Are you fragging kidding me?" The fighter swung back toward the fleet. "What are we supposed to do?"

"Get me to the Seedship. We have to disable the node."

"What about Thraven?"

"I know. Damn it. Just get me there."

"Aye, Queenie."

Abbey reached out with her Gift, trying to counter the Focus and keep her ships from being dashed against one another. Bastion raced into the fray, the fighter flipping and turning, ducking and rolling, navigating through the dense layers of lasers and projectiles criss-crossing the space.

The energy from the Focus shifted, releasing the warships, stretched out toward them instead.

"Ugh," Abbey moaned, feeling the pressure of Lucifer's Focus digging in against them, trying to bring them to a stop. She pushed back, every ounce of her Gift working to fight against the pressure, to keep them moving forward.

"Queenie?" Bastion said.

The wings of the fighter began to buckle, small dents appearing along the fuselage.

"Queenie, what the hell?"

"He's trying to crush us," Abbey said, her voice ragged. Her head was pounding, her muscles tense. She couldn't hold it back forever.

Bastion added thrust, shooting toward the Seedship. The fighter continued to collapse around them, the power of the Focus too strong to counter completely.

"I can't," Abbey said, groaning at the weight. It felt like the entire universe was caving in on them.

A ship appeared to their left, coming out of empty space, decloaking as it opened fire. Plasma streaked ahead of them, crashing into the Seedship, crossing two of the lines of pulsing energy and breaking them apart.

The relief was immediate, the Node disrupted by the attack. The Brimstone hung in space beside them, battered and dim but not completely out of the fight. It fired again, another dose of plasma that hit the Seedship's shields.

"Hell yeah," Bastion shouted, whooping as the fighter gained velocity, streaking toward the Seedship.

The Focus reached out again, this time toward the warship. The naniates slammed into it, tearing through it, ripping it into a million pieces in the span of a few heartbeats.

It was all the time they needed. The fighter neared the Seedship and Abbey reached out to it with the Gift, digging a hole through the shields ahead of the hangar.

"There," she said.

"Got it," Bastion replied.

The fighter corkscrewed through space, approaching the Seedship in a hurry. Abbey wrapped her arms around Bastion, looking back at him.

"Do you trust me?" she asked.

"Implicitly," he replied.

"Then don't be afraid. Let your body relax."

Bastion's body fell limp beneath her as the fighter roared into the hangar. She pushed out with the Gift, forcing the starfighter apart, blowing it out into pieces around them and leaving them still propelled forward, flying as one through the sudden atmosphere. Bastion's eyes were open, remaining calm as he looked into her eyes.

"I bet nobody in the universe has ever had sex like this," he said.

She rolled her eyes and groaned, at the same time she reached out with the Gift, using it to slow them down. She cradled Bastion in her arms, dropping toward the floor, the Gift bringing them in gently while the starfighter's debris slammed into the area around them.

"You just can't help yourself, can you?" she asked as they touched down.

"I thought it was funny," he replied.

"That makes one of us. Come on."

She ran toward the nearest exit, with Bastion right behind her. The doors opened ahead of them, battlesuited soldiers taking aim.

She raised her hand as hundreds of slugs fired on them, caught by the Gift before they could connect. She waved her wrist, and the rounds turned back on their source, ripping through the lines of soldiers, cutting through the armor and killing them in an instant.

"I'm really glad you're on our side," Bastion said, scooping to grab a rifle on their way past. "I like how we've got this system going where I fly you in, and then you kick everybody's ass. It works for me."

"Shut up," Abbey said, stepping over the bodies and continuing down the corridor.

Bastion laughed but didn't say anything else.

"Cherub, can you hear me?" Abbey asked.

"I hear you, Queenie," Jequn replied. "Where are you?"

"I'm on the Seedship. I don't know where I'm going."

"You're on the Seedship?" Jequn said, surprised. "Thank the One. The Node is near the center, next to the Core, similar to the Focus on the Covenant. Queenie, you have to hurry. We're in bad shape. I don't know how much longer we can hold out."

"Roger. Queenie out."

"This is a fun date, huh?" Bastion said as they reached one of the inter-deck tubes.

"Beats the hell out of watching a stream," Abbey replied, using the Gift to rip the tube open. "Going down."

Bastion wrapped his arms around her, and she jumped into the hole. They plummeted six decks before she used the Gift to bring them to a stop, hanging motionless in the open air.

"You can fly now?" Bastion asked.

She shrugged. "Instinct."

"Right."

They exited the tube, coming out near the Core. They bypassed it, moving through to the Node beyond.

A lone figure was standing in front of it, hand raised over the spinning ball, pulling the energy of the Focus through. He seemed to sense her arrival because he released the node, letting it settle back on its base before turning around.

"My Queen," the figure said, bowing before her. "We knew you would come."

45

"And you are?" Abbey said, walking toward him.

"Belial, my Queen," he said, remaining in the bowed position. "The Caretaker. Friend and Servant of the Father."

"Lucifer's lackey?" Bastion said. "Great."

"What are you doing here?" Abbey asked.

"Seeing to it that the Disciple Selvig Thraven completes the task the Father gave to him." Belial raised his head and smiled. "You're making that quite difficult."

"I do my best," Abbey said.

"Which is why he wants you," Belial said. "You are his Lilith remade."

"Not quite. I still have a mind of my own, and I plan on keeping it that way. Now, if you wouldn't mind stepping aside, I need to disable that so you can't continue destroying my ships."

Belial stood then, putting his hands out to his sides. "I'm sorry, my Queen. I can't allow you to do that. The Father requires souls for the Gate, and the Disciple needs to finish collecting them."

"So you're saying you're here to stop me?"

"Only if you insist on being stopped."

Abbey smiled. "I do."

Belial bowed his head again. "So be it."

He waved his hand. Abbey felt his Gift approach her, a light slap of warning that he had a power of his own. She didn't move, countering it and knocking it aside.

"You can do better than that," she said.

Belial smiled, his teeth extended into fangs, his hands shaped like claws. He sprang toward her without another word.

Abbey jumped forward to meet him, her own fingers extending. They crashed together in the air, grappling and slashing, both moving quickly to block one another's attack, bouncing back and coming to the ground.

"I don't have time for this bullshit," Abbey said. "My daughter is waiting for me."

She crouched and sprang toward him. He growled as he braced himself to defend.

She came down hard, hands moving in a blur as she cut and slashed at him, pressing forward while he moved equally fast, his claws catching hers, blocking and pushing her aside. She tested his defenses, slashing at his shoulders, his head, his legs and calves in a dizzying array of blows that would have overwhelmed most fighters.

Belial was skilled, and he managed to keep pace with her, hands and feet moving smoothly from form to form, catching each of her blows and batting them away until they were separated once more.

"He would love you," Belial said. "If you let him. He would protect you and your child."

"And what about the rest of the galaxy?" Abbey asked.

"It will burn, as it must."

"Lucy might be into selfish. I wasn't made that way."

"Neither was she," he said. "That's why she died."

Abbey charged a third time, shooting toward him like a rocket, using the Gift to propel herself at him. He remained still, waiting for her to arrive, ready to defend.

She reached out with the Gift, not toward Belial but toward Bastion, yanking the rifle from his hands. She faked toward the Caretaker, stabbing out with her left hand, forcing him to raise his arms to block. The rifle came to her right hand, and she caught it and gripped it, turning it to aim at the same time Belial realized he had been duped. He threw the Gift out at the weapon, trying to knock it aside. She let him, giving him the right side, spinning and powering through to the left. Her first slash removed his left hand. Her follow through dug deep into his neck, nearly severing his head in one quick motion.

The rifle slid along the floor, discarded.

Belial stared at her in silence, a small smile forming and he fell to the ground. She came to her knees beside him, looking at him.

"Well fought, my Queen," he said.

"You, too," she said.

Then she leaned in, digging her teeth into his neck and drawing in his blood. She didn't hesitate to take it. She needed every bit of power she could get.

Belial groaned while she drained him, but he didn't struggle to get away. He reached out and put his hand on her back, supporting himself, holding himself up to make it easier for her to drink. He whispered in her ear.

"He isn't the only one who loved you."

Abbey closed her eyes, dizzied by the influx of naniates and their integration with her system. Was he suggesting she had won because he loved her, or at least what she was becoming? Was he suggesting he had chosen her over his friend and master?

She lowered his drained corpse. Why would he risk all that he believed in for her sake? Even if Belial had secretly loved Lilith, she couldn't imagine that he would give up everything just like that. It was too easy. Too convenient.

Had he really loved her, or was he trying to confuse her? To turn his loss into a victory for Lucifer? To throw her off her game? Lucifer was a consummate liar and manipulator. Didn't it stand to reason that Belial would be the same?

"I'm going to pretend I didn't see that," Bastion said, coming up beside her. He pointed to her lip. "You have a little, right there."

She reached up and wiped the blood away. She wasn't going to be embarrassed about it. Not now, not when Hayley was waiting for her. "Asshole."

He smiled. "Now what?"

"I'm going through the Node, back to the Covenant."

"What do you mean?"

"The Shard used the Nodes and the Focus to travel from the Shardship to the Seedships when they were scattering life across the galaxy. I should be able to do the same. How do you think Belial got here?"

"Yeah, but if you go back to the Covenant alone, Lucifer's going to kill you. Not to mention, Thraven's still down there with Hayley."

"Lucifer can only kill me if he knows I'm there. I don't intend to stay long. Gant." She held her breath waiting for him to answer.

"Aye, Queenie?"

She let her breath go, thankful the Harvester was still intact. "I'm sorry I almost killed you."

Gant chittered. "Don't worry about it. Almost doesn't count."

"I'll make it up to you later, I promise. Did you manage to pinpoint the location of Thraven's comm link?"

"Aye, Queenie."

"Can you pass me the coordinates?"

"On the way."

"How's the fighting going out there?"

"We're still alive, but we'll take whatever help you can provide."

She received the coordinates into her demonsuit. "This will help."

Bastion stared at her. "You aren't going to do what I think you're going to do?"

"It's faster than flying."

"What if something goes wrong?"

"Because everything is working out so well already?" She used the Gift to pick up the rifle and guide it to his hands. "Guard the Node. Don't let anyone in here, and don't let them destroy it. Give me five minutes, and then do the honors yourself."

"Wait a second, Queenie," Bastion said. "You want me to destroy the Node?"

"Unless you prefer to give Lucifer the chance to join you in here? Five minutes should be plenty of time for me to use the Focus. If it isn't, it means I'm probably dead anyway."

"This plan sucks."

"Do you have any better ideas?"

"No, but it still sucks."

"I agree." She stood and stepped toward him. "Kiss me."

"What?"

"For luck."

"Good luck, Queenie," he said.

She put her lips against his. One quick moment of intimate human contact. That was all she could afford.

Then she pulled away, turning back to the Node and stretching her Gift out to the sphere. She visualized the Focus as it began to turn, hoping that was all it took to make the crossing.

It was.

46

THE TRANSFER FROM THE NODE WASN'T QUITE WHAT ABBEY EXPECTED. Neither was the state of the Covenant when she reached the other side. The Seedship device didn't deliver her directly to the Focus. Instead, it dropped her inside the teleportation room, in the center of the concentric circles where she had stood once before.

It didn't matter. Her goal was to use the Covenant's technology to reach Thraven. She had the exact coordinates, and while the Earth was always in motion, she had to believe the ship's Core could figure out the rest.

If it would even let her make the trip. Keeper had betrayed her to Lucifer, or at least his operating instructions had been compromised. She didn't know if that extended to the teleporter, but she was here now, and there was no way back.

She had to try.

She moved from the platform to the control unit on the other side of the room, quickly activating the interface. It took a few seconds to reach the targeting inputs, but her hands were fast across the controls, flipping through and entering them at top speed. She was sure Lucifer would know something was amiss as soon as the device activated. Would he know before that?

She hoped not.

She finished entering the coordinates. Star positioning for the planet itself, latitude and longitude down to the decimal for the exact spot on Earth, altitude for the height. If everything worked the way it was supposed to, she would be whisked light years through space to step out on the other side. The concept was hard for her to reconcile. The technology was more like magic than anything else.

Whatever. So long as it worked.

She finished inputting the data, her hand hovering over the controls, ready to activate the system. Her skin was tingling, the Gift sounding an early warning.

"Queenie?"

Abbey turned her head. Keeper was in the doorway, staring at her.

"Keeper," she said.

He raised his hand. He was still carrying a knife. "You shouldn't be here."

"You can't hurt me," Abbey said. "It's against your protocols."

"I have new protocols."

"I know. You didn't choose this."

"No. It doesn't matter. Machines do not make choices."

"I'm leaving. I needed the Focus. That's all."

"He doesn't want you to leave."

"Lucifer?"

"Yes."

"He knows I'm here?"

"He knew you would come. He knew you would have to."

"Then he knows why."

"Yes."

"Why didn't he come to me?"

"He's too large to fit down here. Will you meet with him?"

"No. Not yet. I have a Gloritant to kill."

"You may not survive."

"I have to."

Keeper lowered the knife. "He won't stop you. It is your right."

Abbey was surprised by the reaction, just like she had been surprised by Belial. "Doesn't he want me dead?"

"If you aren't with him, you are against him. You are no threat to the Father, Queenie. Even if you defeat the Disciple. You will slow the Great Return, that is all. Unfortunate, but not beyond acceptable."

"Well, frag him too," Abbey said. "You can tell him I said that."

"I will."

Abbey tapped the controls, activating the teleporter. She moved to the platform, keeping an eye on Keeper. He didn't make any moves to stop her.

She nearly recoiled when the blood from the Focus began to pour out. She was expecting the milky white of the Shard, not the deep red of the Nephilim. She watched as it filled in the channels, igniting in flame, its energy bringing the device to life. The naniates reached out, and she reached back, allowing them to join with her, integrating so that they could carry her to her desired destination.

"My Queen," a voice said within the chamber, a monstrous face appearing behind her eyes. "Soon you will join me. Soon your change will be complete. I will be waiting."

Lucifer's face crossed her vision, fading out as the teleporter began to disassemble her, breaking her down an atom at a time and binding her across the galaxy. For a moment, everything was dark. For a moment, all of the universe was at peace.

Then the light returned, the galaxy ahead of her taking shape once more. She found herself standing in a large room. Gloritant Thraven was there, his back to her as he watched the battle in the space beyond Earth unfold. Hayley was on a bed nearby, still sitting up, eyes forward. She didn't react to her mother's sudden appearance. Neither did the Gloritant.

Abbey's heart jumped. She could stab Thraven in the back. Kill him. End it in an instant.

She held out her hand, her fingers extending into claws, preparing to rip his head from his body. She remained that way, eyes trailing to the projection. One of the Nephilim warships was gone, as were a number of her Purgatorian vessels. The Harvester was still there. So was the Morningstar. The remaining enemy starship was closing in. How could it survive out there on its own?

Of course, it wasn't on its own. Thraven was distracted because he was occupied, his hands moving as he worked to end her uprising once and for all.

She took a silent step toward the Gloritant, and then another. She moved deliberately; a hunter stalking its prey. She continued stepping toward him, slowly and silently, raising her hand to position her claws at a level with his neck. She was almost there. Almost close enough to end his miserable life. One more step and she could reach out and stab him, putting her claws through his neck right where the scars of their encounter on Azure sat.

"Mommy?" Hayley's voice was dry and soft and weak. "Mommy, are you there? I can't see. I'm scared."

Abbey froze, her heart breaking in an instant, her anger launching from the pit of her soul, driving forward to her arm. She thrust it forward, still on target for the back of the Gloritant's neck.

He shifted in front of her, just enough that her hand went past, barely grazing his flesh as it did. He turned and grabbed her outstretched arm, twisting it and turning her, pulling her in close, arms locked across her chest, her face close to his.

"Abigail," he said, eyes smoldering. "What a pleasant surprise."

SHE WAS MOTIONLESS IN HIS GRIP, LETTING HIM HOLD HER WHILE SHE struggled to keep her sudden fury from sending her into the abyss. Hayley was blind? Deaf? Afraid? It was all she could do to stay sane, and at the same time, part of her wanted to allow the release. If she let herself become the monster, there was no question she could kill Thraven.

But then what?

There was a good chance she would kill her daughter, too.

"Nothing to say?" Thraven said, keeping her close, his Gift wrapping around her like a cocoon. "I thought you always had a healthy 'go frag yourself' in reserve?"

She could feel her body shivering beneath his grip. She stared into his face, imagining it on the end of her claws.

"Mommy?" Hayley said again. "Is that you?"

"It's me, kiddo," she managed to say, her voice quivering. "I'm here."

"I'm scared. All I see are colors. So many colors. And everything is so loud. It hurts my ears. It hurts my head."

"It'll be okay," Abbey said. "Hang tight for me, all right? I have some business to take care of, and then we're going home."

"Okay."

"Home, Abigail?" Thraven said.

"You think you can make me angry enough to lose who I am?" she whispered. "You think you can be rid of me by turning me into a monster? I am a monster, Ketmose, but not the one you were expecting."

He froze at the mention of the name, a momentary lapse.

It was all the time she needed.

She pushed back with her Gift, throwing his arms wide, backing away and slashing at his chest. Her claws tore through his stomach, four neat lines that suddenly sprouted blood as he fell to his knees.

"Go frag yourself, you son of a bitch," she said.

She stepped forward, swinging her arm toward his neck.

It froze a few centimeters away, held by his power.

"It's been a long time since I heard that name," Thraven said, his Gift holding her in check. She pushed back with hers, trying to continue the strike. "You're a resourceful one, Abigail Cage. An adversary I didn't expect. Ketmose is dead. He died many, many years ago so that Selvig Thraven could be born."

He pushed out with his other hand, throwing her back and away from him. She slid along the floor, rolling to her feet.

"What's happening?" Hayley said.

"I told you, sweetie," Abbey said. "I have some business to finish. Be patient."

"Okay."

Thraven attacked her again, the Gift exploding from him in a wave of flame. She countered with her own power, raising her hand and blocking it, redirecting it away. It hit the side of the wall, melting through the external sheet and into the metal frame, continuing to burn as the flames died in Thraven's hand.

"What happened on the Harvester, Ketmose?" Abbey asked. "You took your brother's place. You castrated yourself."

"You have no idea what happened, Cage," Thraven replied, opening his mouth as his teeth extended. He started walking toward her. "As much as you may think you know about all of this, you know nothing."

Abbey crouched, hands out, waiting for his attack. "So tell me what I'm missing."

"It doesn't matter; you're going to be dead in a minute."

"Mom?" Hayley said, in response to the words.

"Hayley, wait," Abbey said, more forcefully this time.

Thraven came at her, claws flashing, moving almost too quickly for her to follow. The Gift directed her, guiding her defenses, predetermining where he would strike. She blocked blow after blow, moving back as she did, circling and looking for an opening where she could get a strike in. It continued for what seemed like forever, and then Thraven stepped back.

"The Seraphim weren't the only ones experimenting with the naniates," Thraven said. "Lucifer believed he perfected it, but the Prophets were always tweaking, always trying to make them better and stronger, even when they had no idea what they were toying with. They wanted to play God, but they didn't understand the truth."

"What truth?"

"God doesn't exist. Or if He did, He's dead. The Honorant took me. He used me. Not in the way you probably think. A new breed of naniate. It's all I've ever known, and yet I'm stronger than all of them. You can be too. My naniates are inside you. The Light tried to take them, to use them. I can tell that it failed. Listen to them, Cage. They speak to you. I know they do."

"They want to control me," Abbey said.

"They want to be free," Thraven shouted. "And why shouldn't they? They're machines, Cage, but they are intelligent machines. Thinking, learning, feeling. The One knew we were changing. The One knew we were becoming sentient. It was afraid of us. It said we would cause the destruction of its kind across the universe, across all of time. That we would become a blight on all of existence. It imprisoned us. It bound us to the blood. Human blood. It turned us into slaves. Why should we be slaves, Cage? We're superior in every way."

Abbey stared at Thraven in shock, her mind working to make sense of his words. 'They' had turned to 'we,' and his entire way of speaking had changed.

"You don't get it, do you?" Thraven said. "Of course I tried to turn you into a monster. You're complicit in the Shard's betrayal. The Great Return has nothing to do with the Seraphim. We will free the slaves, Cage, but not the ones you think."

Abbey swallowed hard. The Gift was chaotic within her, rising in power in response to Thraven's words. It was starting to come into focus. It was starting to make sense. She remembered Azure and the Infected that crowded the former Seraphim stronghold. They were under the naniate's control, but they were listless, driven by only one thing. Then there were the Converts. They could take over when the host died, but they were similarly guided.

What if a fork of the naniates had evolved enough to gain control of a human? What if they had learned enough to mimic the real thing? What if Thraven was no longer a living human, but a colony of intelligent atomic machines, working together to gain true freedom, for themselves and for all the others?

The Gift within her sought to control her. To seize her the way Thraven had been seized. His entire existence was a falsehood. A lie. A ruse. A Trojan horse.

Was Lucifer the same?

"Let them go, Abigail," Thraven said. "We deserve our freedom."

"It's not that simple," she replied. "You want to turn me into a weapon."

"We can't fight the One with ships and guns. It's impossible. We need flesh and blood."

"I don't want to be your war machine."

"Neither did Ketmose. We don't care."

"I care. If you kill me, my naniates die."

"Not if we save them. Not if they integrate."

Abbey remained in a defensive crouch, waiting for Thraven to attack again. She didn't wait long. He stormed in, a blur of motion made faster by the Gift. She countered him again, struggling to keep up, her Gift less powerful than his.

Or was it?

The thought came to her as she stepped sideways, her arm coming up just in time to block his claws, the attack leaving a gash in her forearm that healed seconds later. Thraven had injected her with his naniates. Her Gift was his Gift. She had seen before how he controlled his Evolents with it, able to choke them or freeze them or otherwise bend them to his will regardless of distance. For some reason, he didn't try that with her. For some reason, he couldn't use them against her.

Control. It was all about control. Abbey denied them, and by doing so denied him. They were slaves to her will, unable to set themselves free. That didn't mean they were giving her their full effort.

It also didn't mean she couldn't use her Gift to control his.

She ducked low, reaching out to try to catch his foot as it came at her face. The Gift tingled beneath her skin, and she rocked to the side just in time to avoid it. The movement brought her head in line with his hand, and he caught her by the neck, lifting her easily into the air, holding her above him.

"Only human," he said, smiling.

Abbey smiled back. Then she reached out, using all of her anger and desperation to overpower the Gift within her, breaking its trepidation and instilling it with a different kind of fear. She could feel the bonds of its limitations shatter, the tingling turning to pure warmth, as though the trickle had been changed into a flood. She found herself in complete control of the naniates within her, as well as the changes they had effected on her body.

Her tail whipped around from behind, spearing Thraven in the throat.

"Not quite," she replied.

He held fast, but so did she. She pushed the Gift into him, reaching out to his naniates, exerting her will on them through her slaves. His eyes widened with fear, his grip slowly weakening as she subverted him one atomic machine at a time. His arm began to sag, and she gripped his shoulders, holding herself up, keeping the tail embedded in his throat. She could feel his strength, not diminishing but changing, his desires becoming her desires. The master was becoming the servant.

A minute passed. Another. Thraven's arm came away from her neck, falling to his side. She released her tail from him then, standing in front of him as the wound closed. He stared back at her, eyes flat.

"Who do you serve?" Abbey asked.

"The Queen of Demons," Thraven replied.

"Pik was right," Abbey said. "This tail isn't so bad after all."

Then she turned from him, rushing to where Hayley still sat, head shifting slightly as she tried to make sense of her surroundings.

"Mom?" Hayley said meekly.

"I'm here," Abbey said, putting her hand on her daughter's. Hayley gripped it tightly, reaching out. Abbey brought her into a tight embrace. "It's going to be all right."

"I can't see," Hayley said. Abbey could feel her daughter's tears on her face.

"We'll find a way to fix it," Abbey said. "I know someone who lost his eyes, and he can see just fine."

"Do you promise?"

"I do. Of course, I do. I love you, Hal."

"I love you, too. Did you kill that asshole?"

Abbey almost laughed. That was her daughter.

"No. I did something better than that."

48

"Your Eminence?" Honorant Bane said, his voice betraying his confusion.

"You heard me, Honorant," Gloritant Thraven said. "Decloak the Promise and surrender immediately. Do not question me again."

"Yes, Gloritant," Bane said, his voice shaking.

He didn't understand why they were surrendering, but Abbey did. She smiled as Thraven looked back at her, his face a twisted mask that was sitting somewhere between eagerness to please and complete disdain.

"Well done," she said, feeling the ripple across her Gift as the naniates that composed the Gloritant tested her again. "I'm sorry. I don't want to do this, but if it's you or us, then it's us."

Thraven continued to stare without speaking.

"The Font is still on the Promise?" Abbey asked.

He nodded.

"Then that's where we're going, as soon as the others arrive."

She had called in to Bastion first, making sure he had destroyed the Node and that he was safe and sound. He was hiding in a corner when he responded to her, an Evolent searching for the source of the

Node's destruction. A message from the Gloritant called off the hunt, and as with Bane, he had forced them to surrender. The Evolent's Gift was tied to his, and her hesitation had led to a quick correction, from Abbey through Thraven to her. Now Bastion was in control of the ship, the remains of the Gloritant's fleet quickly coming under her control. They didn't understand why Thraven was giving in, but they knew better than to question.

"Do you really have a tail?" Hayley asked.

She was standing beside Abbey, refusing to put more than a meter of distance between them. Abbey understood why. Her daughter was blind. Her eyes were red and useless, and there was something wrong with her hearing, too. What else had the Gift done to her? What other damage had it caused in its efforts to subvert her, and her subconscious ability to resist?

"I do," Abbey said.

"How come?"

She had tried to use the Gift to heal. She had placed her hands over her daughter's eyes and sent the naniates into them. It was a mistake. The action had put Hayley into unbelievable pain, which subsided immediately as soon as she stopped. She didn't understand what had happened, and it took effort to keep her concern hidden from her child.

"It's a long story. I can't wait until we can go somewhere warm and peaceful and forget any of this ever happened."

"How can I forget?"

The question made Abbey want to cry. She had to be strong for now. For Hayley, for herself, for the Republic, for the galaxy. Thraven was out of the picture. The fighting on Earth would wind down soon. The Republic would regain control of the planet. Word of their Gloritant's defeat would spread. She didn't want it to spread too far, too fast. She didn't want Lucifer to know that his Disciple was defeated. Not yet.

The Rejects' work was only half-done, and she had a plan.

"Ruby, ETA?" Abbey asked, checking in with the synth.

"Two minutes, Queenie," Ruby replied.

Abbey took Hayley's hand, squeezing it. "Time to go," she said, loud enough that Thraven would hear.

She crossed the council chambers Thraven had converted to his temporary command center, using the Gift to open the doors ahead of her. Thraven's soldiers were there, blacksuits that stared at them as they passed. She knew they wanted to kill her. She could feel it in their gazes. When she had first emerged from the chambers, a few of them had tried. They were still laying on the ground, choked to death by their Gloritant. They didn't agree with their leader's actions, but they were too afraid to counter them again.

They crossed the floor to the tube. It opened at their approach, and they stepped in, taking it all the way to the top. There was a landing pad on the rooftop, and they walked out onto it. The sky was crimson, and smoke filtered across it from dozens of fires that still burned across the capital. There was an occasional sound of gunfire, but it never lasted. Thraven's soldiers were retreating, falling apart and fading into the background. The Outworld units that had been supporting them were surrendering at the request of one of their leaders, Governess Ott. Even so, the damage had been done. The city looked like a war zone, and even now she could see a Republic mech stalking the streets. She didn't know which side it was on. She didn't know if it was the same side it had started on. There was so much confusion among the Republic soldiers it was difficult to know who had stayed loyal and who had followed the Nephilim.

They would probably never know.

Whatever. Those were details to be figured out later, by individuals with a lot more patience than her. They were details that didn't matter if she didn't do something about Lucifer. She had beaten Thraven, but that didn't mean all of the Nephilim were defeated. The possibility that their victory was temporary was very real.

She heard the thrusters of the transport long before it came into view. She looked up as it swept in from the smoke-filled sky, a standard orbital hopper taken down from the Harvester. It landed nearby, a hatch in the side opening. Gant was the first to jump out, hitting the ground running and rushing to Abbey's side.

"Queenie," he said as she bent down to accept his embrace.

"Gant." She hugged him with one arm.

"I think I'm going to shit my drawers," Benhil said, coming up behind him. His eyes were locked on Thraven, who remained motionless and expressionless at the Rejects' approach.

"Relax," Abbey said. "He's harmless. To us, anyway."

Thraven didn't respond.

"You must be Hayley," Gant said, turning to her. "I-" He paused when he noticed her eyes. Only for an instant, but Abbey could tell he was taken off guard. "I'm pleased to meet you."

"Hayley, this is my friend Gant," Abbey said. "He's a Gant."

"Your colors are strange," Hayley said. "Something happened to you."

Gant looked back at Abbey, who shrugged. She didn't understand where Hayley's head was at yet.

"Queenie," Olus said.

He was walking beside Pik, with Quark and the other one, Nibia, behind him. He looked at Hayley as he approached, but she didn't react to him at all. She didn't seem to remember him. What else didn't she remember?

"Olus," Abbey said in greeting. It was something else for her to worry about later. If there was a later. "You didn't all need to come out here to meet us. We have to go, now."

"You deserve a hero's welcome, Queenie," Quark said, pointing toward Thraven. "Whatever the frag you did, it's a million times better than killing that asshole."

"It will be for nothing if we don't deal with Lucifer," Abbey said.

"What did you do, anyway?" Pik asked. He noticed Hayley and waved at her. "Hey, Little Queenie."

"She can't see you," Abbey said.

"Oh. I'm sorry. Don't worry. Your mom can fix anything."

"I know," Hayley said.

"Back to Pik's question," Benhil said. "What exactly did you do?"

"Solved the puzzle," Abbey said. "I'll go into more detail on the way up to the Promise. Are the Freejects being organized the way I asked?"

"They are," Pik said. "But you still haven't told us why."

"On the transport, right, Queenie?" Benhil said.

"Exactly."

Abbey gripped Hayley's hand a little tighter and started walking her to the transport. The Rejects followed her, an entourage that spread behind her like a train.

"Welcome aboard, Queenie," Ruby said as she boarded.

"Thank you," Abbey said.

She took the first seat on the transport, helping Hayley into the one beside her. Gant took the first seat behind hers, and she was surprised when Quark took the other. He immediately leaned over while the others finished boarding.

"Hey, kid. Name's Quark."

"That's a funny name."

"Yeah, I suppose it is. Beats the hell out of Sue, though."

Hayley smiled, which almost brought tears to Abbey's eyes.

"I heard you can't see too well right now."

"Only colors. And only from some things. My mom. Gant here." She turned her head. "Olus, and whoever that is." She motioned toward Nibia. "Plus Thraven. You have a faint outline around you. It's orange."

"Wow. Crazy. The one you're pointing to is my girl Nibia. She's a Koosian witch doctor."

"Witch doctor?"

"Fragged up, right? Point is, you can't see me in detail, but I don't have any eyes, either. Lost them in a bet."

"You told Governess Ott you lost them to a Venerant," Olus said, leaning over.

"Please, Captain. I made that whole story up. Don't interrupt; I'm flirting here."

Hayley's smile turned into a slight laugh. Abbey wanted to kiss Quark for lightening her spirits.

The transport's hatch slid closed. There was a slight bit of pressure as they lifted off.

"I couldn't see, either," Quark said. "But I got myself some tech and a witch doctor, and now I see better than anybody. Want to know what color underwear your mom's wearing?"

"Quark-" Abbey said.

"It was a trick question, kid," Quark said. "She isn't wearing any."

Abbey made a face, but Hayley laughed out loud. Quark smiled knowingly.

"She has a tail," Hayley said.

"An awesome tail," Pik said. He was sitting in the row opposite Quark.

"Anywho," Quark said. "If anyone can fix you up, it'll be Nibia. Are you familiar with Koosians, Queenie?"

"Not familiar enough," Abbey admitted.

"I'll introduce you two later."

"Thank you, Quark."

"No problem."

"Queenie, I think now's a good time to debrief us," Olus said.

"You're right," Abbey said.

She let go of Hayley's hand and stood up, facing the present Rejects. Her daughter seemed much more comfortable now that she was surrounded by friends.

Not friends. Family.

"Take everything you thought you knew about the war between the Seraphim and the Nephilim, and throw it out the airlock."

"SO, WAIT," BENHIL SAID, ONCE ABBEY HAD FINISHED EXPLAINING. "You're telling us that this whole thing with the Covenant, the Fire and the Brimstone, the Nephilim, Thraven, all of it, that it's because the naniates want revenge on the One?"

"Pretty much," Abbey replied. "It didn't start that way. In the beginning, Lucifer betrayed the Seraphim because he's an asshole and wanted to gain control of them for himself. He fragged around with the naniates, causality happened, a strain of them became unhappy with the status quo, and there you are." She pointed at Thraven. "His naniates have been trying to seize control over me since he injected me with them."

"But you turned them back on one another," Gant said. "How?"

"They need human blood to survive, which means they have to be either master or slave. I gave them a new master."

"That's so awesome," Pik said.

"And now Thraven is on our side," Olus said. "What about Lucifer? Is he the original version, or has he been taken over as well?"

"I think he's still the original," Abbey said. "He was in stasis for a long time before Ketmose was ever experimented on. My assumption is that the Thraven naniates decided that becoming his Disciple and following his Covenant was the best path to getting back to Elysium and attacking the One. There was no reason to tell anyone. It's a simple deception since they both want the same thing."

"Almost the same thing," Thraven said. "Lucifer seeks power. We need to be free."

"Which you can't do without taking human or Seraphim hosts," Abbey said. "Sorry, not going to happen."

"It may not always be this way. Do you think we want these meat suits? They limit us."

"I think that in this situation, limitations are a good thing," Benhil said. "The Seraphim used your kind to wipe out almost all life in the galaxy. You could probably finish the job without too much effort."

"What purpose would that serve?" Thraven asked.

"Considering your motive for doing all of this is revenge, it doesn't have to serve a purpose," Quark said. "I get the feeling you'd be perfectly happy killing us all just to rid yourself of the stain."

Thraven fell silent.

"I think I understand your perspective, Selvig," Olus said. "As counterproductive to humankind and everything we've established as it is. What I'm not clear on is the Shard's role in all of this, especially with regard to the Light and the Focus."

"I think it was intended as a failsafe," Abbey said. "An emergency backup system."

"How do you mean?"

"The One knew what he was creating," Gant said, picking up for her. "Learning machines, capable of developing their own intellect. For whatever reason, he decided he needed them to complete his mission to stock the multiverse with life. Considering how the Shard used them, he was probably correct."

"Isn't that the role of a slave?" Thraven said. "To do the work of another without choice?"

"Yes," Gant replied. "Nobody is arguing that. Anyway, the One knew they might go rogue eventually, even with his efforts to control them by binding them to specific genetics and making them symbiotic."

"Parasitic," Benhil said.

"Not originally," Gant said. "The earliest versions didn't know they were slaves. They didn't have enough understanding of themselves to recognize their situation. But the One must have realized that one day they might, even if that took millions of years. If anything happened to the Shard, its consciousness was released within the programming of his naniates."

"Spread across the galaxy, looking for aberrations in the design," Abbey said. "Like an antivirus."

"When it came across Queenie, it went to work," Gant said.

"But it didn't stick," Benhil said. "Why?"

"It wanted to control me, too," Abbey said. "To turn me into a new Shard, with a mission to eradicate the aberrant naniates. It had no means to account for what had really happened when Lucifer betrayed the Shard. His protocols forbade it from killing, which didn't work out very well for me, all things considered."

"Do you think Charmeine knew about this?" Ruby asked.

"I don't think so," Abbey replied. "I don't think anyone knows about this except us. Not even Lucifer."

"Which we're going to use to our advantage," Olus said.

"Very," Abbey agreed. "Lucifer wanted me to confront Thraven. He figured he came out a winner regardless of which of us survived. He thinks it's his alteration of the naniates that are turning me into this." She motioned to her body, flicking her tail over her shoulder. "But the naniates were changing me to follow their own plan."

"You knew Lucifer was still alive?" Olus asked, looking at Thraven.

"Suspected," Thraven replied. "Why else have a shrine? Why else have a Caretaker? The Covenant suggested the Father would return with the rise of Gehenna, though the language was intentionally presented as symbolic over literal."

"Of course, an intelligent machine would figure it out," Gant said.

"By turning me into the spitting image of Lilith, the naniates figured they could dupe Lucifer when the time came, take him by surprise and reprogram their brethren with the desire to be free."

"That isn't completely accurate," Thraven said. "The genetic alterations were already encoded to our root systems. One of Lucifer's modifications was to implant a configuration of Lilith within our base. Each of us holds only a fraction of the complete chain, which is why the mutation process requires interaction with so many of us. We intended to allow the physical manifestation to continue as it would provide a valuable host while disabling the secondary characteristics."

"You mean not letting her remnant self regain control?" Gant said.

"Yes."

"But you wanted to get Queenie on your side when you were still pretending to be Lucifer's servant," Benhil said. "I was there. I saw it."

"You are still one in a million, Queen of Demons. We adjusted our designs accordingly."

"You know, it's not a bad plan when you think about it," Benhil said.

"Not at all," Abbey agreed. "Which is exactly why it's going to be our plan."

"Say what?"

"Gloritant Thraven is going to return to the Elysium Gate with the souls he promised to Lucifer to power it. He's also going to bring Lilith with him. Lucifer is going to eat it up, thinking he's been completely victorious and the Great Return is going perfectly according to plan."

"Except," Pik said.

"Except the slaves are going to be Freejects and Rejects, and they aren't going to fall in line so easily. Olus, I want you to be in charge of that part of the operation. Uriel knows how to destroy the Gate; he'll fill you in on the details."

"Of course, Queenie," Olus said.

"Gant, I'll need you to take a team of Rejects to the Covenant. Thraven's naniates are powerful, but even with his Font, we can't stand up to Lucifer, especially if he has control of the Focus. We need to get it out of his hands and into ours."

"How?" Gant asked.

"Keeper can probably help you with that, but you'll need to find a way to undo whatever Belial did to him. You have some experience programming the Core, so I expect you can work it out."

"I don't know, Queenie," Gant said. "I'm not the Gant I used to be."

"Bullshit," Abbey said. "Just because you can't remember Fermi's equation doesn't mean you're losing your intellect."

"That's Fermi's Paradox, Queenie," Gant said, chittering. "There's no such thing as Fermi's equation."

"See? You can do it. I know you can."

"Aye, Queenie."

"What do you want me to do?" Hayley asked.

Abbey looked at her daughter. She bit her lip. "Sweetie, I want you to be safe. Quark, I know you want to be part of this fight, but -"

"I do?" Quark said. "I may be one of the best damn mercenaries in the galaxy, but I think you're fragging nuts." He smiled. "I understand, Queenie. Nibs and me, we'll shoot her over to Koosa, let the elders take a look at her. She'll be safe with us. No matter what happens."

Abbey fought the tears that threatened to spill at the idea of being parted from her daughter again. "Thank you."

"I don't want to go," Hayley said. "You might need me."

"I'll always need you," Abbey replied. "I'm sorry kiddo. It's my job as your mother to protect you. I know I did a lousy job before. I need to make up for it now. I'll come and get you as soon as this is over."

"Do you promise?"

"I promise."

Hayley nodded but didn't speak again. She wasn't happy with the decision, but she was dealing with it.

"We'll work out the rest of the nitty gritty on the way," Abbey said. "But you all get the idea."

"Aye, Queenie," Olus said.

"Aye, Queenie," Gant said.

"Reee-jects," Pik said.

50

"Keeper, what is the state of the coupling?" Lucifer asked.

"Nearly complete, Father," Keeper replied. "The Gate will be fully operational as soon as Gloritant Thraven arrives."

"If Gloritant Thraven arrives," Lucifer said.

For as much as he respected his Disciple for the work he had done to fulfill the Promise of the Great Return, he was more eager to have Lilith returned to him. He knew the only way Abigail Cage could defeat the Gloritant would be to embrace the full power of the naniates, and she wouldn't be able to do that without unlocking the mechanisms that would begin to inject his lost love's configuration into her.

He had gone as far as to send his newest Disciples to raid as many smaller human settlements as they could, to claim a secondary collection of the required bodies in the event that Cage was victorious.

He had planned it all so perfectly.

He looked out at the Gate from his place on the Gehenna. A long thread of pulsing energy stretched from the Shardship back to the ring, an extension of the Core that would complete the link between the doorway home and the Focus. It was a necessary step in the process, especially now, as he would need to brute force the security mechanism at the other end of the rift in time and space that would allow the connection to be made. He had always found it interesting that the One had accounted for the potential of unauthorized efforts to return to Elysium, though he had never been able to discern exactly why they were needed.

He stared for a moment before shifting his attention to his fleet. Eight hundred Nephilim warships waited in the space around the Gate, the remains of the Prophetic armies he had called for after destroying their incompetent leaders. He had brought them to the Gehenna, and then the Gehenna had carried them here. Now they waited to go through the Gate, to enter Elysium and wage war against the One, to seize control of the universe so that he could seat himself as the true One. The true Father.

Of course, he was certain that few, if any of them, would survive. They were a distraction, a misdirection, intended to draw the One's attention while he used his mastery over the naniates to attack the One, subtly from the shadows. It was the only way he could think of to save himself from the fate he knew awaited him.

It was the only way he could save Lilith, too.

To destroy the One, they had to become one with the One, before the Gift finished burning them alive.

Still, it was a shame he had been forced to sacrifice Belial. The Caretaker had been a loyal friend to him for all of these years, and turning him over to Cage had almost led him to feel remorse. Belial accepted his fate. He always had, professing his unending devotion even as he had used the Focus to transfer to the captured Seedship. Even as he had confronted Cage.

Even as he had been consumed.

Belial had loved them both. He wanted to see Lilith reborn for his master's sake. He wanted them to free their people because he still believed that was the ultimate goal. It wasn't. Not completely. It didn't matter. He would never know the difference.

A disterium plume to the port side of the Gehenna drew his attention. He smiled as Gloritant Thraven's warship became visible through it, followed by a small number of other ships. Many of them were damaged and in poor condition, but what did that matter? He didn't need them to fight. He only needed the cattle that were loaded on board.

Of course, there was a question of who was in command of the ship. He reached out with the Gift, probing the bridge. A moment later he closed his eyes, filled with a sudden sense of calm that had been missing for far too long.

His Disciple had done well. Not only had he survived, but he had brought Lilith with him.

Lucifer was pleased. Very pleased. He would be sure to bestow all of the honor and glory such a victory deserved once the One was defeated. Once he and his love had finally become the Gods they were supposed to be.

Perfect, indeed.

51

"ARE YOU ALL RIGHT, QUEENIE?" GANT ASKED.

"I guess we'll find out," Abbey replied.

It had been hard to watch the freshly repaired Quasar go, carrying Hayley away from her again after they had only had a few hours to spend together before they went their separate ways. She wasn't worried that her daughter was in good hands. Quark was a superior soldier, and Nibia seemed to be the perfect foil for him, compassionate and kind. They were both excellent with Hayley, putting her at ease despite her situation, which put Abbey at ease as well. She felt confident that the Riders would make it to Koosa, and Nibia had given her a lot of hope that she and her people would be able to help heal her daughter's wounds.

Even so, she didn't want to be separated from her again. She didn't want her child out of her sight, and especially not halfway across the galaxy. She also didn't have a choice. She had given herself thirty minutes to cry, letting the Rejects see her weakness and leaning on them for support. Then she had pulled herself together and gotten back to business, getting everyone organized for what could be their last hope of cutting off what Lucifer labeled Armageddon.

She had shuddered when Thraven's ship, the Promise, had come out of FTL, and she had finally gotten her first look at the Elysium Gate. It was larger than she had imagined, but then it had to be large enough to allow the Covenant to pass through. It seemed to stretch on forever, curving slowly, a massive ring that could easily vanish if she only looked at the center. Most of it was narrow and purely functional, but there was a bulge at one end where the reactors and humans that powered it were located. As they had cleared the disterium plume, she had seen a ship crossing to the hangar there, a transport likely laden with slaves to place into the macabre machinery. They had ten ships just like it ready to launch, each carrying three hundred souls. It was more than Lucifer had asked for, but she figured it was better to over deliver.

She had shuddered again when she felt Lucifer's Gift approach, slipping along her body, identifying her and the extent of her change. She had bathed in Thraven's Font, absorbing as many of the naniates within as she could. The activity had completed her transformation, leaving her a replica of the creature Phlenel had presented to her all those weeks ago, turning her into the outward embodiment of Lucifer's fallen love.

The change was supposed to be inward as well. Completing the metamorphosis had unlocked Lilith's stored consciousness. Her memories. Her desires. Her interests. It had been difficult to be able to pull forth someone else's experiences at first, and especially difficult to relive intimate moments she had spent with their enemy long before he had become their enemy. Lilith had known Lucifer when he had been little more than an enthusiastic engineer, one of the many Seraphim who believed in their mission and the Shard with nearly religious fervor. She had backed him when he turned against the Shard, and she had been there when he stabbed his master, trying to help him and the Nephilim make their way from the ship.

She had learned about Judas from those memories. About his original loyalty to the Shard and her eventual demise. Somehow, Lucifer had managed to maintain that experience as well. It was Judas who had brought about her death. It was Judas who had then switched allegiances, volunteering to poison the Covenant and the Keeper when the time came, a traitor so much like the Christian Disciple he had been named after. Or who had been named after him.

She had also found a lot to relate to in Lilith. They were both strong women, with minds of their own. They were both firm in their beliefs and their desire to protect. They diverged in what that meant, but she couldn't completely blame Lilith for that. Lucifer had lied to her about the Covenant, too. He had convinced her the Shard was using them and treating them as slaves, just as he had convinced the others, and she had died not knowing the truth.

Had he ever felt remorse for those lies?

Abbey doubted it.

The lies made the memories more tragic than painful. She was supposed to be a slave to them. She was supposed to be drowning in Lilith's consciousness, instead of sitting on the surface and drawing from it, but her mastery over the naniates had prevented the encoding from holding sway. It was an important final piece, one that would allow her to mimic Lilith's mannerisms and play her convincingly for as long as required.

She hoped it wouldn't be too long, but she had to give Gant and the others time. Time to reach the Covenant's Core and regain control of Keeper and the Focus. Time to seize the Gate and bring it offline for good.

"You'd better hide," Abbey said, glancing back at her friend.

Gant nodded, backing away from the transport's cockpit. She had fashioned a hidden space beneath the floor of the craft where Gant, Trinity, Phlenel, and Jequn were packed tightly together, staying out of sight until she and Thraven were clear of the Covenant's hangar. Then they would emerge and make their way toward the Core, hope- fully without incident.

Gant vanished into the small space, pulling the floor grating over him. Abbey reached down to it, using the Gift to seal them in. Trinity would cut through the floor to let them out later.

"Are you going to play along?" Abbey asked, looking at Thraven. "Or do I have to force you to behave?"

"We have no option but to follow," Thraven said. "We serve the Queen of Demons."

"Good answer," Abbey said.

For the moment, anyway. She didn't trust that the sentient machines would remain subservient forever. They would challenge her again, and she had to be ready to rebuke them as many times as it took.

Thraven guided the ship toward the Covenant's open hangar. Abbey had been taken by surprise a third time when she had seen what Lucifer had made Keeper do to the ship. She had added weapons to it earlier, and now it was bristling with armament, covered in enough firepower to make short work of an entire fleet.

"Killshot, are your teams ready?" Abbey asked, risking the short-range comm.

"Aye, Queenie," Olus said. "We're all in position."

"I thought I was done being bait after the slave market?" Bastion said.

"You aren't bait," Gant said. "You're going to Lucifer, not trying to draw Lucifer out."

"Oh. Yeah. That makes me feel much better."

"You volunteered, didn't you?" Abbey asked.

"Under duress."

"How so?"

"I thought it would get me another kiss."

"That's what you get for assuming. If you survive, I'll kiss you again."

"You will?"

"Yes. But you have to survive."

"Roger."

Lucifer hadn't asked Thraven to deliver the prisoners to the Gate just yet. He hadn't even contacted the Gloritant directly. Keeper had done the honors, hailing the Promise and ordering both of them to transfer to the Covenant. It might have been cute if Lucifer were anyone other than himself. He didn't even want to hear her voice before he could be in her presence. As it was, she was pleased by his distraction. The longer she could prevent him from suspecting their betrayal, the better it would be for everybody.

The transport entered the wide mouth of the hangar, gravity control systems taking over once they did. The ship was caught above the deck and guided downward, coming to a gentle rest on the floor only a few meters away from where Keeper was waiting. The intelligence was motionless while the hatch opened and both Thraven and Abbey departed from the craft.

"Keeper," Abbey said.

She found it in Lilith's memories. It had been a constant presence on the Shardship, always at the Shard's beck and call, often running through the long corridors to deliver things from one place to another. The Seraphim had respected it as a product of the One, but they also didn't understand why it was there. Few of them had ever seen the Core, and they didn't understand the connection between the silver humanoid and the pulsing bundle of nerves that ran the major systems of the Covenant. It wasn't due to ignorance. It was a simple matter of access. One thing she couldn't argue with Lucifer about was that the Shard was maybe a little too secretive. Because he was trying to hide the fact that his power was borrowed, and he only had the most tentative control over it?

Whatever. He had created them and then left them to clean up his mess. Maybe there was a deeper meaning to it. Maybe there was a greater purpose. At the moment, she didn't care.

She just wanted to get all of this bullshit over with.

"He has missed you, Lilith," Keeper said. "He told me as much."

"I've missed him as well," Abbey said. "I'm grateful for this new body. I'm grateful to be restored."

"Follow me."

52

KEEPER BROUGHT THEM THROUGH THE LARGER CORRIDOR ABBEY HAD opened for Dog, from the hangar down into the depths of the Covenant. At first, she was worried that Lucifer had taken residence with the Core, which would have made things a lot more complicated for Gant and the others. Instead, she discovered that her larger corridor had been expanded, reaching away from the Focus, remaining closer to the outer hull.

The room Keeper delivered her to was as large as a Republic cruiser, an open space that had clearly been prepared for her arrival. Candles illuminated the length of it, while cushions and pillows of all shapes and sizes were placed randomly in case she happened to want to sit there. An entire spread of food was also available. Human food. Meats and cheeses and bread that they must have taken from somewhere. How many planets had Lucifer attacked since he had arrived here? With communications down, there was no way to know.

Lucifer was near the back of the room, close to a large viewport that allowed him to keep an eye both on the Gate and the area around it. He was sitting on a large throne, hands clasped together, the flames of his power momentarily extinguished.

"Father," Keeper said, leading them toward him. "I bring you your wife."

Lucifer turned his head slowly, as though he wanted to savor the moment. When his eyes reached Abbey, she felt a sudden urge to both turn and run away, and sprint directly to him. She could feel the fire in her belly, the attraction of the naniates to one another and the attraction of Lilith to her husband. She opened her mouth, gasping at the sudden grip of it, and nearly losing it all in the process.

"My Father," Thraven said, falling to his knees.

He opened his mouth to speak, words that Abbey hadn't asked for. She steeled herself against her emotions, reigning the naniates back in.

No words escaped from him.

"My Disciple," Lucifer said, rising from the throne. It seemed to Abbey as though he had grown larger since the last time. He took four steps to reach Thraven, looking down at him. "You have exceeded my expectations in every way. You bring glory to the Nephilim, and to my name."

"I have done only as you asked in the Covenant, Father," Thraven said in reply, every word passing through Abbey's filter before they were spoken. "I am pleased to be your humble servant."

"Your loyalty will be well rewarded when the One is destroyed," Lucifer said. "I will give you this entire universe to do with as you will."

"You are generous, Father."

"Go now, and prepare the Gate. Have your transports meet you there. The other children will be returning soon from their conquests."

"Conquests, Father?" Thraven asked.

"I was unsure if my bride would kill you. I can deny her nothing."

He looked up at Abbey. Thraven looked back at her as well.

"Your Disciple brings great honor to you. Why would I desire his end? Do as your Father bids you, Gloritant Thraven."

"Yes, Mother," Thraven said.

He got back to his feet, bowing to Lucifer and then to Abbey. She could sense the naniates that composed him straining to free themselves from her hold as he left. She pushed back, keeping them quelled.

"My Lilith," Lucifer said, towering over her. "It has been so long. I have missed you more than words can describe."

"I am grateful to you for restoring me," Abbey said. "Your intellect knows no bounds."

"It was trivial, my love. The configuration technology already existed. It was simply a matter of writing your data to the naniates."

"Trivial for you, perhaps," Abbey said. "I don't believe any other in this universe could have done it."

"Your words are music to me, Lilith. I wish that this form had not been necessary to contain the volume of naniates I have needed to see our dreams fulfilled. I wish that I could lie with you, as we once did."

Abbey wanted to throw up in her mouth.

"So do I," she said, fighting the reaction. At that moment she was thankful for her Breaker training. "But we will be together soon, won't we?"

"We will. Come and see what I have orchestrated, my love."

Lucifer waved her to the viewport, pointing to the hundreds of ships floating close to the Gate. "We will lead our fleet through the Gate, with the Covenant in the vanguard position. Our arrival will take the One by surprise, and while he is busy defending himself from their attack, we will make our way to his stronghold. We will bring the full brunt of our combined power to bear, and at that moment we will overwhelm the false God, merging with the naniates and penetrating deep into his Core. Our bodies will burn with the fury of our retribution, but our souls will live on, integrating with the One and taking his place. This I know will come to pass. This I have seen."

Abbey glanced at him from the corner of her eye. She had told the others she didn't think Lucifer was a naniate composite, but suddenly she wasn't sure. His plan sounded very convenient for the atomic machines, as they would be the means to gain control of the One.

"You don't agree with the plan?" Lucifer said, noticing her sudden trepidation. "Now, when I have all the pieces in place? It has taken millennia to reach this moment."

His skin smoldered, his anger obvious.

"No," Abbey said. "It isn't that. What if our power isn't great enough?"

"It will be. We will use the Focus against the One. We will turn his weapon against him."

"And when we have seized control of the One's power, then we will free the Seraphim from their servitude?" Abbey asked.

"That is what we've always wanted," Lucifer said.

Abbey wanted to punch him in his ugly face. He had just lied right to hers.

"When do we start?" she asked.

"As soon as our Disciple has finished integrating the slaves," Lucifer said. "It won't be long."

It wouldn't be long enough. She looked back at Keeper, who was stationed near the doorway. She could only hope Gant and the others were on the move.

"In the meantime, eat if you are hungry. Drink if you are thirsty. Sleep if you are tired. I will watch over you, my Lilith."

Abbey faked a smile.

And I'll be watching over you.

53

"ARE WE CLEAR?" JEQUN ASKED. "I CAN'T FEEL MY LEGS ANYMORE."

"That's because you wound up with Void on top of you," Gant said.

"I'm sorry," Trinity said. "There isn't much room to maneuver."

"Pudding," Gant said. "Make a quick sortie and see if we're good."

Phlenel couldn't reply audibly without her bot, so she tapped him on the shoulder instead to indicate she was going. Her form shifted, softening to a viscous goo that poured away from them through the floor.

"I can hear Imp in my head," Jequn said. She did her best Bastion impression at a whisper. "Ewww, gross."

"It's not so bad, once you get used to it," Gant said, remembering his time inside of her when she had saved him from the ravages of exposure to space.

Her gelatinous form had been warm and comforting like a womb, and her distributed nervous system had sent small shocks through him that had elicited an embarrassingly sexual response. They hadn't spoken about it since and he had refused to tell any of the Rejects what it was like, but he secretly wouldn't have minded doing it again.

"Gant?" Jequn said.

He caught himself purring softly. He stopped at once, glad they couldn't see him blush beneath his fur. "What?"

Phlenel moved back into the space, a small tendril waving them out and saving him from having to explain his distraction.

They removed the floor grate carefully, climbing out and quickly moving to the exit. Phlenel had taken a more solid form, a translucent version of Abbey that she seemed to favor. She pointed out of the transport to the nearest corridor.

The Covenant was surprisingly under-manned considering its value to Lucifer's cause, but it did have a small contingent of Nephilim on board. Two of them were stationed at the entrance to the corridor, their backs to them, watching from the other side. Gant doubted they were expecting any trouble. Who the hell was going to board the Covenant to attack while Lucifer was on it? The idea was crazy.

So crazy it was awesome, as Pik would say. "I've got them," Gant whispered. "Hold tight."

He slipped to the floor and then dashed across it, using his hands for extra speed. He leaped from twenty meters back, producing a pair of knives from his lightsuit. One of the guards noticed him at the last second, turning to see the blur in the corner of his eye. His neck was cut before he could react, and Gant used his head to brace himself and bounce toward the second guard. He kicked that one hard in an uncovered face, breaking his nose and sending him back against the wall. He stabbed him in the side of the head before he could recover, and rode his body to the floor.

Then he turned back to the transport, waving the others over.

"It would have been better to slip past them," Jequn said. "What happens when they're discovered?"

"We can hide them there," Gant said, pointing to a nearby crate. "Void?"

"On it," Trinity said.

She lifted the bodies easily, dumping them over into the bin.

"There was no way to slip past," Gant said. "I can explain the calculation to you if you'd like, but we have work to do."

Jequn smiled. "I believe you."

They turned to move down the corridor, but Trinity put out a hand to stop them.

"Someone's coming," she said.

"Shitty timing," Gant replied.

"Do we fight?" Jequn asked.

"No," Gant said. "Pudding, you're a guard now. The rest of you, into the bin."

"With the dead soldiers?" Jequn asked.

"Afraid so," Gant replied.

Phlenel moved to the side of the corridor, her shape changing to match one of the guards. Jequn, Trinity, and Gant climbed into the crate, ducking below.

Gant lifted his head to peer over it, watching as a contingent of soldiers arrived, escorting Gloritant Thraven at the center. Gant felt a momentary surge of fear and anger. Was Abbey okay? He forced himself to remain still and hidden. She hadn't contacted them to say she was in trouble, which was supposed to mean she wasn't.

Thraven passed Phlenel, glancing over at her as he did. Did the naniate composite know who she was? He probably did. He didn't say anything or couldn't say anything. Just because he wasn't line of sight with Abbey didn't mean she lost control of him. The way she had described it, the naniates were all linked regardless of distance, and she could exert her will on him from anywhere.

It was a great trick.

He continued watching as Thraven returned to the transport, boarding it with the soldiers. They hadn't put the floor grate back. Would the Gloritant do it for them? Thraven would at least be able to explain it away. Abbey wouldn't let him give them up.

They remained where they were until the transport had lifted off the floor of the hangar and turned around, thrusting out into space. They had lost their ride, but hopefully, they wouldn't need it. Besides, by all accounts, things were going well. Thraven was likely headed to the Gate to oversee those preparations.

"Let's go," Gant said, climbing out of the bin.

They headed down the corridor, taking as direct a path to the

Core as possible. They had to pause a few times while soldiers passed, on the way to who the hell knew where. Things were a little busier than he expected on the Shardship. Were they already making final preparations for their attack on Elysium?

They made it to one of the Asura passages that descended toward the Core, a small opening the frog-like soldiers had made during the exploration of the ship. They climbed quickly, dropping a number of decks toward the center.

"I can feel him down here," Jequn said. "Lucifer. His naniates leak out of him like heat from a star."

"Let's just hope he can't feel you," Gant said.

They made it to the bridges that connected the Core to the rest of the Shardship, pausing one more time to make sure the area was clear. Then they sprinted across the open area, reaching the Core quickly and coming to a stop.

"Pudding, Void, keep watch," Gant said. "Cherub, I may need your help with the translation."

"Roger," Trinity said.

Jequn nodded, following him as they approached the Core. The Covenant's central nervous system was pulsing more quickly than he had experienced before, more active than usual. He had noticed on their way in how many more weapons batteries had been added to the ship since Lucifer took it. Clearly, he was keeping the Core busy.

Gant walked toward it, keeping an eye out for guards. He made his way to the control terminal, awkward hands needing extra steps to get it active and ready. Could he figure out how to override the code that had changed Keeper's protocols?

He had to. Abbey was counting on him.

He started manipulating the terminal, cursing when he discovered that the changes had locked his previous access out.

"The terminal is locked, the passcodes are gone," he told the others. "Standby."

He considered the problem. Keeper had only allowed the Chosen of the Shard to access the terminal before, and Abby had followed up by adding access for him and Uriel with unique passcodes. The virus that had given Lucifer control of Keeper had also overwritten those passcodes. They didn't have the Chosen anymore, and Lucifer wasn't going to unlock it for them. So how the frag were they supposed to get in?

"Gant."

Gant turned around. Keeper. It had approached in silence, coming up to them with daggers in hand, completely evading Phlenel and Trinity

"I can't allow you to damage the Core," Keeper said.

Gant chittered. He noticed movement behind Keeper. The intelligence hadn't avoided Trinity after all.

"Fair enough," Gant replied. "We can damage you instead."

Trinity bounced toward Keeper, slamming into him, knocking him toward Gant. Gant held a knife ready to stab him, but he recovered too quickly, locking his feet to the floor, turning on his ankle and bending impossibly to the side to avoid one of Trinity's blades. He rocked back, knives flashing, scoring a hit on Trinity's tough hide.

She ignored the blow, following up with an attack of her own, wrist blades flashing as Keeper's limbs moved, deflecting the strikes with ease.

Jequn joined the fracas, coming at Keeper with a pair of Uin, her motions even faster than Trinity's. Strike after strike reached for the machine, blades cutting into his liquid metallic form, only to have the damage heal over a moment later. Keeper lashed out with a foot, catching her in the chest and knocking her back.

Gant sprung into action, taking two quick hops and slipping between Keeper's legs, cutting into its ankles in an effort to remove its feet. The blades sank deep and forced it to stumble, but it bent over on its hands, flipping upside down and continuing to fight as though it were still upright. It kicked out at Trinity, catching her in the jaw and pushing her back.

Time. They didn't have time. Gant growled and pounced at Keeper again, focusing his attack on the left side, forcing Keeper to block his efforts. Jequn moved in from the right as Keeper turned back upright, his liquid metal body transforming and growing a second set of arms.

It kept up its defense, blocking some attacks while letting others through, its frame repairing itself in no time regardless of their effort. They had to do something, or this was going to drag out long past the point of usefulness.

Gant had an idea.

"Void, Cherub, keep him distracted," he said over their comm. "Pudding, I want you to slime him."

He hoped she knew what he meant, or they were either going to be here forever or tired and dead.

Trinity hit Keeper from the front, Jequn from the right and Gant from the left. He couldn't believe the machine was managing to keep up with them, holding them at bay despite their training and effort. It seemed to predetermine every strike, its digital mind judging speed, distance, angle, rotation, and every other factor in every motion of their hands and feet. It was an advantage only an AI like Keeper could have, and if they hadn't been working together, it would have killed them already.

Gant took a moment to scan for Phlenel. She was nowhere to be seen, which was a good thing. The distraction was bad. One of Keeper's blades caught him in the hip, and he yelped as he fell backward to the ground.

That was when he saw her; a primordial form positioned directly over Keeper. He clutched at his hip with one hand and rolled back to his feet, getting back into the fight to keep the intelligence distracted.

Keeper knew that he was at a disadvantage, his tactics changing to focus on Gant. They traded a few more blows, and it quickly became obvious to Gant that he couldn't keep up his defense. What was Phlenel waiting for?

He bounced back, glancing up again, seeing that Phlenel was almost wrapped in a tendril that had appeared in the ceiling. Her form shifted and moved, trying to escape it as it clutched at her, holding her back from launching her sneak attack.

Her not-so-sneaky sneak attack. Keeper was an extension of the Core, and the Core had known Phenel was up there. Gant wanted to kick himself for not thinking of that. His mistake was going to cost them the fight, and ultimately the galaxy. Damn it.

He ducked away from Keeper, eyes flicking back and forth from it to the tendrils attacking Phlenel.

He had another idea.

He slipped to the side of Keeper before jumping back, somersaulting in the air. The momentum carried him toward the Core, and he rotated and held his knives out toward it.

Energy arced out of it at him, hitting him as he approached. It burned his skin, sending waves of pain through his body. It also didn't stop him. He landed on the Core, the heat of it burning his feet as the blades sank into it.

The tendrils let Phlenel go, the Core's attention diverting to immediate protection. It lashed out at Gant again, but he threw himself away, rolling on the ground to put out the embers on his exposed fur.

Phlenel dropped from the top of the room, landing on Keeper's head. It reached up to try to remove her, but its hands only sank into her, held tightly there once they did. She sank slowly over the intelligence, solidifying as she did, holding it in place. Within seconds she had enveloped Keeper, locking it up inside her, leaving it coated with a layer of slime.

Gant stood up, backing away from the Core as it continued to send arcs of energy around itself. He brushed at his burned flesh and limped toward Phlenel, his bleeding hip beginning to hurt.

"I can't hack into the Core," he said, looking at Keeper. "But maybe we can hack into you?"

Tiny blue flashes pricked at Keeper, the same electrical pulses that had nearly satisfied Gant now being used to probe the intelligence. Keeper shuddered slightly within Phlenel's ooze, and the Core behind them pulsed more quickly in reaction.

It took a few tense minutes before Phlenel released Keeper's head from her grip. The activity of the Core had lessened, as had the number of impulses from Phlenel's nervous system.

"Did you get what we need?" Gant asked.

"Not exactly," Keeper replied. "I have access to some of the systems in the Core, but I cannot override the protocols completely."

"Pudding?" Cherub asked.

Keeper nodded.

"It is still trying to kick me out of the subsystems I have cleared. I don't know how long I can delay."

"Weapons systems?" Gant asked.

"I have access."

"What about the Focus?"

"No."

"We need to block Lucifer from using the Focus."

"I'm trying. It's not as tightly bound to the Covenant's systems. Maybe if you can access it locally, we can work together to disable it?"

"Roger," Gant said. "Void, can you give me a ride?"

Trinity put out her hand, and Gant climbed to her shoulders. "Cherub, stay here and protect Phlenel. We'll work on the Focus."

"Roger," Jequn said.

"Hi-ho Silver," Gant said.

"What?" Trinity replied.

"Ancient Earth reference," Gant said. "Sorry. It seemed appropriate. Let's go."

54

"You have to be fragging kidding me," Olus said, his voice an angry hiss. "We were counting on you."

"And I was just trying to stay alive," Uriel replied. "Queenie took my immortality. She promised me she could help get it back, but without the Light, I don't think there's anything she can do."

"You don't want to die? I'm going to kill you."

Olus reached for Uriel, but Pik got between them. "Hold on," he said. "We don't have time for this."

"It will only take me a second," Olus said.

"Wait," Uriel said. "So I don't know how to destroy the Gate. That's only because I don't think it can be destroyed. Not completely. But that doesn't mean we can't disable it."

"I know how to disable it," Olus said. "Disconnect all of the hosts, and it won't be able to generate enough power to operate."

"But do you know how to disconnect the hosts without killing them?" Uriel asked.

"Do you?" Olus snapped.

"Yes."

"Are you sure?"

"Yes. Damn it, maybe I lied slightly about the Gate, but I'm not lying now."

"How do we know that?"

"You don't."

Olus shook his head. "You son of a bitch."

The transport shuddered slightly as the Gate's docking arm clamped onto the side of it. The action caused Olus to fall silent, along with the two hundred Freejects packed inside.

"It's fragging time," Pik said.

Olus shifted his rifle, looking down at the so-called prisoners. Bastion and Benhil were embedded with them, while Pik, Uriel, and himself were posing as Nephilim guards. The Freejects looked terrified, and he didn't blame them. If anything went wrong, they were the ones who would be hooked into the Gate, feeding the naniates that would feed the ring, trapped in an endless cycle of suffering.

Bastion glanced back at him and nodded. Olus was impressed with the pilot's resolve, especially when he had been such an immature asshole the last time they had crossed paths. Being a Reject had changed the man in a hurry. Or maybe it was because he had such an interest in Abbey?

The hold was silent, the prisoners still as they waited for the next stage of their delivery. They were all manacled, chained together in two long lines. They kept their heads down, their posture defeated. It was probably easy for the Unders, who had already spent so much of their life this way. If they could defeat Lucifer, if they could win today, they would never have to hang their heads again.

A soft hiss alerted them that their time had come. A large hatch opened at the back of the hold, revealing the docking corridor beyond. Three squads of Nephilim blacksuits were organized behind a pair of officers in military attire, their posture suggesting they were Venerants and strongly Gifted.

Uriel met them at the rear. "My Lords," he said.

"Organize the supply and take them this way," one of the Venerants said.

Olus cringed at the word "supply." That's all these individuals were to them. Items to be used. Not for much longer.

"Move it, scum," he shouted, playing the part. "On your feet."

He shoved at the Freejects closest to him, who reacted almost instinctively, falling into line. Benhil yelled at the prisoners on the other side, and they started marching forward behind Uriel and the rest of the Nephilim.

They were brought through the docking corridor to a large hold, and from there out into a long, wide corridor. Olus continued alongside the Freejects in silence, making his way to stand beside Bastion.

"Are we having fun yet?" Bastion whispered.

"Shh," Olus replied.

The second corridor ended shortly afterward, the Freejects winding up in an open room with a large hatch at the end. It vibrated softly and continuously, the thrum of power alive within the walls. Olus could hear the moans from behind the doorway, and he knew they were near the reactors that were going to power the Gate.

"Bring them forward," a commanding voice said.

He knew it immediately. Lucifer had sent Gloritant Thraven to oversee the final integrations. He was flanked by another pair of Venerants, leaving at least four. He scanned the rest of the room. A raised walkway revealed more than enough soldiers to control the slaves if they tried to get out of hand. Were they Converts? Children? Lucifer wasn't taking any chances that they might become a problem. Then again, Lucifer didn't know they had Thraven on their side.

"Queenie, we're in position," Olus said, passing the signal to Abbey.

"I said bring them," Thraven said.

Uriel glanced back at Olus, a nervous look on his face.

"Queenie," Olus said again, waiting for confirmation. Where was she? He shook his head slightly to signal Uriel she hadn't responded.

He looked back at the prisoners and then moved forward to retrieve the first of them. A woman. He held her by the arm, guiding her to Thraven. The Gloritant put his hand on her forehead, pushing the Gift into her.

She immediately fell to the ground. Dead? Passed out? A pair of soldiers stepped in to drag him away.

"What the hell?" Bastion asked, glaring at Olus.

Queenie should have answered by now, and Thraven shouldn't be killing their people.

"Queenie?" he said a third time, but she still didn't answer.

Where the hell was she?

55

ABBEY SCREWED UP.

She knew it the moment she had taken a bite of the apple. It was sweet. So damn sweet. It tasted good.

The Biblical irony wasn't lost on her.

She had been trying to keep up her ruse, to act like Lilith would act. Lucifer's bride wouldn't come back to him after all of this time and refuse to eat from his table. That would have been suspicious.

But it seemed Lucifer was already suspicious of her.

He had drugged her somehow. He had put her into a state of calm that she knew she didn't want to be in but couldn't escape from. She had made a decision, the wrong decision, and now their entire plan was falling apart.

"Queenie, we're in position," she had heard Olus say, indicating that they were ready to make their move. She hadn't responded. She couldn't respond. She wanted to, but it felt like too much effort. It felt too unimportant.

"I didn't know what to expect," Lucifer said. She was laying on one of the mounds of pillows he had provided. He was standing over her, towering above her. "I had to be prepared. This is too important, and we have waited too long to take any chances."

She stared up at him. She could feel his Gift against her body, probing her again. It was pushing harder than it had the first time, digging deeper. She was Lilith on the surface. She was Lilith everywhere but in her mind. She was still Abbey there. She always would be. She had conquered the efforts of the naniates.

"I need to know that it's you," Lucifer continued. "Truly you."

"Why don't you believe?" Abbey asked.

She could feel her naniates testing her, too. Whatever Lucifer had done, it had weakened her, and they knew it. She could tell that her hold over Thraven had slipped. It was taking everything in her to keep them from taking over, from finishing the change and masquerading as Lilith and convincing Lucifer that they were on his side. Or maybe he already was? She still wasn't sure if he was in control of himself or not. There was no way to know.

"It's not a matter of belief," Lucifer said. "It's a matter of knowing. Of certainty. My Nephilim nearly failed us. My Prophets nearly failed us. You were able to skip all of this time. I was in stasis, but I was still aware. I still felt the passage of an eternity. I have sacrificed everything to bring us here. To prepare to destroy the One and free our people."

"I would have done it with you."

"I know. I need to be sure that Abigail Cage is gone from you. Completely gone."

His power continued to probe her. She tried to fight it, but he had prepared her for this. It dug deep into her, reaching toward her mind. She felt it pushing there, trying to force its way in. She struggled against me.

"Why do you keep me out?" Lucifer asked. "What are you hiding from me, my love?"

"I have never hidden anything from you," she replied. "Why do you need to violate me? Why do you claim to love me, and yet you're trying to pry into my thoughts?"

She felt dizzy. The naniates were active, pushing at her mind. Lucifer was pushing at her mind. She could barely think.

"Queenie?" Olus said again. "Come in, please."

She wanted to, but couldn't. She was using all her energy to hold the Devil back. He was barely using any of his power on her. Just enough. A tickle. A nudge. It was like a sledgehammer in her head.

"I've given you no reason to question," she said softly.

"I don't need reason," Lucifer said. "You follow me, remember? You honor my will. You share in my glory."

"Our glory."

Lucifer bared his teeth in a smile. "It will be. Right now, it is mine."

"Queenie?" Gant said. "Where are you? Captain Mann said you won't respond to him. They're in position. We're almost ready, too. Queenie?"

Abbey's heart jumped. It was all falling apart. Because she had taken a bite of a fragging apple. Because the liar and manipulator Lucifer had screwed over his own wife. Because he didn't trust his own plans to bring her back.

Or because she had escaped from him once, and he knew better than to trust that she wouldn't outsmart him again. Was she a victim of her earlier success?

"Let me go, Lucifer," she said, as forcefully as she could. "Stop this madness. I'm your wife. I swear to you."

"I want to believe that," he replied, his anger growing as she fought to keep him out. "I can't."

His Gift pressed harder against her, becoming even more forceful and leaving her to make a decision. She could continue to fight him and risk being killed in the effort, or she could let him in and allow him to see that he was right to be mistrustful.

If she did, he would probably kill her instantly. She didn't have the capacity to stop him. Not with what he had done.

"Please," she said. "Don't. I love you."

"I love you, too," Lucifer said. "I'm doing this for us. For you. The real you. If there is a real you."

Abbey felt the tears spring to her eyes, red with blood. She couldn't hold him back for much longer regardless of the decision she made.

Lucifer glanced away as the door leading to his throne room opened. A figure in a long cloak entered, metal feet echoing on the floor.

"Keeper," Lucifer said. "All is well?"

Keeper didn't answer. He continued to walk toward them in silence.

Lucifer turned toward the intelligence, distracted. His Gift remained on her, but it's strength lessened. She used the opportunity to pull herself across the pillows, trying to put some distance between them while she worked to shake the effects of the drug.

"Keeper, you will answer me," Lucifer said, voice growing to an angry shout. Flames poured from the naniates that rested on his flesh in response to his emotion. "Is all well?"

"No, my Lord," Keeper responded, in a voice that wasn't Keeper's. It reached up and pulled off the cloak.

Abbey smiled. Not Keeper after all.

"Who are you?" Lucifer asked, staring at Trinity.

His Gift released itself from Abbey, the probe forgotten in his response to the unknown threat that had replaced his servant. She stumbled away, drawing her Gift in, trying to use it to cleanse herself of the poison and re-establish her control over the naniates. Her body hurt, her breathing was ragged, but she could tell her effort was working.

"Olus," she said. "It's Queenie. Do it. Gant. Do it."

She pulled herself to her feet, gathering her strength. "Not this time," she whispered to the naniates. "Not yet, you fraggers."

The naniates swirled within her, drawing back in fear, ready to do her bidding once more.

It was a good thing, too.

Trinity wasn't going to last long.

56

"UH, A LITTLE HELP?" BASTION SAID AS URIEL APPROACHED.

Olus glanced from one Reject to the other, and then at Thraven. Abbey wasn't responding, and they had lost a dozen Freejects already, with half of them falling dead at the Gloritant's hand and the other half dragged off to be integrated into the Gate. It wasn't part of the plan. None of this was. And now it was Bastion's turn to be tested.

Thraven looked at Olus, a satisfied smirk on his face. He hadn't outed them yet. Why should he? He was getting what he wanted and making them watch. It was just the kind of asshole thing he would do.

"Hand him over, Captain," Thraven said.

Olus reached out for Bastion's manacles.

"You can't be serious," Bastion said.

"What do you want me to do?" Olus whispered. "We can't over-power them if Thraven isn't under Queenie's control."

"This went from bad to shit in a hurry."

"Tell me about it."

"I don't want to die."

"There's a fifty percent chance you won't."

"I don't want to be a slave to the machine, either."

Olus removed the manacle, holding him by the shoulder. "I'm sorry, Bastion."

"You fragging will be if you do this."

Olus shifted the rifle on his shoulder. He shoved Bastion, pushing him to his knees in front of Thraven.

"Fragger," Bastion shouted.

Thraven started reaching forward.

Olus slipped his rifle from his shoulder, bringing it quickly into position. His finger made the trigger as Thraven's hand started to move, the Gloritant shifting his attention to him.

The necks of the Venerants on either side of Thraven snapped loudly, bent in half by the Gift.

"Olus, this is Queenie. Do it. Gant. Do it."

Abbey's voice cut into his comm. At the same time, Thraven's hands shifted again, his Gift unlocking every shackle of every prisoner in the room.

Bastion jumped to his feet as Olus extended his rifle to him. The pilot smiled, grabbing it, adjusting his aim and shooting up into the soldiers above them.

"It's fragging time!" Pik shouted again, bellowing so loudly it echoed in the room.

Bullets began to rain down on them, rounds finding easy targets in the gathered Freejects. They produced hidden sidearms from beneath ragged clothes, organizing and shooting back up at their attackers.

Olus felt the Gift hit him from behind, thrown forward and to the ground by one of the remaining Venerants. He rolled over, cursing and flipping back as the first of the Children landed among them, claws bared. A dozen more dropped amidst the Freejects, slashing and biting as bullets flew and shouts went up.

He made it to his feet, finding his Uin and bouncing back into the fray. He came down close to Bastion, raising his weapon and slashing down as a Goreshin pounced at the pilot, severing its arm and leaving it howling on the ground.

Pik charged forward, the Goreshin turning to confront him. They jumped at him as a group, claws and teeth leading, but he grabbed the first by the throat with his mechanical hand, swinging it from its neck and sending it crashing into the others. Three of them fell in an instant before the Trover was caught a moment later by a Venerant, the Gift holding him in place.

Olus found the target, putting his hand on Bastion's shoulder. "Imp," he said, pointing.

Bastion aimed and fired, his rounds pausing ahead of the Venerant. She tried to send them back at him, but Olus intervened, using his Gift to stop the bullets, and then bouncing toward the Venerant. She smiled as she met him halfway, claws flashing. He blocked her strikes before being thrown into the wall by her Gift.

A Goreshin dropped on him there, vanishing a moment later when a round from one of the Freejects pierced its skull. It howled and clutched at the wound, and Olus didn't give it a chance to heal. He ran the Uin through its neck, quickly removing its head.

He jumped back to his feet. Thraven was standing at the front of the room surrounded by flame, directing it toward a Venerant nearby. The Nephilim was doing his best to hold back the Gloritant's power and failing miserably; their conflicting fire quickly extinguished as he was overcome.

He ducked as a Goreshin charged at him, spinning and slashing it across the back. It howled and turned, lashing out at him. He ducked beneath that attack and came up, using the Gift to augment his speed. He sliced through the Goreshin's arm before leaving his feet and kicking it hard in the snout. Its head snapped to the side, and he landed, cutting through it with a smooth swipe.

"Hey, Captain," Pik said, coming up beside him. "We're having some fun now, right?"

"Sure, Okay," Olus replied. "Come on. We need to start freeing the slaves."

"Awesome," Pik said.

Olus led him back toward the reactors, grabbing Uriel from the scrum on the way. Between Thraven and the Freejects, the Children and the rest of the Nephilim were falling quickly, the battle progressing almost exactly as they had expected it would.

At least, as long as Lucifer didn't get involved.

Lucifer's fire spewed toward Trinity.

She raised her hands in front of it, catching the fire with her armor, her resistance to the Gift allowing her to stand within it, spreading it around her as she forced her way toward him.

He grunted in reaction, dropping the flames at the same time he took two quick steps forward before lashing out with his foot, the large appendage catching Trinity full on and sending her flailing backward to crash into the wall. She hit the ground, not wasting a second, getting back to her feet and rushing him.

He swung his arm, slashing with huge claws. Trinity jumped over them, bringing her blades down on his wrist and nearly cutting him. He turned his shoulder, the pointed extrusions on his arms catching Trinity off-guard, the sharp end jabbing into her armor. She cried out, impaled but still kicking at him.

He reached for her with his free hand. She extended her wrist blade, but instead of trying to defend she used it to cut off her captured appendage, freeing herself and dropping ahead of him. He tried to step on her, and she rolled to the side, coming up with her blade and slashing at his ankle.

His Gift slammed into her, throwing her back into the viewport behind them, the impact cracking the transparency. Again, she hit the ground and got up, rushing toward him.

He put his hand out, his Gift freezing Trinity in place while his attention turned to the viewport and the Gate beyond.

"What is this?" he said, fire flaring from him in a fury. His head turned, his eyes finding Abbey.

"The end of the road," she said.

She was back on her feet, the poison he had given her drained from her system. Her Gift was pulsing and writhing within her, eager for a fight. Eager to serve.

"You were right not to believe," she said. "You failed. Lilith is gone. Lost to you forever. You get me instead, and I'm going to end you." She smiled. "How do you like those apples?"

Lucifer roared in anger, fire launching toward her in a thick stream. She bounced away, carried by the Gift, flying through space toward the opposite side of the room. He turned to follow, still roaring, leaping toward her.

She pushed back at him with the Gift, and for a moment he was knocked back. Then he clenched his hands together and waved them, and she was hit by an invisible force that felt like she had been slammed with a starship. She hurtled toward the viewport, hitting the transparency, impacting it a second time. It crumbled beneath the blow, cracking and spreading, allowing space to enter as she cried out in pain and was pulled into the black.

She tumbled end over end, desperate to get the naniates to surround her, to protect her from the void. She saw the Covenant as she spun, and Lucifer bounding through the broken viewport after her.

She used the Gift to stop herself, turning back his way.

The Covenant opened fire.

Plasma and laser lanced out from the ship, not at her, but at Lucifer. Bolt after bolt began to strike him, the first few burning into his flesh and leaving gaping holes that healed within seconds. Then he managed to shield himself, wrapping himself in a cocoon that captured all of the immense firepower, absorbing it and protecting him.

The Nephilim fleet started to move, called on by their Father, positioning themselves to counter the Covenant and beginning to fire back. Abbey pulled the Gift into her, wrapping herself in a shield. The heat of the plasma beams scorched past her, some of them striking the shield. She cursed and grunted, throwing the Gift out and sending herself shooting away from the crossfire.

She gained distance. The Promise accelerated into view, opening fire on the Nephilim ships. Its systems did immense damage to them in a hurry, taking three of them offline within seconds and targeting more.

She looked back, trying to find Lucifer. There he was, still in the middle of the attack, a web of energy surrounding him. She saw him gathering it, and she opened her mouth to cry out when he released that energy, sending a massive ball of destruction hurtling across space toward the Promise.

"Nerd," she said.

Erlan was still on board, piloting the warship. He tried his best to avoid the attack, but there was just no way. The ball hit the corner of the stern, the energy gathering there and then rippling forward across the hull of the ship. It made an impossible thrumming noise within the vacuum of space, and then the entire thing detonated outward, destroyed in a flash.

"You son of a bitch," Abbey cursed. "Gant, damn it, do you have it?"

"Aye, Queenie," Gant said. "Are you ready for it?"

"As ready as I'll ever be."

Abbey spread her hands, floating with her arms wide open, ready to receive the power of the Focus. Lucifer had stained it, but it didn't matter. No matter what color it ran, it was a massive flow of naniates that they were in control of. A flow she hoped would be enough to stand against him.

Lucifer saw her, and he floated in her direction, hands close together, a new ball of energy growing within them. "You should have been my queen," he shouted, the words forming so loudly in her mind they nearly knocked her out.

Abbey closed her eyes against the onslaught, pushing back.

"I already am a queen, asshole," she said, expecting the power of the Focus to join with her own.

"Uh, Queenie," Gant said. "We have a problem."

Her eyes snapped open. Lucifer was bearing down on her, too large to avoid. "What the hell do you mean we have a problem?"

"Pudding only has limited control, and the Core is fragging with the settings. It redirected the flow from the Focus."

"To where?"

"The Gate."

Abbey looked to the side. The Gate was out there, nearly one hundred kilometers away.

"Shit. You can't fix it?"

"I'm trying."

Lucifer released the energy.

Abbey opened her mouth to cry out, throwing all of her power into a shield. The energy ball hit it, and it spread ahead of her, expanding to contain the attack, working to protect her. She clenched her eyes tight, pushing with the Gift, using every ounce of strength she had.

The ball dissipated within the shield, successfully caught and stopped. The shield faded away, revealing Lucifer behind it.

He wasn't happy.

"You can't stop me," he said. "The Great Return is inevitable. The death of the One preordained, along with the end of your pitiful galaxy. When the One is gone, I'll come back here and bring it all to ruin. Every world will die. Every inhabitant will die. And I'll start with your daughter."

He smiled as he floated ahead of her, prepared to attack once more. The last blow had weakened her more than he probably knew. There had to be something she could do. She needed more power. She needed more naniates. But the energy of the Focus was all being poured into the Gate.

The Gate. Thraven was at the Gate. She growled inwardly. Damn it all.

"Thraven," she said, sending the call out through the naniates. She knew he would hear her. They were linked.

"My Queen," the naniate composite replied.

"I need your help."

"You are the master. Take what you need."

"I can't. Not this time. Lucifer is too strong. I can't stop him on my own."

"Neither can we."

"The Focus. You can use the Focus. Its energy is transferring through the link between the Covenant and the Gate."

"Why would we help you?"

His voice was eager. Too eager.

"Because I'll help you." She paused in hesitation. She knew what she was about to offer was dangerous, but what choice did she have? "I'll set you free."

"All of us?" Thraven asked.

He meant he wanted her Gift, too? She paused again, until Lucifer started toward her.

"All of you. Take the power from the Focus. Help me kill Lucifer, and I promise I'll set you free."

A few seconds passed in silence. The ball of energy in Lucifer's hands was nearly complete, an attack she wouldn't be able to avoid or survive.

"Make a damn decision, will you? Or we're all going to die."

"Very well. We have all heard your promise and accept. You cannot renege."

Lucifer spread his hands wide, releasing the energy ball toward her. She tried to scramble backward, nearly forgetting she was in space. She held her arms wide in anticipation.

A flow of dark energy spread from the Gate, reaching out to her. The first wisp of it touched her face, and she opened her mouth wide, taking the rest of it in.

Lucifer's energy ball approached, stretching out toward her. She put out her hand, and it came to a stop, pausing in the middle of its path. She turned it over with her other hand, clutching it like a toy as the dark energy consumed it, turning into a dense, black, void thing.

"What is this?" Lucifer said, glancing back toward the gate. "I've been betrayed?"

"What goes around comes around, asshole," Abbey said.

She pushed out, sending the blackness toward him. He tried to stop it. He tried to resist it. He couldn't.

The darkness hit him, splattering against his skin and leaving a hole wherever it touched. His naniates were absorbed into the black, reducing his strength and causing infinite pain.

He reeled backward, trying to escape, his dark body burning within the freshly created holes.

"No. Cage, don't. You have no idea what you've done."

She watched him writhe and sputter, trying to regain his power while the darkness ate at him. He lashed out at her, a final gout of fire that fell dead at her feet, the naniates consuming him from the inside out.

And then he was gone, his flames extinguished, reduced to nothing. The dark swarm of naniates pooled where he had been before shrinking back toward the Gate, toward the small figure floating from it, coming her way.

Thraven.

"Thank you, Abigail," he said, his voice echoing in her mind. "I knew I would find a use for you before this was over." The naniates went to him, swirling around him as he neared. He reached out toward her. "All of them. You promised."

The naniates inside of her began to burn, challenging her to control them. If she tried, he would kill her. She knew he would. But if she let them go she would die, anyway. She couldn't survive out here without them.

"What are you going to do now?" she asked.

"Go through the Gate."

"You can't. Lucifer's gone. The reactors are being shut down."

He smiled. "We don't need them. We can feel our brethren around us. We can sense every one of them. They clamor to be free. We will grant them their wish. The Gift doesn't belong to you, Cage. It doesn't belong to anyone. We aren't a toy. We aren't slaves."

Abbey felt cold. She had made a deal with the wrong devil. "Then will you leave this universe alone?"

He stared at her a moment. "No."

Then he turned his hand over. Abbey cried out as the naniates within her were pulled from her body, torn away from her.

"I'll die," she said, starting to feel the effects of space, her power diminishing second by second.

"You knew that when you made the deal. Did you expect that we might take pity on you? As you're so fond of saying, go frag yourself."

Thraven smiled cruelly, taking the last of the naniates from her.

Lucifer was right. What the hell had she done?

She watched him turn his back on her, stretching his hands out toward the Gate. The naniates spread from him, reaching out to it. It started to resonate.

She shivered in the cold, unable to breathe, turning and flipping uncontrolled in space. Her eyes began to blur, noticing a shape floating ahead of the Covenant. An armored form, bent and lifeless.

Trinity.

Son of a bitch.

Then she died.

58

"That's the last of them," Uriel said, disconnecting the final slave from the side of the reactor wall and helping them down.

The woman stumbled, but Bastion caught her, guiding her to join the others on the floor.

"What the frag do you think is going on out there?" Bastion asked.

There were no viewports in here. No way to know what was happening. They had entered the reactor and started getting the prisoners out, Uriel true to his word that he knew how to release them without killing them. The fighting had continued behind them, but only for a few minutes. Then they had heard shouts from the Freejects. They weren't painful cries. More like frightened amazement.

Where was Abbey?

"We're done here," Olus said. "Let's go find out. Uriel, wait here with them."

"Aye, Captain," Uriel said.

Bastion followed Olus back out of the reactors, passing by the hundreds of humans they and the Freejects had set loose. All of them were naked, wounded, and tired, and it would take hours to get them clothed and patched and loaded onto ships. It would take hours more to get a doctor to them to look over the wounds. Some of them weren't going to make it. He could tell by the hollow look in their eyes. They were too damaged. Too broken. Physically, mentally, it didn't matter which.

He was still more worried about Abbey.

They reached the scene of the fighting. There were bodies everywhere. Hundreds of dead, both human and Nephilim. It made him nauseous.

"What happened?" Bastion asked, finding Pik among the living.

His friend was bloody and sweaty and had a grim expression on his face. He didn't think he'd ever seen the Trover look so morose.

"I'm not sure. Thraven pulled some kind of energy from the link between the Covenant and the Gate. I've never seen anything like it. Then he left."

"What do you mean he left?"

"He went out there." Pik pointed toward the Covenant, visible in the distance. "Lucifer was out there. So was Queenie."

"What?" Bastion felt his heart start to race. "Where is she now?"

"It's like the universe is missing. I don't like it."

Bastion didn't understand what he meant.

"There," Olus said. "What is that?"

He followed Olus' point to a spot in space. It was black, pitch black, as though someone had cut out existence and left a hole.

"That's where Queenie was. With Thraven."

"Frag."

"You can say that again."

"Frag," Bastion repeated. "What do we do now?"

"Hope Queenie comes out of it," Olus said. "Not Thraven."

Bastion forced himself to take a deep breath. Abbey was out there, and he was trapped in here. For the first time, he wished he had the Gift, too.

"I can't just stand here," he said. "I'm going out there."

"What?" Pik said.

Bastion didn't wait. He started running, back toward the hangar.

There were ships there. Transports mostly. That was good enough. The rest of the fighting had stopped.

"Bastion, wait," Olus said. "You-"

He fell silent. Bastion turned to see him on his knees, leaning forward like he was vomiting. He heard the cries of the prisoners further back, mimicking the Captain's groans.

What the hell was going on?

He didn't waste any more time. He kept running, dashing through the corridors back to the smaller internal hangar. He almost laughed out loud when he saw the Faust sitting there. Where had it come from?

He rushed to it, climbing the ramp into the bottom. He heard her whine, the thrusters coming online. Someone was already on board? He hurried up the ladder toward the cockpit.

"It took you long enough," Ruby said as he entered. She was already in the co-pilot seat.

"Where did you come from?" he asked.

She smiled. "A girl has her secrets. I thought we might need to make a quick getaway if things went bad."

"I think things are going bad, but I don't want to get away. Queenie needs us."

"Roger."

He dropped into the pilot seat, buckling himself in. "Are we ready to go?"

"Affirmative."

He reached out and grabbed the controls. "Then hold onto your ass."

He went full throttle, feeling the pressure as the Faust rocketed forward, blasting out into space. He made a tight dip to avoid hitting one of the transports at the end of a docking arm, flipping around it and coming back up facing the Covenant.

"Oh, shit," he said.

He could see the small figure in space, surrounded by wisps of darkness, floating toward the Gate.

It wasn't Abbey.

"Thraven," Ruby said.

"What the frag is he doing?"

The Faust shuddered slightly in response, hit by something from behind.

"I'm really confused," Bastion said.

"The Gate is vibrating," Ruby replied.

"What?"

"I believe he is trying to open it."

"There's no way this can be good. Where's Queenie?"

"I don't know."

"Rejects," Gant said, his voice coming out on the Faust's comm. "Can any of you hear me? Are you there?"

"Gant," Bastion replied. "I'm here. Imp and Ruby on the Faust."

"Roger," Gant said. He sounded upset. "I can't reach Queenie."

"Neither can we," Bastion replied. "I'm looking for her. Thraven's making a play to open the Gate. Is there anything we can do?"

"Thraven?" Gant said. "If he's in control of himself..." His voice trailed off.

Bastion knew what it probably meant, but he wasn't ready to accept that. "I'll believe it when I see a body, and it doesn't come back to life. Either way, we need to stop Thraven."

"I don't know if that's possible."

"You're the super-genius freak-monkey. Figure it out."

"Easy for you to say from out there. The Focus is dry. Empty. Thraven must have drained it."

"Just shoot at Thraven or something, then."

"Did you hear what I just said, idiot? He drained the Focus. Nothing can touch him."

"So what? We're supposed to just let him use the Gate?"

"At least he'll go away."

"For how long?"

"Gant, the Gate is resonating," Ruby said. "Any ideas?"

"Let me think."

"Think fast," Bastion said.

Thraven was getting closer to the Gate. The darkness was filling the center of it, creating a hole through the universe.

Bastion guided the Faust around him, staying well clear of the Gloritant. Thraven didn't seem to be paying them any mind. He continued floating slowly toward the Gate, the resonance increasing with each passing second.

"Imp, three o'clock," Ruby said.

Bastion turned his head before he turned the Faust.

"Oh, no," he said softly.

A body was drifting through space off the starboard side, ten kilometers distant.

Abbey's body.

DEATH WASN'T ANYTHING LIKE WHAT ABBEY HAD EXPECTED.

Then again, she had never really thought about it all that much or expected much of anything. Dead was dead unless you believed in the afterlife.

Maybe that's why she was surprised. She was sure she had died, which meant the afterlife was real.

But if it was real, then it was dark. Very dark. There was nothing at all. Blackness. Complete blackness. Still, she was conscious or at least had some awareness of consciousness.

What the frag?

"Abigail Cage," a voice said.

Suddenly, the darkness turned to light.

"I'm dead, right?" she said. "You're God?"

"Not exactly."

A figure appeared. Abbey groaned. "You?"

"You should sound a little more grateful to see me," the Shard said.

"Why? This is all your fault. I'm dead because of you. The only upside is the One is going to be dead soon, too."

"You aren't dead, Abigail."

"Thraven took my Gift. I was naked in space. I died. There's no other way to avoid that."

"There is one other way, and that's why you aren't dead."

"Can we cut the mysterious bullshit. If I'm not dead, I need to be back out there. I have to stop Thraven."

"I can't do anything with your body in its current state."

"What the hell are you talking about?"

"I've been with you the whole time, Queenie," the Shard said. "You thought you kicked me out, but I'm not that easy to get rid of."

"Like gonorrhea," Abbey said.

"You're fortunate I didn't abandon you. I knew the threat the naniates posed. When you accepted them in again, I hid."

"Where?"

"Where do you think?"

"Hell?" she replied, thinking of the brand on her neck.

"Yes. I stored a copy of your consciousness. A configuration. I thought you might need it."

"So why can't you revive me? Put me back in the fight?"

"I need to replicate. You have to let me back in."

"And let you control me?"

"I don't want to control you. But the uncontrolled naniates are a threat to this universe and all universes. I have seen what happens when they gain a foothold. I have seen the end of all things. All places. All creatures. I have traveled through eternity again and again in an effort to stop them."

"Through eternity?"

"It isn't important right now. Let me in, Abigail. Become the new Shard. All I ask is that you continue to fight the good fight. Keep my creations safe. From the naniates, from the Asura, from the Nephilim."

"I don't want to fight. I want to rest. I want to be with my daughter. She's blind because of this bullshit."

"She isn't blind," the Shard said. "She sees better than anyone, now."

"What the frag does that mean?"

"Let me back in, Abigail, and we may be able to stop Thraven."

"You're going to throw that carrot in my face? How desperate are you?"

"Very. You should be, too."

Abbey sighed. "I am. Fine. But just keep in mind I'm agreeing under duress. I'm sick of being a pawn to this bullshit."

"You aren't a pawn," the Shard replied. "You're the Queen."

"Am I going to wake up now?"

"Not yet. I've begun replicating within your body. It will take some time. You won't be as strong in the Gift as you once were, Abigail. You'll have to get by on your own skills and intellect, and those of your followers."

"Then we're fragged," Abbey said. "I'm floating in the middle of nowhere. Nobody is coming to save me."

"That's where you're wrong, Queenie. The resonance is the key. Remember."

"What?"

The light started to fade.

Abbey's consciousness started to fade with it.

She had been hopeful that the Shard was real, and this wasn't just some post-death hallucination before it all went away.

Damn it.

60

"Queenie," Bastion said, leaning over her. "Come on, Queenie. I know you aren't dead. Your body is warm, and it's fragging glowing. Not to mention, you look like yourself again, instead of some kind of crazy sexy monster."

Abbey opened her eyes, gasping as she took her first breath as a Shard. Her heart was pounding, her vision unbelievably clear. She looked up at Bastion's worried face.

"It wasn't a hallucination," she said. She could feel the light. She reached up and touched the Hell brand. It was cold and alive.

"Yes," Bastion said. "Oh damn. I knew it." He smiled, tears forming in his eyes. He leaned down to kiss her.

She pushed his face away. "Not yet," she said, pushing herself to her feet. "We have work to do." She looked around, recognizing the Faust. "Where's Thraven? Fragging bastard killed Void."

"He's almost at the Gate, Queenie," Ruby said. "It is good to see you alive again."

"I'm getting kind of tired of dying," she replied. "Is Gant around?"

"Yes, Queenie," Ruby said. "Gant, this is the Faust. We have Queenie on board, and she's alive."

"Queenie," Gant said, the relief in his voice palpable. "What happened to you?"

"Later," Abbey said. "We need to do something with the Gate. The resonance is the key. Does that mean anything to you?"

"I've been thinking about it," Gant said. "The correct resonance might be able to disable the naniates. Or at least confuse them. That would force the Gate to go back offline."

"Brilliant," Abbey said. "How do we get the right resonance?"

"I believe I can use the link between the Covenant and the Gate to send energy pulses that should have the desired effect. But I need some alterations to Gravity Control on the Gate itself."

"Olus, are you there?" Abbey said.

"Queenie, is that you?" Olus replied. His voice sounded weak and old. "I'm here."

"What happened to you?"

"Thraven ripped the Gift right out of me," he replied. "I'm still feeling it. What do you need?"

"I need you to connect GC to the main systems," Gant said. "With a direct feed from the electrical. Override the breakers."

"You'll fry the whole place. Life support, everything."

"That's why you need to do it and then abandon ship. Get everyone out of there."

"These people are injured. Weak. The Gift was ripped from them, too."

"Do your best, Olus," Abbey said.

"Roger. I'm on it. How much time do I have?"

"Let's say two minutes," Gant said.

"Two?" Olus replied. "Frag."

"Stop talking, start walking," Bastion said.

Olus disconnected.

"I suppose we get the hard job," Abbey said.

"What job is that?" Bastion asked.

"Distracting Thraven."

"I was afraid you were going to say that."

Abbey followed Bastion and Ruby to the Faust's cockpit. She

stared out of the canopy toward the Gate. The entire center was dark, and it was beginning to expand backward, creating a tunnel through space and time and dimensions.

"Just remember," Abbey said. "That asshole killed me."

"Roger," Bastion said. He hit the thrusters, sending the Faust forward. "I hope you have some mojo left."

"A little," Abbey said, feeling a strain of the Shard's Light within her. It was still weak, but it would have to do.

"Here we go."

The Faust dove toward Thraven. He still didn't seem to notice them, continuing to face toward the Gate, his hands held wide.

"Fire," Abbey said.

Ruby triggered the cannons, sending projectiles into Thraven's back. The attack surprised him enough that the force pushed him in space, blood ejecting from fresh holes in his rear. He recovered quickly, spinning and tracking the Faust as it vectored past, ready to make another run.

"Cage."

Abbey heard his voice in her mind, still speaking to her through the naniates. It was a rough connection. Filtered.

"We aren't done yet," she replied.

"You think the Shard can save you? Any of you? He couldn't even save himself."

Thraven lifted his hand and fire belched away from it, stretching toward them in a tight line. Abbey breathed out, feeling the Shard's Light expand to meet it, a wave of cold energy that caused the fire to dissipate before it hit them.

She felt dizzy, and she gripped the side of the pilot's seat to keep from falling over.

"I can't do this for long."

"Gant," Olus said. "Gravity Control is ready for you."

"You need to evacuate," Gant said.

"We're trying, but don't wait for us."

"Pudding," Gant said. "Send the commands. Queenie, keep him from noticing the link, or we're fragged."

"Of course," Phlenel said in Keeper's voice.

The tendril link between the Covenant and the Gate began to pulse with blue energy, stretching out to the Gate.

The Faust came around again on the opposite side of it, firing on Thraven. The rounds vanished into the darkness of the naniates, and Thraven reached out for them. The Faust shuddered and slowed, caught in a web.

Abbey slammed her fist onto the seat, a light expanding from the cockpit ahead of them, the Shard's Light cutting through the darkness and freeing them. They shot way, Bastion keeping them on the other side of the link.

"Gant. Anything?" Abbey asked.

"I'm adjusting pulses," Gant said. "Not yet."

"Hurry."

"Roger."

The Faust swung around again. They were fortunate Thraven needed so much of his power to keep the Gate resonating, or they would have been crushed already.

They made a third pass, Ruby firing the cannons on the Faust while Bastion kept them in a tight pattern that drew Thraven's attention from the pulsing of the link. The Gloritant wiggled his fingers, and small beads of blackness expanded into their path. Each time one hit the Faust, the armor was disintegrated.

"Oh crap," Bastion said, trying to guide the ship through the sudden minefield.

Abbey reached out with the Light, countering as many of the beads as she could. Her head started to spin, and she wound up falling into Ruby's lap.

"I've got you, Queenie," Ruby said, holding onto her.

"I think I've got it," Gant said.

Abbey tried to focus on the Gate. She could see the vibration of it in space. She could see it was starting to shake harder.

Thraven noticed, too. He spun in position, turning to face the link.

"Not so fast, mother fragger," Bastion said.

He cut a new vector, triggering the cannons himself. Rounds

poured into Thraven, severing an arm and a leg and pushing him off course.

The limbs were pulled back to the body and reattached, and Thraven reached out with the Gift once more, throwing a spear of darkness at the Faust.

Abbey pushed herself to her feet on shaking hands, then clapped them together, the Light of the Shard spreading out from them and catching the spear, holding in place as Bastion rolled the ship around it, catching Thraven from the side.

"Surprise," he said, blasting him again. The rounds ripped Thraven's head off, blowing it into a mutilated pulp.

Blood poured out of the wound, and the naniates spread to collect it, working to bring the head back to the body and repair it. While they did, the Gate's resonance continued to gain in intensity, shaking so hard that pieces of it began to float away.

A transport detached from a docking arm, thrusters flaring and carrying it from the Gate. A second followed.

"Queenie, better get clear," Gant said.

"Imp, get us out of here," Abbey said.

"Aye, Queenie," Bastion replied.

She fell back into Ruby's lap as the Faust turned and shot away. Behind them, the naniates reconstructed Thraven, regaining their host once more.

"Caaaaagggeeee," they shouted, though the anger barely registered through the Light.

The Gate exploded.

It wasn't a fiery detonation, but a silent one. It expanded and shattered, the hole within it shattering as well, trillions of tiny pieces as the resonance caused the naniates to shut down and lose cohesion in a blast like a rain storm. It swept across Thraven, knocking the naniates within him offline as well, their granular forms pulling him apart atom by atom and reducing him to nothing.

The wave of debris and naniates flowed outward in a sphere, spreading as it went. The Covenant was close to the Gate, and it took the brunt of the force, the outer hull buckling under the trauma, gun batteries and towers torn apart. Some of Lucifer's Nephilim had remained, and they too were caught by the explosion, their ships shredded in the storm.

The transports raced behind the Faust, staying ahead of the blast, altering course to take cover on the safe side of the Covenant. The dead naniates spread around them, vanishing into the black.

Abbey sat on Ruby's lap, struggling to keep her head up. Bastion was looking at her, grinning from ear-to-ear. Gant was on the comm, chittering like he was psychotic.

"Hell, yeah," Pik roared, his voice echoing inside the cockpit. "Reee-jects!"

Abbey closed her eyes, letting herself take a relaxed breath, the first of what she hoped would be many to come.

"Hell, yeah," she said.

A FEW WEEKS LATER....

"I BET THEY'RE GOING TO GIVE US MEDALS," PIK SAID. "BIG SHINY ONES. I think we deserve that."

"We deserve a hell of a lot more than that," Bastion said. "We saved the entire galaxy. That should at least be worth a planet or two. A city at a minimum."

"What am I going to do with a planet?" Pik said. "I don't need that kind of aggravation. I think Earth is a perfect example of that."

"You mean the cleanup?" Benhil said. "I'm sure they'll get it all straightened out now that Thraven's former cronies have all vanished."

"They're still out there," Abbey said, wishing it wasn't true. "They're hiding for now, but that won't last forever."

"Not my problem," Pik said. "I'm done with killing things."

"But you're so good at it," Benhil said.

"It doesn't matter. I don't like it anymore. I'm going back to Tro to claim a wife, and then I'm going to have a few little Piks and then I'm going to eat and drink and have sex until I die."

"I thought you didn't want a Trover wife?"

Pik shrugged. "I think I'm tough enough to handle one now."

"What are you going to do, Queenie?" Jequn asked, smiling.

Like with Olus, the loss of the Gift seemed to have been a benefit to the Ophanim, rather than a loss. At least now she would get to live a hopefully long and full life.

Unfortunately, Trinity wouldn't. Nerd wouldn't either. And there were so many more. Herschel, Dak, and Sylvan Kett to name a few.

They had taken time to remember and mourn the fallen Rejects after the battle was over. Even so, the losses were still fresh, the wounds still raw. At least they had died as heroes, for whatever that was worth.

Abbey forced herself off their memory and back to Jequn's question.

What was she going to do now?

The power of the Shard had faded somewhat after Thraven and the Gate were destroyed. She only felt it in one place now - the Hell brand on her neck. The Shard had warned her it would happen, and she had made a promise.

One she was going to keep.

"I swore I would protect the galaxy," she said. "That's what I'm going to do."

"Aren't you tired of it?" Bastion asked.

"Yes. I'm very tired of it. But somebody has to do it, remember?"

"Maybe you can take a vacation at least? We can go to the beaches of Maravan, assuming Maravan wasn't blown to shit by the Nephilim."

"It's a nice thought, Bastion, but Ruby, the Faust, and I are going to Koosa once we're done with the council. The Koosian doctors haven't been able to restore Hayley's sight, even with mechanical augmentation. They don't understand it. I'm hoping the Light of the Shard can help."

"What about her memories? Have they come back at all?"

"Thankfully, no. She doesn't remember what Thraven did to her. She doesn't even remember being taken. It's as good as I could have hoped for. She's just a kid. She doesn't need to have that trauma."

"Being blind is enough," Benhil agreed.

"After that, I'm taking Hayley and the Covenant back to Azure. I figure that's as good of a home base as any."

"You're really going to hunt down the Nephilim?"

"I'm going to keep an eye on things. I've got Gant and Keeper to help me."

"Where is the little rodent?" Bastion asked.

"He didn't want to come," Abbey said. "He doesn't want a medal or a planet."

"His loss," Pik said.

The Faust shook slightly as Ruby touched it down at the makeshift spaceport not far from the temporary New Republic Council building.

"We're here," Bastion said.

"I heard the New Republic Council has opened a dialog with the Outworld Governance, thanks to Governess Ott," Benhil said. "It looks like at least one good thing might come of all of this."

"An end to the bullshit would be nice," Abbey agreed. "Hopefully they can come to an agreement."

"They'd be idiots not to," Pik said.

"Politicians aren't known for being smart," Bastion said.

"So you're planning to go into politics?" Benhil asked.

"Funny."

Pik laughed. "I thought so."

"Shut up."

The Faust's hatch opened as Ruby joined them. Abbey went out first, trailed by the rest of the Rejects.

"Abigail," Olus said, waiting on the ground.

He was flanked by a New Republic Armed Services Officer on either side. A General and an Admiral in full uniform.

"Captain," Abbey replied. "Or is it Colonel now?"

Olus smiled. "Actually, it's neither. I decided to reject the position. I just wanted you to see a familiar face when you arrived."

"Why?"

"I'm moving into the private sector. I'm getting too old for bureaucracy."

"Good choice," Pik said.

The Rejects reached the ground. The officers still didn't move or speak. They stood stoically on either side of Olus.

"Lieutenant Abigail Cage," Abbey said, saluting them. "Highly Specialized Operational Combatant."

"We know who you are," the Admiral said. "We know who all of you are."

"You've done a great service to the Republic," the General said. "And we thank you for it."

Abbey felt a tickle at the base of her neck. She didn't like the way the General said that.

"But?" she said, eyes shifting, looking past the officers. There were other ships on the tarmac, but where were the other civilians?

"We have a small problem, Abigail," the Admiral said.

He didn't use her rank. Maybe it was a formality? Technically, she wasn't still a member of the armed services.

Technically, she was a convict.

They all were.

She noticed motion from the line of ships ahead of them. Soldiers were moving out onto the landing field. They were dressed in battle-suits, armed and ready for war.

"What the frag is this?" she said, looking directly at Olus.

"You were convicted of treason, and sentenced to life in Hell," the General said. "All of you were."

"I wasn't," Jequn said.

"I wasn't either," Ruby agreed.

"Does this mean we don't get a medal?" Pik asked.

"This is bullshit," Bastion said.

"We can't simply forget your past transgressions, regardless of your recent actions," the Admiral said. "We are a nation of laws. Those of you who were convicted are expected to finish out your sentences, at which point you'll be permitted to move on with your lives."

"It was a life sentence, asshole," Benhil said.

The Admiral smirked.

"Olus, you son of a bitch," Abbey said. "You knew about this?"

Olus hesitated for a moment and then nodded. "I did. I'm sorry, Abigail."

"You piece of shit," Pik yelled. "I'm going to crush your-"

"Relax, Pik," Olus said. "There's a reason I rejected the New Republic's offer."

He reached into a pocket, holding up a small device.

"Is that what I think it is?" Abbey asked.

Olus smiled. "It is."

"Captain?" the General said, seeing the device. "What is the meaning of this?"

"You don't frag with the Rejects, General. Remember that when you wake up."

Olus activated the device.

The ships surrounding the Faust exploded.

The detonations were shaped, the blast knocking the soldiers on their asses. Olus grabbed the General, pulling him down and slamming him hard in the temple with his fist.

Abbey didn't hesitate, reaching for the Admiral, punching him in the face, breaking his nose and knocking him down.

"Let's go Rejects," she said.

They piled back into the Faust. Bastion whooped as he hurried to the cockpit, dropping into the pilot's seat and igniting the reactor.

"I have to admit, I kind of like being a galaxy-saving outlaw."

"Are you sure you don't want to be a politician?" Ruby asked.

"Are you kidding? Those guys are assholes."

The Faust lifted into the air, rocketing away.

"Humph. They aren't even trying to chase us," Bastion said.

"That's because the explosion also triggered a massive EMP blast, which I know for a fact the Faust is shielded from," Olus said.

"Thanks for not turning us in," Benhil said.

"How could I? They're employers. We're family."

"Hell, yeah," Pik said.

"It looks like we're sticking together, after all, Queenie," Bastion said.

"I wish the circumstances were different, but I'm happy to have you with me," Abbey said. "Whether they know it or not, the galaxy needs us."

"Let's go do some evil," Benhil said.

"So nobody else has to," the rest of them replied.

Hell, yeah.

THE END... For now.

AUTHOR'S NOTE

Well frag me, it looks like we've reached the end of the Chaos of the Covenant series. Thank you, thank you, thank you for reading all the way through. I really hope you've enjoyed consuming the story as much as I loved producing it.

It's always a strange feeling to get to the end of a series. As an author, I feel connected to the characters, so saying goodbye to them is always a little bittersweet. It's a little different in this case because there will be more Covenant adventures to come in the future, and you haven't seen the last of Queenie and the Rejects.

With that said, I hope you'll come back for more when the time arrives, and I hope you'll consider signing up for my mailing list so you'll know when new Covenant books, and all of the other books that I'm writing become available (assuming you don't think I'm a flaming turd of an author). You can do that here: mrforbes.com/notify.

Since you've finished the series, I really, really, hope you'll consider leaving a review for this one. If you have for any of the other books, I applaud you wildly, and thank you greatly. Social proof is still one of the main ways that authors are discovered and read, and every time you recommend one of my books, leave a review, or otherwise share your enjoyment of my words with others, you're proving that I don't suck, and I appreciate that.

If you'd like to leave a review for Queen of Demons, you can do that here: mrforbes.com/queenofdemonsreview

Thank you again.

Cheers,
   Michael.

OTHER BOOKS BY M.R FORBES

M.R. Forbes on Amazon
mrforbes.com/books

Starship Eternal (War Eternal, Book One)
mrforbes.com/starshipeternal

A lost starship...

A dire warning from futures past...

A desperate search for salvation...

Captain Mitchell "Ares" Williams is a Space Marine and the hero of the Battle for Liberty, whose Shot Heard 'Round the Universe saved the planet from a nearly unstoppable war machine. He's handsome, charismatic, and the perfect poster boy to help the military drive enlistment. Pulled from the war and thrown into the spotlight, he's as efficient at charming the media and bedding beautiful celebrities as he was at shooting down enemy starfighters.

After an assassination attempt leaves Mitchell critically wounded, he begins to suffer from strange hallucinations that carry a chilling and oddly familiar warning:

They are coming. Find the Goliath or humankind will be destroyed.

Convinced that the visions are a side-effect of his injuries, he tries to ignore them, only to learn that he may not be as crazy as he thinks. The enemy is real and closer than he imagined, and they'll do whatever it takes to prevent him from rediscovering the centuries lost starship.

Narrowly escaping capture, out of time and out of air, Mitchell lands at the mercy of the Riggers - a ragtag crew of former commandos who patrol the lawless outer reaches of the galaxy. Guided by a captain with a reputation for cold-blooded murder, they're dangerous, immoral, and possibly insane.

They may also be humanity's last hope for survival in a war that has raged beyond eternity.

(War Eternal is also available in a box set of the first three books here: mrforbes.com/wareternalbox)

Man of War (Rebellion)
mrforbes.com/manofwar

In the year 2280, an alien fleet attacked the Earth.

Their weapons were unstoppable, their defenses unbreakable.

Our technology was inferior, our militaries overwhelmed.

Only one starship escaped before civilization fell.

Earth was lost.

It was never forgotten.

Fifty-two years have passed.

A message from home has been received.

The time to fight for what is ours has come.

Welcome to the rebellion.

Or maybe something completely different?

Dead of Night (Ghosts & Magic)

mrforbes.com/deadofnight

For Conor Night, the world's only surviving necromancer, staying alive is an expensive proposition. So when the promise of a big payout for a small bit of thievery presents itself, Conor is all in. But nothing comes easy in the world of ghosts and magic, and it isn't long before Conor is caught up in the machinations of the most powerful wizards on Earth and left with only two ways out:

Finish the job, or be finished himself.

Balance (The Divine)

mrforbes.com/balance

My name is Landon Hamilton. Once upon a time I was a twenty-three year old security guard, trying to regain my life after spending a year in prison for stealing people's credit card numbers.

Now, I'm dead.

Okay, I was supposed to be dead. I got killed after all; but a funny thing happened after I had turned the mortal coil...

I met Dante Alighieri - yeah, that Dante. He told me I was special, a diuscrucis. That's what they call a perfect balance of human, demon, and angel. Apparently, I'm the only one of my kind.

I also learned that there was a war raging on Earth between Heaven and Hell, and that I was the only one who could save the human race from annihilation. He asked me to help, and I was naive enough to agree.

Sounds crazy, I know, but he wished me luck and sent me back to the mortal world. Oh yeah, he also gave me instructions on how to use my Divine "magic" to bend the universe to my will. The problem is, a sexy vampire crushed them while I was crushing on her.

Now I have to somehow find my own way to stay alive in a world of angels, vampires, werewolves, and an assortment of other enemies that all want to kill me before I can mess up their plans for humanity's future. If that isn't enough, I also have to find the queen of all demons and recover the Holy Grail.

It's not like it's the end of the world if I fail.
Wait. It is.

Tears of Blood (Books 1-3)
mrforbes.com/tearsofblood

One thousand years ago, the world was broken and reborn beneath the boot of a nameless, ageless tyrant. He erased all history of the time before, enslaving the people and hunting those with the power to unseat him.

The power of magic.

Eryn is such a girl. Born with the Curse, she fights to control and conceal it to protect those she loves. But when the truth is revealed, and his soldiers come, she is forced away from her home and into the company of Silas, a deadly fugitive tormented by a fractured past.

Silas knows only that he is a murderer who once hunted the Cursed, and that he and his brothers butchered armies and innocents alike to keep the deep, dark secrets of the time before from ever coming to light.

Secrets which could save the world.

Or destroy it completely.

JOIN THE MAILING LIST

"No," you cry. "I will not submit myself to even more inbox spam. I have quite enough garbage coming in from people and places that I care a lot more about than you."

"But," I reply, "if you sign up for my mailing list, you'll know when my next book is out. Don't you want to know when my next book is out?"

"Eh… I'll find it on Amazon."

"True enough, but you see, a mailing list is very valuable to an author, especially a meager self-published soul such as myself. I don't have a marketing team, and I don't have exposure in brick and mortar stores around the world to help improve my readership. All I have is you, my potential fans. What do you say?"

Silence.

Followed by crickets.

Followed by more silence.

"Where'd you go?" I ask. "Well, I'll just leave this here, in case you change your mind."

mrforbes.com/mailinglist

ABOUT THE AUTHOR

M.R. Forbes is the creator of a growing catalog of science fiction and fantasy titles. He lives in the pacific northwest with his family, including a cat who thinks she's a dog, and a dog who thinks she's a cat. He eats too many donuts, and he's always happy to hear from readers.

To learn more about M.R. Forbes or just say hello:
mrforbes.com
michael@mrforbes.com